## SECRETS FROM

George Hamilton studied at the University of East London, majoring in development economics. He spent several months during 2002 in Australia researching Koori (Aboriginal) culture at the Koori Centre, University of Sydney, amongst other places, and some of that work is reflected in the novel. He currently lives in London, England.

## Reviews:

4/5*
'Harrowing, beautiful and thought-provoking, Secrets From the Dust is an impressive novel from George Hamilton. With its shocking conclusion it deserves an audience…'(Shelleyrae @ Book'd Out)

5/5*
'This one hits on the heart of the dreaming and the repercussions of stealing the indigenous from their "country"…'(Karyn @ Goodreads)

5/5*
'…it was a superbly written, thought provoking book that I just didn't want to put down.'(Joo @ KUForum)

4/5*
'The characters in this story all form a connection with the reader. You don't just read this book, you live it, and that is due to the amazing writing of George Hamilton. …this is an eye opener book that should be read by lots of people as a way to put some sense into them.'(Guta @ murphyslibrary)

4/5*
'A fabulous read. Wonderfully written and well researched. I found the character of Margaret an absorbing one.'(Larelle @ Goodreads)

5/5*
'This book was very hard to put down once I got started reading… This book is very well written and the characters are so easy to become connected with. I feel like this book will be enjoyed by many.'(Lynn @ Readers Favorite and Amazon.com)

4/5*
'Secrets From The Dust is a well written book which pulls at the heartstrings… Thoroughly enjoyable read would recommend it to my friends.'(Rosemary @ Amazon.co.uk)

4/5*
'I loved how the author painted the vastly different experiences of Aboriginal history between rural and urban Australian life in the 50s, 60s and 70s… The book would make great discussion for a bookclub.'(Megan @ Goodreads)

# SECRETS FROM THE DUST

George Hamilton

**BR**
Browsing Rhino

Published by Browsing Rhino 2010

WWW.browsingrhino.com

A CIP record for this book is available from the British Library

Paperback ISBN: 978-0-9566861-2-1
Ebook ISBN: 978-0-9566861-1-4

# Acknowledgements:

Proofed by: Alasdair McKenzie

With thanks to the staff at the Koori Centre, University of Sydney, for their assistance in researching this novel.

Thanks to Aisha, Kevin, Owen, and Penny who read and commented on drafts.

For my parents, Delores and Lloyd

# Chapter 1

The *pang pang gooks* all laughed as their several tiny fingers raced over the bushes, plucking at the wild *riberries*, which were fat with juice. The girl that they sometimes called *Snake-woman-child* darted in and out of the scrub with an athletic ease, eager to reach the biggest fruit ahead of the others, with whom she would share them afterwards anyway. They were eating more than they saved for the elders, who were dancing and singing up some spirit back at camp, and the luscious red juice ran down mouths and across cheeks, adding to the days-old stains that had already accumulated on their T-shirts and dresses.

A cloud of red dust billowed and raced towards the berry pickers, even though the sun was sitting high in the belly of its expansive sky and there was no hint of a breeze. They first noticed that the flock of chattering budgerigars, which had waited patiently on the wing for their chance at the scrub, had flown off, and when they stopped listening to their own rowdy voices, they heard the roar of the truck towards them, and turned to see it at the head of the dust cloud. The little ones ran off as the truck careered closer, remembering the warning of their parents. But Snake-woman-child stood still, in a game of dare, as she knew the elders had mostly warned them about *cunnichmen*—who could do more than arrest drunks and thieves for breaking 'white man's laws'—and what they had called 'smart-dressed types', driving big black cars.

The truck stopped in front of her, and two fellas, farmer types, jumped out of either door. The men's skins were only lightly touched by the sun, and when one of them lifted his *Akubra*, his head was bald and his ears white, like the colour of a dead man's bones. "G'day. You know where we can get some water, love? Our radiator

1

is as dry as this here track." He kicked at the ground, and the dust landed on his shiny new boots. He appeared to ignore her when she didn't answer, then he lifted the bonnet of the truck and stuck his head inside.

The younger man, who had a few days' growth on his chin, waggled a water bottle over his gaping mouth to indicate it was empty, but still she said nothing, and didn't attempt to close the twelve feet between them. Her narrow nose, and translucent blue eyes looking out from behind her rusted gum tree skin, mesmerised him. He pulled himself away from her spell, went back inside the car, and brought out some candy, which he held at arm's length whilst gingerly closing the gap between them. All of the remaining berry pickers took a few steps back, but Snake-woman-child stepped forward, holding out a handful of berries for the exchange. She could feel the eyes of fear from her kin heavily on her back, but knew her actions would be sung and danced up when the others tasted these new treats. They would sing that Snake-woman-child truly had the spirit of her totem serpent, and she would hide any hint of individual pleasure and sing them up too, so that no one person could take the glory for all that had gone on that day, and no one person would be without recognition too, because that was the way it had always been.

The men spoke to each other in hushed tones, but the one with the candy kept his hunter's eyes on her just the same. She remembered a few of the words she could hear, like *slowly* and *pretty blue-eyed one*, because it was less than two years since her mother had liberated her from the settlement school to go walkabout with their *mob*. This way she would be able to parent her in their *mob's* ways, and she could be closer to where her husband might find work as a sheep shearer or cattleman, as he was always on the move.

"Grab the little mulatto bitch!" the bald-headed man shouted when the one bearing gifts was within a foot of the exchange. It was then that she noticed the coarse sack hanging from his back, and he pulled it out and threw it in an arc, like a whip. It was over her head by the time she had turned and taken two lithe strides in the other direction. The other children scattered like frightened rabbits. The girl kicked, clawed and screamed more violently than a hare caught in a trap, but the two fellas were too strong. They tied a rope around the sack, and one of them carried the writhing bundle on his shoulder to

2

the back of the truck. He threw her into its empty belly real hard, and she hit her head and passed out.

When the girl came to, it was dark, like the deep caves at Walara, and she sniffed the oily air in the truck through two holes in the sack. The vehicle lurched over uneven ground, and its inners rumbled more ferociously than angry thunder. The fear woke in her, and she pushed her arms against her bindings, but it made breathing the already stale, hot air burn her lungs. So she lay still and sang to herself, and each time the fear in her rose, she sang louder, so as to block out the screams that were leaping from her heart.

***

They arrived at Radley Domestic Training Home for Girls in the dead of night. Radley and other segregated training institutions like it had been set up by the Chief Protector of the Government Protection Board in each of the states. They were the legal guardians of all Aboriginal children, and homes like these were usually the first stop for those children taken from their families due to 'neglect', 'destitution' or because they were 'uncontrollable', or so the state authorities said. Before the state began to take the children, the growing Australia had been in need of a cheap source of labour, and when the European settlers had first spread out across the outback, they had met fierce resistance from the natives with whom they fought over rights to land, food and water sources. Once the settlers had won those battles, they had then kidnapped Aboriginal women and children to provide what labour and recreation they required. Later, the policy was carried out in a more formal manner when the Government and missionaries took the mixed-race children to train in 'European values and work habits', before they were employed by the settlers in exchange for rations.

The men took the sack off the girl in the back of the truck, so it couldn't be seen how they had trussed her up. Then they presented her to a rotund woman standing in front of the stone building in her dressing gown, with both fists pressed into her doughy hips. She carried a two-foot long leather sheathed truncheon in one hand, and slapped her foot against the gravel with open impatience.

"This is the girl," the bald man said, scratching his head.

3

"Well, does she have a name?" the woman demanded. The men looked at each other and then back at the girl, but she seemed to stare straight through them as if they were ghosts.

"Margaret," the bolder man said, stroking his coarse chin. "Her name is Margaret."

"Then thank you and goodnight," the woman said as she spun on her heels and flung the heavy, wrought iron clad, oak door open. "Get in," she commanded, and the girl, who was now Margaret, followed her extended arm into a long, pine-floored hallway.

"You will address me as Matron Blythe," she said as she marched a pace ahead. Margaret felt as if she were floating, and her mind had lost all of its ability to navigate on its own, so she followed Matron Blythe. They climbed a stairway to the first floor, and Matron Blythe stopped outside a varnished French door. She looked Margaret up and down and tightened her nose as if slamming a door. "You're filthy, but it's too late for you to wash now. The water is turned off at seven. You'll have to wash the bed sheets in the morning." Her voice fell off. "You will go straight to bed and I'll have no whimpering out of you to wake the others, or else there'll be no breakfast for you in the morning." With that she eased open the doors and led Margaret into a large dormitory. Thirty or so iron beds with thin mattresses ran in straight, regimented lines down either side of the dormitory, and more than half of them were occupied with girls fast asleep or keeping as still as they could, so as not to provoke the wrath of Matron Blythe. They stopped at an empty bed and Matron Blythe pointed Margaret towards it. She climbed in wearing the same sweaty dress she had been trussed up in all day and pulled the thin blanket over herself. Only then did Matron Blythe leave the room.

***

Margaret lay awake for the longest time while struggling to unravel her thoughts, wondering how it was that they had become tangled now. She knew she had to escape before these people tried to get her to forget her mob's ways—her mother had always advised her to if she was caught—but each time she tried to think of it her mind spun a web, and she would be left hanging some place, unable to move. Was it a dream? She closed her eyes tight and then sprung them open to end the lurid nightmare, but she was still in the dark dormitory. A steady breeze floated in through one of the grilled windows, left slightly ajar, and it seemed to revive her, so she turned her head in the direction from which it was coming and breathed more deeply. The cool air blew away some of the webs and she started to knit together ideas again. She looked around her for some means of escape. She had made no plans, but pushed the blanket off her and swung her legs onto the floor. Before she could stand, an elfin voice sang out, "Don't do it, Matron will getcha." She stuttered, wondering if the voice was part of the dream. When she didn't hear it again she got up and started across the well-waxed floor. "Matron will getcha I tell you, she sleeps real light."

"Shut up, Lilly, let her get caught if she wants. We'll get her breakfast in the morning," another voice said.

"Who wants that stinky stuff?" another added, and there was a cacophony of giggles around the room, as most had stayed awake to see who the new girl was.

The doors of the dormitory crashed open and Margaret froze, snared in the blinding light of a torch. "What is all that talking, and why are you out of bed, Margaret?" Matron Blythe demanded. The words for a response were coming back to her, but too slowly for Matron Blythe's lean patience. "Well, girl?"

"I—I wanted to go toilet, Matron," she lied, looking down at the floor, where she was making shaky patterns with her foot.

"I told her she had to ask you first, Matron Blythe," said the thumbnail voice belonging to Lilly, "because there is no toilet after bedtime, but she's new and didn't know."

"I would prefer you to mind your own business and go back to sleep, Lilly."

Matron Blythe turned her furious attention back to Margaret. "Didn't I tell you there is no toilet after bedtime?"

"Yes, Miss—I mean Matron Blythe," Margaret said when she saw the stony look on the woman's face.

"Then you'll go back to bed like everyone else and hold it in until morning." Matron Blythe pointed the torch towards the bed. "And let me tell you we don't tolerate pee-the-beds here at Radley. They are good homes you girls will end up in, and I will not have them thinking badly of the training you receive here at Radley." Margaret climbed back into bed wondering what new home the woman was talking about when she already had a mob and a home. She pulled the blanket over her, and Matron Blythe spun on her heels and left.

Margaret woke to the cock-a-doodle-doo of a rooster somewhere in the grounds, and the girls all around her jumped out of bed and made them, with sheets folded back precisely one forearm's length over blankets as they had been taught—Matron Blythe's forearm, that was. Lilly, who was as slight as a thin gum tree and about a foot shorter than Margaret, even though they may have been the same age, had slept in the bed next to her, and kept smiling her small broken teeth at Margaret each time she did a fold that she wanted her to follow, but there was no talking. When all of the beds were made, the girls stood straight-backed with chins out, at the head of their beds, with a white towel rolled exactly four times under their left arms and a toothbrush in their right hands, all neat and tidy, the way Matron Blythe liked it. Some of the girls looked at Margaret hard, trying to weigh up if she had enough white blood in her to be Matron's pet and their enemy. They ranged in colouring from near white to a dark coffee, although when Matron lined them up to be inspected by prospective foster parents, she would have the girls she called half-castes at the back, the quarter-castes or quadroons in the middle, and the octoroons—whom the girls at the back hated—at the front. There were no full-blood Aboriginals in the home, as unlike the mixed-race Aboriginals it was felt their numbers were in decline, and the strict control of them in segregated settlements and who could marry an Aboriginal would speed that process.

The girls stayed by their beds for ten minutes, waiting until the squeak of Matron Blythe's loafers, which they said sounded like farting, told them she was on her way. Margaret saw her more clearly now, and she had a sagging chin and two or three rolls of fat around her neck. She strode down one side of the dormitory and up the other with her flat feet turned outwards, slapping her truncheon against the palm of her hand as she inspected beds and the girls' preparation for the wash. When she had done, she crossed over to Margaret's bed and ripped all the bedclothes off, leaving them in a pile. "You'll wash these by hand this morning, Margaret. And in future you will make sure you're clean before you go to bed. Don't for one minute think that because you're all little black girls I can't see the dirt on you." She addressed the last part to all the girls, then slapped her hand twice with the truncheon and commanded,

"Dismissed." The girls filed out of the dormitory, down the corridor and into the communal washroom. As always, they had to leave the door open, and Matron Blythe sat in her office across the corridor with its door ajar, so she could watch them.

***

By the time Margaret had finished washing and hanging the sheets, breakfast was almost over. She trudged into the dining hall dizzy from the hunger which was biting her like a rabid dog, and the dehydration which had set in, as she had drunk nothing since the previous day. The clean, cast-off frock that Matron had given her to wear was already sticking to her sweaty skin, and every now and then she peeled it loose. She went up to the serving counter where a woman the girls called Matron Cook was standing behind a large pot with ladle in hand.

"You must be the new girl—Margaret?" Matron Cook said, her meaty smile revealing the two gold teeth on one side of her mouth.

Margaret chewed it over on her shredded gums. She didn't accept the new name, but her mother had told her to pretend she agreed if she was ever caught, until she could run. "Yes, miss," she said.

"Matron Cook," the woman whispered as if in a conspiracy, and Margaret repeated her name.

"Afraid there isn't much left, Margaret," Matron Cook said as she slingshotted gooey lumps of porridge into a bowl. It caused her upper arm to wobble like jelly, and the porridge stuck to the dish like cement.

Margaret took the bowl, scanned the faces at the four long tables which dominated the room, and went to sit at the table where Lilly was. Lilly grinned at her through her jagged teeth, and Margaret managed a twisted raise of her cheeks. The other girls had already scraped their bowls clean, and some had even washed them with their tongues when Matron Cook wasn't looking. Margaret screwed her face up at the mess in the bowl, and the heavy whispers from the girls around the table softened as they waited.

"You best eat it, Margaret. There'll be nothing more," Lilly said.

Beatrice, the darkest and hardest girl to place in the home, who had short nappy hair and a bulldog's build, bared her teeth at Lilly and shot her a kick under the table. "It's her porridge, Lilly; leave her

7

alone." Lilly clutched at her bleeding shin and her eyes watered, but she didn't cry out; they had their code.

Margaret sliced through a piece of porridge with her spoon and moved it slowly to her mouth. The sugarless mass caused her to heave, and Beatrice pulled the bowl away from her so that what came up landed on the table. "You want it?" Beatrice asked, with her spoon at the ready. Margaret shook her head whilst wiping her tongue with the back of her hand, and Beatrice shovelled the mass into her own mouth. "You'll be glad for it soon enough," she said between mouthfuls.

Matron Blythe arrived with the day's duty roster when the girls finished eating, having been served breakfast in her office. "Cathy, Sheila One, Kate, clear the tables and then cooking skills with Matron Cook. Molly, Joan, Sheila Two and Beatrice, go to Matron Thomas in the sewing room. That table there, I want the building scrubbed and polished from top to bottom. Lilly, Margaret and you two, I want the vegetable gardens weeded. The rest of you are with me for domestic lessons." It was the same everyday in Matron Blythe's quest to train the best domestic girls in all of the state. The younger girls who were fair enough would be fostered or adopted, and those of around thirteen years old, or who looked big for their ages, would be sent out to work as domestic servants or farm labourers for their keep. "Chop-chop!" Matron Blythe gave her two 'get moving' claps, and the girls jumped to attention and filed out of the dining room in all directions.

***

Margaret followed the other two girls out through the door that she had entered the previous night, into the blazing heat, and really saw the sprawling, walled-in, two and a half acres of grounds that made up Radley for the first time. The ten foot high red-brick wall encircled the property like a noose, except for huge double iron gates at the front, which were left permanently open. A gravel drive cut down the centre to the front door of the two-storey institution, which years before had been a monastery. To one side of the drive was a large vegetable garden with peas, tomatoes, cabbages and several other plants in various stages of growth. On the other side was a small orchard of apples, pears and oranges. Three or four bees' nests scattered through the orchard pollinated the plants and provided honey, and behind the trees was a chicken house.

The girls went over to a small wooden tool shed, where Mr Ralph, the beanpole, leather-skinned gardener, whose back had started to curl forward from age and so much bending, was waiting. He handed them wooden rakes, pointed out where they should weed, and told them to be careful with his garden, before trundling off to work on a patch of ground himself without even noticing the new girl.

Margaret watched Lilly rake up rampant weeds from a bed of peas and followed her. She was wilting like an exposed leaf scorched under the sun, but didn't want to show it. "Where you from?" she suddenly asked Lilly, to help herself to keep going.

"Not from round these parts," Lilly said. She continued to weed, not looking at Margaret as she spoke. "Social workers come to our house and looked in all the empty cupboards and said us children were being neglected. Me mum said if we were entitled to Social Security like you people then they wouldn't be, but they pushed her out of the way and took me and me brother both. Mum come running after us, grabbing hold of the *cunnichman's* leg, but he kicked her off and said he'd arrest her if she didn't behave. I ain't seen her or me brother since."

"I got caught yesterday near our camp," Margaret said. "Me mum's going to find me dad and they're going to come get me." Lilly peered at her out of the corner of a sceptical eye, as though she knew differently. "How long you been here, Lilly?"

Lilly's eyes turned from her, like someone not wanting to douse her flickering flame so soon. "Eleven months," she said, and Margaret buckled at the knees so much that she had to support herself on the rake.

"Eleven months! Me mum loves me too much to leave me here all that time."

"My mum loves me too," Lilly made her know, then turned away, unsure.

Margaret lowered her voice. "You tried to get away?"

Lilly's neck retracted into her shoulders like a turtle into its shell, and she looked about her. Mr Ralph was busily ignoring them. "I thought about it, but I don't know where to go. Some of them other girls tried it, but Matron always catches them, and then they get locked in the box room without food for four days."

"Who wants to eat that rubbish anyway?" Margaret's stomach burped, as if to remind her that she hadn't eaten for more than a day. "I'll wait until we get some of this for dinner." She rested her rake on a fat pumpkin.

"That's not for us," Lilly said. "Well it is, but Matron uses it for herself and sells the rest."

"So what do we get?" Margaret demanded, gripping the rake like a fowl's broken neck.

"Bread and jam with water for lunch, but we get milk with it for supper." Lilly sang out the milk part as though it was some great concession. Margaret's stomach moaned several times in succession, and she swayed a little. Tears rose to the corners of her eyes, but she gritted her teeth and blinked it back. She tugged at a patch of weed, and when it wouldn't come easily, she strangled it in her hand and pulled it free.

Margaret scanned the grounds to make sure that Mr Ralph and the other girls weren't close. "Let's take some of these and have them later." She held a tomato, its blood flesh eating into the green.

"We can't," Lilly said, and stopped raking, as though reconsidering whether Margaret was going to be a safe person to have as her friend.

"Why not? You scared?"

Lilly clammed up, turned her back on Margaret, and continued to weed.

"I didn't mean it like that," Margaret offered in a truce.

Lilly ignored her for a while longer, and then said, "I'll show you in the morning."

***

Early the next morning, before the cock had crowed, someone shook Margaret out of her sleep. "Hmm?" she said as she rubbed her knuckles into the corners of her gummy eyes.

"Shh!" Lilly pressed a finger over her narrow mouth. She signalled for Margaret to follow her to one of the barred windows from where they could look down into the grounds. Matron Blythe was marching up and down the rows of vegetables, scribbling notes into a little red book. When she had done there, she crossed to the orchard to do the same, and the girls ducked as she went under their window.

"What's she doing?" Margaret asked.

"She's counting," said Lilly.

10

"Counting what?"

"All them vegetables, all them fruit, all the chickens and their eggs, and all the honeycombs. If any goes missing and the person doesn't own up, we don't get to eat, all of us. She does it every morning."

***

Margaret ate the cement porridge on her second full day at Radley, and within a few days she was licking her bowl clean like the rest of the girls when Matron Cook's back was turned. Then she started making tracks when she thought no one was looking.

"What you doing?" Lilly asked when she saw Margaret twisting in the red earth.

Margaret stopped and clasped her hands behind her back as if stillness bore innocence. "Nothing."

"I won't tell," Lilly said.

Margaret shrugged her shoulders and shuffled to wipe out the markings with her heel.

Lilly scratched at her calf with a foot to mask her rejection and then turned to go.

"Okay," Margaret said, "but if you tell I'll sing you up a bad thing."

Lilly rose on her toes and giggled like a frolicking kitten. "I know, my aunty got that done to her when she stole somebody's husband."

"I'm making my sign, so me mum and dad can follow it and find me."

"How they going to do that?"

"I was born under the totem of the snake, and so if I make my tracks like a snake they'll come and find me."

Lilly watched her make more snake tracks without saying anything, then, "You want to come and play skipping?" she asked, changing the subject to something they could make happen. Margaret finished her tracks and then the two girls hopped off like wallabies to find a rope.

***

It didn't rain much in these parts at this time of the year, but rain had already washed away Margaret's markings four times. Still, she kept making them. On the morning that she and Lilly were given the job of cleaning out the chicken house, her stomach was shrivelled to a hardened bean. Matron Blythe had already counted the eggs and one

11

of the girls had taken them to Matron Cook. The girls piled the dirty hay in one place ready to burn, and the chicken manure in another, ready to feed the gardens. It was one of the few things that Matron Blythe didn't weigh or count, and if she could have squeezed it through her hands and scribble a number in her red notebook, she would have. Margaret smiled; maybe one day she would get to make Matron's tea and find some nutritious use for it, like the spreading on of mouth-watering cream that the girls who had taken cooking lessons with Matron Cook described.

A commotion in the yard, over by the front gates, drew her eyes from the pile. She and Lilly peered like sunlight through the gaps in the trees to see what was going on. A towering black man, wearing an *Akubra*, was arguing with Matron Blythe. "Daughter, is that you?" the man called out, and he started running in her direction.

"It's me dad," she said, almost jumping with glee. He had been away sheep shearing or working as a cattleman for much of her life, and she had only seen him five times in the last two years. He was all of six foot five with a hardy stockman's build. His skin was a high black, which when the sun shone on it gave hints of a transient mauve, and his face was a complex landscape of peaks, ridges and valleys.

"You stay right there, Margaret," Matron Blythe shouted. "He's not allowed onto the property." She pushed him back with the tip of her baton, but he palmed it aside like a twig and took giant strides towards his daughter. He stopped in front of Margaret, a cavernous grin splitting his face, but not able to hug her as he wanted, as the years apart made them both feel uncomfortable. Margaret had forgotten her food hunger, but the hunger them government workers never measured when they took her, the one for family, came rushing back and filled her up to bursting. She swung from side to side, trying to hold back her laugh behind the fear of upsetting Matron Blythe, but the dam burst, and the laughter came flooding out until she had to put her hands over her mouth and bend at the waist to hold the spillage back.

"He is not allowed, Margaret. You are not to say anything to him," Matron Blythe warned in her sternest tone.

"So they changed your name, daughter?"

Margaret nodded a shy response, and the pool of laughter overflowed again.

"Your mam sent to get me, girl. Told me they took you. We've all been worried sick."

"The police are on their way. See, Matron Thomas has called them." Matron Blythe pointed to Matron Thomas, who was waving frantically from the doorway. "If you don't leave now, you'll be arrested."

He held Margaret's hand, and a charge ran up her arm, switching her to gushing laughter again. She'd known they'd find her tracks. Her mother had always said what a good reader of the signs her father was, and she had always dreamed he would show her how, one day. Now even Lilly would believe her.

"We'll get you back, girl. We're going to keep trying until we do." Margaret buried her fingers in the rich soil of his hand like a vine when she realised that he wasn't going to take her, to hold him back. Matron Blythe pulled Margaret's hand away from his as though tugging at a weed.

"You must leave now or you'll be arrested. That will only upset Margaret."

He looked into his girl's pleading eyes. "You people done upset her and our family more than anything else you can do, Missus."

Matron Blythe shuddered, as if to shake off the touch from the implied familiarity of the word Missus. "You will leave now!"

"You getting enough to eat, love? You need any money?" He dug a few shillings out of his pocket.

"She is in no need of anything. We provide all her needs." Her father gave her three shillings anyway. Matron Blythe held out her hand for them. "I will take care of that for you, Margaret." Margaret delayed handing them over a little longer than she should have, so that she could remember the ridges on the shillings her father had given her, but she eventually relented, knowing she wouldn't see them again. Her father rested a hand on her shoulder. "Can her mother write to her, Missus?"

"I am Matron Blythe to the girls, Miss Blythe to you, and the welfare office doesn't allow letters or contact, and neither do we."

"Well, I'll be going to see those welfare people about getting our girl back."

"She is in much better hands now."

"Hands that don't even feed her. Look at my girl."

13

"If you don't leave now, not only will you never see Margaret again, but I will make sure you spend a long time in jail for trespassing."

"Okay, *Missus*." He winked at Margaret as he emphasised it this time, and she gifted him a smile as if to hold him longer. "I'll be taking my leave, but we'll fight you to get our girl back. Me and her mam will be back for her soon." He raised his Akubra to her, and patted Margaret's reeling head. "I'll be back with you mam soon, love."

Matron Blythe watched him leave with Margaret and Lilly, whose mouth had opened to fresh hope throughout the whole event. Then she stayed by the chicken house until the girls had finished and ordered all of the girls to stay inside for the rest of the day.

\*\*\*

Margaret went to bed thinking of the way her father had stood up to Matron Blythe. All the girls were talking about it and it made her heart swell but feel empty at the same time. She dreamed of the shillings that Matron Blythe had taken from her and what they could have bought. The girls who had already taken the week long cooking lessons with Matron Cook spoke incessantly about washing, chopping, seasoning, mixing, baking, roasting and boiling beef, legs of lamb, and cakes with icing on the top and other treats. The girls feasted on these stories at night and it filled them up, because they were not allowed to eat any of the food they cooked—although three of the girls who could remember said that when the inspectors came, if they behaved, they got to eat good. But just that one day. Whatever wasn't sold to a shop in town or to local people who had made orders was eaten by Matron Blythe or taken home by Matrons Thomas and Cook, both of whom lived in town. The waste would be given to Mr Ralph to feed to his pigs. But when her father came back she would get to eat good.

\*\*\*

The following morning, the girls had been standing to attention in front of their neatly made beds for nearly an hour before Matron Blythe came to inspect them for the wash. Margaret, Lilly and some of the other girls spied on her from the window as she wandered in and out of the chicken house. She stuttered out, leafed several pages back in her red notebook, scratched her curly head with her pen and went back inside.

"What do you think's wrong?" Lilly asked.

"Chickens must have laid so many eggs today she can't count them. We're all going to have a good feed of fried eggs for breakfast," Sheila Two said, and infected the room with laughter. Some of the girls ran to take a peek and then scampered back to their inspection positions, as if Matron Blythe could materialise from the chicken house to the dormitory in a second.

"I think Margaret's gone and stole Matron's eggs," Beatrice said. She had been baiting her since the first day. "You won't be needing any breakfast then, will you, Margaret?" Margaret ignored her. "And you, Lilly, I can have your porridge this morning, can't I?" Lilly dropped her head like spilt milk and said nothing. "Can't I, Lilly?" Beatrice repeated with a growl.

"If you want," a bird-like voice came back. Margaret jabbed Lilly in her side and tensed her cheeks, to encourage her friend to stand firm, but Lilly's eyes remained downcast on the floor.

"Lilly said she's as hungry as all of us and she wants her porridge," Margaret said. Lilly glanced with timid admiration at her friend from the corner of an eye. She hadn't seen what Beatrice could do to those who upset her, yet.

Beatrice crossed the room and shoved Margaret in the back. "Lilly can speak for herself." Margaret kept her back to Beatrice and tilted her head, but not so that her submission was conspicuous to the other girls. Beatrice wanted to fight, and Margaret knew she was no match.

"Matron!" one of the girls cried. All those not already by their beds ran back. Beatrice walked, snarling at Margaret all the way.

"Margaret, Lilly, what have you done to my chickens?" Matron Blythe marched into the room pointing her truncheon at them.

Margaret looked at Lilly and shrugged her shoulders. "Nothing, Matron Blythe."

"This morning there were only half the eggs I counted yesterday. That has never happened before." She waited for an explanation. Margaret couldn't think of anything to say, and her head shook in spasms of denial. Lilly's fretful eyes never left the floor. "Your father didn't put some jiggery-pokery on my chicken house, did he? Not that I believe in that sort of thing, but you can never rule anything out

15

with you people." She took one step back from Margaret when she said that. "Right, I can see I am not going to get an answer. There will be no breakfast for any of you today or any other day until I get to the bottom of this. Have your wash and I will meet you all back here in fifteen minutes to give you your duties." She slapped the truncheon against her palm, and the girls scurried out of the dormitory.

*\*\*\**

Margaret, Lilly, and nine other girls did classes with Matron Blythe that day. She taught them the rudiments of reading, so that they could follow the recipes their mistresses would want them to cook; the basics of mathematics, so that when those same mistresses sent them out to shop for groceries they could ensure they received the correct change, and anything else it was felt would help them in the cleaning of their mistresses' homes, which wasn't much. They were taught nothing purely for themselves, as they were thought most unlikely to need it.

Margaret usually liked the classes. Often, she tried to read the words that Matron Blythe hadn't taught them, and when she had to clean the classroom or prepare it for Sunday service—which only ever happened if a preacher bothered to come out to the home from town, as the good Christian townspeople didn't welcome their sort in church—she would sit and practise reading one of the books. She was distracted by thoughts of her mother and father coming to get her, and wondered how she would persuade them to take Lilly, also. The way her father, usually a quiet man, was riled up surely meant that they would be coming soon.

The girls were still not getting any breakfast because the egg count remained low. Throughout the day they watched each other like circling vultures for any signs that would show who knew what was happening to the eggs. At lunch, Margaret sat gazing at Beatrice as she wolfed down her two pieces of bread and the two half slices she had confiscated from two other girls. "What you looking at?" Beatrice said when she realised. Margaret played with the edge of her plate, but her ferreting stare didn't leave Beatrice.

"You found any reason why them hens didn't lay?"

"Maybe they did lay. Maybe you and Lilly ate all the eggs and so that's why we didn't get breakfast."

"Yes, that's right," Margaret agreed, "they laid ten eggs and me and Lilly ate five each, so we didn't want breakfast anyway."

"Well, in that case you won't want this either." Beatrice leaned over, snatched a slice of Margaret's orange-jam bread, and devoured it in one go. Margaret stretched across the table and wiped her face with the other slice like a rag. Beatrice leapt on her, knocking cups and plates off the table. She grabbed hold of Margaret's curly black hair, which showed a tendency to wanting to grow straight, and yanked at it as if it had offended her. The other girls flocked into a circle, cheering.

Matron Cook ran to call Matron Blythe, who cracked her baton onto a table and shouted for quiet. The screaming girls remembered where they were and ran to their seats, but Beatrice remained on top of Margaret. Matron Blythe swiped her once across the backside with the baton, and she grimaced in pain and scrambled to her feet. Then Matron grabbed Margaret by the shoulder and struck her the same way. It cut through her like lightning and she coughed up an involuntary scream as tears shot from her eyes before she could hold them back.

"Into the middle, you two." Matron Blythe pointed to the centre of the room with her baton. "Up!" All the other girls stood with their hands behind their backs. Some were quaking in their frocks, wondering if they would be next. "Would the rest of you girls like to remind these two how they must act if they are to improve their lot in life?" There was a bloodcurdling silence. "Now!" She banged the baton onto a table.

The girls all recited it in a chorus. "We must think white, speak white, look white and act white if we are to improve our lot in life."

"Do you think these two were doing that?"

"No, Matron Blythe."

"Do you think they will find nice husbands?"

"No, Matron Blythe."

"If the only husbands they can find are full black men, then what will happen?"

"Their children will be blighted, Matron Blythe."

Matron Blythe paced between the rows of tables. "Even the darkest of you can have a good life if you observe those rules and behave in the right manner. Albert Namatjira was a black, blacker than any of you." She waved the baton at them as if she were

17

conferring damehoods for their good fortune. "He was granted honorary citizenship of Australia because he acted right." Some of the girls squinted at each other as if to ask what citizenship was and why they didn't have it. Did it mean you got to eat good if you had this citizenship thing? "You all have a better start than him. Don't let me see you behaving like these two." She pointed her baton at Margaret and Beatrice. "Out. Animals stay out in the yard."

\*\*\*

The stifling heat of daytime dissolved into a freezing night, and Margaret and Beatrice stood trembling in the yard whilst the others slept. Several times Margaret thought about running away, but she wasn't sure where she was and in which direction to run. Anyway, her mother and father would be coming for her soon, and she would get them to take Lilly, too. On one occasion she thought about lying on the grass and going to sleep, but Matron Blythe had left her light on, and every few hours she peered out into the blackness to check on them. They were allowed the morning wash, but no breakfast. Then Margaret was assigned to digging the gardens with Lilly and two other girls again. She was flagging, like a struggle-weary fish at the end of a line.

"Here, Margaret," Lilly said. She took a piece of crusty bread from the pocket of her frock and handed it to Margaret, who grabbed it and wolfed it down.

"Where did you get it?" she asked, her hunger still unsated.

"It's yours. You left it on your plate last night and I hid it for you."

"Thank you, Lilly. When my father comes back to get me I want you to come with us." Lilly said nothing, and dragged her rake through the brittle, red soil. "You do want to come, don't you? We can take you to go look for your mob." Margaret gazed at Lilly, whose frown said she didn't like playing this game. She appeared not to believe in it, even though Margaret's father had come. Although he was as big as an ox, Margaret sensed that she thought Matron Blythe could sweep him away like flood currents, and to continue playing this game hurt her too much.

"You think he'll really take me?" Lilly decided to play to satisfy Margaret's hunger.

"If I ask him he will, I'm sure of it."

"Okay then, Margaret, I'll come with you and your mob."

18

The following morning after they were surprised with breakfast, Matron Blythe told all the girls to change into a clean frock. Then without warning they were told to gather in the dining hall. The tables and chairs had been pushed to the sides, and a heavy-jowled man and a small bespectacled woman that they didn't know sat erect behind a table at the far end of the hall with Matron Blythe and Matron Thomas. They were talking and making notes into a heavy, leather bound book. The girls stood in five lines at the other end of the hall, the octoroons at the front. After an hour or so they heard cars pulling up outside. They craned their necks to see out of the too-high windows, but the occupants of the cars soon came in anyway. They were mainly women on their own, or husbands and wives, and sometimes a small family group. Many had seen the girls advertised in newspapers or church magazines, and after meetings with the Welfare, they felt it their Christian duty to ensure the girls had a family upbringing, at the same time getting domestic service on the cheap. After they had spoken to the panel at the front table, they approached the girls and walked up and down the lines inspecting them. It wasn't like Matron Blythe's inspections. Some would hurry down the lines, hurry back to the front table and out again. One woman walked down the lines with a white handkerchief over her nose and her shoulders turned away from the girls. When she bumped into one of them she jumped back startled, waved her handkerchief at the front desk and ran out of the dining hall. Others took their time and stopped to inspect the girls' physical stature with a farmer's buying eyes, but no words were exchanged. A few of the couples even smiled soothing reassurance at the girls, but most of their children were either indifferent, or making faces and laughing at them, and one mother slapped her son on the back of his head for this.

A man with bushy eyebrows and runny lips hesitated in front of the older girls in the last line. They were the darkest, and so had been at Radley the longest, but his plain and strident wife kept insisting on looking at the lighter and smaller girls at the front. She won the argument on which line, but only if she agreed with his choice of girl, which was Cathy. His eyes wouldn't leave her pure honey skin and gangly limbs, and they went back to the front desk and had what appeared to be a heated discussion with the panel. The man stood up and pulled his wife to go, but Matron Blythe called them back, and in a flurry of activity papers were filled out at the desk. Matron Thomas, a straight-backed woman with a quiet and gentle demeanour, came over to Cathy. "Come, Cathy, we have to go pack your things," she said, and they disappeared.

"What's going on?" Margaret whispered.

"They could be our new foster parents," a voice replied.

"But we got our own parents, so what we need new ones for?"

"They're going to take Cathy away."

"They're going to take you too, Margaret," Beatrice said from somewhere behind her, "so you mum and dad won't find you."

Margaret's legs began to shake like a wet and bloody lamb, as she now understood what these people were here to do.

"Can't be any worse than here," someone whispered. "At least we'll get fed better."

"You'll have to work a lot harder though."

"I'm not going anywhere," Margaret said. "Me dad's coming back to get me soon."

"You see the way that man looked at Cathy?"

"Yeah, he wants Margaret, too," Beatrice said.

Matron Thomas returned with a tear-smudged Cathy and a small sack containing her other frock and some undergarments. She handed the trembling girl to the woman, and she and the man with the bushy eyebrows led Cathy away. There were no goodbyes.

As they went through the door they bumped into a woman wearing a wide-brimmed white hat with a black band tied around it, which hid most of her sun-worn face. She had been rushing and apologised several times before heading for the front table whilst searching her bag. Some of its contents spilled onto the floor, and she stooped to pick them up and apologised again, but to no one in particular this time. After a few minutes with the panel she walked down the lines, throwing tremulous smiles at the girls in-between dabbing at her face with her handkerchief. She stopped at all of the youngest girls in the first line, two in the second, and Margaret in the third. "How long have you been here?" the woman asked, in that high-pitched, phoney voice they heard Matron Blythe use when she was on the telephone as though she were sucking on a stone.

Margaret kept her eyes to the floor. "Long time, miss. They say I'm too bad to place," she said in her worst English, causing some of the girls around her to giggle. The woman showed a flicker of a smile, then hurried down the fourth and fifth lines, as if she was obliged to look because the girls had been waiting, then she went back to the panel at the front before leaving.

***

It took several days for Margaret to get over the inspections from the foster parents and feel satisfied that she wasn't about to be taken again. Cathy had been the only girl chosen, and life at Radley fell back into its normal routine, except for the *chooks*, whose eggs were still below average. Matron had asked Mr Ralph to check them for diseases and to buy another rooster, if only to excite them into laying more unfertilised eggs, but still they were laying half as much as they had done previously.

Late in the afternoon, when they had nothing in particular to do, Margaret and Lilly sauntered down to the chicken house. They circled it several times to make sure that they were alone, then Lilly kneeled at the back of the hut and allowed Margaret to stand on her back to peep through a gap in the weatherboard. "That lady who talked to you when the foster parents came seemed nice," Lilly said.

"A dingo will act nice until it gets close enough to bite you," Margaret said.

"But some of them won't bite, and then you become friends."

Margaret ignored her and concentrated on the chicken house. The *chooks* seemed all right to her, and she had seen one of the other girls collect their eggs that morning. Then she noticed it. A large brown egg sat in one of the hens' nests; it must have been laid after the girl did her rounds. Margaret squeezed her hand through a gap in the weatherboard and took hold of the warm egg. "What you got there?" Lilly asked. Margaret showed her the egg and then hid it in the long grass. She pushed her face back up against the hole to see if there were any more. She winced as nails bit into her ear, and jumped back from the chicken house in pain.

"What are you two up to?" Mr Ralph asked, his face twisted in scorn. He had Lilly by the ear also. "Been stealing the eggs, eh?"

"No, Mr Ralph, we're not doing anything," Margaret said.

"Right then, it's off to Matron Blythe with you two."

21

Matron Blythe marched them back down to the chicken house, and on the way they saw Beatrice coming from that direction. "What are you doing, Beatrice?"

"Nothing, Matron Blythe," Beatrice said, standing to attention with her hands behind her back.

"Idle hands make for mischief, run along and find something to do and stop making a nuisance of yourself." Beatrice scurried off and Matron Blythe carried the other two to the back of the chicken house. "Well, explain to me what you were up to?"

"We were watching them for you, Matron Blythe. To see if we could tell why they weren't laying."

"Yes," agreed Lilly.

"And?"

"We don't know, Matron Blythe," Margaret said. She was watching Matron's steps with concern, as she was treading close to where she had hidden the egg.

"Do you know what happens to little liars?"

Lilly did, and she started to cry.

"No, Matron Blythe," Margaret said.

"I'll give you one more chance to tell me the truth."

Margaret was saying nothing. No matter what Matron Blythe did to her, she wasn't going to lose that egg. She only hoped that Lilly could hold out too. Matron Blythe swung away from them, "Have it your way, then. Wait here." She looked in the grass, right where the egg was, and retrieved a dry twig. Margaret's throat shrunk dry, but Matron didn't find the egg. When Matron Blythe went into the chicken house, Lilly's shrieks drifted higher, as if she were calling for absolution. Matron Blythe returned with the twig, and there was something on the end of it.

"Put out your tongue," she ordered Margaret. Then she smeared the chicken shit onto it. Lilly got the same. The bitterness would eat away the lies.

"I will get to the bottom of this soon," she promised as she waddled away from them.

Margaret plucked a leaf from a tree, wiped her tongue clean, and spat out the rest. Lilly was still crying with her white-grey smeared tongue hanging out. Margaret used a leaf to wipe it for her. "When we eat that egg it will all have been worth it, you'll see." Lilly shook her head as if to dislodge Margaret's words. "I'll let you have most of

22

it," Margaret said. She pushed back the grass to retrieve her egg, but their nest was empty. She continued to search but couldn't find it. They ambled back through the orchard like outrun dingoes. Beatrice was sitting against an apple tree, sniggering at them.

"Margaret, put out your tongue," she called, whilst waving a twig at her. Margaret poked her tongue at her with a wide-eyed glare. Beatrice returned the tongue wagging, but there was a yellow egg yolk sitting on hers.

*** 

The cooking lessons gave the girls another opportunity to be around food, and sometimes steal some, and that's why they all liked them. They also liked the fact that Matron Cook was easy-going when Matron Blythe wasn't around, and then you could just call her Matron. She made jokes about some of the girls' cooking and shared her heaving laugh with them, and those that made a really good effort she would pat on the head and say well done to them. She told the girls that when they did the cooking for their masters and mistresses they should taste it, because that was the best way to tell how good it was. But she was sorry that she was the only one allowed to taste the food here, because Matron Blythe disapproved of them tasting things. The girls weren't sure if it was because Matron Blythe felt scorn at the thought of them putting spoons into their mouths and then back into the food, or if she just wanted to deprive them. If it were up to her she would make them taste it, Matron Cook had said, but you know how you girls are, in no time it would fly back to Matron Blythe. So she instructed the girls on what to do and waltzed around the kitchen dipping her finger into sauces, slicing off bites of meat, and filling her spoon with stew.

Margaret was into the third day of cooking lessons, and already she was getting the hang of making roasts in an iron oven, and stews using a gas fire. She had learned some of these things with her mother, but they had done it in an old three-legged oven when they lived on the settlement. Even so, with the rations of second-rate flour, unrefined sugar, tinned meat and last grade tea that they were given—which had to be supplemented with *tucker* they surreptitiously gathered from the bush, and a sheep that her father would send with someone from time to time—her mother and the other women could concoct sticky fig pies, roasts that melted in the mouth, and cakes that didn't last long after they had been baked. And if any of the families in the settlement ran out of their small rations after a few days, which they often did, they would always share. Her mother and some of the other women had been thrown out of the settlement by the new manager, because they objected to being fenced off from their kids and obeying all his rules. But he had only let them take their black kids with them. The half-castes and above couldn't go, he said, but her mother had sneaked back with some of the other women and taken their kids to go walkabout. Sometimes she hankered after those walkabouts as though in a deep grieving. On these extended holidays to their own tribal areas, at times when they were teeming with game and other bush *tucker*, her mother showed her how to hunt rabbits by sneaking up on them from behind and falling on them. Her mother was also a good shot with her father's rifle, and when she shot a wild pig, swan, emu or kangaroo, it would be cooked in a large hole in the ground, wrapped in leaves, with hot rocks on top. There were days when she licked the air to remember the taste of roo tail soup, or emu liver with bush tomato, and her stomach would argue even more, as it was doing now.

The girls all wanted to try a taste of the food they were making, but the penalty for being caught was expulsion from the cooking lessons, and it might mean that Matron Cook wouldn't put extra porridge into their bowls for breakfast, or extra jam on their bread at lunch and supper. So mostly they obeyed the rules and memorised the smells, textures, consistencies and amounts, so that they could elaborate on their stories when they told them to the other girls.

*Matron cook made us cook something real fancy today.*

*After you roasted it you had to put these white shoes—or was it hats?—on them.*

*The food's getting dressed to go out. Now I know why we don't get to eat any!*

*Well, when the fat was spitting from the frying pan I made some of it hit me on my lip, and I tasted it.*

*I didn't wash my hands after like Matron said we should, and when I came out I licked it off.*

*Well, I made some of that batter stuff spill onto my frock, and I ate it off when I came out. See, there's a bit left—you want to taste it?*

On the last day they made cakes. Because she had done well during the week, Margaret was allowed to make the cream cake. After the sponges had been baked and the cream churned, she spread the jam onto the cake. A drop of jam fell onto her finger, and she considered it for a moment. Matron Cook was at the other end of the kitchen with another girl, and so she plunged the finger into her mouth. The next time she shook the knife to encourage the jam onto her finger and licked it off. Lilly saw her and wore a snigger laced with envy behind her hand. Margaret spread thick mounds of cream onto the jam, and then placed one sponge on top of the other. Then she loaded the rest of the cream into a piping bag. She piped some onto her finger and tasted it first, the richness fogging her caution.

"What does it taste like?" Lilly asked.

"Fluffy clouds," Margaret answered, and Lilly bounced as though she could float. "You want some?" Lilly shook the craving from her head and hurried back to what she was doing.

The slapping of truncheon against open palm told them that Matron Blythe was approaching, and everyone, including Matron Cook, fell silent and doubled their efforts to look busy. Matron Blythe strolled around, inspecting the girls' work without comment. Then she addressed Matron Cook from the other end of the kitchen. "Matron, will you have the cream sponge and an apple pie sent up to my room for supper."

"Yes, Matron Blythe," Matron Cook replied in her best voice, genuflecting from her corpulent waist.

Matron Blythe started to leave, and then with sudden thought spun back. "Would you like to have cake and sandwiches with me for supper, Lilly?"

"Me, Matron Blythe?" Lilly touched a palm to her chest to hold back her surprise.

"Yes, you, Lilly."

Margaret was shaking her head 'no'. She could see Matron Blythe rolling the truncheon between her fingers like some extension of herself. But Lilly was too overcome to see Margaret.

"Yes please, Matron Blythe," Lilly accepted with her eyes glazed over.

"Then you will be responsible for bringing up the cakes for supper," Matron Blythe informed her, and she turned around and waddled away.

"Don't go, Lilly," Margaret said, her forehead creased with worry.

"Why?" Lilly demanded.

"Because I don't want you to."

"You had a taste of it."

"Yes, but it wasn't that nice."

"You said it tasted like fluffy clouds."

"When my father comes for us he'll give us shillings and we can buy cakes."

"He may never come!"

"He will, I promise he will."

"I think you're just jealous that Matron asked me."

"No I'm not."

"Yes you are." Lilly swung away from her.

Margaret shuffled closer to her and whispered, "Some of the girls say she uses it like—like a man thing."

Lilly stared at Margaret as if she were an untravelled trail. Her bottom lip enveloped her top one, sealing in her anger that her best friend should try to prevent her from eating cake. They didn't talk again.

***

All the other girls were in bed long before Lilly slithered into the dormitory as if she were stepping onto hot coals, sniffing back tears. She climbed with halting spasms into bed, and with each movement to get there she belched out a sharp moan. Margaret got up and crept to stoop by her bedside. "You all right, Lilly?" There was no response. The moonlight rested on Lilly's face, which was ashen and vacant, and her red eyes were swollen with tears. Her two hands rested between her legs like a broken shield, guarding that place. "My father is going to come and get us soon, Lilly, you'll see." Lilly looked straight through her as though it didn't matter now.

Margaret spent much of the night by Lilly's bedside, brushing her hair, talking and singing to her, but she expected and received no response. When the new rooster crowed the following morning, Margaret woke to find herself still kneeling by Lilly's side.

***

Matron Blythe removed Lilly from cleaning duties and had her sit in what went for reading and mathematics classes. There was much cleaning of the dormitory, bathroom and kitchen that week. Extra girls were put out to weed the vegetable gardens, and Matron Blythe inspected everything three times and for twice as long, but she wore false pleasantness now. She stopped to ask some of the girls how they were, which shocked them. "Fine, thank you, Matron Blythe," they all said. She even praised some of them on their work, which encouraged them to do more.

"What's going on?" Margaret asked some of the other girls, but they just shrugged their lightened shoulders now that their burdens had been eased. Then Matron Cook was asked to select some of the better cooks to prepare food for the next two days. Margaret was selected to bake cakes and pies. Matron Cook was pickled with animation, waltzing around the kitchen as she tasted each dish.

"What's happening, Matron?" Margaret asked.

"Oh, all right, then. It's tomorrow, but you mustn't tell." She was bursting like bloated crackling to tell the secret herself, and the girls gathered round. "You all get to eat this tomorrow, if you're good."

There was a malnourished silence. Then Margaret broke it. "Why? Does she want us to forgive her for Lilly?"

Matron gave her a stern schoolmistress's glare, and Margaret's gaze fell to the pies she was making. "There is an inspection tomorrow by the Inspector of homes, and if you are all good,"—her words stopped like an upturned stall on Margaret again—"you get to eat what you have been preparing for the last two days. So let's hope no one spoils it. Now do your best, as it's all for you." She chirped as if she was the one expecting to eat a good meal for once, and her elation filled the girls, and they poured this into their cooking. But Margaret was still brooding over Lilly.

*** 

The Inspectors from the Aboriginal Protection Board were supposed to visit and inspect the homes every few months, but they rarely did. Radley hadn't been visited in more than a year. Mr Simmonds was a short, balding man with a pleasant round face, who removed and wiped his steel-rimmed glasses with nervous frequency. Like Matron Blythe, he was fond of taking copious amounts of notes in a diary he carried for the purpose. Matron Blythe led him around the vegetable garden and he was impressed at the variety of vegetables the girls had to eat, and expressed his wish that other homes were run to the same high standards. They wound their way through the orchard and past the chicken house, and Matron Blythe told him how they were buying in eggs now because for more than two months their hens hadn't laid

27

properly. Mr Simmonds kept chickens himself, and told her about a remedy for worms that might get them laying again, and she accepted his suggestion because it pleased him, not telling him that Mr Ralph had tried that but it hadn't worked. Mr Simmonds insisted on seeing everything. He ran his hand along window ledges as they climbed the stairs, noting in his book that they were immaculately clean. Then they walked through the dormitory, where he tested the firmness of the beds, and he took one of the girls' frocks from a cupboard and examined it for cleanliness and any tears. But Matron Blythe had been nothing but thorough herself, and all was in order.

Last of all, Mr Simmonds was shown to the dining hall, where the girls stood assembled like a choir. As she walked through the door, Matron Blythe stopped and introduced him. "Girls, this is Mr Simmonds, the inspector from the protection board."

"Good day, Mr Simmonds," they sang out in chorus.

"G'day, girls," he replied. He took off his glasses and cleaned them again, as if to confirm what he was seeing. All four of the long dining tables were overflowing with sumptuous fare. A small pig sat at the centre of one table, and then all the tables had whole roasted chickens, a leg of lamb, potatoes, carrots and peas, fruits from the orchards, freshly baked bread, butter that had been churned that morning, pies and cakes and clotted cream. He licked the aroma from his lips. "I don't want to keep you from this marvellous lunch, girls, so I will be brief."

"We hope you will join us for lunch, Mr Simmonds," Matron Blythe said.

He looked at his watch. "I wish I could, Matron, but I have another visit to make today."

"Then you must make Matron Cook pack you some lunch." She raised her hand in command and Matron Cook set about it.

"That would be most welcome, thank you," he said, moistening his lips again.

He walked towards the girls assembled in a line away from the tables, Matron Blythe now making him lead. He stopped at the beginning of the line to ask the girls how they were doing. Did they enjoy the home? Were the matrons good to them? He didn't ask if they received enough to eat, as going by the fare on display that was patently obvious.

"Good."

"Yes."

"Yes," came a consensus of replies. The girls all knew what to say if they expected to partake of the feast, and he noted their answers in his book.

Margaret stood towards the end of the line. She wiggled her toes, clasped her jittery hands behind her back, and hoped the smiling man would walk past her, before she could ambush him with the truth, which was unfurling in her aching belly, to rob the others of the only good day that they would have for the next six months—at least, until the next inspection. The inspector walked past her, to the next girl, and the other girls breathed a collective sigh of relief, like nervous game that had avoided being snared on their way to some succulent grazing, because they could now allow themselves to taste the aroma; it wouldn't be long now.

"Margaret, you were asked a question," Matron Blythe said, causing her to jump out of her wilful reverie.

"Do you get enough to eat?" Mr Simmonds directed his question to her again, from his position in front of the girl next to her. Even though he was satisfied by the evidence he had seen, it was on his list of questions and he wanted to put a tick next to a girl's answer.

"No, sir, we don't." The answer escaped before she had time to trap and strangle it.

"But look at all this." Mr Simmonds gestured to the food on the tables.

"The worms out back eat better than us, sir. All this fancy stuff is just for show."

"Margaret has a problem with telling the truth, Mr Simmonds, don't you, Margaret? I said, don't you, Margaret?" Matron Blythe repeated.

Margaret bowed her head as if bearing shame. "Yes, Matron Blythe."

Mr Simmonds ticked yes for the answer and finished his questioning. He collected his packed lunch, thanked Matron Blythe for showing him around her remarkable facility, and swaggered away.

Matron Blythe waited until Mr Simmonds' car had sped through the gates. Then she instructed all the girls to leave the dining hall except Margaret. If one failed, they all failed. There would be no sumptuous lunch. She ordered Margaret to pack the food away to be taken to town for sale. "I will deal with you personally tomorrow," she promised. It probably meant more chicken shit spread on her tongue again, Margaret thought. She would wipe it off like the last time and eat a stolen carrot to get rid of the taste. But she knew the other girls would want their revenge.

***

The following morning no one spoke to Margaret at breakfast. Matron Blythe had said nothing to her, and she wondered when she would receive her punishment. As soon as breakfast finished, Matron Blythe strode into the dining hall. "Margaret, Beatrice, go to the dormitory and pack your things." Margaret's mind grew cataracts again, the way it had when she was caught and taken to Radley. But both she and Beatrice went, and Matron Blythe accompanied them. As soon as they had packed, she escorted them down into the yard where Mr Ralph's car was waiting, its engine shuddering. Some of the other girls must have been standing on their chairs, because Margaret could see their bobbing heads at the windows of the dining hall. Lilly was standing at the door pulling at her dress, her eyes welling up. She had said nothing since the day she ate cakes with Matron Blythe, and her mouth parted as if to say goodbye, but nothing came.

"But me mum and dad are coming for me, Matron Blythe," Margaret protested. She had even laid down new tracks in the yard last night in case they had lost their way.

"Where you are going they will never find you," Matron Blythe said. She ushered her into the back seat with Beatrice, and she sat in the front next to Mr Ralph.

The car jerked forward and rolled towards the gates. Beatrice squeezed herself into a corner like a rodent in a cage, but Margaret was still protesting. Then she turned to look out of the rear window at Lilly. "Tell me mum and dad they took me, Lilly. Tell them to find me. I'll always be your friend, Lilly," and she started to cry.

# Chapter 2

Margaret wasn't sure how long they had been driving because she had been raining tears. The car had left the dusty roads some miles back and sped along a straight tarmac highway, which rose and dipped gently all the way for miles. The land to either side was unchanging red earth, which was dry and bald, but here and there a hardy gum tree broke through the congealed soil and sharp tufts of spinifex grass salted the plains. As they went over one rise, a tall peak appeared as a dot on the horizon, but it was more than three hours before they reached the mouth of the canyon which was outlined by the peak. It took another hour to drive through the canyon, and Mr Ralph followed a sign to the left towards a small town. They were journeying further away from where her parents might find her. Since they had left Radley they had passed only seven other vehicles on the road, and those were mainly huge road trains transporting farm produce. They veered away from the town before they reached it, and stopped by a leaning farmhouse. Matron Blythe had a word in Mr Ralph's ear and then climbed out of the car.

"Beatrice, get your things and follow me."

Beatrice, who had not moved for the whole journey, eased herself out of the car like an infirm old woman. Margaret stared at her arching back, her heart screaming like thunder as she realised she would be on her own. Even though she and Beatrice had not gotten on, hers was a familiar face, a known adversary. Beatrice turned to shut the door. "Bye, Margaret." Her voice, which would normally drown out all around her, was unusually shallow. Margaret couldn't sound the words, and Beatrice pushed the door shut and followed Matron Blythe up onto the veranda. Margaret pressed her face up against the glass as if to see better. Somehow she hoped the people in the house wouldn't want Beatrice, and she would get to come with her. The Beatrice she knew at Radley was like a cornered boar, desperate to survive. That wasn't the real Beatrice. She needed to be with someone she knew, even if it was Beatrice.

31

After a few minutes Matron Blythe came back onto the veranda followed by the man with the runny lips, his wife and Beatrice. Cathy was nowhere to be seen. Matron Blythe climbed into the car and Mr Ralph pulled away again. Margaret gazed out the back at Beatrice fighting to raise her hand, but it resisted, and instead she waved it from where it rested against her side. Margaret flattened both her palms against the window so that Beatrice could see them.

"I just polished that glass this morning," Mr Ralph said. "Did you hear me, girl?"

"Margaret ... Margaret," Matron Blythe called, but their cries were like far-off echoes.

*** 

They drove for another few hours before stopping at another girls' home as dusk rolled in. There, they shared supper and had beds for the night, and then they set out again as the sun rose. This time they drove on an unsealed highway for several hours, over land where there were even fewer tufts of spinifex breaking the barren soil. Some of the yellow spiked grass leapt out of nowhere to slash at the tires of the car, and Mr Ralph sometimes swerved to avoid it. No other travellers traversed this road. Margaret began to take note now, whereas before she had not. If she were to leave tracks so that her mum and dad could find her, she would have to know the country they had driven through.

Finally, they broke out of the choking desert into an oasis of life and growth, and Matron Blythe coughed up her relief. Red river gums grew up to eighty feet high in the middle of a streambed, and Mr Ralph sped the car down one side of them, throwing sand up against their rock solid, mottled grey, white and red trunks. Before long they came upon a forest of acacia and eucalyptus trees, which were interspersed with desert oaks. They followed a rough path through these for over twenty miles before they came upon a dust track, and there was a large bullet-riddled sign nailed to a tree with the name of the town, Malee.

They drove for another five miles before they saw any sign that human life existed in these parts. At the dusty intersection of the unsealed road into the town, they could make out the start of a ploughed field behind a hedgerow of acacia bushes. Mr Ralph waited while Matron Blythe looked down at her directions, and she told him

32

to turn left, away from the town. A few hundred yards up the bumpy road they startled a freckle-faced boy on his pony, his head protected from the fierce sun by a straw hat. He stopped to stare in curiosity at the strangers, and Matron Blythe wound her window further down and leaned out of it. "Good day—"

"G'day, miss."

"Do you know where the McDonalds' place is, young man?"

"Yes, miss." He continued to stare his unshielded amazement. "Well?"

The boy leaned off his pony and pointed behind him, but his inquisitive eyes never left them. "Follow the track back there and it's the first homestead you'll see. It's the only one up that ways."

"Thank you," she said as Mr Ralph thrust the gear into first and hurried the car into a turn. They went past the boy and turned up the path, between more of the acacia. At points the bushes thinned, and Margaret's mouth fell stone dry as she saw the homestead with its green corrugated iron roof get closer. They drove into a clearing in front of the homestead, which stood on stilts, its weatherboard walls freshly painted white. On the side of the homestead was a small barn with a hardy variety of bougainvillea climbing up over it. The tank stand stood taller than the two-floored homestead, with a tank that carried several months' water supply. Furthest from the house was the dunny, which stood on the edge of a forest of malee trees. Margaret's eyes flitted about like a buzzing bee, but she tried to keep her body still, so that she would feel the vibrations of the place and take in all those stirrings that her eyes couldn't pick out. Swallows flew back and forth from under the barn roof and, somewhere, a log from an old malee was singing out a hollow death song. Margaret shuddered at the vibrations from marching ground insects and reptiles rising into the air, as she was surprised at how much her senses were still alive, having spent countless nights away from the desert floor where they had been honed. She eased herself high in her seat to look at the two dogs lying lazily under the shady tank stand. Then she saw the woman heaving an axe over her head and letting it fall onto the log at her feet. She could only have been twice the length of the axe, but her arms were thick and her back firm. She raised the axe to strike again and saw the car approaching. Without stopping in her motion, she dropped the axe and ran into the house through the back door.

33

They waited in the car, expecting that the woman who had run into the homestead had gone to call someone, but no one came. Mr Ralph was about to hit the horn when a woman wearing a beehive hairdo, a pleated dress, and white stilettos stepped out onto the veranda. She stumbled a little coming down the steps and had to hold on to the banister for support. She walked towards the car, swaying a couple of times in the high heels, and she shielded her eyes from the sun with a fan. When she recognised who it was, she stopped like a felled log. Matron Blythe climbed out of the car to meet her. "Good day, Mrs McDonald."

"Good day, Miss Blythe, I didn't expect you until—Well, until I had got back in touch to confirm it."

"I had to drop off another girl not far from here, Mrs McDonald, so I thought it best to bring Margaret today. You do still want her, don't you?"

"Yes ... Yes," Anne McDonald said, looking around Matron Blythe for the girl.

Matron Blythe turned to her side and didn't see her. "Margaret, Margaret, come here, child." Margaret slid out of the car and crept towards them. She scratched her leg through her frock and then started to pick at her nails. "Have you forgotten your manners, Margaret?"

"Good day, Mrs McDonald." Margaret gave a curtsey like she was told, her head bowed all the time, but it still felt silly.

"Good day, Margaret." Anne McDonald pursed her lips into a weak smile and nodded at her. Then she turned to Matron Blythe. "Lets get in out of this infernal heat. I'll never get used to it." Matron Blythe silently concurred and followed.

Anne and Matron Blythe stepped on the path an army of ants were busily crossing, but Margaret remembered to step over it, and she followed the two women up the five steps onto the veranda, which was shielded with a fine mesh gauze to hold back the flies which were milling outside. The doors to the house had been left open to allow cool air to circulate, and Anne showed them through into the lounge. She put her head round the door and called out, "Elizabeth." An auburn haired girl, not much older than Margaret, but prematurely widening at the hips, hurried into the room.

"Yes, Mum."

"Elizabeth, this is Matron Blythe and Margaret. Margaret is coming to live with us."

"Hello." Elizabeth directed it to both of them, standing as erect as a stone-built fence.

"Hello, Elizabeth," Matron Blythe said, then she poked at Margaret's arm, before she could say anything. "Have you lost your tongue, child?"

"Good day, Elizabeth." Margaret gave her a curtsey too.

"Elizabeth, can you fix some supper please?" The girl was already on her way to the kitchen.

"Not for me, Mrs McDonald. We have such a long way to go."

"It wouldn't be proper not to have you and your driver eat before you go, Matron Blythe. It shouldn't take but a few minutes." Anne directed her to a seat. "We can have some cold ham with a salad. I did have a joint to roast for Wednesday, but that will take too long. Would you like some pineapple juice? It's freshly squeezed from my husband's crop."

"All right then, Mrs McDonald, but we really must be on our way within the hour."

They called in Mr Ralph from the car, and soon Elizabeth had set five large plates of sliced ham, tomatoes and salad leaves on the table. She went back and forth a couple of times to bring in bread and butter, a jug of pineapple juice, and a strawberry cake that they had made specially for another day, but she looked glad to eat now. As they ate she watched Margaret through lowered lashes.

Margaret had never sat at a table with their kind, and Matron Blythe warned her not to shame them with a peppery stare. She ate like a turtle, chewing every morsel as if she expected it to be her last. And on two occasions she slipped slices of bread under the table to hide in her frock.

"This is an excellent meal, Mrs McDonald. We'll certainly be stronger for the drive back."

"It's a pity you're in such a hurry and can't stay the night," Anne said. But Margaret would later learn that the offer was only out of courtesy, as Anne McDonald felt sure that the accommodation she had to offer was probably not as comfortable as what they were used to, and she hated subjecting her home to anyone's scrutiny.

Matron Blythe slipped more ham into her mouth and finished chewing on it. "I must tell you that the girls at Radley don't appreciate such rich food, Mrs McDonald. There is certainly no need for Margaret to have the same meals as you."

"Would you like strawberry cake, Matron Blythe?" Anne held the dish in front of her, then she passed it to Mr Ralph and then Margaret, who looked for Matron Blythe's approval first, but when she saw that she was too involved in her own meal she took a slice. She bit into the cake and pinpricks ran through her as she remembered splashing as she swam in ponds with a dozen other children, mulberry juice running down her cheeks as she sat in a tree eating the fruits, and chasing goannas with her mother. The high went soon after she had finished eating the cake, as she remembered what Lilly had been forced to do to eat cake.

Margaret helped Elizabeth to clear the table whilst the two women completed the formalities of signing the various forms. At the door Matron Blythe remembered something. "Now I'll tell you this for what it's worth, Mrs McDonald. Margaret's a spirited girl, but she is also a little liar. I don't expect you'll be able to train it all out of her, but she does have some intelligence and is good at domestic chores. With any luck she'll be able to get work as a housemaid when she's a little older, and find a half-cast or quadroon that will marry her. At least that way her children may stand a chance, although I doubt it." She waited for Mrs McDonald's reaction, but when there was none, she spun around and hurried to the car, which Mr Ralph had already started. Margaret stood in the hallway, where she had heard Matron Blythe's parting remarks. She watched as the car started its long journey back to Radley, and its spinning wheels spat up dust at the outback homestead.

\*\*\*

The tight knots in Margaret's stomach loosened a little as the car disappeared. She realised that Anne McDonald was the same woman who had been chopping wood as they pulled up to the homestead, as she had seen her hastily discarded boots by the kitchen door. What other changes would Mrs McDonald make now that Matron Blythe had gone? Fortunately, she had hidden two slices of bread under her frock, just in case. Sure, Anne McDonald had given her strawberry cake right when Matron Blythe had more or less forbade it, but was that so she could pass the inspection?

"Elizabeth, get Margaret that old brown dress that you've grown out of, that should fit her. We can't have her doing work in this one." Anne cast an eye over Margaret, trying to measure her size. "We'll have to see what else of yours she can get later." Elizabeth ran upstairs followed by her mother. Within moments Anne returned, dressed in an old pair of pants and shirt, with a scarf protecting her beehive. "Margaret." She followed after Anne, who scurried like a foraging mouse to the storeroom at the back of the house. The woman's movements seemed familiar to her. "This will be your room. We were going to get it ready for you, but you'll have to help Elizabeth to do that now. Mr McDonald never seems to have the time to do anything in this house." The room was murky with floating dust and packed to within a pace of the door. Anne turned back and scurried past Margaret into the kitchen. She reached into a cupboard and pulled out pieces of dusting cloth. All the time Margaret was watching each move she made, trying to weigh up when and how much she could untie her knots. Had the strawberry cake really told her anything?

Margaret changed into the brown dress in the kitchen, taking care to hide her two slices of bread in its pockets. The frock caught her mid calf. Anne pinned it at the shoulders because Margaret was slighter than Elizabeth, then she gave both girls a broom and duster each, put on her boots by the kitchen door and hurried out of the house back to the logs.

The girls stood in the doorway of the storeroom and stared at the crates and boxes of all sorts, but they were really tracing the outlines of each other's personalities. "I suppose we oughta move the boxes first." Elizabeth froze at the sound of Margaret's voice.

"Well—okay, we can put them in the barn; Daddy won't need it for storage for a few months." There was someone else. Elizabeth had called him Daddy, and her mother Mr McDonald, and Margaret was already wondering about him. What would he be like? Not many men had worked at Radley; something to do with the way Abbo girls seemed to cast a spell over them, offering them favours and all sorts, or that's what she'd heard. Some of the matrons were used to saying anything in front of them—maybe because they considered them like Mr Ralph's pigs, too dumb to understand and have feelings.

37

They humped several of the crates and boxes into the barn, sometimes single-handed, and when the boxes were too heavy for one, they carried them together. When they carried one box they faced each other, and Margaret searched Elizabeth's face with a prying stare. It made Elizabeth glow warm, and halfway to the barn she turned to carry her end from behind. When they put the box down, Margaret sat to rest on the bed of hay scattered over the barn floor, still staring.

"We're not going to finish if you sit there."

"We can take a rest, can't we?" Margaret said.

"Mum never rests until bedtime, and she's okay."

"Well, at Radley we learned lots of ways to rest so that the matrons couldn't see us."

"Sister Ruth says you're all lazy."

"Who is Sister Ruth?"

"She's my teacher at school."

"She doesn't know my dad, then. He works so hard that we only see him once or twice a year."

"He can't be a very good dad if we have to look after you."

Margaret didn't answer. She was beginning to wonder that herself, as he had promised to come back for her, and he had waited so long that Matron Blythe had moved her before he came. Now she wondered if he would be able to find her in this new place.

"Sister Ruth told Mum that she couldn't take any more Aboriginals in her class."

"Why's that?"

"Well, for one, a lot of the parents don't like it, and Sister Ruth says she doesn't want to drag the school down."

Margaret felt like hopping when she heard this. She did like school, but if she couldn't go then maybe they would have to send her back to Radley where she would see Lilly, and her father would certainly find her there.

"Mum says she'll get you in one way or another, though. But I don't think Daddy agrees."

For a while, they observed each other like eagles circling prey.

"What do you like to play, Elizabeth?"

"Everybody calls me Liz, except Mum."

"Why's that?"

"She says the full name has a regal ring to it."

38

"What's regal?"

"Like Kings and Queens and so on."

"You a Queen, then?" Margaret asked, with serious eyes.

"No, silly."

"What you like to play then, Liz? I like to swim, hunt rabbits, climb trees and run after spirits and things. How about you?"

"Those are boys' things. I go to school, read and play the piano; and Mum is teaching me about etiquette."

"What's that?"

"It's just something white ladies have to learn so that—well, so that we become proper ladies and find a nice husband."

"Are—Are you a real live Aboriginal?" Liz asked as though she was unsure about the wisdom of the question. Margaret shrugged her shoulders as if easing off dust. "Well, do you eat slugs, roots and babies?"

Margaret laughed. She leaned back on her hands, put the soles of her feet together and flapped her knees like wings as she laughed. "You ever seen anybody eat babies?"

"Well, no. But Sister Ruth tells us that you do." Liz circled her foot in the hay as if to ease her smouldering discomfort. "I don't think you are, anyway. Sister Ruth showed us a picture of some once and they were real black. Like charcoal. But she covered up the bottom bit and wouldn't let us look long because they didn't have any clothes on. She says this girl and boy in our class are half-caste, and if they are halfway between something then they are nowhere at all."

Margaret continued to flap her limbs and watch Liz. She knew she was going to feel at ease with her.

"We had better go and finish that room, otherwise Mum's going to be mad."

"We can rest just a little bit more."

Liz headed for the barn door and Margaret scrambled to her feet behind her. Then a shower of hay landed over Liz's head and shoulders. "What did you do that for?" She spun around, brushing hay out of her auburn hair, which was tied in a ponytail that reached the small of her back. Her freckled face, which was otherwise milky white, glowed.

"Because my mind told me to," Margaret said as she waited for Liz to join in the game.

"Well, you better watch what your mind tells you to do around here. Daddy is in charge, then it's Mum and then me. Sister Ruth says your people aren't capable of making decisions. We'd better finish your room now." Liz strode out of the barn in a fabricated humph with Margaret skipping behind her. When they came within view of Anne she stopped skipping, but as soon as they were in the house she started to skip again, and grinned as Liz fought back her laugh, because it wouldn't have shown that she was in charge.

They took a few hours to finish the room. The remaining boxes and crates were carried to the barn, and then they piled those things that could be burned in the yard. After that, they wiped the insides of the windows clean, swept the room of dust, hundreds of spiders and cobwebs, and wiped down a spring bed and mattress that they found buried in a corner. When they had finished, Margaret followed Liz upstairs to find bedclothes and curtains. "This first room is mine." She pointed it out. "This is Daddy's bedroom, and Mum sleeps in here." The room at the end of the landing was light and airy, the floral prints on the walls, bedclothes and curtains blooming like the desert after a heavy rain, and the scent circulating sweet as lavender. It was the only room in the house to have a carpet. The rest of the house had polished floorboards and painted walls. Liz opened a chest at the foot of the bed, took out a wide-brimmed white hat, and laid it on the bed. Now Margaret remembered where she had seen Anne McDonald's walk. The woman who came to Radley to look at the girls and dropped the things from her handbag had worn the same hat. Liz pulled out two sheets and a blanket. A large pile of letters bound together with string fell onto the floor, and Margaret put them back into the chest. Liz handed the sheets to her. "Once every week we have to change and wash them. Mum does hers and Daddy's."

After they had made the bed and hung a piece of hessian over the window, Liz led Margaret out the front, grabbing a stick lying on the veranda as she went. The sun was already sliding out of the sky, making it much cooler. She used the stick to beat the clumps of spinifex as she wound her way towards the tiny shed on the edge of the woods, being careful to see if anything came out of it before she advanced. "What you doing that for?" Margaret asked.

"You have to mind out for snakes and spiders when you're going to the lavatory. That's where we're going now. Daddy calls it the dunny, but Mum doesn't think that's proper."

"A snake's not going to do you no harm if you walk peaceful, like."

"And how is it going to tell if you're walking peaceful?"

"Step soft, so that the vibrations you leave don't rush up on them too sudden," she said matter-of-factly. But Liz glared at her with her hands on her hips.

Margaret slowed her walk and was careful to step over any clumps of grass that she couldn't see through. Something glinted in the sun and she stopped to look at it. It was what she thought. It must be a sign. She couldn't collect it now whilst Liz was watching, but she would come for it later.

Liz got tired of waiting for her and continued beating the grass all the way to the dunny. The door creaked as she pulled it back, so that Margaret could see the wooden box on which she had to sit. "Mum won't come in here. She does hers in a pail and then Daddy empties it. She says if he gets us one of those indoor lavatories, like people in cities use, then he won't have to do it anymore."

A patrolling column of ants had captured Margaret's attention and she wasn't listening. So Liz marched back towards the house, and Margaret ran to catch up with her. "Mum says she's heard that Mrs Cartwright has a lavatory inside her house. Right inside her own house! Can you imagine that? And it's made of real china as well." But Margaret wasn't showing any interest, and Liz sighed as if it was to be expected and what Sister Ruth had said about them not being cultured was right.

***

Sean McDonald sauntered into the house well after dusk. He went straight to the table in the dining room and slumped his tall, lean body in the chair. As he prised off his dusty boots with his foot, Anne left the plaiting of Liz's hair and caught them before they hit the floor. She deposited them on the veranda, where she would clean them before going to bed, and then she fetched his dinner from the kitchen. She also gave him a wet towel, so that he could at least wipe the caking grime from his hands before he started. Margaret regarded him from the floor in the corner of the room, and when he looked at her, her gaze flitted back to the red-gum fire.

"She's come then," Sean said to Anne.

"Yes," Anne said, through new hoarseness, her uncertain eyes never leaving Liz's hair. She waited to see if Sean had any more to say on the subject. He was silent as usual, but over the years she had learned to sort the different grades of Sean's silences.

"Introduce yourself then, Margaret." Anne said.

Margaret curled her head towards her body without turning to face him. "Good day, I'm Margaret."

"G'day. I'm Sean." He nodded in her direction, his mouth full.

"Mr McDonald," Anne informed Margaret, while her fingers rushed through Liz's hair. Margaret turned to acknowledge him and flinched from his stare brushing her cheek. She pulled her knees tight under her chin, wrapped her arms around them and escaped deeper into the dancing flames.

Sean discarded the knife and shovelled spoonfuls of the food into his eager mouth. His plate was piled high as usual, but his body seemed to burn away the food before it reached his stomach; but that was how it had always been, however much was put in front of him. He used the towel to wipe the salty grime from his elongated axe of a face and then dragged it down his long sinewy arms, which, like the rest of his body, was the colour of a ripe pineapple. The towel was already blackening as he wiped his hands on it, but it wouldn't get the soil out from under his nails. This didn't disgust him in the way it did Anne. This was the rich soil, whose blood flowed through the food they ate, and Sean brought his hands to his face to smell his land. "Didn't get a chance to clear that storeroom." Anne heard but chose to ignore him, and Liz winced as her hair was pulled tighter. Sean wiped the towel over his jet-black hair, which generally hung to the right. One strand of grey stood out in it, but it wasn't the sort of thing that worried Sean McDonald. Most of his contemporaries were bald or greying and had wild boar guts. "She could probably sleep in the barn tonight," he said. Liz was stirring a foot as if trying to tell him without betraying her mother.

Anne finished with Liz and beckoned Margaret. She held her curly hair between her fingers and wondered what she could do with it. She dragged a comb through it several times, but the curls sprang back into place. If it were cut back, would that get rid of them? One of the ladies at church was bound to know, and she would ask them the first opportunity she got. For now she plaited it into one corn stem; that would help to straighten it out.

42

Liz took up Margaret's position in front of the fire with a book, which she was unable to disappear in whilst the air in the room had frozen over. "We put Margaret's bed by the window, Mum, and I used two of the sheets and a blanket that was in your chest. She'll be warm tonight." Sean smiled and winked his thanks at her. He got up to go to the kitchen and brushed her hair as he walked by, which earned her collaborator's smile. He came back with the aluminium pail of milk and a glass, which was only for Anne's benefit, then he switched on the radio, turned it down low and sat in the armchair to listen to the world.

***

Margaret knelt at the foot of her bed and said the Lord's Prayer like Mrs McDonald had asked her to. Besides, it was mandatory at Radley, and she would probably have done it out of habit anyway. Liz had given her one of her nighties, and Margaret burrowed under the blanket to escape the cold. She found it odd that when she had slept under the stars with her *band*, even though they wore next to nothing and had only a small fire to warm them, they could store the heat from the scorching days in the very depths of their stomachs and then call on it at night to fall asleep with consummate ease. Now she had to wrap the blanket around her like a shroud to fall asleep.

The room fitted her loosely, like reams of cloth that could be shared. She had never slept in any place on her own before. She had mostly slept with her mother, brothers and sister, and when these older siblings had gotten married, her sister had moved away to join her husband's mob, and her brothers, although remaining with their mob, had arranged their own sleeping places, so then she had slept with her mother. Even at Radley she had shared the dormitory with more than twenty other girls. She couldn't sleep with a sharp and harsh vacancy for the familiar being driven through her heart, and wondered how much longer it would take her mother and father to come. She had left secret messages with trees and birds that she knew were friendly with her *band*, and her mother knew magic and was friendly with certain spirits, and they would surely show them the way. She dreamed the band by a campfire in the cold desert night, in loud, animated conversation about which trail to follow. Father was rolling a gummy black ball of *pituri* around his mouth and spitting the narcotic juice when mother overruled one of his ideas, and she remembered the foot-raising laughter they used to get from these exchanges. The thought that they were still searching comforted her like fluctuating breezes and set her off into a light sleep.

In the middle of the night the door creaked open and woke Margaret, the sound pinning her to the bed like a ghostly robber. She had heard the results of entrances into the dormitory at Radley whilst lying in a cold sweat and gripping her blanket tight, hoping it wouldn't be her call. The weighty presence sucked the air from the room, and she realised that the blanket was off her shoulders, which made her shiver with cold again. After a few wheezing breaths the heaviness left the room, closing the door behind it. Margaret lay frozen until her veins thawed. When she saw a shadow pass by her window she came up onto her knees and peeped under the edge of the hessian curtain as if she were being hunted. Mr McDonald was strolling by the tank stand smoking a cigarette. He didn't stop by the dunny either, but kept going into the woods and disappeared. She stayed like that, waiting for him to re-emerge, until the cold grabbed hold of her spine again. Then she dived back under the covers and spent the rest of the night alternating between light bouts of sleep and waking to every sound.

# Chapter 3

Anne rose before sunrise as if she had always been used to the rhythms of a farmer's wife. Each morning she did for Sean first, as it was part of a wife's duty. She went to his room, pulled back the curtains so that he would see when it was light, laid out his clothing for that day and took away the things he had worn the previous day. These she would wash later in the morning, so that they would be ready for him to wear again in a day or two. His breakfast had to be started, and she went down to the kitchen to stoke the stove. Within a few minutes there was the toasted scent of fresh bread rising through the house. She scurried between larder and stove, and soon there were a series of pots and pans lined up with thick cut ham being fried, beans being heated, and water being boiled for coffee.

Sean sauntered down, filled a basin at the sink, and took it out back where he washed his face, shaved, and brushed his teeth in the morning heat, which had already risen to a simmer. When he was finished he tipped the water onto the vegetable patch, the way they always did to conserve it. As he came back towards the house he saw Margaret searching in the grass over by the dunny, and he sidled up to the side of the house where she wouldn't see him.

\*\*\*

She knew it was still out there somewhere, and Margaret stepped over and around the clumps of stinging spinifex until she saw it. She picked up the moulted snakeskin and hung it around her neck. It was already drying out, so she would have to find some oils to preserve the crinkly, transparent hide. She walked past the dunny to the edge of the woods. This is where she would start it, and it would go all the way around to the window of the storeroom, which was now her bedroom. With measured steps, she placed her right foot behind the left and twisted in the red earth towards the back of the house. Sometimes she twisted sideways; this way her mob would feel the vibrations and know it was the track of a Snake-woman-child.

"Margaret! Margaret! What in heavens name are you doing?" Mrs McDonald was standing by the kitchen door with a floured hand on her hip. Margaret froze in her tracks, clasped her hands behind her back, and swung her body like a pendulum. She wondered if they would know about these things. The matrons at Radley hadn't figured it out, so perhaps it was something white folks didn't know.

Margaret shuffled away from the tracks towards the kitchen door. Sean had gone in for his breakfast when Anne had come to the door. "What is that disgusting thing hanging from your neck?" Anne recoiled. "Get rid of it, now." Margaret threw the snakeskin into the spinifex. "Come in and wash your hands and get changed. I want you to help Elizabeth sweep off the porch before breakfast."

Margaret was washed, changed and helping Liz to sweep fishy-smelling millipedes off the veranda, which Mrs McDonald called a porch, within a few minutes. The thread-thin, black, worm-like creatures had crawled up out of the ground in their hundreds during the night, and were trying to take up refuge in the house, but all the points of entry had been well sealed, and as soon as one was breached, Anne McDonald would find the source and seal it. Although she had not been particularly squeamish whilst growing up in England, here she had had to be more vigilant, when her home could be overrun by thousands of ants, spiders and millipedes, not to mention the flies, within a few minutes. Margaret had carried out similar duties at Radley, and although she didn't understand their ways, she swept the creatures into a pile with Liz, scooped them up onto a piece of cardboard, and deposited them in a smouldering trash can by the side of the house. Once when Liz wasn't looking, she threw the contents of her cardboard into a bush, then she asked the *Creative Ancestors* to forgive her for the ones she had burnt, without even eating their flesh so that their spirits could live on through her body.

***

"I'm thinking about seeing the sisters again to ask them if she can start school," Anne said as she shared out the girls' breakfast and left them on the stove to keep warm. Sean wiped the last drop of sauce from his plate with a piece of bread.

46

"I don't see what for; their education is out there." He threw a hand towards the vast outback. "Besides, Sister Ruth has already said no more Aboriginals in her school."

"But she's not an Aboriginal."

Sean's face opened like a question mark.

"Not a full one, anyway," Anne reasoned.

Sean pushed back his stool to go. Anne put down the pot she had started to scour and hurried to the porch to fetch his boots, which she put in front of his stool before going back to finish her pots. "You could do with some help around the house," Sean said. "Get her to help you on the vegetable patch." He pulled on his boots and tramped through the back door. A nauseous acid rose in Anne's stomach. She knew what this was leading up to. She scoured harder to push it further away.

✳✳✳

The girls drifted in from their chores. "Have you washed your hands?" Anne asked. She was already filling the basin for them. They washed and dried their hands and sat at the workbench, which doubled as a breakfast table. Liz hurried her food, but ate with more decorum when she caught her mother's gaze asking her to show a better example to Margaret. As she ran upstairs to fetch her satchel, Margaret gazed after her like an abandoned pup, not wanting to be left alone with Mrs McDonald. Mrs McDonald wasn't easy to talk to like Liz, and she didn't play, nor, it seemed, stop to listen to the songs of birds, or feel which direction the wind was blowing from. She must have taken a wrong turn somewhere, and hadn't figured out how to get back on her trail. "Bye Mum, bye Margaret." The door slammed and Liz was gone.

They spent all morning washing clothes and bed linen. Anne washed the things in the kitchen sink and passed them through the window to Margaret, who rinsed in a basin outside. They hung the laundry to dry behind the house and then threw the water over the vegetable plot. A little after midday they drank lemonade and ate bread and cheese for lunch, then they started again, this time on the vegetable plot. Anne showed Margaret how to weed between the rows of cabbages, carrots, tomatoes and peas, but Margaret was too chilled by shyness with her to say she had already been shown how at Radley. They cleared the irrigation channels and prepared more

47

ground for planting by chopping down some *buckabunge*. Margaret thought how silly it was to chop down this wild plant, which after the rains would grow two to three feet high and be luscious and tender for eating. It meant that they had to labour long hours over things which were not natural to the land, and which would take more of the scarce water and sometimes poisons to stop their rejection. But that was their way, and she didn't understand.

Their cotton frocks were soaked through and stuck to their bodies, and at times Margaret started to flag, but she stole mouse-sized bites from the bread she had hidden at the previous day's meal when Anne wasn't looking, even though by now she had figured that she would eat the same meals as the McDonalds.

"Have you ever been to school?" Anne asked. It was the first words they had spoken all day that required an exchange and was not an instruction of what work to do and how to do it.

"Yes, miss, ma'am." Margaret realised that she didn't know what to call her, and she kept her eyes firmly fixed on a head of cabbage as she answered.

"What did you do?" Anne persisted.

"A little reading and writing, but domestic training mostly."

"Would you like to go to school?"

Margaret shrugged her shoulders and then remembered it was the type of thing that could get you a clip around the ear at Radley. "Don't know, miss." Was there one answer that was better than another, one that would get her more favour? If there was, she didn't know which it was yet, and so she'd have to try and outguess Mrs McDonald until she knew her better.

"Well, I think God wants you to go to school, Margaret."

She had heard of Him before when they had services at the settlement and Radley, but she had never seen Him. She remembered that one of the elders at the settlement had told a pastor, who had been real excited about this God replacing their *Spirit Ancestors*, that if he couldn't read the signs on the land, then how was he capable of hearing this God fella, because it seemed to him the land spoke more clearly than some purely spirit God. From what she could figure out, this God was one of their *Creative Ancestors*, a real important one. He was only supposed to do good, but probably He had shared out so much of the good that there hadn't been any left for the likes of Matron Blythe at Radley. If she had to stay then she wanted to go to

48

school, too. She liked all that reading and writing stuff, and it would probably mean she spent the day with Liz instead of Mrs McDonald. But she didn't know if to give Mrs McDonald a yes would have meant no. So she mostly kept quiet and surrendered the pious talking to Mrs McDonald.

***

Anne knew her mind was made up. Margaret had to go to school, but she had to get Sean's agreement, and she didn't like what she had to do to get him to agree to something.

After they had finished on the vegetable plot, they moved up to Sean's bedroom. Anne wouldn't have him in hers. Whatever was to be done would have to be done in there. The room was sparsely furnished with a bed, a wardrobe and a chest of drawers with a mirror on top; and if it had not been Anne's doing, the room would have had even less. She stripped the bed whilst Margaret dusted the reclaimed-pine furnishings. Then she wiped down the mattress with a solution of water and lye, and while this dried out Margaret swept and mopped the floorboards. When all this was done, Anne dressed the bed with a fresh set of her best sheets, using tight tucks and folds as if covering a gaping wound.

***

Margaret emptied the bucket from the mopping in the yard, and as she turned, she saw Liz drifting up the path like an unhurried grazer. She was about to break into a run to meet her, but she stopped herself and gobbled long strides instead, so that they met at the bottom of the steps. "What you do today?" she asked. Liz sat on the top step and pulled a book from her satchel. Margaret sat close and leaned over her shoulder to see it.

"We did history today. We studied how Captain Cook discovered Australia, and when he met the Aboriginals he offered them mirrors and metal pans, but they didn't want them."

"How come he discovered Australia if he met those Aboriginals there, then?" Margaret asked, her chin in the palm of her hand.

"It says so in the history books." Liz's forehead creased in annoyance. "I suppose it's like, well, those dogs over there." She pointed under the tank stand. "They couldn't discover anything; only people can discover things."

49

"We used to have two hunting dogs, and they were always discovering rabbit holes, and this girl I knew, her band had a cat that was always finding rats in their hut," Margaret said.

Hurried footsteps on the veranda stopped them. "Elizabeth, can you come and get supper? You can show Margaret your work later."

"Yes, Mum." Liz jumped up and scurried to it.

"Margaret, you need to have a wash and put one of these on." Anne gave her two more of Liz's outgrown dresses, which she almost snatched as she stared at the departing stopper of her lesson with Liz. But Anne was too deep into her preparatory trance to notice.

***

Supper was hurried and in silence, and as dusk enveloped the land, Anne went out and started the engine, which pumped water from an artesian well into the irrigation channels of the vegetable patch. This underground water was used for irrigation, laundry and bathing, whilst the rainwater from the tank stand was for cooking and drinking, although the artesian water could be used for those purposes if the rainwater ran out. If they had done the watering during the day, the heat would have licked the moisture from the soil, and the plants would have wilted like raisins. Anne allowed the flowing water to hypnotise her for an hour or so, moving the hose every now and then, as if to wash the night's encounter from her mind. When the ground was well soaked, she struggled back into the house with the cast iron bathtub, which was stored on the wall outside the kitchen.

The girls were still at the table, poring over Liz's homework. "I would like you in bed by nine, girls," Anne said, and then she went on filling the tub, not noticing when they had gone. She brought her Bible down with her towels and read from it up to her neck in hot water. When she finished, she put on a light airy dress, cleaned the bath for its next occupant, and sat by the tub waiting for Sean to come home.

The front door slapped against its hinges and woke Anne from where she was dozing in the kitchen. Sean stomped in and fell into the dining chair as normal. Anne brought his dinner to the table and picked up his discarded boots. "I've fixed you a bath for after," she said, without looking at him, and then walked out of the room with the dusty boots. Sean's mouth locked open as he watched her

50

stiffening back go through the door. He would have liked to say something, but what eluded him. He had never really been comfortable with women, except maybe one. Being the third youngest in a family of nine boys, the eldest of whom were all hardened hands on a sheep and cattle station, hadn't helped. It was during one of the severe drought years that he had left. He had only just reached his teens. Every man had a right to make it on his own, he had figured, and he had now been making it without them for more than thirty years. Even if he could write, he doubted whether he would have found the time or inclination to send them a letter just to say he was alive and well, and he didn't think this would have bothered the McDonalds, being as concerned as they were with just getting by. Years spent criss-crossing the outback as a *wagonner*, delivering essential supplies to remote homesteads and small towns, had made him used to an isolated life; that was what he knew. With increased transport after the war, he made the right decision to get out of the business, buy his own piece of land and go into farming. It was hard work, but he was still out under abundant skies where he could drift like a solitary cloud.

Anne had been the result of an advert placed in a newspaper by one of his former customers as payment for his services. He had done well there. Had she not been recently arrived from England, part of the migration after the war, probably an advert by a pineapple farmer with more than three hundred acres in the outback wouldn't have impressed her as it had. In England, a man with three hundred acres was probably overflowing with wealth. Out here it was a struggle to survive with that when a man could own several thousand square miles of land without turning a profit, and in some ways he was raked with guilt for cheating her of her dream.

She hadn't poured him a bath for more than two years now, and after that they bought one of those American refrigerators. He had come to know the routine now, and if that was the way it had to be, he would savour it like a rare eclipse. He wasn't used to forging connections or starting a conversation, and if one did start, he preferred it to be about the land, and that it should smoulder for no longer than necessary. He knew that nobody really understood Sean McDonald, not even Sean McDonald, and the easiest way to deal with that was to stay out and caress his land with the sun pouring over his back, because they didn't ask who he was. They mostly didn't seem to mind, and if they ever needed to know, he somehow felt they could tell without him having to say.

Anne poured the last of the water into the bathtub and Sean let his clothes fall to the floor and climbed in. His knees protruded over the top of the tub as he soaped himself down, and then Anne brought him his razor and a mirror. When he was done he stepped out of the tub onto a towel and she wrapped another around him without taking time to notice his bronze cast body.

Sean climbed the steps to his room and waited for Anne, as this was what he remembered. He could hear her cleaning the bathtub and hanging it back on the wall outside the kitchen, and then she hurried up the stairs and into his room in the same unbroken rhythm she used for cooking a meal, chopping firewood, darning a dress, or any of the other multitude of things that she would do outside of sleeping. She turned off the light, sat on the edge of the bed to remove her dress, and Sean watched her with guarded hope that she would pull down her hair, but knowing she wouldn't. As she lay back on the pillow her lips were sealed like cold steel, her eyes in a trance, and they said nothing to each other as he rolled over and mounted her.

\*\*\*

The carnal negotiations in the McDonald household continued for another week. Then they ended as abruptly as they had begun. The following morning, after washing the dress she had worn the previous day, helping Liz to sweep invading millipedes from the veranda, and having breakfast, Anne gave Margaret an exercise book and a pencil. "You're going to school with Elizabeth today." Margaret's eyes flickered like a dozen candles, which she hid the moment she saw that Anne's lips were still curled into a tight ball, the way they were when she had first seen her. Even so, she wanted to say something to Mrs McDonald that would uncurl her lips, but she couldn't think of anything to say that would do that. She remembered her own mother's gap-toothed smile when she was asked to tell the story of how she had been chosen to be guardian of the dreamtime secrets. This reminded her that she would have to weave fresh snake tracks to her window that night, and it drummed a hollow rumble in her just-fed stomach, and so she tried not to think of this; they would come. In any case, it didn't seem as if Mrs McDonald had any stories to lift

52

her, so she made up her mind to help Mrs McDonald even more in the vegetable patch, because she knew how tending to things which were growing could cure some parts, even though Mrs McDonald didn't show any signs of it.

As the girls walked to the door Anne remembered something. "If Sister Ruth asks where you are from, you are to say Southern Europe, Margaret." Greeks and Italians lived in the district, and Anne had heard that other foster parents compared their Aboriginal kids to them. Both girls waited for her to explain, but Anne left them by the door and went back to her work.

Margaret kangaroo-hopped off the last two steps into the yard. Liz stopped at the top with her hands on her hips. "The sisters don't allow any playing in school."

Margaret ignored her and skipped off towards the path. Liz shook her head, put on a wide-brimmed bonnet to protect her freckled skin from the boiling sun, and followed after her. They walked for a way along the narrow path between the acacia and gum trees, and when Margaret saw a flock of resting galahs, she ran off the path and weaved in and out of the trees like a hunting dog to see if she could track anything else. They came out of the forest onto the bend in the dusty road, and when they went around this, the five-building town emerged to greet them. Their dresses wore dark stains under the armpits, and Liz was already wiping back streaks of dust-bearing sweat from her forehead. "Mum said you've done some schooling."

"Yes," Margaret said, "I was taught reading and writing in the settlement and at Radley."

"Were ...Were your teachers nice?"

Margaret shrugged her shoulders and kicked up some dust.

"Well, our teachers are Sister Ruth and Sister Agnes. When you can't see Sister Ruth you should hold your body tight."

Margaret curled her exercise book in half and pressed the point of the pencil into her thumb. "Why's that?"

"You just should, okay?"

53

# Chapter 4

The dust road came to an end and the five wooden slat buildings were arranged in a semicircle some distance from each other. The steepled church with its small cemetery, the whitewashed house of the priest and sisters, a rickety grocery store which was also the post office and pub, Malee school, and the community hall. The girls walked towards the far side of the semicircle, where chattering children were already gathering like swallows under the overhang of the school roof to escape the roasting heat. Two others, an Aboriginal boy and a girl the same rusted gum tree colouring as Margaret, were standing some distance off. Liz slowed her pace as if deciding what to do. She turned towards the Aboriginal boy and girl, stopped, and gave Margaret a look weighted with meaning, as if to say 'You wait here.' Then she hurried on. Margaret hadn't understood and followed her.

A woman wearing a habit opened the door of the school and rang the bell as if she were sprinkling holy water. Liz ran to go in behind the children who had waited under the overhang, and Margaret reached the door in time to go in ahead of the other two.

Light leaked through the window slats and flooded the room, which had about thirty-five wooden chairs and desks fixed to the floor, as anything from twelve to thirty children could turn up for school depending on the weather, the type of work taking place on their farms and, for some, whether they felt inclined to. Most of the desks were on one side of the room, for the primary school children, but the sisters also taught secondary school to those children who hadn't been sent away to board, and there were twelve desks in a separate group for them.

The front rows were taken by the pupils who had entered the room first, and the two Aboriginals walked unnoticed to the back. An empty desk sat next to Liz, and Margaret went to stand next to her as if she were seeking refuge. Liz nudged her. "You've got to sit with them," she whispered.

Margaret gazed towards the back at the two who had their lifeless eyes cast down. "Why?" Some of the children stole a look and giggled under their breaths. Liz turned away from her and stood erect with her arms like broomsticks by her side. One of the sisters, a short, busty woman, whose face was like fine print to read, was hustling her way towards them.

"Who is this, Elizabeth?"

"It's Margaret, Sister Agnes, we've fostered her and—"

"Didn't Sister Ruth tell your mother that we would be taking no more Aboriginals?"

"Yes, Sister Agnes, but mum says that Margaret is from Southern Europe."

Sister Agnes scrutinised Margaret more closely.

"Did you tell her where to sit?"

"Yes, Sister Agnes, I—"

Sister Agnes already had Margaret by the arm and led her like a convict to sit immediately in front of the two Aboriginals. "This is where you will sit from now on. And you would do well to keep your head down."

Sister Agnes strolled back to the front of the classroom with the shafts of light playing on her pudding of a face. Margaret avoided the gaze of the other two. She felt as if she had tripped on a conspicuous rock, but tempered this by telling herself that at least she wasn't made to sit right at the back; there must have been some meaning in that. As soon as she knew what she had to do, she was going to get to sit at the front alongside Liz. She didn't hear the register called in her soothing reverie, and in any case, her name and those of the two behind her were not called. The girl behind pulled her down when it was time to sit, and that's when her daydream stopped. Liz must have told her the wrong sister to watch out for, not that she would have known which was Sister Ruth and which was Sister Agnes in any case. Her mother had always said one snake in the open was worth five in the bush, and so she was glad to know which sister to keep an eye on. She watched Sister Agnes surveying the class from her position at one side of the blackboard, her hands clasped behind her back. She wore a black headscarf, which hung down to her shoulder, but unlike Sister Ruth, she did not wear a habit. Instead, she wore a plain blue dress to just below her thick calves. Margaret dropped her head when their eyes met, and the breath rushed out of her like steam from an opened pot.

Sister Ruth slapped the register shut and her chair scraped the floor as she stood up. She put the thick record aside and picked up her social studies textbook, which she opened to the appropriate page. The gaunt woman pushed her oval rimmed spectacles up her wrinkled nose and brought the book close to her face. "We will start with chapter nine today." A quick ruffle of fingers slid over paper, and then the room fell silent again. Margaret looked around her for a textbook but there was none. She held up her hand to attract Sister Ruth's attention, but Sister Ruth continued her lesson without seeing her. After she had changed arms twice, both were sagging like slender branches overburdened with fruit, and she kept them down.

Sister Ruth marched towards the back of the class, where there was a large map of Australia on the wall. "Now who can show me what part of the desert the men were in?" Like the children at the front of the class, the two behind Margaret had turned towards Sister Ruth, although the boy was still gazing with forlorn hope at some spirit far too elusive to be held within the four walls of the classroom. Margaret kept a wary eye on Sister Agnes, who patrolled the front of the class like a warder. Their eyes met, and Sister Agnes stopped and circled her index finger in the air, as if she were mixing a light cake. In the foreground, Liz kept clenching and unclenching her fists, each time rolling the ball like stiff pastry.

*Thwack!*

Margaret's hand jumped to her right cheek too late. A red wheal was already rising like a molehill from just below her eye down to her chin. It sizzled like raw meat thrown onto hot charcoals, but she remembered not to scream or shed tears, like her mother had taught her. "Look this way, child!" She turned, and Sister Ruth was standing over her, still clutching half of the broken ruler.

Margaret could feel it building in her, and it filled her mouth with words of poison, but she swallowed the sounds and instead sung Sister Ruth to death in her heart; even though she already knew it wasn't as effective against white folks as it was amongst her own people.

With the girl's attention now assured, Sister Ruth went to the big poster next to the map. It showed a number of Aborigines sitting at the end of a big wide road, and they were playing cards, gambling and drinking. She pointed to the words, and the class read them aloud for Margaret's benefit: *"Wide is the road that leads us into destruction, which leads into hell."* Sister Ruth moved to the other half of the poster, which had a number of nicely dressed white people on a narrow road, and she pointed to the words under this: *"Narrow is the road that leads us into the kingdom of life or the kingdom of God."* She stood in a clinical silence until they had all swallowed the words. Sister Ruth was one of those nuns who felt it her duty to emphasise the differences between the races and the need to keep them apart. She had spent time in a town next to one of their settlements, and she had witnessed, first hand, the effect of what she considered a heathen, tribal people could have on otherwise hard-working European men, reducing them to atheist, salivating predators with a penchant for all manner of bestialities, and if left unchecked, the backward and lazy could flourish like weeds, stifling all the good that civilised man had created. That was at least how those like her, who felt they had been chosen to do God's work and prevent such an eventuality, saw the world.

\*\*\*

At lunchtime, Margaret stood between the children under the roof overhang and the two out in the centre taking shade under a ghost-gum. Liz strolled over and gave her a sandwich and a bottle of home-made fruit juice. She looked at the wheal on Margaret's face and winced as her gaze flitted away. "There are two more lessons before we go home. I'll see you then," she said, and then went back to join the children under the overhang.

Margaret squatted on her haunches like a market seller, ate the sandwich and drank the warm drink. While she was making circles in the dust with the empty bottle, the girl from under the ghost-gum walked across and her shadow fell over her. "G'day, I'm Isabel." Margaret peered up from the shadow of the girl, who was thickset with wide shoulders and hips. She would have been on the verge of celebrating the ripening of her womb if she was with her band, but here she was still a child. She wore a curly matt of brownish-red hair, and her face was broad and strong, with wide, firmly shut lips, as if they were holding back some rage. "You can come and sit with us if you want." She pointed over to the boy. "He doesn't talk, but I think he understands some things." Margaret hadn't made up her mind who she wanted to sit with, and she continued to draw in the dust.

Isabel waited for an answer, and when she received no response she went back to the boy. Then Sister Agnes came to the door and rang the bell for the last session.

***

They walked home for most of the way in silence. Margaret left the path when she saw a eucalypt, and she plucked several of the leaves, crushed them in her hand and let them caress her cheek. "Mum will have something for that," Liz said, but Margaret ignored her, plucked more of the leaves and released the oils before holding them against her cheek again.

"How do you decide which group to sit in?"

Liz slowed her pace, and her nose and mouth wrinkled like dried fruit. "Well—you just know, don't you?"

"I know in class I have to sit in front of the ones at the back, but when we're in the yard, how do I know?"

"I saw Isabel come over to you. Didn't she say you could sit with them?" They were in sight of home, and Liz lengthened her stride as if to hasten her retreat.

"Can I sit with you tomorrow?"

"What for?" Her voice leapt like a windswept kite and Liz realised and reined it in. "It's not just my decision." She ran up the steps onto the veranda. "I've got to hurry and get supper ready."

The girls went through into the kitchen as Anne bustled in the back door with a basket full of dried washing. "Afternoon, Mum," Liz said.

"Afternoon," Margaret repeated, still not sure what to call her.

"Afternoon, girls." Anne caught sight of Margaret's face and raised a querying brow at Liz.

"It was Sister Ruth. Margaret was turning the wrong way."

Anne put down the washing and turned Margaret's cheek towards her. She pursed her lips. "You must pay attention next time. If you keep your head down then it should soon stop. You do still want to go to school, don't you?" Margaret nodded.

Anne took the first aid box out of the cupboard by the pantry and dabbed antiseptic onto the wound with cotton wool, which made Margaret wince. "I'd like you both to get supper ready and iron these things." She put the basket of clothes on the kitchen table and hurried out the door.

58

Liz showed Margaret how to do the ironing and then she started supper. The back door was left opened, and the mesh around the veranda allowed whatever breeze there was to flow into the room whilst keeping out the flies. But today there was no breeze, and the heat boiled what little air there was. A wide-bladed ceiling fan stirred the hot air, which circled the room like a stiff porridge.

Without warning, Anne rushed into the kitchen like an agitated hen and knocked over the broom by the back door. She didn't stop to pick it up as she headed for the hallway. "Get the kitchen tidy, girls; Mrs Cartwright is coming." She scurried upstairs.

Mrs Cartwright had never been to their home, and Liz rushed to peer out of the window to see her brand new Rover Coupe pulling into the yard. She raised her head and snorted as if it hadn't impressed her. "We probably won't eat supper until late now."

"Why's that?" Margaret asked.

"Mum will want to pour lemonade as though it's champagne, and it won't do for Mrs Cartwright to know that we don't eat steak every day." She went back to the kitchen and started to clear the work surface. "Margaret, pack away the ironing in your room and then put on one of your clean dresses. Mrs Cartwright is coming." She ran on the spot in mock haste, and Margaret laughed. But she saw the startled urgency with which both Liz and her mother were scurrying, and she followed them.

***

By the time Helen Cartwright knocked on the open front door, the girls were sitting at the kitchen table doing homework, and Anne was coming down the stairs dressed for a Sunday afternoon stroll. "Hello, Mrs Cartwright," Anne said in her best voice.

"Hello, Anne, you look wonderful."

"Thank you, Mrs Cartwright," Anne said, even though she felt sure that Helen Cartwright dampened other women's qualities.

"Oh please call me Helen, Anne. I don't suppose Sam Cartwright would mind me not using his name."

"Thank you," Anne said, with an ounce too much thrill. "Please come in."

They went into the living room and Anne walked behind, admiring Helen's wide-brimmed white hat, one of those new polka dot dresses which were fashionable in America, high heels and matching purse. A small brown parcel was tucked under her arm. Helen Cartwright looked around with eager anticipation, as if she were searching for something. "Is she here yet? I've bought her a few things, I do hope they fit." She held out the parcel to Anne. Anne wasn't sure exactly who had told Helen Cartwright about Margaret, but the gossip had reached Malee the day she arrived, and Helen knew full well she was there. But if it meant having the company of Helen Cartwright, she was quite prepared to play along. She usually only saw Helen Cartwright at church, and mostly from the back, because Helen Cartwright had paid for the church roof to be rebuilt, and so she had the privilege of sitting in the front pew with Joshua, the mute Aboriginal boy she had fostered. It was a little after this that Anne had thought it might be a good idea to foster, but it had taken her a while to persuade Sean, and even now she still wasn't sure that he was in full agreement.

"Thank you Helen, but we were planning to go into Langley and get her some things."

"But I'm sure she'll like these, Anne. Why not let her try them on?"

In spite of their difficulties, Anne McDonald was sure that she had convinced everyone in Malee that they were doing well. She kept a better homestead than most in the area, and she had never asked for any help. She hadn't gone to church for the few weeks that Margaret had been with them, because Margaret didn't have any dresses which were nice enough to wear, but she had been hoping to go into Langley soon to buy material and make some. "She's doing homework with Liz at the moment. If she likes them then I'm sure it will be fine, Helen. Would you like some tea?"

"Oh yes, thank you, Anne, it's been so dry and sticky today. I really need something to put the moisture back into my skin."

Anne wondered how Helen Cartwright could ever feel dry and sticky when she lived in such a grand homestead. Billabong Lodge was designed so that there was a constant flow of air from one room to another and then out again, or so she had been told, and then it wasn't as if she had to do any physical work, because although Mr Cartwright, whom Anne had never met, had died years before, he had left enough money to give Helen a more than comfortable life.

Anne waltzed through into the kitchen to where the girls were, making sure to shut the door behind her. "Elizabeth, can you show

Margaret how to make some of that tea we have for special occasions? And get her to serve it in the good china. You can also take some lemonade to Joshua. He's standing out by Mrs Cartwright's car."

When Anne glided back into the living room, Helen was looking out of the window. "You have such a lovely vegetable garden, Anne. How do you manage to keep it so well?"

"Sean has one of his workers tend to it. He says it's not a lady's place to be doing that sort of work in this infernal heat."

"I have to say I agree with him," Mrs Cartwright said.

Margaret pushed the door open with her shoulder and walked gingerly across the floor with the tray to where the women were sitting on the sofa. "Oh, she's beautiful, Anne," Helen squealed. Margaret balanced the tray on the coffee table in front of them and Helen took hold of her arm. "Hello, Margaret, I'm Helen Cartwright." She grinned her protruding front teeth up at her. Margaret looked at Anne, and when she saw the expectation growing in her face like a runaway weed, she curtsied. "Good day, Mrs Cartwright."

"And she's so polite. You must have met my son at school? His name is Joshua. He doesn't speak, but I know you two are going to become good friends. What do you like doing, Margaret?" Mrs Cartwright asked.

"I like hunting, chasing rabbits, and fishing."

Anne pursed her lips as if to swallow Margaret's words, "Those are men's things, Margaret. You are going to learn to be a lady now."

Margaret stared at the floor as if the gaps in the joints would reveal the things she was to say. "Well—I like reading the Bible," she finally said when she saw Anne gazing with unbridled expectation at the book on the side table, "and helping Mrs McDonald to tend the vegetable gardens."

"We don't tend the garden," Anne cut in. "Sean's labourers do that." She stared at Margaret with firm lips, hoping the girl would understand. Margaret's hand jerked against the tray when she realised her mistake, and one of the cups fell to the floor and broke into two pieces. "Oh, Margaret," Anne said.

"I'm sorry, miss." Margaret tensed like taut rope, as if waiting for the slap she would have gotten at Radley, but when Anne didn't move, she pushed the tray further onto the coffee table and picked up the broken cup.

"It was an accident, Anne," Helen Cartwright assured her, and rested a downy hand on her arm.

"Ask Elizabeth to give you another one," Anne said, and Margaret left the room with the broken pieces.

"I am just trying to teach Margaret what little I know about the garden," Anne continued. "I don't want her fraternising with Sean's labourers, and you can never tell when she might need it. She may not have the luxury of a husband like Sean who refuses to let her work the grounds."

"She's quite fair, Anne, she may only be quarter-caste, what do you think?"

"They said her mother was quadroon and her father was—" Anne sneaked a concerned look at the door to make sure that Margaret wasn't there. "Well—you know, full-blown. So I suppose that makes her half-caste."

"I was speaking to Mrs O'Hare," Mrs Cartwright said. "She tells me that they have something called a recessive gene, so once they mix with whites, their skin colour changes as does the shape of their nose and there is no going back, even for future generations." Anne nodded sagely. "Sometimes I think it's more a case of our men having no control than the Aboriginal mothers having loose morals, Anne. There are so many single men out here."

Anne's cheeks flushed as she fought to hold back her deflating breath. This wasn't the type of thing she talked about. She had come out here to be with one of those single men. If only she had known.

Margaret came back into the room with the new cup and the women stopped the conversation. "What about school, Margaret?" Helen asked, "Do you like school?"

Margaret's lips spread like thin butter, and her hand rose to cover the wheal on her cheek, but she stopped when Anne shook her head to tell her no.

"I don't think Sister Ruth is too keen on having her, Mrs Cartwright—I mean, Helen."

"Why ever not?"

"Well, she says the school is full."

"Poppycock. She tried that with me when I enrolled Joshua."

Anne's shoulders jumped, as though she was alarmed at a woman of Helen Cartwright's standing using such language. "She was ignored in class and hasn't been set any homework."

"I tell you what, I'll have a word with Father Beir. He'll see to it that she's allowed to go." She brushed Anne's arm again.

"Margaret, get Elizabeth to finish showing you her homework." Anne said.

***

Margaret hurried out of the room and drew grateful breath, even though she had been transfixed by Mrs Cartwright's flowery scent and attention, and by the fact that she was so much more elegant than any of the women she had seen in Malee, or Radley for that matter. She certainly wasn't younger than Mrs McDonald, and the feathery touch of her hands said she had never worked as hard, but something about her said she had more energy. Her face may have been narrow, like her hips, and her protruding teeth meant that her nose and mouth were on the same line at the front of her face, but she had a poise which attracted attention. She found Liz mixing the lemonade for Joshua. "How did you break the cup?" Liz asked.

"Mrs Cartwright asked me what I liked doing and I said I like tending the garden with your mum."

Liz caught her shower of giggles between her fingers. "Mum doesn't tend the garden, Daddy's labourers do that. We're not poor, Margaret. Didn't we have strawberry cake when you came?" Margaret stared at her, her eyes like a wiped slate. "It's a game, Margaret. Mum likes to play it for some reason, but you have to be quick enough to know when she is playing it, so that you don't say the wrong things."

Liz finished making the lemonade and started for the door with a glass for Joshua. "I'll take it if you want," Margaret offered. Liz gave her the glass and went back to her work.

Joshua was standing by Helen's car, staring into space, or maybe it was at a spirit so elusive that no one else could ensnare it. He stood one head above the car roof, and there was a sweaty gloss to his mahogany skin. His golden-brown hair had been left curly, but cut back so that you saw all of his narrow, closed face. There was no smile. He looked right through you, and no speech escaped his lips. Margaret crept up behind him. "I've got some lemonade here for you, Joshua." She had to know for sure, and when he didn't turn around,

63

that satisfied her eager curiosity. She glided in front of him and handed him the glass. He took it and emptied it as if he had scooped it from a stream whilst wondering by himself. She had never met anyone who couldn't hear in the real world before. Her mother had shown her many people who could translate vibrations disturbing the air, but couldn't attune to the spirits of their ancestors or their hidden enemies, which was most dangerous of all. But Joshua seemed in the presence of many voices from the other side, and he couldn't share it. If he couldn't do this, then how would he pass on the secrets that the spirits had chosen to reveal to him? Margaret wondered if he could dance his secrets, and she moved out a distance so that she couldn't be seen from the house before she started. She kicked up the first swirl of dust, and it floated like confetti into her hair. Before long the spirits accosted her and she was lost to the now as she stamped, twirled, leaped and threw herself into a sweating frenzy, where only she could hear the beat of time.

"Margaret! Margaret! What are you doing? Stop that silliness now." Anne's shrieks were like a chain, ensnaring her. She stumbled to a halt, panting like a wild horse. "Come inside, we're going to have supper now." She looked at Joshua as she went past him, but she could tell he hadn't seen her dance. "Mrs Cartwright bought these for you." Anne handed her the two dresses and Margaret's eyes bloomed like a flower seeing daylight.

"Thank you, Mrs Cartwright, thank you."

"That's all right, Margaret. They'll look beautiful on you." She turned to Anne. "I'll see you in church then, Anne."

"Yes, Helen, and thank you again." They watched Helen Cartwright as she doe-stepped off the veranda and walked back to her car like one of the leading ladies in the Hollywood movies that they would later get to see at the theatre house in Langley, and a cocktail which wasn't quite envy appeared to stir on Anne McDonald's face. They stayed watching until the car was lost to the forest and scrub, and then they became ordinary again, and went inside to change into their work clothes.

\*\*\*

Sean ploughed down his food like a hoarder, each spoonful reaching his mouth before the previous one had been fully chewed and swallowed. Even so, he ate with a reverence that only people who

64

plucked their meals from their own land could fully appreciate and understand.

Anne could see that he was happy with himself even though she was now back in her own room, and she wanted to ask him before he sat by the radio and fell into a sleep. She got to the end of the plait in Liz's hair and summoned Margaret from in front of the open fire. "I was hoping we could go into Langley soon," she said, as if to no one in particular. "We need to get some things for the girls and stock up on provisions." Anne also needed to see a town with more than five buildings at its heart in order to remind her that she lived in the real world.

"Can't do it this Saturday," Sean said. "The Abbo boys are having some ceremony next weekend, so I need to get them to finish the planting this week. We'll go next week." With that, Sean got up, stretched his arms and rolled his neck, and then he walked out of the house and into the woods.

Anne's fingers jumped to a dance in Margaret's hair. They usually only went to Langley four times each year, and they had used those up already, but now he was prepared to go without any demands. She imagined herself walking down the street looking at people, new faces, probably summoning up the courage to say hello to one or two, and hopefully they would strike up a conversation, which, although she would shiver with stuttering unease, she would savour more than the iced cream from the general store. Just to talk out loud to someone other than the children or the women at church and get an interested response; if that was all she did, then the trip would be worthwhile. And maybe Sean would allow them to see one of those Hollywood movies at the theatre house, or with some luck they might have one of those Ealing movies on, and she might get to see what London looked like now.

"What's an Abbo?" Margaret asked. The question caught Anne like a trap, and Liz stopped reading her book, but she kept her head down into the pages and waited to hear her mother's answer.

"Why do you want to know that, Margaret?" Anne asked, trying to give herself time to think it through.

"Because Sister Ruth talked about Abbos at school, and Mr McDonald, he just talked about them, so I just wanted to know."

Anne coughed up time enough to consider her answer and continued with the plaiting. "Well, they are desert people, really, and I think some of them live in the bush. We have some of them close by and they help out on the farms and things like that."

Margaret's forehead remained wrinkled, as though Anne hadn't said anything to help her understand what she needed to. She tried again. "Am I Abbo?" Margaret pressed her thighs against her hands like a vice, as if to squeeze life out of the possibility.

"No." Anne chuckled haltingly. "Whoever gave you that idea?" Margaret shrugged her shoulders, and Anne tapped them with the comb to remind her not to do that. "You look more like a Southern European, I told you, and that's what you're to tell Sister Ruth if she asks. The Aboriginals like to keep to themselves and have different ways about them, so you should leave them alone. And from now on when you go outside I want you to wear a bonnet to keep the sun off your face." Anne tied off the end of the plait. "Now run along and get your things ready for school. And when you get back from school tomorrow I want you to take the scouring brush and scrub the kitchen floor as white as new."

"Yes, Miss—Mrs McDonald."

\*\*\*

Margaret had sensed it was time to call Anne McDonald something else, and she had introduced it as though she were probing a hornets' nest. When Mrs McDonald didn't object, in fact didn't appear to notice, she decided that's what she would call her now.

\*\*\*

She went to her room and took out the dress she would wear in the morning. There wasn't much picking, as the two that Helen Cartwright had bought her were for church and she had four others, one of which she was now wearing. Mrs McDonald insisted on them being changed and washed in the morning before school and then ironed when she returned in the afternoon. When she had been with her mother the only clothes she had were the ones she wore, and she wondered why her mother had not gotten her some more, or even a pair of the shoes which she now wore to school or had to put on at home when Helen Cartwright came by. She took off the shoes and wiped off the fine dust with a rag. Then she spat on it and buffed it until her reflection shone through. She hadn't laid any extra tracks for a few days, but she didn't mind if her parents took a little longer to

66

find her now, because she quite liked the idea of going to school, even though she had to sit near to the back of the class. Maybe if Sister Ruth knew she was a Southern European like Mrs McDonald said, then she wouldn't have to sit at the back. But if she was a Southern European, then what was her father, mother and the band they had been with? The band had not treated her mother any differently, even though she had special powers and could talk to the spirits and the like, because it was not good to caress a person's ego, in case it meant that when it was their time to leave the physical world, their *ego spirit* would be too inflated to go willingly. But also because they all prized independence, and this could only be maintained if no one was elevated to a position where the others would have to depend on them. Even she had learned to feed herself as soon as she could crawl, and her mother would sometimes leave her near bushes where she could pluck berries, whilst she and the other women dug for edible tubers and water. It was on one such occasion that her kinship to her totem animal, the mulga snake, was confirmed. Her father had already created this tie when he had fed some of the mulga's meat to her mother, who had remained barren for many years after her first four children, and it was only after this that her mother had become pregnant with her, her last child. Then on that day when she had been left by the bushes as the women dug for tucker, they returned to find her playing with a poisonous snake, which had done her no harm. That's when the band realised that she would follow her mother, learn the secrets and speak with the spirits, and they gave her the name Snake-woman-child, but still they had treated her the same as all the children. Maybe these Abbos took Southern Europeans in the way she had now been taken, and this set her off to thinking in another direction. All these thoughts were running, leaping and dancing into each other, so that when one of them started, it never had time to reach the end before three or four more had mingled like blown leaves. Margaret lay back on her bed and closed her eyes. If she could rake in some of these thoughts, she might be able to imagine what these Southern Europeans looked and sounded like. Soon the wind that was driving her thoughts ebbed away, and she fell into a deep sleep.

\*\*\*

Anne dragged the hose across the ground and further into the vegetable patch. She dropped it into one of the irrigation channels and watched the water pump out of the severed artery. This was her nightly ritual. It was also the time at which she thought most about what she had given up to come here. Both her mother and Carol, her best friend, had been against it, and had her father not been killed at Dunkirk, he would have been too. But she was determined to leave a country struggling to recover after the devastation of the war, so that she would not have to struggle too, and she sighed at the wicked irony of that. Now her evenings watching the water soak into the soil were the times when she wondered what life would have been like had she stayed. Surely she would not have mostly been drowning in loneliness and work, and at the very least she would have been able to attend her mother's funeral. At first she had avoided listening to the radio programmes that brought news of another world, for fear that the continued recognition of that life would have been too traumatic for her. But now it gave her pulse a rhythm, together with conversations with the women at church, Carol's letters and magazines, and her four-times-a-year trips into Langley, which reminded her of a small English town.

After the ground had received a soaking for an hour or so, she turned off the pump engine and walked back to the house. She knew it was for the best, what they, she in fact—because Sean was playing no part, and if it were up to him it wouldn't have happened—had done for Margaret. How could anyone want to live out here the way her people did? She would get an education, go on to find herself a job and a husband, although Anne couldn't find anything to recommend that besides the fact that it was expected, and at least she would lead a better life, of that Anne was sure. She sat on the back step, cleaned off her boots and left them on the porch before getting ready for bed.

*** 

Early Saturday morning was prickly cold and mist had descended below the roofline, but the girls knew it wouldn't last, and they hurried to sweep the millipedes from the veranda and wash their bedclothes. Then Margaret used the kitchen brush to scrub the floorboards in her room clean, as Anne had instructed, and only then did they have breakfast.

68

By nine o'clock the sun was cruelly hot, but still, after breakfast the girls picked their way through the woods at the back of the house into Sean's pineapple fields. Margaret wore the straw hat Anne had given her to keep the sun from adding any more colour to her skin, and as they broke out of the woods they saw Sean and three or four Aboriginals in the distance inching towards them in an empty field, but this was surrounded by fields filled with swords of serrated pine leaves in various states of growth. Margaret followed Liz over to a clearing at the edge of the woods, where dozens of crates of reeking pineapple tops sat ready for planting. Liz pulled her floppy wicker hat from the bag that she carried and hung the bag in a tree next to her father's Coolgardie, to protect the food from marauding ants and marsupial mice.

"Can you manage a crate, Margaret?" Liz put on her hat and pulled one of the crates up to her waist.

"Yes," Margaret said as she copied Liz.

They walked straight-legged and curve-backed with the weight of the crates from under the protection of the trees, and the sun sat on their backs and added to their burden. Margaret pulled her arms shorter and then let them out to ease the weight. When Liz stopped and put her crate down, Margaret's body flopped forward with grateful release, and after a short respite Liz set off again. "Let me know when you need to rest, Margaret."

"I'm okay," Margaret said, even though she was already swaying, and she picked up her crate and followed. They stopped two more times before they reached where the men were, and Liz smiled and waved at her father.

"You and Margaret stop working when you get tired, you hear?" Sean shouted. He knew working out under these wide blue skies could make a man's spirit soar, but it took a high price in the energy it sucked from you, sometimes without you even noticing until it was too late. He had seen strong men wilt and die in these conditions.

"All right, Daddy," Liz said as she found them a spot to start. With a small trowel she dug a hole in the ground and buried the crown of the pineapple in it, being careful to leave the four to six big leaves at the centre of the stem clear of the soil. Margaret watched her do it two more times and then started to plant the crowns from her crate. She cut her thumb on the serrated leaves of the first one she planted, but she sucked the blood and continued to work, hurrying to keep pace with Liz. She was more careful with the others that she planted and, before lunch, they went back to the woods for three more crates each and to drink cool water.

Sean McDonald gazed up at the position of the sun; then he took off his Akubra and wiped his brow with a sinewy forearm. He looked across to where the Aboriginals were working, and his face rolled into a ball to hurl at them. "Nipper, what the bloody hell are they doing?"

"The boys are going as fast as they can, Mr McDonald." Nipper straightened onto his spindly legs and his hard belly protruded over his shorts. Margaret watched the confrontation with one eye and the knife-sharp leaves of the pineapple crown with the other.

"There're another bloody hundred and fifty crates to go. When are you going to finish them?"

The other three Aboriginals were already hurrying between the rows of ploughed soil, and when they heard the confrontation they started to scurry like ants. "The boys will be finished by tomorrow, Mr McDonald. I'm sure."

"Not if you bastards have your way and get drunk tonight." Sean knew Nipper and his boys liked their Saturday night grog. They had been banned from the centre of town and it was illegal to sell booze to Aboriginals in the state, but they still found some way to get it.

"No grog tonight, boss, we got a ceremony coming up," Nipper said.

"You're always finding some bloody reason not to work," Sean said.

"Only reason to work is when we need something, boss, and we don't find all the things to need that you fellas do."

"If any of those crowns get spoiled I'm taking it out of your pay." Sean walked past Nipper and headed back towards the trees.

Nipper held his hands behind his back and an ingratiating smile lined his face. "None of them is going to spoil, Mr McDonald," he said to Sean's back.

"And make sure they only take half an hour's break," Sean retorted. They were good people, but lazy bastards, these Abbos, and you had to let them know what you expected all the time, or else they would easily fall into their old ways.

"Girls, come on." Sean waved them towards him. "Let's go get some lunch."

Margaret jumped up and hurried to catch Sean and Liz. "Hello, little sister," Nipper said as she went past. She threw him a smile restrained by caution and opened her hand to him, but not so that Sean and Liz could see. Then she broke into a run as he took a step towards her.

*** 

The ute bounced and clattered over the track, throwing up a blanket of dust behind it, but Sean revved the engine and raced the vehicle towards Langley. Although he never said, he liked the trips to the small outback town as much as Anne and Liz. While they shopped, caught up on news and sometimes went to the little theatre house, he would savour several cold beers at one of Langley's two public houses, and listen to farmers tell stories about how they were winning the battle with their land, although he rarely had much to say. Sometimes he would watch the cricket or racing on the pub television, because even though he didn't follow either sport, the television and the radio news helped to make him feel knowledgeable about the outside world.

All four were tightly squeezed into the long seat of the Holden. The two girls sat in the middle and Anne sat at the window, so that she could feel the full force of the air blasting in her face. Sean spied her static gaze. Unlike the others, it never occurred to her to take in the arthritic ghost gums or stunted desert oaks going by. A flock of galahs exploded from a leaning eucalypt when the ute suddenly swung under it, and a curious emu kept pace with them for a mile or so, but she took no notice of these either. This land was all the same to her, not fit for human habitation.

As they approached the edge of the town, Sean noticed her sit higher in her seat. Her eyes became greedy for the sights, and her breathing grew short as her senses were caressed. The town of a hundred or so buildings was arranged around a wide main road cut through the centre, and he always drove slowly the full length of it, because he took pleasure from how Anne lost her self-consciousness and swivelled at everything they went by, stripping away her guard. The quiet outskirts boasted single-storied houses with well-kept gardens, but as they approached the commercial centre with its three and four-storied art deco buildings, the town seemed to come alive. Anne turned in his direction and blushed peach when she caught him

71

watching her pleasure. "Can we get out here, Sean?" He pulled the ute to the side of the road and Anne climbed out, followed by the girls.

"Meet me at the Langley hotel for supper when you're done," Sean said, wanting to prolong her unfamiliar pleasure. Anne seemed about to ask if they could afford it, but he pulled off before she had the chance.

*** 

A car's horn screamed as Sean swerved into its path, but even this angry blast and duel between two vehicles made a change to the silences of Malee.

Saturday afternoon was the busiest time for the high street, and Anne looked up and down at the afternoon strollers, some, like her, taking sustenance from seeing other people. Women loitered with two or three children in tow, and the parking bay of the general store was full. Most of the vehicles belonged to farmers from outlying areas, stocking up on groceries, and a group of them were talking and drinking on the boardwalk outside of a bar. She knew exactly where she had to go to buy the cloth for Liz and Margaret's dresses, but she wanted to take a lingering stroll first, to steep herself in the life of the town. Several women were looking through the window of a new dress shop, and Anne and the girls crossed the road to join them. She stood at the end of the half circle peering through the window. Some of the women were giggling like pubescent girls and already in muted conversation. A burly woman turned to Anne, "Could you imagine me in one of those? Mind you, I'm sure my Alfred wouldn't mind." Her eyes, like Anne's, were hungry for the sight of others, and her mouth and ears craving conversation. It was something that outback wives had in common.

"Does anyone really wear those?" Anne said, her usual reserve cloaked in the mist of her smouldering elation.

The dress ended halfway up the mannequin's thigh, and the shoulder straps, which held it up, were hung low, revealing an ample amount of cleavage. On the wall behind the mannequin was a blown up photograph of the English model Jean Shrimpton, wearing one of the new minis at the Melbourne Cup.

"They're all the rage in London. We were there a month ago," another woman said, and all turned towards her, an authority who had been in contact with the real world.

***

From the moment that they had entered Langley, Margaret had been scrutinising every feature of all the people she saw. She had seen mainly whites and could tell right off that some were more closely kin than others. A few Aboriginals were going in and out of the shops, and when they nodded an acknowledgement she returned it behind a hidden glare. There was an unusual-looking couple that Mrs McDonald discreetly pointed out and said they were Chinese, but she hadn't seen any Southern Europeans who looked like her, and didn't want to ask Mrs McDonald to point them out. The Southern Europeans she had imagined had two or three children, all the same pale rusted colour of a gum tree like herself, and they drove a car like Mrs Cartwright who looked after Joshua, although it wouldn't have mattered if they drove an ute. She stopped to watch the two Chinese that Anne had pointed out, not noticing that Anne and Liz had gone on. She decided to follow these two, because they might live in a part of town where the Southern Europeans lived.

Like the roots of a plant seeking out more nourishing soil, she followed the two down a side street and watched them go into a butcher's shop, where the floor was covered in sawdust. They bought various cuts of meat, which the butcher wrapped in newspaper, and then she followed them further away from the main road. They stopped at a clapboard house, and she knew if she let them go inside she wouldn't get her chance, and so Margaret crossed the road and walked up to them. The woman turned and waved Margaret off with a porcelain coloured hand, protecting her groceries with the other. "No money, go away, go away." Margaret kept her distance so as not to alarm her any further.

"Do you know where the Southern Europeans live?" She asked. The woman looked at her husband. "I'm looking for the Southern Europeans."

"We are Cantonese, we don't know Southern Europeans. We thought you were Abbo," the man said, with a smile oozing regret.

"Mrs McDonald says I'm a Southern European," Margaret assured him.

He smiled more easily and the woman released her grip on their goods. "You look on main road." He thrust a finger in the general direction; then he and his wife went into the house and shut the door.

Margaret took his advice and headed back towards the main road. Mrs McDonald had said they were Chinese, but he had said that they were Cantonese, and so that made her wonder whether Mrs McDonald had gotten it right about her. She came out onto the main road and looked up and down it. On the far side, three boys were hurling insults at a stumbling old Aboriginal, who was drinking beer from a bottle wrapped in brown paper. The man staggered into the road and a car swerved to miss him, its horn screaming. "Get the fuck out of the road, you drunken wog," shouted one of the boys, and the others burst into fits of laughter.

"Chalkie, show us a dance, come on."

The old man raised his brown paper bag to toast them and then proceeded to stomp his bare feet like an irate emu in the middle of the road. When he had run out of beer he dropped the bottle and weaved across the road towards Margaret. She gave him a slit-eyed stare.

"Hello, little sister. You got any beer money?"

Margaret shrunk back from his stale smell. "My father said grog's no good for you, *Nakuppa*."

"You too young to understand, little sister; wait until you grow up."

The discarded bottle bounced off Chalkie's head back into the road. "Hey, Chalkie, you didn't tell us you had a girl. You're too drunk to get it up, so you'd better leave her to us." The boys swaggered over to where Margaret had frozen against a wooden beam, and one of them lifted her dress. Chalkie batted them off like flies, but most of his strikes missed, and all three boys danced around them, laughing and pulling at her dress. Margaret pressed her back further into the post and tears welled up in her eyes, but she forced them back, because she knew that a cornered *joey* could escape if it didn't whimper.

"What are you doing? Leave her alone!" Anne McDonald came charging up the boardwalk and clouted one of the boys around his head with her bag before he had time to duck.

"What's it to you? They're only friggin Abbos."

74

"She's not a bloody Abbo, so leave her alone." Anne tugged Margaret by the arm and marched her off down the road.

"Abbo lover," shouted one of the boys, and then he followed his friends after Chalkie.

"Where have you been? I've been looking all over for you." Anne hurried her across the road and lowered her voice. "I told you to stay away from the Aborigines. You'll only get yourself into trouble." Anne was in such a hurry that it was obvious she didn't want an answer, and so Margaret didn't give one.

She pushed open the door of the general store and the cold air stung Margaret's skin, so that she became aware of sensations other than her recent encounter on the street. An assortment of smells hit her as she went past sacks of flour, rice, sugar, tea, coffee, stacks of oily boxes leaking their tinned fish contents, huge mounds of cheeses and humming freezers filled to their guts with rock-hard meat. They went through an alcove towards the back of the store, and Liz was waiting for them in front of a mirror. She turned and stretched out her arms to show off the dress to her mother. "What do you think?"

*\*\**

Anne moved slowly around her daughter, running her hands over the dress and committing measurements, pleats and tucks to memory. "I like it," she said. "Only, it's a bit too narrow in the waist for you."

As Anne took up another dress and held it towards Margaret, a shop assistant who had been spying on them from beneath the hem of a petticoat on one of the displays hurried over. "We've got some bargains on the cloth if you want to make her a dress yourself," she said with a smile.

"How much is this?" Anne held up the dress.

"You can make two or three dresses for what that will cost you," advised the woman, who had curly brown hair and the name Maureen pinned to the breast of her white blouse.

"Margaret, go over there and try this on," Anne said, handing her the dress.

Maureen snatched the dress from her as though it were the last bargain at the sales, and her overly pleasant demeanour crumpled. "She can't try them on."

"Why ever not?" Anne demanded.

The woman considered Margaret to make sure, and her nose wrinkled as if to avoid a foul smell. "Everyone knows the rules; they can buy but they can't try, and they can't return, either, in case you get any ideas."

All the petty annoyances and indignities of living in such a hostile place seemed to converge on Anne at the same time. She heard when Liz said, "Mum, what are you doing?" But by then she was enjoying the unfamiliar indulgence of snatching dresses from displays, wielding them like a matador's cape to avoid the lunging woman's reach, and pressing them against Margaret's stunned body.

"That costs forty-five dollars. Don't you dare," the woman said as they both came to a breathless stop by a party frock. Anne took up the dress and slid her fingers over its silk waistband.

"You can have this one for her at half price,' the woman whispered, holding up another dress. Anne hesitated, as though assessing what had been said. "I'm shopping for two," she said, nodding towards Liz, who had a hand to her mouth and had edged behind a rail of clothes to hide from the startled gaze of other shoppers. Anne took the two dresses for the price of the cloth she had come to buy whilst ignoring the stares of the other customers as she paid for them. Then she walked down the sidewalk towards the hotel bar where Sean was waiting with a slight smile on her lips, a growing pride in her stride.

# Chapter 5

There's a band of six or seven of them, right inside our front gates, Matron Blythe had told the police when she spoke to them. The last time he came, my chickens stopped laying. The police said there were not enough of them on duty, and it would take them several hours to get someone out there. Matron Blythe accused them of leaving a white woman to face marauding blacks on her own, and she went down to the gates with her baton.

"Where's our daughter?" the wild-dog-eyed black man asked again. He was there with his wife, two of his sons and one of their wives this time. They had left their grandchildren with the other adults in the ute some ways off. The children had been smothered in crushed charcoal mixed with animal fat, so that white folks would only see black kids from a distance.

"And I tell you, you are not supposed to be here," Matron Blythe said.

"Miss Matron." A slight woman with piercing sapphire eyes stepped forward. Her straight hair was tied back in a scarf and she had a light honey colouring. "Our daughter is very special. We have been aching for her, Miss Matron."

"The girl is being better provided for than you can manage."

"But, Miss Matron, can you tell her the stories about her grandparents that she needs to know to tell her own children? Do you know and love her history like we do, Miss Matron? When they start to tell her that her kind is no good, she will need someone to turn to, Miss Matron. I have been through it."

"The girl has learned domestic duties, been taught to fear God, and she might one day have a family and bring them up in a real home."

"Miss Matron, if you think your life is more important than ours, or your religion is more real than ours, then you have no place bringing up our children, because you can only harm their spirit." She hung her head and shuffled about as if to conceal her insolence. "Our girl might act like one of you, but she can never look like one of you, so she will never be accepted, Miss Matron. I know my girl, she won't stop until she feels a part of something, and the trying will kill her."

"Margaret is a strong and sometimes spirited individual, and I'm sure she will survive."

"You bloody people." One of the woman's sons broke from the group who were milling behind and charged like a steaming bull towards Matron Blythe. He grabbed her by the throat and near lifted her off her feet. She swung to hit him with the baton, but he swiped it from her hand as if he were ploughing through grass. "Where's my little sister? You've taken our bloody land, leave us with our children."

Matron Blythe was choking. "The police are on their way, I tell you. I called them."

His mother and father reached out to pull him off. "Let her go, son," his mother said. "We don't want the cunnichman to come and arrest you, we've already lost one child."

"Where's my sister? We want to see her," he repeated, shaking Matron Blythe like torn grass.

"She is not here," Matron Blythe spluttered. He dropped her. She put a hand to her throat, picked up the baton and heaved to recover her breath. "It's you who has blighted the girl—you." She stabbed a finger poisoned with accusation at the woman. "If you had married a quadroon like yourself you would have given birth to an octoroon, a near-white child. Instead you took up with a full-blood Aboriginal and blighted her to become a half-caste mongrel. We sent her away months ago and you will never find her, never."

Mr Ralph appeared out of nowhere. He was clutching a garden fork, ready to spear someone, anyone. "You wogs better go now if you know what's good for you." He took a couple of tentative lunges with the fork, his hands shaking.

"Miss Matron," the woman tried again, "have you ever lost anything you loved?"

Matron Blythe's eyes glazed over like a stale fish, and her body began to quiver. "You get out now. Now." She threw the baton at the woman and it struck her a heavy clunk in the middle of the forehead. Fresh blood trickled down her face and into her mouth, but she made no move to wipe it.

"Come wife, we'll find her ourselves."

Her husband put his arm around her and led her away, but even when they exited the gates, she looked back over her shoulder at Matron Blythe. She had met others like her when they lived on the settlement. They always thought that they were helping, trying to do the best for them. Her own mother, a half-caste named Alice, had grown up on a government settlement. When she reached fourteen they had sent her to work as a servant on a white farm, labour for which she was paid in rations of food and clothes. They sent her back to the settlement each time she became pregnant, and Daisy became the third pregnancy for which she was returned. She said the white farmers wouldn't leave her alone, but the Government-appointed missionaries said she needed to curb her promiscuity, for which they prescribed hard and longer hours of work. She only held each of her children until they were four years old, and that's when the missionaries took them and placed them on the other side of the chicken wire, which ran down the middle of the dormitory, so that there would be no contact. That's why the mothers kept them children on their breasts for such a long time, so that they could give them a lifetime of loving and touching in those four years. Soon after this the mothers were sent out to work, and by the time they returned with their next pregnancies, their older offspring had been moved into segregated children's dormitories, so that they could be converted to the Christian values and work ethics without risk of cultural contamination. Daisy and most of the other children found ways to break the strictly regimented rules that governed settlement life, and they sneaked across fences to make contact with the women—all of whom would act as their parents and let them call them auntie, whether their real mothers were there or not. Sometimes they even dug under the fences to go and spend time in a blacks' camp close by. But one day the missionaries looked at her and agreed that she had too much white blood to live with the others, and they gave her to a white family. The family said the girl had some kind of spirit in her, and they were frightened of this, so when she escaped to live in a blacks' camp, they didn't complain. She grew up there learning their ways, and when she was old enough she became Toby's woman, only getting tied in their customary way, because it was illegal to marry an Aboriginal without the white protectors' permission. Their mob had been drawn back into a settlement because the Government was still trying to force their people off the land, but the management there had not been so keen on separating them from their children. She had allowed her kids to go to school, but secretly she still taught them their ways, until a new manager came and everything changed. He applied the rules the way they were written, and rations were reduced or denied if they continued to go fishing, hunting or tucker gathering, as well as if they spoke their own lingo or refused to put their kids up for adoption. But Daisy and her mob kept breaking the rules, and so he threw them off the settlement, telling them to see if they could survive on their own, but without their mixed-race kids. They went back for them kids, and then they had kept moving to stay close to where their husbands were working and steer clear of the cunnichman and the Welfare. She hoped she had taught her daughter enough to survive until they got to her. She had seen how much their girl liked to do good at their schooling and always wanted to be as good as them other kids, and it worried her, because she knew she wouldn't be allowed.

# Chapter 6

Margaret was enjoying school some, even though the Sisters never gave her any of the textbooks, asked her any of the questions or looked at any of her work. Still, she took in all of the talk, did the sums in the exercise books Mrs McDonald gave her, and when she got home she sat on the veranda or in the kitchen with Liz, who showed her how to do the homework. She especially liked when they did geography, which Sister Agnes took, and she would talk about the snow-covered peaks of the Alps—which Mrs McDonald said looked like the cream she sometimes bought from a farm across the ways— the long fjords along the Norwegian coast down which Vikings used to sail, and most especially about Great Britain and its long river Thames, which cut through its chief city, London. She spoke more of these places than Australia, which made it appear that hers and the pupils' hearts lay elsewhere. They also shared an understanding, so that even though they were distant from its source, they could still quench their thirsts from it. When she spoke about the people that lived in these places, Margaret sat forward and listened with her soul, waiting for words that might bind her to some of them, but mostly they never came, or the ones that seemed likely, such as those Eskimos that drilled holes in ice to fish, or the Pygmies that hunted in the Congo rainforests, always sounded lesser somehow, and would sometimes draw the sniggers of the children.

When the boy that sat in front of her bothered to come to school, Margaret tried to look over his shoulder at his textbook without him knowing. He never seemed to be following the lesson, never answered any of the questions, and if there was homework, which there usually was, he would sometimes go missing for several days.

"What is the longest river in the world?" Sister Agnes asked. Margaret's hand shot up again, even though by now she knew she wouldn't be asked. But at least if her hand went up she was signalling that she knew.

"The same few with their hands up as usual," Sister Agnes said as she scanned the room. "What about the rest of you?"

The boy in front of Margaret turned his head to his desk so that his eyes wouldn't meet Sister Agnes's. "The Amazon," Margaret whispered at his curved back, not quite knowing whether she had done it to help him or have the satisfaction of someone knowing that she knew. The boy ignored her.

"Laura." Sister Agnes pointed to the girl whose long corn-ripened hair hid one side of her face.

"The Amazon, Sister."

"That's right, well done, Laura."

Margaret tapped her foot to give herself a mark and smiled in satisfaction. The boy in front of her hadn't moved.

"And through what country does most of the Amazon run?"

Again the same hands went up, Margaret's included. "Brazil," she whispered to the boy's spiny back. Again he didn't move, and Sister Agnes asked two other pupils before she got the right answer. When the boy heard Brazil, he turned like a basking lizard, his back still folded, to look at Margaret. She smiled a greeting at him, and he swung his head back to face his desk.

"Can anyone tell me the main language they speak in Brazil?"

Fewer hands went up this time, and Margaret's was one of those. "Portuguese," she whispered. She had learned a lot from Liz in only a few months. The boy waited, then he put his hand up as if through thorny brush. Sister Agnes turned towards him, and he tried to pull his hand down, but she had seen him.

"Federico, did I see your hand up?"

"I don't know, Sister Agnes," he mumbled.

"Well, is that your hand or someone else's, Federico?" Federico looked at his guilty hand and the class roared with laughter at his fumblings.

"I'd better ask the hand then, shall I?" Sister Agnes walked over to Federico and held his hand to her mouth like a megaphone. "Did you go into the air to answer a question?" The class were now in stitches, and Federico's blood rose to the surface of his hot butter skin.

"Yes, Sister," Federico admitted.

"Ah, the hand has spoken," Sister Agnes said, as if she were in a Shakespearean play. "And the answer is?" She put the hand to her ear this time.

"Portuguese," Federico answered.

"Bravo Federico, bravo." Sister Agnes clapped as if he had won a race. Then she pinched his cheek. "You see, we see so little of you, but you do have it all there, Federico. You must come to school more often." Then she went back to the front of the class to continue the lesson. Margaret's knees flapped under the table as if she herself had answered the question and received Sister Agnes' praise, and she rubbed the right side of her cheek, where Sister Agnes had pinched Federico. She had never liked coming second to other kids.

That's how it started and continued for the first few weeks. Margaret would whisper an answer to Federico, and he put his hand up and answered if he was chosen. Sometimes he was wrong, and he smiled shyly and looked back at Margaret like a drowning child asking to be fished out of a pond, but more often than not he was right. Federico began to come to school more often, and after a while, when he noticed Margaret looking over his shoulder at his textbook, he held it up so that she could see more clearly. Then as she wrote out her answer to an essay or another problem the sisters had set, she watched to see if Federico looked unsettled, and if so, she whispered what she was writing. But apart from this, they never spoke or played or stood near each other in the schoolyard. Secretly giving answers and sharing textbooks was the extent of their relationship.

***

Most Sunday mornings Anne and the girls walked the two or so miles to St Peter's church in the centre of Malee. But on the Sundays when Sean was not working his land, he drove the family to church before continuing the few hundred yards to the general store, where the grog would unleash his tongue enough for him to confer in the back with one or two of the other irreverent men.

Margaret took off her white gloves to push the door on the ute shut, so that the dust on the car wouldn't blacken them. Then she followed Anne and Liz up the creaking steps into the church, which was packed with women beating fans against the air like hummingbirds on the wing, fidgeting boys in white shirts and bow ties, competing girls in pastel nylon frocks, and four or five stalwart men wearing wide-lapelled suits. Father Beir was conducting his fortnightly sermon at his home church today, instead of travelling to bring the word to another community, and so one had to get there early to be sure of a seat. There was always space at the front next to Helen Cartwright and Joshua, but Anne was too shaken with self-consciousness to sit at the front, and so she found a pew a few rows back, from where she could still see Helen. All three edged their way to their seats. Margaret smoothed out her frock under her as she sat down, the way Anne had taught her, and she rested her plastic purse, containing a hanky and sixpence for collection, on her lap.

Mrs Jones was banging out 'Bringing in the Sheep' at the piano, even though none of the Malee farmers reared the fleeced ruminant, and Margaret swung her white-socked foot in time to the music, but not so that Anne could see. She had been coming to church for some time now, and it hadn't escaped her how the spirits these people prayed to were saddled with a chilly solemnity, especially when Mrs Jones' husband, the chief elder, filled in for Father Beir. Like now, while Mrs Jones was playing the piano, it took her spirit to get up and sing, because she had already learned many of the hymns by heart, but that wasn't allowed until you were told. And there was certainly no dancing, nor did the spirits invade and abduct the bodies of the living so that they could writhe to worldly pleasures again. Maybe it was like the elders had said, that everybody turned as white as skeletons after death, and so these people were already dead. They could be the dead ones whose spirits hadn't yet found their way up to the sky, and that was why they couldn't make exciting ceremonies.

\*\*\*

Father Beir sauntered out from a door at the front of the church flanked by Sisters Ruth and Agnes, both of whom were now wearing their habits and carrying large unlit candles as though they were heavy swords. The sisters peeled off to seats either side of him and Father Beir headed for the pulpit as the piano playing rose to a crescendo then died. He opened his Bible and looked out over the congregation, where a number of female hearts fluttered on silken wings. The women stopped fanning long enough to open their Bibles to the page he announced, and the few children who had Bibles did the same. Anne held her well-fingered copy out in front of her, so that the two girls, who were sitting either side of her, could see.

Margaret was sure that the Bible contained the secrets of their *spirit ancestors*. She wondered, if the stories were so precious, why they had not embedded them in their minds, so that they could extract them at

84

any time, and pass them on like sparkling gifts when the need arose. Even Father Beir, their custodian, had to read the words from his book. How could all the secrets of a people's spirit ancestors be kept in something so small? And then that they should all be able to have knowledge of it, even the young ones. Mrs McDonald never tried to hide the book, and she had positively encouraged her to read it on many occasions. But what surprised her most of all was that none of the women taught the secrets in their sacred place, like her mother did. Mostly it was left up to Father Beir and Mr Jones. But then if you were a woman, according to Mrs McDonald, you weren't supposed to hunt or fish either, you were meant to learn etiquette, which was like stitching your energies up into a womb and leaving them there to fester. How was a woman meant to fly like an eagle if she couldn't do those things?

Father Beir finished the passage and bowed his head. "Let us pray."

Some of the congregation shuffled to their feet and others kneeled. On one occasion Margaret had tried to kneel to see if she was closer to this God, but Anne had summoned her up with a stern finger and whispered through clenched teeth, "You'll ruin your dress." So now she stood next to Anne, bowed her head, but left her eyes unlatched so that she could see if He made an appearance.

"Our Father, we pray for all those who will be harvesting crops over the next few weeks. We pray that the harvest will be bountiful and reward the community of Malee for the hard work it has put into the land—"

Margaret spied on the congregation for sight of these hard workers. Some of the men were leaning on the pew in front of them and, she was sure, falling asleep through exhaustion. Women with their minds shut to their isolation were still fanning themselves, while young children were scratching calves with a foot, picking noses, and now and then poking or pushing a sibling. None of the Aboriginal farm workers or their children were in church, and the only Aboriginals in church were Joshua, who Helen Cartwright had fostered, and Isabel, the girl Margaret sat in front of at school, who had been fostered by the Nicolaideses.

After they had sung another hymn, Margaret sat down with the rest of the congregation. Father Beir wiped the sweat running down his ruddy face, which needed to be kept out of the sun, and then searched through his papers on the pulpit. He turned and looked towards Sister Ruth, as if asking for assistance, but she kept her head down in her Bible and ignored the fumblings of the heavyset man who had told everyone that he had been born in the Swiss Alps. Through various conversations she had overheard, Margaret had learned that for the five years after Father O'Connor had died, Sister Ruth had wanted to take the services, and on one or two occasions she had, but many of the congregation refused to be preached to by a woman, and the Archbishop in Sydney had sent word that Jesus had chosen twelve men as his disciples, and so it was obvious that God had given men the task of passing on his word. That is when Elder Jones started to take the sermons at St Peter's, ably assisted by Sister Ruth in its planning. Then they had sent them this colossus straight out of training in Rome, town gossip had reported Sister Ruth as saying, and now she was relegated to carrying candles, pouring wine for communion and ensuring that there were enough hymn books in the pews, as Elder Jones continued to take the sermons when Father Beir visited another community.

Sister Agnes crossed the floor and handed Father Beir a copy of the Holy Baptism before his fumblings bore panic. He conceded a child's guilty grin, wiped his brow again, and turned to face the congregation. "Today is a special day, as we are about to welcome Elsie and Bob Neil's baby Alexander, and young Laura Wilson into their new life in Christ."

Elsie carried baby Alexander in her arms to the front of the church followed by Bob and the two godparents. Laura Wilson glided forward like a regal bride, proffering smiles to either side of the congregation as she went, with her proud parents and godmother in support. The group stood either side of the pulpit, and Margaret's mouth fell open as if she had sucked in a spirit bearing revelations. Laura Wilson, who she had seen in school but had not spoken to—in fact she had not spoken to any of the children apart from Liz, Federico and the two Aboriginals, and Joshua couldn't hear or speak back—looked like one of the angels she had read about in Mrs McDonald's bible. Her ivory dress dragged along the polished floor, the same one she would wear for Holy Communion later in the year, and she wore a translucent string of beads around her neck, which Margaret would later learn were pearls left to her by a grandmother. Her head was also covered with an intricate white lace scarf.

"Parents and godparents, the Church receives these children with joy. Will you pray for them, draw them by your example into the community of faith and walk with them in the way of Christ?" Father Beir asked.

"With the help of God, we will," the parents and godparents answered.

"Do you reject the Devil and all rebellion against God?"

"We reject them," said the parents of Alexander, on his behalf, with youthful bemusement.

"I reject them," said Laura, her voice travelling all the way to the back of the aisles. Margaret could see her glowing like kindling in the distance, and her feet appeared to have left the ground so that she floated above the others, but there was no sign of the wings she had read about.

"Christ claims you for his own. Receive the sign of the cross." Margaret was sure that as tall as he was, Father Beir had to rise up onto his toes to sign the cross on Laura's forehead. This part of her now seemed whiter than the others, but this whiteness was spreading like poured milk across her forehead.

Father Beir summoned all the participants, and they followed him a few paces to the corner where the baptismal font stood. Laura had her back to Margaret, and she wished she could be where Father Beir now stood, because he could see it happening, he could see Laura shedding her skin. Margaret had seen snakes do it, and she had been called a Snake-woman-child since her birth, but she had never thought about shedding her skin. The revelatory spirit rose up in her, so that she wanted to stand and run forward to see Laura change, but she was hemmed in between Mrs McDonald and another woman, so she gripped the back of the pew and fought her invader whilst praying for Laura to turn around.

"Do you believe and trust in God the Father?"

"I believe in God, the Father almighty, creator of heaven and earth," the reply came from most of the congregation.

"Do you believe and trust in his Son Jesus Christ?"

"I believe in Jesus Christ, his only Son, our Lord, who was conceived by the Holy Spirit, born of the Virgin Mary—"

Margaret didn't yet know the words, and she didn't want to read them from the programme in case she missed the moment of Laura's conversion. So she stayed unblinking, waiting. After Father Beir had dipped Alexander's head into the font he called Laura forward. He held her head over the water, and she pulled back the scarf from her head so that it rested on her shoulders as if it were the hide she was discarding. Father Beir took a handful of the holy water and poured it like ointment over her head. "I baptize you in the name of the Father, and of the Son, and of the Holy Spirit. Amen."

Sister Ruth lit two candles and handed one to Alexander's father and the other to Laura. "God has delivered us from the dominion of darkness and has given us a place with the saints in the light," continued Father Beir. Laura was now floating near the rafters and the spirit that invaded Margaret was struggling to join her. Father Beir rested his hands on Laura's and baby Alexander's heads. "You have received the light of Christ; walk in this light all the days of your life."

Laura Wilson turned, and her smile engulfed the light from the candle so that her whole body merged with it and became one. The transformation was complete, and a potent breath leapt from Margaret's chest so that she was overcome with exhaustion, as if it were she who had been reborn. Her eyes glossed over, and she didn't have the strength to sing the final hymn or join in the final prayer, so she slumped back in the pew and drew breath.

When the church had emptied, Margaret slinked up to the baptismal font. She was sure it was here that Laura had shed her previous skin, and she had decided to take it home and keep it under her mattress with the snakeskin she had found. There was nothing on the floor, and when she looked in the holy water Laura's lace scarf was lying in it. She scooped it from the font like a flower petal and squeezed it out so that the water ran down her arm. "What are you doing, Margaret?" Sister Agnes made her jump, and she hid the wet scarf behind her back.

"Nothing, Sister Agnes."

"Then you can help me to collect the hymn books."

After Margaret had collected the hymn books and left them in a pile on the front pew, she ran outside into the searing heat. The women were standing in little groups, filling each other in on any news that was available; who was expecting, that new mini-dress thing at the store in Langley, and they all laughed as if to cast off their seclusion and said they would never be seen in one. Mrs Rossi, Federico's mother, brought up the young woman who had married the farmer next door to their farm and left after two months. "I heard she went back to her family in Brisbane," she said. They were hushed for a while, as if they could hear the muted screams of the young woman when she had realised, and wishing they had been brave enough to do the same when they had first come to the outback.

"It's a pity," someone said.

"This life isn't for the faint-hearted. It takes a strong woman to live out here," Mrs Wilson said, clenching her fist.

"You were born here, Mrs Wilson, so it's different," Anne offered.

"She should have come to us, we would have helped her," Mrs Jones said. "That's what we have to do out here, stick together and help each other."

"The general store in Langley put those washing machines from America on sale," Anne said, changing the subject, as though the thought of that woman escaping to Brisbane was too much for her to bear. They talked about how much easier it would make their lives, and Mrs Wilson said if she helped her husband in the fields, on top of her other jobs of tending the vegetable garden, rearing their chickens, cooking the meals, making many of the family's clothes, cleaning the house, tending the illnesses and more, they could take one on credit. They all agreed that if they worked additional hours they could get a little more, and none of them questioned where the time was to come from. Sundays after church was the one chance most of them had each week to speak face to face with another woman, and it felt good, but it never occurred to them to extend it to other days of the week; there was work to be done. On many Sundays the talking could go on for two or three hours, especially if the men decided to go for a beer at the back of the general store, which wasn't a place that decent women frequented.

The children separated into groups of their own, and some ran in circles playing tag, a few played a ball game, and some stood in the group which was congratulating Laura Wilson on her baptism and admiring her new dress. Joshua was sitting in the infernal heat of Helen Cartwright's car, staring into space, and Isabel was standing outside the grocery store with Mrs Nicolaides, who didn't speak much English, and became nervous whenever she was too far away from her husband, Costos. But in any case, Margaret didn't want to be with them now. She stood on the steps of the church watching Laura, hoping that she would be left on her own for a while. When it became obvious that it wasn't going to happen, she pulled the ribbon in her hair tight, smoothed out her frock and sauntered over to the loiterers. "I'm happy for you, Laura." The children's conversation and laughter died as if buckshot had brought them down, and it seemed to Margaret that she was sinking in the swamp of their contempt. Then Laura's lips turned up for an instant, and that seemed to release her feet and she departed. The children clucked like chickens as they turned back to their conversations as though nothing had happened.

\*\*\*

Helen Cartwright finished talking to Father Beir and came down the steps towards the women. "Hello, ladies," she said.

"Hello, Mrs Cartwright," came back a choir of voices.

"Hello, Helen," Anne said with a stutter, but loud enough for the other women to scrutinise her with admiration for being on first name terms.

"Could I speak to you for a moment, Anne?"

"Yes, excuse me." Anne followed Helen towards her car.

"I saw Mrs Nicolaides in church, Anne, but I don't know her very well. How is this pregnancy going?"

"The doctor saw Aithra two weeks ago, and he said both she and the baby are doing well. He did advise her to take some more rest, though."

"You will let me know if there is anything I can do to help, won't you?" She brushed Anne's arm.

"I will, Helen. Thank you."

Helen Cartwright smiled as if conferring comfort, and then climbed into her car and drove away.

\*\*\*

Whilst the others were at church, Sean parked the ute at the back of the general store and went in through the back door. Perry, the proprietor, was serving cold beer from behind the log bar, which he had built himself. Most said that Perry never kept a fan in the hot place because it encouraged the customers to buy more beer, but it also attracted flies. The door behind the bar led into the store, and Perry left it open so that he could move between the two rooms and serve customers when Fiona, his wife, was out front pumping gasoline; not that the store ever saw many customers at one time.

"G'day, Sean," said the waif-of-a-man from behind the bar.

"G'day, Perry," Sean said, and kept going towards the table in the dark corner of the tiny room.

Costos Nicolaides jumped out of his seat, and the loose flesh on his arm made waves as he shook Sean's hand heartily and slapped him on the back. When he had first gotten to know him he had tried to hug and kiss him in the way that was common amongst Greek men, but Sean had held a manly resistance in his body, and now this was the most intimate greeting Costos could extend to the man who had saved his life. "How are you, my friend?" Costos asked. Sean loosened his grip, and Costos realised that he had held on to Sean's hand a little longer than was comfortable for him, and so he let go and poured him a beer.

"As good as can be, Costos." Sean leaned back his head and downed half the beer in one mouthful.

Costos' stomach eased back the table as he sat. "What do you mean by good?" he asked, well accustomed to Sean not saying all that he had to.

They had met serendipitously. Costos had done his two compulsory years and a few more in industry as a new citizen in the rapidly growing Australia after the war. Then he had gone in search of land with his savings. He had heard that there was good farmland in Queensland, and, leaving his wife to wait for him, he had gone in search of it, only to find himself lost in the Outback with a spinifex clogged radiator and overheated engine. Sean found him close to death from thirst and heat exhaustion while on his way to complete the sale of his second crop. He gave him water and then food. After that he dropped a flaming petrol-soaked rag down the front of the car radiator, to burn out the dry spinifex grass and seeds which had clogged it and couldn't be cleared by hand. Then when Costos' car was running at normal temperature, he showed him where he could buy good farmland in Malee. Costos Nicolaides was forever grateful to Sean McDonald.

"Finished planting half of the crowns yesterday," Sean said.

Costos grinned corn-yellow teeth at him. "All of mine been planted, Sean. You're not working your boys hard enough. They used to this heat." Costos wiped his brow with a forearm and flicked a glassful of sweat onto the floor. "You promise them the beer after and they work like ants. I afford to go home in ten, maybe twelve, years." Costos was in a hurry, but Sean was already at home with his three hundred acres, although much of it hadn't been cleared and planted yet. "Now I get them to clear another two acres and plant next year."

"There's not enough water in the district to support much more planting, Costos."

"My water tank's full, Sean, and my bore about half full, I think. We will get big rain soon, you see."

"We haven't had good rains for three seasons. The Wilsons are clearing more land, and someone's been trying to buy up land behind Helen Cartwright's place."

Costos slapped him on the shoulder. "You worry too much, my friend."

Sean carried the empty jug to the bar and Perry refilled it. He poured glasses for himself and Costos, gulped his whole glass and refilled it again. Both men had shared four jugs of ice-cold beer by the time they tottered out of the pub, Sean more so than Costos. Sean followed Costos around to the front to say hello to Aithra, and she still greeted him with a mousy smile, after all this time. "You see, I have two beauties, Sean." Costos worked his way between his wife and Isabel and placed both their arms around his ample waist. Isabel made hers slip away as if over lard, and Costos took it firmly in his hand, strung his arm around her shoulder and supported himself between the two women as they started the journey home.

***

All that excitement of Laura Wilson's baptism in church had been dancing on her mind, and Margaret couldn't fall asleep. She rolled out of bed, pulling the blanket around her shoulders, crept into the kitchen and lit the lantern. Then she tiptoed through the back door, making sure she hadn't woken everyone with its piercing squeak. She hurried through the cold to the dunny, where she lifted the loo lid and waved the lantern at a couple of redback spiders which were foraging on its underside, and they disappeared into its dark recesses.

When she came out, Mr McDonald was standing on the veranda sucking on a cigarette and watching her. She quickened her steps, and when he started down into the yard, she broke into a run, slammed the back door behind her and ran to her room. She sat on the edge of her bed panting up a sweat, the blanket held tight under her chin, and watched the window and the gap under her door for any shadows.

When she saw nothing, she edged back the curtain and watched as Mr McDonald went into the dunny. When he came out he continued into the forest. It was only then that Margaret heard her thunderous breath and swayed from her body pounding like a river crashing against rocks. She watched the trees to make sure he was gone, and then she took her snakeskin and Laura's lace scarf from under her mattress, draped them around her neck and climbed out the bedroom window.

She went to the edge of the forest and weaved snake tracks into the ground, right up to her window, as she had done on previous nights, and then she went to stand under the water tank. She pulled Laura's scarf up over her head and leaned back over an imaginary baptismal font. She hadn't seen any Southern Europeans who looked like her since Mrs McDonald had told her that's what she was, and no one else talked about them. And even though she had continued to make her snake tracks from the forest to below her bedroom window and sometimes in the schoolyard, she had seen no signs of her mother and father. They would certainly be coming, but maybe it would take a little longer. She wondered about how hard it would be for her to come to the Lord and be baptised. She wouldn't do it for long. Just long enough to see what it was like. Then, when her real mother came, she could gift her some of their secrets. But she would have to think about it hard, because there were plenty of things these people did that she didn't think was none too smart. Like the way Mrs McDonald always kept her and Liz sweeping at them ants and millipedes when she knew next morning they'd be right back. Or the way she would root up and burn good natural tucker from the soil, then plant those things that didn't belong, and which would struggle and require her devoted attention to survive. Her father used to chuckle when he came back to the settlement from his stockman's work, as he told them how the white fellas tried to kill off the kangaroo, good eating meat, because they said it was a pest. Then they brought in sheep and cows that didn't know where to find the best grazing and waterholes, and the stockmen would have to spend most of their days guiding these stupid beasts, so that they had little time left to themselves to make ceremony and touch their spirit selves, and in that way know why they were here. He at least could stroke his spirit whilst riding over the land, because they were chiselled from the same rock. To the white fella it was merely something to be bought, sold, owned and controlled. But how can you control something that has been here longer than you, has survived more changes than you, and has acquired more knowledge than you? Their way was like a small scratch in the sands of time, he would say, and eventually those same sands would blow over and cover that scar so that no one would know it had been there. She had seen how Mr and Mrs McDonald never had enough time to sit down and embrace each other or watch the night sky passing by. They did everything that you should savour and enjoy real quick, and the things that you shouldn't spend too long on they kinda struggled at with a sadness in their eyes, like deep down they knew that wasn't how it was meant to be. Even the moaning she had heard in the room above hers hadn't lasted long, and she hadn't heard it now since she had started school, while out in the bush or settlements, the older folks moaned all the time; to make them happy, to mend a quarrel, to make the cold nights warm, and just because they liked to, and it didn't seem to matter to them who heard their squealing, laughter or breathlessness, so long as they were happy. Back-to-front people, that's what they were. But she was beginning to like some of the things these back-to-front people did and had.

A slight breeze had picked up, and the night smelt as wholesome as freshly cut herbs. Then without warning, heavy bombs of rain fell onto Margaret's snake tracks, wiping them out. She would have to retrace them later. In the meantime, she held her arms out to the elements, her face up to the rain, and made it wash over her. Streaks of lightning shot across the sky, the heavens screamed, and mushrooming fireballs ripped holes in the fabric of the night. A blade of fire swooped down and sliced through the branch of an old eucalypt, severed the limb and left the stub smoking. The branch fell close to Margaret, and she ran into the house, where she listened to the percussion on the corrugated iron roof, and watched small streams grow and wind their way down to fill the artesian bores below the soil.

# Chapter 7

At lunchtime Margaret sat out under the ghost-gum with Isabel and Joshua, but she was careful to keep a little distance between them. She watched Laura Wilson, who had ignored her smiles and attempts at eye contact more completely now than she had done before her baptism. Margaret was sure it was because Laura was more special now, and she wanted to know how they could become friends. She couldn't ask Liz, because she had a different group of friends to Laura's. Laura's group were lively and played ball for short periods when the heat would allow, or took turns to ride the pony of one of the boys who came to school that way. When the test matches were on the radio, someone would bring a bat and ball, and they took turns at being Bradman or McKenzie. Liz sat in the shade reading books and talking with a small group of children, some of whom were derisively referred to by others in the class as dagoes, balts, jugos, wops, or poms.

Isabel peeled an orange and handed a piece to Joshua, and he ate it in muted solitude. She waited until the other children weren't looking their way before offering Margaret a piece, because that was the only time she took it. Margaret took the offered fruit, regained her distance and watched Laura as she hit a ball and ran between the wickets.

"How did they catch ya?" Isabel asked.

"Nobody caught me." Margaret turned further away from Isabel and rested her head between her raised knees. "My mother's a Southern European and she gave me up for adoption because she knew it would be better for me."

Isabel looked at Joshua drawing in the dust as if to hide her unblinking scepticism. "I've never heard of them Southern Europeans. Where they from?"

"We're from a really beautiful island, and lots of us live in nice houses in Sydney as well."

"Me and me three brothers got taken by the Welfare," Isabel said. "Me mum told us to watch out for the Welfare. Don't play outside or

95

the Welfare will get you. Don't be bad or the Welfare will get you. Eat you tucker or the Welfare will get you. Do you school work and stay clean or the Welfare will get you. We were in the class when they pulled seven of us kids out, including me and me brothers. Slung us in a big black car and took us to the children's home. I hate bloody school."

"Your foster mum and dad nice?" Margaret asked.

Isabel shrugged her shoulders. "They chose me from the children's home. Said I looked like a strong worker."

"Mrs McDonald gave me strawberry cake to eat the very first day. And I got my own room and covers with flowers on them. She even took me into Langley to buy me a new frock." Margaret watched Isabelle finger the crescent-shaped fold of skin on the back of her calf. "How'd you get that?"

Isabelle stopped playing with the scar. "I don't know. Me real mum said I was born with it, and it was the same size when I was born. She said a dingo spirit may have tried to take me while I was still inside her." Margaret twisted her lips, as she didn't know whether to still believe in such things after what they had been taught in school and all, and she certainly wasn't going to admit it out here in the open. Isabel saw her and scratched at her arm as if to conceal her inferior's embarrassment.

"Have you heard from your mother, Margaret?" Isabel asked to break their silence. Margaret lowered her head and made impressions in the hot, red dust with her fingers. "I heard from mine," Isabel whispered.

"You're a bloody liar." Margaret jumped to her feet, ready to go.

"I can prove it," Isabel blurted out, as if in desperation to hold onto the only familiar person she had to talk to. "I've got secrets." Margaret stopped with her back to her and gouged deep channels through her earlier fingered impressions with her heel.

"Me mother's written to me and I've got one of her letters."

Margaret swung back with her hands on her hips. "How did you get the letter? At Radley they never give us any letters. I bet you can't show me the letter."

"I was cleaning me foster mum and dad's bedroom, and I steps on the loose floor in the corner. When I lifted it I find where they hide their money and lots of letters from me mum." Isabel looked over to the schoolhouse to make sure no one could see her, then she put her hand under her skirt, pulled the folded letter out from her panties, and handed it to Margaret. "I couldn't read all the words." The Nicolaideses weren't fussed about education, there was too much work to be done, and when Isabel did come to school she resided inside her silence, partly because that was all that was expected of her, but mainly because she hated school. "Can you tell me what it says?"

Margaret unfolded the letter, and the right hand corner where the sender's address should be had been torn off. She sat in the dust with her legs crossed under her. It took her a while to scan the letter and compose herself. Why hadn't her mother written? *"My dear daughter, I keep asking the Welfare, but they still won't tell me where you or your brothers are. I would love to see you. My heart and your father's is weeping. I go into the yard every day to cry so that the others don't see. They must think I am a silly old woman, because it's been so long now. Will you write to me, my daughter? I love you.*

*Your mother, June."*

"They told me she was a drunk and a prostitute and didn't want anything to do with me." Isabel cried. Her tears fell onto the hot ground and were greedily evaporated.

Margaret held out the letter to her. "If you bring me the others, I'll read them for you."

Isabel wiped her tears with the edge of her skirt. "There hasn't been any new letters for more than a year. She must think I'm dead or I don't care."

"We could write to her."

"They tore her address off the letter, see." Isabel pointed a finger ruled by tremors to where the address had been torn off. "How we going to write to her?"

"The welfare people stamped it and here's their address," Margaret showed her. "We can send the letter to them and maybe they'll send it to your mother."

Isabel's stare was like blunted stones, and her shoulders shrunk back like a cornered dingo. "If me foster mum and dad knows I've wrote her they'll know I've seen the letters."

Margaret knew that the Welfare would probably vet the letter before passing it on to Isabel's real mother, if they bothered to forward it at all. "We'll have to figure out a way to do it."

*\*\*\**

All the way home, Margaret wondered if her mother had written to her. She knew her mother could write, as she had been taught to at a settlement school and then by a farmer's wife at one of her husband's early jobs. Sometimes she wrote letters to their father when he had been away for a long time, and on a few occasions they had received a reply, which he had probably had to pay someone to write, as he himself didn't read or write. Whether her mother would know where to send a letter was another matter. Parents were usually denied addresses and would have to send their letters by way of the Welfare. But would Mrs McDonald have shown her the letters if she had received them? She remembered the pile of letters in the trunk at the foot of Mrs McDonald's bed, and she determined that she would have to search them.

***

Mrs McDonald was hanging washing on the line, trying to catch the afternoon sun, when Margaret came round the back. She stood a little way off with her hands firmly clasped behind her back. "Afternoon, Mrs McDonald."

"Afternoon, Margaret." Anne went to hang another sheet on the line, and then she stopped, as if in spiritual contemplation. "Margaret, I am thinking that maybe it's time you called me Mum, now. I was in town speaking to Mrs Cartwright—Helen — and she was saying how nice it would be for Joshua to call her Mum if he could speak." Margaret's mind wavered as if seized by sunstroke. All the way home from school she had built herself up to ask; now Mrs McDonald was pouring in more doubts. "What do you think, Margaret?" She shrugged her shoulders. Anne grasped one of her offending shoulders and held it still. "Don't do that, Margaret. Unlike Joshua you have a tongue, so use it to speak."

"I don't know," Margaret said, although she knew that it would feel more comfortable to call her Mrs McDonald or nothing at all, for now in any case. Her tongue just felt tied when she thought about calling her Mum.

"Well you think about it," Anne said. She carried the basket further down the line and Margaret took out a piece of washing to help her.

"Have any letters come for me?" She didn't look at Anne when she asked.

98

"Letters, what letters?"

"From my mother. Has she written to me?"

Anne stopped as if she had been stunned by poison. "Your mother abandoned you, Margaret. She didn't care that you had a roof over your head, enough food to eat, clean clothes to wear and a decent Christian education. How any mother can have her children wondering half naked about the bush like—well, it's just beyond me." Sweat was straining to form pools on the bridge of her nose, but the stalking sun evaporated them before they settled. Her forehead knotted in her rejection, and the heat suddenly caused her to sway. "She's forgotten about you, so it's time you did the same and forgot about her." Anne caught her falling forehead and hurried past Margaret towards the back door. She forgot to take her work boots off and slammed the door behind her.

Margaret finished hanging the washing and helped Liz to prepare the supper of boiled meat and vegetables, which melted when they came into contact with one's mouth. Anne joined them for supper with a cold towel wrapped around her head, after she had rested on her bed for half an hour. They ate in breath-held silence. After Margaret had washed the dishes, Liz showed her how to do her homework, because the sisters still gave her none of her own. When Margaret saw Anne go out to water the vegetable garden, she got up from the table. "Where you going?" Liz asked.

"To the dunny," she said. But she went out into the hall and crept up the stairs.

Margaret pushed open Anne's bedroom door, and the sweet scent of lavender captured her senses and drew her in. She shut the door behind her and turned full circle in the middle of the hidden oasis, forgetting why she was there. It reminded her of a sweet watering hole her mob would visit after heavy rains had fallen, where they would find birds in their thousands, rock wallabies and other game, and where sweet clumps of mulla mulla with their white cotton-budded blossoms would fight for attention with blood-red desert pea, carpets of purple parakeelya, and hundreds of other transient desert flowers. They would enjoy that hole with relatives from other distant clans for a few days, until the waters subsided, but Anne McDonald kept this refuge all to herself. Cut glass pots summoned her like mysteries from the dresser, and Margaret opened them one by one to see and smell what was inside. In one she found a round powder pad, and she lifted it to see the white powder underneath. It looked like the ochre pigment they had used in *corroborrees* and the colour Laura had turned when she had been baptised. She rubbed some onto her cheek with the pad and looked at herself in the mirror. Now she could be a spirit or Laura Wilson and she laughed with abandon. She dabbed more powder onto her face until it was cloaked in a white mask, and then she floated around the room as if she were an angel. This set her free and she started to spin. Margaret span until she knocked her shin on the edge of the trunk, and the pain which scurried up her leg like a fleeing rodent reminded her why she was there. She opened the trunk and took out the crisp letters wrapped in the rubber band. As she made for the door she heard tramping on the stairs. It was too late to put the letters back in the trunk, and she couldn't hide them under her frock. She looked around the room. The wardrobe. She threw them on top of it as Anne opened the door.

"Margaret, what are you doing in here? And what's that on your face?" Margaret touched her face and some of the white powder came off on her fingers. "I hope you haven't been practising anything in here." Anne poked her head through the door and peered around as if she were searching for demons.

"No, Mrs McDonald. My face was hot, so I borrowed some of your powder stuff."

"I told you to wear your hat. That will stop your face from getting hot."

Margaret looked down onto her shin. A trickle of blood was running down from where she had knocked it. "And I was looking for a bandage, Hmm." She couldn't voice the appellation 'Mum', but that's what Anne seemed to hear, and it brought a smile to her face. But then her pleasure vanished.

"You are not to come into my room again. Come downstairs." She took Margaret by the arm. "You'll get blood onto the carpet."

The following afternoon, Margaret stood on Anne's regency make-up chair, which was rarely used, and retrieved the letters from on top of the wardrobe. She left most in the trunk, but smuggled a few out of the house and hid them in the barn, where she could read them later.

In the night, Margaret lit the lantern and crept out the back door into the barn. Cicadas were humming and the night air bit cold, causing her to wrap a blanket around her shoulders. She retrieved the letters from where she had buried them in a corner under some hay, sat on one of the crates and pulled off the rubber band. Her fingers ran through the pile, which were all addressed to Anne McDonald at the Lodge, c/o Malee Grocery Store, and soon she recognised the long thin flowing lines of script as all being from a woman named Carol, in some place called London. She threw them down, hot with anger that not one letter from her own mother was amongst them. Mrs McDonald had said her mother didn't care, and this proved it. She wouldn't make any tracks for her to follow tonight. If she couldn't be bothered to write, then why should she make tracks?

Margaret picked up one of the scattered letters, turned it over and started to read. Anne McDonald's mother was dying. She had something called lung cancer, and Carol was asking Mrs McDonald to come and visit her. She said that she knew how proud both of them were, and even though they hadn't spoken or written to each other in more than ten years, she was sure her mother loved her and had forgiven her for going to Australia. Margaret looked at the date on the letter, and it was more than three years old. She gathered up all the other letters, put them into date order, and hid them in the same place. She would read them each night when she had the chance. Then, before she went to bed, she went out and channelled her snake tracks anyway.

# Chapter 8

On her way to school in the morning, Margaret skipped off the path and, when she was far enough away from Liz, she ran off into the trees. She crossed to the other side of the woods and went into one of the Nicolaideses' orchards, where the apples were ripening and had started to fall off the trees. She picked three of the biggest and reddest fruit, put them into her satchel, then ran like a hound chasing hares. She climbed a fence to get onto the Rossi place and continued scurrying across it in the direction of school. When she reached the edge of the woods, a bird's shrill call disturbed the air. Margaret stopped and looked towards the trees, but they were as still as mountain rocks. She ambled on, and there was another sonorous shriek before she saw Federico step from behind a tree. "Hello, Federico," Margaret said as she hurried towards him.

"Hello, Margaret," he said, and then looked down at his shoe, his hot butter skin turning a shade. Margaret handed him her exercise book and Federico sat with his back against a tree and copied the answers to the previous day's homework into his book. Some he had already attempted, like Margaret had told him, and he checked his answers against hers and had to correct them in most cases. Margaret watched the way his olive eyes soaked up the words, his long thin fingers raced over the work, and it prickled her skin to know that she could help him the way Liz helped her.

"What is this word, Margaret?"

Margaret followed his finger to the word. "Con-tin-uously … continuously." His olive eyes narrowed to a slit as if to ask her the meaning. "Well, it's like when you keep doing something." She thought of the way Federico would ask the same question time and again, that was continuously, but she knew if she used that example it would make him look at the ground again, and for some reason, she wasn't sure why, she preferred it when Federico looked at her. "Sister Ruth used it yesterday, remember?" Federico's broad-mouthed frown

102

said no. "When she said 'The same people continuously put up their hands to answer my questions.'"

"Yes, I remember—con-tin-uously."

"That's it," Margaret said. "We better hurry or else we're going to be late."

Federico rushed to finish copying the work then handed Margaret her exercise book. "Thank you, Margaret," he said, lingering, but when her eyes fell against his as if witnessing the first bloom of the season, he ran off.

Margaret slipped the book into her bag and ran on a slightly longer route. When she saw Laura Wilson, she slowed to a gait that would make sure she caught her before they were in sight of the school. "Good day, Laura," Margaret said when she was within touching distance.

Laura jumped around clutching her bag to her chest. "You almost scared me to death. What do you want?"

"I thought you might like to walk to school together. And I bought you this." She held out the best of the apples for Laura.

"No thanks. And I can walk to school by myself." Laura recovered the birthmark on her cheek by draping her corn-ripened hair over her left shoulder, and her buoyant strides lengthened as she hurried towards the rise of the hill.

"I thought you looked really nice at your baptism," Margaret said, as she strode to keep up.

"You already told me that."

Margaret could tell she was being deaf-eared, but at least they were walking together. Her mother had once told her that it takes time to find the sweetest berry, and so while the other children had often ended up with handfuls, she would find the biggest and juiciest, and these satisfied her thirst even more. She knew Laura was worth the waiting.

When they reached the crown of the hill where they could see the school, Laura broke into a run. "Bye, Laura," Margaret shouted, but she didn't look back.

\*\*\*

Margaret hurried into school behind the children who sat at the front, and this time she turned right, so that she would go past Sister Ruth's desk. Isabel stared a taut warning at her, as though concerned that the heat had scorched her mind, but Margaret ignored her. There was only an orange on Sister Ruth's desk that morning. Many of the children's parents had already harvested their crops and sold it to the cannery. Margaret placed two of the apples on the desk as she went by, and then she took her place in front of Isabel and Joshua.

"What did you do that for?" Isabel whispered. "She won't have them."

"She will. That girl bought her some yesterday and she had those. Then when it was question time and the girl raised her hand she got to answer two questions." Margaret folded her arms in unbending defiance, waiting for the apples to disappear into Sister Ruth's bag.

"She doesn't even call our names in the register. We're not here," Isabel said.

"Well I do all my work and Liz and Mrs McDonald, they mark it." She wanted to say she even helped Federico with his homework, but she had promised not to tell.

"I don't know why you're trying so hard anyway. You don't need all this stuff to clean and cook."

"I'm not going to clean and cook."

They held their heads down and stilled their tongues whilst Sister Ruth surveyed the room like a market buyer. "So what you going to do then?" Isabel asked when the buyer was done.

"I may be a teacher, I don't know yet."

"Who you going to teach? They won't have you teach their white kids." Margaret preened her neck like a peacock, because she was teaching one already.

***

They did arithmetic and biology, which Sister Agnes, being the more technically minded of the two teachers, took, and work was placed on the board for the children to do according to the ability streams in which they were put. When Margaret had first come, Anne had figured out that she was at least four streams behind Liz, and she had told her to follow the work for that stream, as the sisters had made no attempt to grade her. But Margaret was as eager as a newborn to learn, and it had only been a few months before Anne told her to do work three streams behind Liz. Now she was doing work that Liz had done eighteen months ago, and trying to do some of Liz's current work when they were at home, also.

When they went into the yard for lunch, the apples were still untouched, and after the break, the orange had gone, but the apples were still there. All through the afternoon's English lesson Margaret's eyes were attracted by the magnetism of the fruit on the desk as if they were on opposite poles, and she tried to think of an occasion in her mob when food offered had not been accepted, but she couldn't remember one.

While one of the children cleaned the blackboard, another recited a passage from the bible, and then the sisters ended the school day. Margaret plodded in clearing her desk so that she could keep an eye on the table at the front. When Sister Ruth picked up the apples by their stem, the joy leapt up inside her and a smile spilled from her face. Then the dustbin rattled as Sister Ruth dropped the apples into it and hurried from the room. Margaret crept, crippled by rejection, towards the door. Not even avowed enemies refused an offering. "Come on, Margaret, hurry along," Sister Agnes said, and escorted her to the door.

***

Margaret was picking at her supper as though still aching from her rejection when Costos' jeep screeched to a halt at the front. He ran into the house, slamming the screen door behind him, "Anne, Anne!"

Anne met him in the hall. He was perspiring, his huge stomach heaving, his flaming eyes leaping out of his moon crater face, wild with fear.

"How is she?" Anne knew immediately that it was Aithra. She had already miscarried twice, and the doctor had warned them if it happened a third time she wouldn't survive.

"She is bleeding, Anne. I go to the general store and call the doctor, but they not get here for hours. You must come, Anne." He had a hold of her arm, which, even under the circumstances, made her rigid cheeks twitch with unease.

Anne patted his hand, easing it away with determined inconspicuousness at the same time. "I'll be ready in a minute, Costos." She was halfway up the stairs when she leaned over the banister and shouted down for Elizabeth. But Liz was already standing at the cracked door with Margaret.

"Yes, Mum."

"Get me the medicine chest."

When Anne arrived Isabel was wiping Aithra's forehead with a damp towel. She was as pale as a ghost gum, and each guttural moan that rose from her rigid body clung to them like the rotting stench of death. "Get some fresh water, Isabel, and put more on to boil, lots more." When Isabel had gone, Anne pulled back the bloody sheets. The foetus had already come, and its fetid odour ploughed into her face, making her gag. The heat had already started to claim the flesh, and she took it from between Aithra's shrivelled limbs and wrapped it in a towel. Costos was too afraid to come into the room, so Anne took out the fast decaying remains to him and told him to dig a deep grave, which he did with great energy, as if that would temper his anger with God. She then went back to try and save Aithra.

Anne took off all the sheets to clean her up and shook her head. Her limbs were still that of a frail girl, the same as when she had first met her. She rinsed the rag in the basin at the foot of the bed to wipe her again, and Aithra let out a wail lacerated with contractions, which hurried Anne back to her side. Aithra gripped Anne's arm, gritted her teeth and pushed with a moan straining with prayer. The second child slid out of her with a gush. It was a boy. The child's face was blue with breathlessness. Anne looked from him to Aithra, not sure which to work on. She decided on Aithra. As she went to wipe her face, Aithra pushed her hand away, towards the boy. Anne tried to wipe her again, but again Aithra summoned the strength and pushed her towards the boy. Isabel had brought in more hot water and stood watching them as if it was all part of life's curve, as it was not uncommon amongst her own people to dispatch an unhealthy newborn, who could burden a trekking mob. Anne opened the baby's mouth and cleared the mucus with her finger, then she took the rag and cleared his gummy nose, but still he didn't move. Her mind was tumbling through her options without conclusion. What were those things she had read in the medical encyclopaedia again? It was in her medical chest on the floor, but she didn't have time to look at it now. She held the child on its front and slapped its behind, once, twice, three times, but still there was no response. Aithra's sapless mouth was working from the bed, willing her on, but no words came. Isabel crept over to Anne and blew a gentle stream of air at the baby's nose, the way she had seen the old folks do it. Anne remembered and

106

followed suit; three breaths, a light pump of the chest with two fingers followed by a slap; three breaths, pump, slap. She slapped the baby and he coughed. Then he coughed and spluttered like an engine straining to fire, and he started to wail. Anne's eyes sprung shimmering pools, and she turned them on Aithra who had no energy to smile, but Anne could sense it seeping from her, along with her life's force. She cut the cord, wrapped the baby in a sheet and lay him next to Aithra.

Throughout the night Aithra's temperature rose, and Anne wiped her down with wet towels and made her sip solutions of lightly salted water and weak broth. She could hear Costos' hod carrier's feet pacing the hall, and several times she sent him to check on the progress of the doctor. On the afternoon of the next day, the flying doctor arrived with a nurse and took over.

Early the following morning, the tired, dishevelled doctor, whose rough beard concealed his youth, walked around to the side of the house, where Anne was laying flowers on all three graves, the last of them freshly filled. "She will live, mostly thanks to you, Mrs McDonald."

"And the boy?" Costos asked, in a voice barely clutching onto hope.

"You have a healthy son, Mr Nicolaides, but your wife won't be able to have any more children."

Costos hugged the doctor, who was stilled with embarrassment. "Thank you, Doctor, thank you." Then he hugged Anne, and in his tactile celebration did not feel her slippery stone body. "Thank you, Anne. We call the boy Andrew."

"But ... But surely you want a Greek name?" Anne said, concealing her pleasure like a sealed vault.

"Andrew, so that he remembers who helped to bring him to us, Anne."

"The nurse will stay with her for a few days, Mrs McDonald, so you can go home and get some well earned rest. And Mr Nicolaides, I think it would be a good idea if you slept in separate rooms for a year or so."

Isabel stood by a corner of the house, at the edges of their world, and the coming of the child made that world grow.

# Chapter 9

The summer night had roused Margaret from her weightless sleep, and she came out of the dunny and stopped to listen to the cicadas competing to outsing each other and watch the moon pull faces at her, as she wasn't allowed to do these things when Mrs McDonald was around, as there was always work to be done. She turned off the lantern and left it by the back door before slinking off into the forest thinking that she might find some wild berries and plums to eat. Every now and then she stopped as she heard scurrying in the undergrowth, but the nocturnal residents were too elusive, and she never caught sight of them. She thought if they could hide from her she would do the same, and each time she heard the ruffle of leaves or the snap of a twig, she pressed herself against a tree or stooped like a hare in the undergrowth. Once, when she pressed herself up against a tree, the crackling of trampled leaves refused to die. She arched her back like a hunter's bow and cat-toed her way to the nearest hiding tree from the sound. She stayed pressed against the gum tree until her breathing and heartbeat were like the silent pulsations of its trunk, and then she peered around the side. The large animal was in the middle of a clearing, close to the ground, playing with dry twigs and leaves. The leaves suddenly bloomed into flames, and the animal unfurled its body and stood on its two hind legs. It was a boy. As the flames silhouetted his gangling body, stripes of white and red ochre reflected from his legs and torso. He kicked his legs high and threw his arms to the sky as he danced around the fire. Then a pulsating groan erupted from the pit of his stomach like a dozen tones fighting to be heard, and he sang out in a tongue that Margaret didn't understand, with the resonant night sounds accompanying him. The light flickered against his body, and sometimes it caught him so that the white X-ray lines were dancing by themselves.

Margaret wished she could join him and wanted to see better. She moved around the tree and started towards one on the other side. A dry stick squealed under her foot. The singing and dancing stopped.

The boy took sharp turns around him, and Margaret hovered over the stick with her outstretched foot. The boy drowned the fire with dry earth and trotted off into the shadows.

Margaret waited to make sure the boy was long gone, and then she went into the clearing. When the moonlight struck them, some of the boy's footprints could still be made out where the ground was clear. Margaret stepped into them to draw his energy and retrace the dance. As she turned, the X-ray skeleton stood up out of the undergrowth. She jumped back, almost falling over. The *Mungee*, eater of children, had come to get her. But the monster didn't move.

"Joshua?" she exclaimed, when her fright had abated enough to give her back her sight and tongue.

"My name is Nannup," he said, with clenched teeth. But Margaret failed to hear the exact words, as she was too rooted in surprise at the sound. How was it that Joshua, who everyone believed couldn't, had deceived them all with his self-imposed silence?

"You can hear and talk. How come?"

"You going to tell?"

Only then did Margaret notice how tightly he was gripping a dead branch, and she swallowed some courage. "Not if you don't want me to, Joshua."

"I said my name is Nannup."

"If I call you that then they'll know." She really liked Joshua better anyway. Mrs McDonald had shown her parts in the Bible where he had done important things.

Nannup appeared to agree but said nothing, and looked as though he was deciding if she could really keep his secret. "You know what happens to people who give secrets away?" Margaret shook her head, no. Nannup raised the branch above his head and Margaret pulled her neck into her shoulders and covered her head with her hands. He swung the branch around several times and brought it crashing across the face of a tree. It shattered into pieces.

Margaret started to breathe again when she saw his knotted arms untie. "Why you watching me?" Nannup asked.

"I liked what you were dancing. But why were you singing with all that lingo? The sisters wouldn't like it."

"Because it's mine. I don't care what the sisters like." He walked off at a pace, and Margaret trotted to keep up. "I want to be like a gum tree," he said. "Them gum trees never forget what they are." His words singed her skin.

"Why's that?" Margaret asked, eager to hide her wounds.

"You can have a big fire sweep through this place and it will burn that gum tree so that it looks dead, and that gum tree will pretend for years that it have no life in it. But what you don't know is that its lifeline run deep into the heart of the tree, so that fire might scar the outside, but the next time that tree get some of that rain that it like, them leaves just start blossoming again." The moon traced their steps, and Margaret caught hold of each of his words like falling fruit, because she liked the way he told the story. "Who's your mob?" he asked.

"They want me to be a Southern European, but I haven't seen any of them."

"So what you going to do?"

Margaret shrugged her shoulders and then remembered Mrs McDonald's instructions. "I don't know yet." She didn't want to tell him that she was a Snake-woman-child and she could shed her skin, although she hadn't decided if she wanted to do that yet. He wouldn't understand, and he would either try to stop her or he wouldn't talk to her again. And she liked it that she was the only one Joshua talked to; apart from when he was singing to the shining spirits that stood guard in the sky at night.

"Can I come back next time?" she asked.

"What for? You don't like *Koori* things."

"I do. My mother kept all our secrets, and I'm just learning theirs so that I can show them to her when she finds me."

"They have too many secrets, you'll never learn them all."

She was about to say I will, but decided to wait until she could show him. Nannup stopped and pointed down a track, "You'll get home that way." Margaret was waiting for him to tell her that she could come again, but he turned and walked back in the direction from where they had come.

"Bye, Nannup" she shouted, but he had already disappeared, so she ran up the path towards her home.

***

School always finished in the early afternoon, and the children headed home to do their chores on the family farms. Liz saw Margaret heading across the town square towards the church, and she said bye to her friends and ran to catch up with her. "Where you going, Margaret?"

"I'm going to see Father Beir," she said. "I was thinking that maybe he wants someone to help him keep the church tidy or something."

Liz's faced turned sour. "Don't you think we have enough work to do at home? We have to help clean the house, wash the clothes, sweep creepy-crawlies off the veranda—sometimes twice a day—help Mum with the vegetable garden and Dad with the farm, read the Bible when we wake and before we go to bed. Sometimes I'm too tired to do my homework."

"You won't have to help."

"But you know—"

"Shh!" A lone worshipper shushed them from the pew as they had already entered the church, and Liz reined in her voice.

"You know Mum is going to want me to help."

"If she does then I'll do your share and you can sit in here and do your homework. That way she can't call you away to do something else."

Father Beir emerged from the vestry at the front of the church and Margaret gulped air and looked around him.

"Hello, girls. What are you looking for?" Father Beir gazed over his shoulder in the direction Margaret was looking.

"I was wondering if Sister Ruth and Sister Agnes are going to be here?" Margaret said.

"Not today, I'm afraid," he said, and Margaret smiled in relief. "You are Margaret, and you are Elizabeth, are you not?" He shook both their hands with an overdose of animated gusto, but it was the nervousness of a man trying to be accepted.

Liz's cheeks tightened as though she was grinding her teeth. "Most people call me Liz, Father."

"Okay, then, that's settled. Liz it shall be," Father Beir said, and he let out a rousing laugh, which caused the girls to raise probing eyebrows at each other, and the woman that was trying to pray stared firm-lipped, as if to admonish them from afar.

"Have you come for confession?"

Both girls said no in unison. Father Beir frowned like a man whose journey had been wasted. "I have had very few confessions since I have been here. Have the people of Malee nothing to confess?"

"Nothing interesting happens here, Father," Liz admitted.

"Oh, you are but a little child, Liz." Father Beir rested his hands on both girls' shoulders and led them to sit in the front pew. "When you reach the world of an adult you will realise that everyone has something to confess, my child." Liz's lips puffed with annoyance.

"What is it—" A Bavarian accent broke free, and Father Beir stopped, re-incarcerated it and started again with what sounded more like Swiss German. "What is it I can do for you, then?"

"We were thinking, Father—" Liz glared at Margaret. "I mean, I was thinking that maybe you needed someone to help you with cleaning the church and things." Father Beir looked up and down the aisles. He had managed to take care of the church with the sisters, but Sister Ruth frowned on the very idea of a Father getting down on his hands and knees, except when prostrate before God. And she was not keen on polishing floors herself. "You'd have more time to catch things in your net, Father," Margaret continued.

"You've seen me in the woods?" Father Beir asked. Margaret nodded. "I'm a lepidopterist." Margaret's face creased. "I've been catching and logging some of the wonderful species of butterfly you have here in Australia," he said in explanation. He put a finger to his lip as though the idea had some merit. "I have been thinking that I would like help for some time. Come with me." The girls followed him to the vestry, Liz dragging her heels, and Father Beir pulled back the black curtain across the doorway. The light bounced off the gold plated goblets and jewel encrusted plates used for communion, most gifted to the church by Helen Cartwright, and bathed Margaret's face like healing ointment. "You could polish the goblets and plates once a week and the church floor also. So that would be two days."

"We'd be able to do that, wouldn't we, Liz?" Margaret beamed, as if drunk on gold.

"We'll have to ask Mum first," Liz said, and then creased her lips.

"That's settled then." Father Beir shook on the deal, and Liz hurried towards the exit. But Margaret stayed looking at the goblets and contemplating Father Beir. "Is there something else, Margaret?" She put her hands behind her back and swung like a smoke-filled urn.

"Sometimes your voice sounds funny, Father. I was wondering where you're from?"

The heat suddenly seemed to accost Father Beir, and he looked faint and breathless. He loosened the button at the neck of his robe and cleared his throat. "I'm from Switzerland, Margaret. That's where I was born," he said with a slow and deliberate control of his accent.

"Is that near to where any Southern Europeans live?"

"It's a lot closer than Australia, Margaret."

"Have you ever seen any Southern Europeans, Father?"

"Well, the Rossis and the Nicolaideses can be considered Southern Europeans, but there are many others who I haven't seen, Margaret. But why all this interest in Southern Europeans?"

She scratched her thigh and stared at the cross resting on his chest. "I was wondering if Southern Europeans could get baptised and go to heaven, Father."

"All God's children can get baptised and go to heaven. Even you, Margaret." He touched her shoulder as he said it, and she looked into his unmasked eyes.

"Thank you, Father," she said. Then she held back her leaping until she got outside, and she bounded all the way home.

***

"What made you think of asking Father Beir to clean the church, Margaret?" Mrs McDonald asked when they told her. Margaret rested the iron on the board and pulled the creased part of the sheet round to the front.

"I like being in church, and I think it might help me with my Bible reading." She knew Mrs McDonald would like to hear that. Helen Cartwright was able to act charitably and give funds, ceremonial plates and goblets to the church. Mrs McDonald had never felt she had anything that they would want, but now her daughter and foster daughter had donated their time to the church, and Margaret knew that Father Beir would mention it from the pulpit on Sunday, which would please both her and Mrs McDonald. Still, Mrs McDonald wasn't able to convey to them the full extent of her indebted pleasure. Somehow it remained drowning inside her, as though struggling to float on her chest, and sometimes it swam up to her throat, but it couldn't escape the torrent inside her.

113

She finished stitching Mr McDonald's worn out pants, bit the end of the thread and took off her reading glasses. "Now you know it mustn't get in the way of your chores around the house?"

Liz was straining boiled vegetables at the sink, and cast an 'I told you so' glance in Margaret's direction.

"It's only two afternoons a week, Hmm." The word still wouldn't come out of her. "And I'll make up my chores when I get home. I promise."

"What about your homework, have you been doing it?"

"Yes, Hmm."

Mrs McDonald looked at Liz, who she was increasingly relying on to keep an eye on Margaret's progress. She had done much herself in the first few months that Margaret had been with them, but the freshness of it all had disappeared like a too long harvested fruit, especially when Andrew had come along, and Costos and Aithra had asked both her and Mr McDonald to be godparents. More than a year-and-a-half had eluded them since his birth, and Mrs Nicolaides now brought the unsteadily walking boy over at least once a week. At other times Mrs McDonald found some excuse to go to their farm so that she wouldn't miss out on any of his changes.

"She's done her homework, Mum, and it's getting quite good now," Liz said. Margaret suppressed the smile which was unfurling its wings. She swallowed learning as if it were pure air, and those were the times that she and Liz found that they had most in common and thrived like well fed roses in each other's company.

"Have the Sisters marked any of it?" The question spoiled Margaret's pleasure like an insipid meal. She had grown accustomed to the sisters not marking her work. But she could sometimes judge how well she was doing by the marks Federico received, especially if he had copied her work exactly, when he would get B's, and on one occasion he even got a B+ and some nice words from Sister Ruth. Liz looked away and busied herself in getting supper ready.

"No, Hmm," Margaret admitted. "They haven't marked my work."

Mrs McDonald seemed to turn over her admission like a coin between finger and thumb. "I've been thinking I should come to see Sisters Ruth and Agnes," she said to no one in particular. Both girls looked at each other as if they had stumbled in the dark. Liz shook her head at Margaret and mouthed "No!" Then she turned back to the food before her mother could see her. Sister Ruth did not allow parents to tell her what to do in her own school, and those whose parents had tried gave the other children ammunition to aim at them for weeks.

"I'm learning just fine as it is, Hmm, really I am," Margaret said.

"Just fine may not be good enough," Mrs McDonald said. She sat in her reverie for a while longer, and then she took Mr McDonald's mended pants up to his room.

"You better stop her," Liz whispered as soon as her mother was gone.

"It's not my fault. I didn't tell her to come."

"Sister Ruth is going to stop asking me questions, and you know what the other children will say. She might even stop you from coming to school." Liz went over to the door and looked up the stairs to make sure her mother wasn't coming. "If you don't stop her then I won't talk to you."

The stairs squeaked under Mrs McDonald's footsteps, and both girls hurried back to their duties in silence.

\*\*\*

On Wednesdays the children did arithmetics in the morning and their answers were checked after lunch. Margaret sat in the schoolyard with her back against a tree, and she wrote the number of the question and then did the sums and the answers right there in the red dust, saying it out loud as she worked. Federico leaned against a tree three yards behind, so that their attestable separation was obvious to all. From there he could see Margaret's doodling, and he corrected those sums that he had gotten wrong. Most of the other children were sitting in the shade of the school veranda, but Joshua was out under the old oak by himself, as Isabel had not been to school for a while.

"Margaret—your mother," Federico said, and she looked up to see Anne shuffling down the road in her white high-heeled shoes, the ones she rushed to put on when someone important came. She put Andrew down to totter alongside her, his shiny black hair sometimes spilling like wine to stain his excited face. Margaret looked for Liz on the veranda, but she had already seen her mother's approach and separated from the other children to hide behind a roof post. Margaret hoped, through hasty, fervent prayer, that she might be on her way to the grocery store, but she had on her important shoes, so

115

it was unlikely. She opened her exercise book to the previous night's homework. Federico had already been given a B for his. Sister Ruth's tick was long and curved at the end like a sickle. She practiced the tick twice on another page and then inserted it next to her homework with a B. Then she got up and ran out past the church to intercept Anne.

"Good day, Hmm."

"Good day, Margaret," Anne said, whilst steadying the giddy Andrew with a firm hand.

"I got a B for my homework." Margaret opened the book and showed Anne.

"Sister Ruth marked it?" Anne asked, surprise tugging at her voice like an angler with an unexpected catch.

"Yes," Margaret lied. She would say three Hail Marys at church in the evening, but she wouldn't confess to Father Beir.

"That's good, Margaret. When you and Elizabeth get home can you start supper? I am going to meet some of the other ladies for prayer and tea at Father Beir's house."

"So you weren't going to see Sister Ruth?"

"No," Anne said, "and it seems there is no need to now. I'll see you this evening. And put on your hat."

"Yes, Hmm," Margaret said as Anne headed towards the Father's house.

***

Isabel hadn't been to school for several weeks. The Nicolaideses needed her to help out on the farm and around the house, even though the yields from the fields had not been high. Most of the farms were just breaking even, and Costos did not want to spend his savings on hiring extra help when the girl was quite capable. Sometimes, when she could get away, Margaret met her in one of the fields, or at the edge of the woods, and they read more of the unanswered letters from Isabel's mother. Margaret had also continued to secretly read the letters from Anne McDonald's friend in England. When she had decided how they were going to do it, Margaret told a reluctant Isabel to steal some money from the pile that Costos kept under his floorboards, and she bought some stamps and envelopes at the general store.

116

Margaret hurried across the fields under the light of thousands of flickering stars on a balmy night, and when she reached the Nicolaideses' homestead, she hid in the undergrowth at the back and let out two owl hoots. She watched Isabel's bedroom window, waiting to see if she would climb out, but instead she saw a lantern swaying to and fro from the cracked barn door. She ran through the brush and into the barn, where Isabel, still in her nightie, was waiting. "Me foster dad doesn't sleep too sound, so we'll have to be quiet."

"Do you have the letter with the address of the Welfare?" Margaret asked. Isabel gave her the letter and they sat on the dusty barn floor.

"How you going to write to me mum without the Welfare knowing?"

"I'm going to write the letter from Mrs Nicolaides."

Isabel's face stiffened like plaster and her hands began to shake. "But me foster mum can't write, and what happens if me mum writes her back?"

"They won't know that Mrs Nicolaides can't write, and you'll have to be the first to check the post box every week." Margaret was already doing this at her home to check for letters from her mother and Anne McDonald's friend. The absence of any letters from her own mother sometimes caused her to kick the letterbox stand or hurl stones at the resting dogs, but as soon as she saw Anne McDonald, she threw a covering smile over her acts. "If it's a letter from the Welfare—and you can tell by the stamp here; see, it's from Brisbane—then don't give that letter to your foster parents."

Margaret placed her exercise book on the floor, and in her best hand she addressed the letter from Mrs Nicolaides to the Welfare. "What do you want to say to you mum?" she asked. Isabel put a hand over her mouth as if to catch the decaying words and laughed. Her eyes glistened like treacle and her breaths were deep and audible.

"Tell her ... Tell her I love her and I want her to come and get me, and I want to see me brothers and dad." Once she had started, she rattled off a list of basic wants as if they could be ordered, while she made circles in the dust with a finger. Margaret didn't write anything.

"We've got to pretend the letter is from your foster mum. She'll say things like how you're getting by and so on."

"Like what?"

"I don't know," Margaret admitted. "Well, like—she's getting on well in school, has good food to eat and likes it here."

Isabel's charcoal eyes burst into flames, "I can't say that. Me mum will think I don't want to come home."

"Well, something simple. Then if you mum writes back we can think of what else to say."

In the end they agreed on:

*Dear Mrs Anderson,*

*Your daughter is doing well with us. She goes to school and is healthy. She is wondering how you, her brothers and her father are doing. Sometimes she says she wishes she had a photograph to remember you all by. She sends her love.*

*Yours truly,*

*Mrs Nicolaides.*

Then Margaret suggested adding: '*The rains here have not been good and we have only had a reasonable harvest of pineapples, oranges and apples this year. We truly hope that God helps us and that next year there is more rain.*' This she did because she said the Welfare were bound to tear off the address if they sent the letter on to Isabel's parents.

***

Liz slouched in a pew doing her homework whilst Margaret took a broom and swept the slightly raised stage from where Father Beir gave his sermons. The baked red dust seemed to find its way in through every crack, and even though the church was cleaned regularly, the desiccated bodies of insects still littered the floor and newly woven webs hung in the corners. Hundreds of tiny newborn spiders were climbing up the walls. They must have been *dreamed* by the *ancestors* a few nights earlier. Instinctively, Margaret knew that she must protect their *dreaming*; that inner consciousness where all that they could be already existed, and which she knew resided in all things. But the waves of the dreaming were ebbing lower in her spirit each day, especially since she had seen Laura baptised and glowing, and Father Beir had told her that she was one of God's children and all God's children could be baptised. This was so even though she had heard Sister Ruth tell the class that God already knew all that they would do in their lives, and they too should try to visualise those things they wanted to achieve, to sleep on it as well as pray, and then one day it would come true. She picked up the spiders on the edge of the broom and made several trips outside to deposit them by an old

118

desert eucalypt. But she didn't hold her face to its trunk, which had survived harsh centuries, and whisper to it to guide them with the abundance of wisdom and magic it had gained in that time, as she would have done some months previously. How was she to hold onto dreams when her parents had not followed her tracks and come for her, so that she was making them less often now? Besides, Mrs McDonald had told her that she was a Southern European, and maybe those people hadn't been her real parents. They hadn't bought her cloth to make new dresses like Mrs McDonald, nor had they given her a room for herself, so maybe they didn't love her like Mrs McDonald.

When she came back inside the church she was racked with self-conscious doubt about what she had done, and wondered if Liz had seen her. She stopped at the piano and rattled the keys, but stopped when Liz *shushed* her. She swept and mopped the rest of the church, and came to a stop in front of the pulpit. The Jesus man was hanging with outstretched arms in front of her, and she curtsied and gave the sign of the cross, the way Laura had on the day of her baptism. Then she went over to the font, but it was empty, so she pretended to wash her face in it, but she didn't glow pure white like Laura.

"Liz, you think Father Beir would baptise me, and then maybe give me Holy Communion?"

Liz stopped her work and stared saucer-eyed at Margaret. "Why do you want to know that?"

Margaret shrugged as if through wet sand, and then rested her chin on the broom handle. "I just thought it might be nice to get baptised. You know how I've been reading my Bible and I like all the stories and things."

Liz sat up, indignant with trained pride, "It takes a lot more than that to get baptised and have communion." Her back settled to a plumb, her face grew taut, and she reminded Margaret of Mrs McDonald. "It takes years of going to church and not just reading your bible, but understanding it, before you can get baptised and communion. Then Sister Ruth will ask you questions about it, and recommend you to Father when she thinks you're good enough."

Sister Ruth had something to do with it. Margaret's body sagged like half-filled sacking. She wanted to be as good as all them other kids. If Father Beir didn't baptise her soon she was going to do something one day to make sure he would. She finished the last of the

119

mopping and put the broom, mop and bucket back into the cupboard. When she came back Liz was packing her books away.

"Liz, you been baptised or had communion?"

"Hmm hmm," Liz said, without looking up.

"What's it feel like?"

Liz stopped packing and with pensive strokes combed her memory. "All right, I suppose." Then she remembered. "Mum bought me a beautiful white dress. She normally makes them, but that was special."

"Did you fly like Laura?"

"Fly? How do you mean."

"When Laura got baptised she was floating and flying above everybody."

"Don't be silly, people can't fly."

Margaret went to retort, yes they can, when she remembered that not everybody could see that well, and she hadn't really met any white folks who gave her the impression that they could. But if Laura could fly then maybe she could see everything, or at least more than most, especially from up that high. Then again, if she couldn't, maybe she could help her to see, and then Laura would help her to get baptised and have communion. She went to stand in front of the cross on the pulpit and pressed her body like bandages against the prostrate Jesus, sealing his wounds.

"Margaret, you can't do that." Liz said, alarm ringing in her tone.

"Why not?"

"Well—it's not right. And besides, he doesn't have anything on."

"He does too, otherwise I'd be able to see his man thing." Margaret pointed to his loin cloth. "I've seen them before, you know."

Liz slammed her eyes shut and crossed herself four times in quick succession, "Holy Mother Mary, forgive us for we have sinned. Holy Father, forgive us for we have sinned."

"Was Jesus a black?" Margaret asked, out of nowhere.

"No," Father Beir replied as he entered the church, causing Margaret to release her embrace and jump back from the cross.

"I told her it wasn't right, Father, I did tell her. You won't tell mother, will you?" Liz pleaded.

"There's no need to do that. I sometimes kiss him as well." Father Beir held up his redeemer's cross dangling from his neck and touched it to his lips. "But I'm interested in why Margaret wanted to know if Jesus was a black."

Margaret stared in her ignorant embarrassment at Father Beir's boots, which jutted out from the hem of his robe. "I—I thought maybe it was only blacks who deserved to die on the cross."

"No one deserves to die on the cross, Margaret. But he did it for all of us, to atone for all our sins. As for his colour, I can't be sure, but I think he would have been of a Mediterranean hue. Much like the Nicolaideses or Federico and his family."

"Is that white?"

"I suppose it is. But all God's colours are equally important."

Margaret clenched her fist in victory. She knew it, she had caught Father Beir in a lie, or at the very least he wasn't as clever as everyone thought. How could anyone believe that all God's colours were the same? Matron Blythe had made it known that if she married a half-caste or quadroon then her children would stand a better chance. But what if she married a white? She almost looked like one of the Mediterraneans herself, so her children could be higher up, and they would get to sit at the front of class in school, be asked questions when they raised their hands, and be given homework which was marked. They would even be able to try on dresses when they went into Langley to buy them, and sit where they wanted in the picture theatre when they went to see one of the Hollywood films, although she couldn't understand why Mrs McDonald had been upset when they had gone and the usher had pointed at her and said she would have to sit at the front. She wasn't able to sit at the front in school and felt quite special being the only one sitting in the front row of the picture theatre, even though it made her eyes hurt. But then maybe she wouldn't want to get married at all. She didn't know whether she liked boys that much yet anyway, although Federico was all right because he said thank you when she helped him with his homework, even though he only did so when the other children couldn't see. And she was beginning to like Joshua—which she liked calling him better than Nannup—and she would like him more if he allowed her to come dancing and singing with him in the forest at night.

\*\*\*

121

When they came out of the church into the blazing heat, they saw Laura on her way home from the general store, and she crossed their path. She smiled a greeting at Liz. "Hello, Liz."

"Good day, Laura," Liz and then Margaret said. Laura made as if to stop, but Liz kept on going and so she did too. Margaret stopped.

"What's wrong?" Liz asked, still moving to get home into the shade.

"I've forgotten something in the church. I'll catch you up." Margaret ran back towards the church, but she didn't go in. Instead, she walked around to the back and watched from there until Liz was out of sight. Then she ran across the field to follow Laura from a distance where she couldn't be seen.

She tracked Laura all the way back to her homestead, and stood in one of their orchards, close to the house, watching Laura and her mother cooking together. They were talking and laughing with familiar ease, and sometimes her mother brushed her hair or touched her cheek, and this made Margaret's body tingle with the bald memory of recognition. It reminded her of the times she went to gather food with her mother and other kinswomen. The female elders always dreamed the best places to forage the nights before, and as they gathered berries, dug for tubers or fished for water lilies, they played, laughed, told old stories, danced, sang, gorged themselves and slept a little before starting again. Then when they returned to camp they would share their harvest amongst the rest of the clan and sing and dance like wallabies again, and the memory made her weak for lack of their vibrations. Those food gathering trips had always been more exciting than when they had to queue at the manager's office on the settlements and wait to be handed their rations of flour, sugar and tea. But those times were beyond her grasp, so she pushed them away like an unfinished meal.

She contemplated with swelled yearning how she could dream into being a plan to bring her and Laura into a friendship. She hadn't dreamed anything into existence for some time now, partly because at one time she had thought the matrons at Radley could read her dreams. Then when she had realised that they didn't see dreams, or not in the way she did anyway—as a desire which was sculpted in the mind before it could become a concrete act—they put the fear of God and the Devil into her, so that she wondered if her dreams were the Devil's instructions. And she certainly hadn't been able to sing

122

any of them to death when they had done her something so wrong as to force her retribution. So maybe the spirits that protected them were armed with more defences. But the dream that she would have now would be one to strike up a friendship, and she was sure that God wasn't going to be concerned with a dream like that.

Margaret curled like a well-fed cat under an apple tree, and her body jerked in stirring bursts and spasms as the dream took shape. The dreaming was always vivid to her, each instruction very clear, and she walked through it like a rehearsal for some part she would have to play, noting each scene, each line of dialogue, and every action, so that when it occurred, she would know that it had happened before.

She was woken by the ear-piercing blast of a shotgun and shouting coming from the homestead. "What are you doing on our land?"

Margaret rubbed her sleep-fed eyes and stood up to see Laura's mother standing in front of her homestead with a shotgun pointed towards the sky and belligerence in her stance. She raised the gun to her broad shoulder and fired off another shot. It jerked her Nordic frame back three feet and she had to brush her golden hair out of her face, "Get off our land, you bloody thief."

"I wasn't stealing, miss." Margaret walked towards her. "I was just—" The gun was lowered and buckshot screamed over her head and brought down branches, apples, and leaves. She turned and ran through the orchard, leaping the wire fence like a fleeing dingo, and not stopping until she was on McDonald land.

By the time Margaret walked down the path towards the McDonald homestead, the orange sun was falling out of the sky. Anne stood in front of the house with her hands on her hips and a razor sharp scowl across her face. "Where have you been?"

"I went back to the church because I forgot to do something. Then I decided to pray for a little while." She knew how Anne wanted her to like religion.

Anne clipped her around the back of the head. "That still doesn't explain why you're only getting home now."

"I tried to take a shorter way because it was getting dark. I got lost." Anne clipped her again and she stumbled up the steps.

"Do you think I was born yesterday? There is work to be done around the house. You have ironing, your room hasn't been swept, and your supper's cold." She gave her one last clip for good measure. "Don't let it happen again."

"No, Hmm," Margaret said, and she smiled with inward satisfaction at having gotten off so lightly.

*\*\**

After Mr McDonald had carried out his nightly ritual of disappearing into the woods, Margaret stuffed her pillow under her blanket and put a several-months-old letter from Anne's friend in the pocket of her frock. Then she clambered out of her window and hurried off into the woods, towards Nannup's ritual place. When she arrived she gave him a start, and he kicked more dirt over the ground where he had just buried something. "What you doing?" she asked. He brushed past her without a word and started to collect firewood. "I know the best wood for burning fires, and I can light them too." Nannup continued to ignore her, but she trailed him like a boisterous pup. "Sometimes we used to make a fire that was so big it burnt everything. Then when it rains the plants grow back better that way, my mother said. You know—"

Nannup turned and threw up a hand to stop her. She saw that he had gathered white ochre on a saucer-sized piece of bark. He spat into it and mixed the paste to a workable consistency with a twig. Then he painted a shilling-sized dot in the centre of her forehead. "This is to open your mind to take in the teaching," he said, "and it is also your third eye."

"What does it do?" Margaret asked. She didn't recognise the initiation from any that her mob had held.

Nannup ignored her and painted a stroke above her left eyebrow. "This will help you to look and see so that you don't get lost. You can pick out landmarks when you use your third eye for survival."

"I have very good eyes, and I'm always finding things."

Nannup pursed his lips in soaring frustration with her, as if the object of his teaching was misplaced. Then he painted a stroke behind her right ear. "This is to help you listen, so that you can hear the birds, the wind and the rain."

"I have good ears, too; I can hear when Mr and Mrs McDonald are talking through the walls, although he doesn't say much."

Nannup then painted a dot below her lips. "And this is to seal your lips—"

"I can talk real good—"

"So that you can *shut up!*" Nannup flung a hand an inch from her face. "Then you can listen and learn."

Margaret swallowed her words like whole onions then went to say something, but Nannup raised a stern finger and she nodded as if hypnotised instead. She now knew that this was one of the times when he was dreaming up an adventure, and she followed at his shoulder in muted anticipation.

Each time that Nannup came across a tall tree, he stopped and looked high into its branches before striding off again. This went on for several trees until he came to one that seemed to be humming his name, and he put his ear to the trunk as if to listen to its heartbeat. Margaret stared up into the tree, but she could see nothing through the black canopy that enveloped it. As her blurry eyes travelled back down, she saw Nannup hugging the wide girth of the trunk with his arms and pushing himself up with his bare feet. He pulled himself tall with his arms and pushed with his feet, pulled and pushed like a giant koala seeking refuge until he had disappeared into the canopy.

\*\*\*

When he reached halfway into the canopy Nannup stopped and stared out to the end of a narrow branch, where a possum had not yet woken to start its nocturnal feed. He waited for its twitching, which told him it was still dreaming, to stop—because no creature was to be killed whilst it was still in conversation with the ancestors—then he wrapped his body around the branch and slid snake-like along it towards the sleeping rodent. When he was within striking distance he drew a short boomerang from the waist of his pants and held it tight. In a flurry of inaudible chanting he asked the spirit of the furry rodent not to escape into nothingness, but to join with his, so that together they could be more in touch with the creators, and for that he would give its body a swift death. And as he visited that thought, he grabbed hold of its long, fatty tail and brought the boomerang crashing down onto its skull while it slept, in the certainty that it knew nothing of its death, only that suddenly it had a larger knowledge of itself and all things.

\*\*\*

125

Margaret heard a crack and almost immediately a body came tumbling out of the tree into the night's shadows. "Joshua?" she screamed and ran over to where the body had fallen with a loud thud.

"Ka, ka, ka, ka, ka."

She heard the broken laughter sliding down the tree before she reached the body of the possum, and she marched over to Nannup as he jumped the last few feet to the ground. Her eyes were like raging seas and her fists rock hard. "I thought that was you, Joshua. That's not funny."

"My name is Nannup," he said with a broad grin, and he grabbed the possum by its tail, slung it over his shoulder and headed towards camp.

Nannup started a raging fire within minutes and threw the possum onto it to burn off its fur. When this was done, he took the swelling animal off the fire, pulled a glinting knife from his waistband, and scraped the burnt fur from the skin.

"I've got one of them letters from Mrs McDonald's friend in England," Margaret said, hoping to capture his attention. Nannup continued to prepare the tucker by slitting the animal's belly from its tail to neck and scraping two handfuls of bloody intestines out of the cavity. He took the entrails and placed them on known animal tracks where they would be eaten, and in that way continue the cycle.

When he came back Margaret took out the crumpled letter and started to finger it to distraction. He buried the carcass of the possum in smouldering coals and sat on his haunches like a wise old man. "What's Mrs McDonald's friend like?" he asked.

Margaret sprung to life again, and she sat up and unfolded the letter. "Well, she's the same age as Mrs McDonald, because they went to school together, but she doesn't have a husband or any children."

"Why not?"

Margaret shrugged her shoulders. She remembered she wasn't supposed to, but knew Nannup wouldn't mind. It was one of the reasons she liked being with him. "I think she has her own shop, selling nice frocks that Mrs McDonald calls 'couture' and other things, so she doesn't have the time."

Nannup laid back and gazed at the silvery stars that littered the sky like confetti. "You notice how they don't have much time to do things they like?"

"But that's because there's so much work to do."

"I just got our tucker, and now we can talk, laugh, dance and watch the stars."

"Yes, but they have to get more things." Margaret picked at the hem of her frock and slipped into her uncomfortable self, because she knew that she wanted some of those things.

"But when they have to do so much work, they don't have no time to enjoy those things. Or sometimes after they seen them and touched them a few times, they don't like them no more." Nannup rolled over onto his belly to look at her. "It's like Mrs Cartwright keeps buying me lots of shirts and pants, and she even wants to buy me a bicycle, but I get more fun out of hunting, watching the stars at night and listening to the trees and things."

Nannup regarded Margaret as if he were weighing up their friendship. "You want to know what I buried in that there hole, don't you?" She bit her lip and shook her head as if it had come unhinged. "I buried a blanket and some food."

"What for?"

"'Cause I'm going to run away."

"What you going to do that for?"

"'Cause I want to live our way."

Margaret stirred the dust with her finger, as if considering the sweetness of tea. "Mrs McDonald has some tins of Spam. She won't miss that if I bring one. He smiled a cautious satisfaction and dug the meat from the ashes, placed it on a bed of leaves, and divided it into portions. He offered Margaret the best portion, and they ate the succulent meat until they were full. Nannup laid back and held his bloated stomach. "What's Mrs McDonald's friend say in the letter?"

Margaret drew close to the glowing embers and rested on her elbows.

*Dear Anne*

*I was so happy to hear from you. I see that the mini has reached Oz. It's all the rage here now, and I've simply sold stacks full. It's pretty cool still getting wolf whistles as I walk down Kings Road. That's how I met Freddie. He's a guitarist in a band, and only 25 with a hard bod. Yes I know what you're thinking, it won't last, but what does today love, apart from your marriage to that Sean of yours, who I am dying to meet one day. I've sent you the last three months of 'Marie Claire', and if you let me know your size, I'll send you one of those minis. Only joking. I know that as the lady of a large homestead it wouldn't be proper, but your Sean would love it. But joking apart, how about Liz, and the girl you've taken in, Margaret, I'm sure they will like them.*

*I saw one of those new Rover Coupes that your Sean bought you. They are beautiful, or real cool, as most of my friends in London would say now. If you let me know where that jerk from Brisbane who redecorated Billabong Lodge and left it a mess lives, I'll come over and sort him out. Thankfully, with the success of your farm you can afford to have it put right.*

Nannup sat up and stared at Margaret like a madman before she had finished. "That's not about Mrs McDonald, she's talking about Mrs Cartwright."

"I know," Margaret said. "Mrs McDonald pretends she lives in your homestead and has the things that Mrs Cartwright has."

"Why's that?"

"I don't know," Margaret said. "In one of the letters from a long time back, Carol says Mrs McDonald's mother, Betty, is dead."

Nannup *shushed* her, and his finger rushed to cover his lips. "You shouldn't speak a dead spirit's name, Margaret."

Margaret's hand shot to her mouth as if to reclaim the spoken words. "Sorry, I forgot." They both looked around them with soaring fright for any signs that Margaret's name calling had summoned the dead woman's *ego spirit*—that part of the spirit that was jealous of the living and would, if it could, refuse to depart. The air was standing still, and there was only the calling of cicadas and the occasional rustle from a nocturnal rodent. When Nannup felt it was safe to continue, he said, "That's why I don't speak or hear when I'm with them, Margaret, because I will forget our ways."

Margaret's gaze scurried to the smouldering embers, to seek refuge from Nannup's scolding glare. Yes, she wanted to do good at school and liked some of the other things, and maybe she had forgotten some of the ways, but she wasn't even sure it was her way now, after what Mrs McDonald had told her about being a Southern European and all. She didn't mind if she could be like Nannup when she was with him, and more like Mrs McDonald when she was with her. But that was kind of confusing, because you could just jump into one way whilst forgetting who you were with. "I'll try to remember from now on," Margaret said, "especially if you let me come with you when you run away." Nannup didn't answer. He was in one of his dreamings again, and Margaret watched him in anticipation and wondered what it would tell him to do now.

# Chapter 10

Margaret wandered off the path into the woods on her way to school and headed for a tree where she had seen some. First she stopped by a eucalypt and picked two bunches of its leaves. Farther into the woods she climbed a tree and used a stick to scoop the black tar out of an open knot. She wrapped the tar in a bunch of the eucalypts and continued to school. She didn't need to meet Federico that morning, as she had scrawled out the answers to their homework the previous afternoon in the dusty yard at the front of school. Margaret waited until lunchtime as the dream had instructed her, and after the children had finished eating and left their satchels on the veranda to play hide and seek, she slinked up onto the veranda. She saw Laura's red satchel in amongst the others, and stepped over them with furtive strides to smear a thin coat of the tar on its underside. Then she slipped unnoticed back into the yard.

When school ended Margaret hid against the side of the building so that Liz wouldn't see her. Liz waited several minutes in the bitter sun, and then she sighed as if releasing her burden and started home. Margaret knew she had to hurry, and she ran like a cyclone in the direction of Laura's home. A light breeze stole her hat several times, and eventually she held it in her hand. By the time she saw Laura, she was already flailing her arms like a windmill at bees. Her swipes grew wings of desperation, and she squealed in lightning bursts and took flight, still flapping her arms. She turned to swipe a bee that had rested on her birthmarked cheek, and tripped and fell. The bees swarmed into a dark cloud, and as Laura covered her face, Margaret reached her. She ripped the satchel from Laura's shoulder and threw it to the side. The bees followed the bait. Margaret crushed the remaining bunch of eucalyptus leaves between her hands and rubbed its oily ointment onto Laura and herself. Laura made her do it, still cowering behind her hands. "I was in the woods and heard you screaming, Laura, so I came," Margaret said.

"I don't—I don't know where they came from," Laura said. Margaret offered her a hand and she took it with grateful relief. Margaret felt the smoothness of her skin and admired its peach-white tone before she pulled Laura up. "My satchel, they are all over it," Laura said, as she wiped away a tearstain from her cheek. "It has my homework and everything in it."

"I can get it for you if you like," Margaret offered. Laura squinted at her through bloodshot eyes, fear rising from her scent like smoke from fire.

Margaret crushed the leaves between her hands again and went over to the satchel. She stretched her eucalyptus-scented hand towards the bag, and a few inquisitive bees sat on it to investigate. Then they flew away, closely followed by the rest of the swarm. She wiped the remnants of the tar stain from the underside of the bag with the leaves and held it out to Laura. Laura withdrew her hand as if from an open fire.

"I think you must have spilled some lunch on it, Laura. You should be okay now; I wiped it off for you."

"Can you carry it a little way for me, Margaret? My arm is hurting."

"Okay, Laura." Margaret glowed like moonlight on the inside, and she silently thanked the spirits. As she had dreamed it in the Wilson orchard, so it had occurred.

They walked for a way without exchanging words. Margaret searched through her catalogue of memories for what she thought it appropriate to say, and she sensed Laura was doing the same. She didn't want to say anything that would spoil the friendship before it had ripened. They stopped at the entrance to the Wilson homestead, and Margaret handed Laura the satchel. "Thanks," Laura said as she swung around and hurried through the gates, as if hoping that had said it all.

Margaret continued along the path with a tugging at her back, as if something had been left unsaid. "Margaret," Laura called out, "what way are you going to school tomorrow?"

Margaret ran back to the Wilson fence and jumped onto the lowest rung. "I'm going through the woods tomorrow," she said, with an expectant glaze coating her face.

"Me too," Laura said, and she waited, as if to draw more flavour from a brewing teapot.

"I'll walk with you to the edge of the woods, just before we see the school, then you can go first and I will come after."

"Okay," Laura agreed, and she turned and walked away again. Margaret waved after her until she was out of sight, then she bunny-hopped the rest of the way home.

***

After the incident at Radley Domestic Training Home, Toby and Daisy Winmati's youngest son, Joe, was arrested for assaulting Matron Blythe. He spent thirty-six months in a state prison—most of it added time for bad behaviour—and Toby took on stockman's work close by so that the kinfolk could go to see him. In the meantime, Daisy wrote letters. She wrote to the Aboriginal Protection Board asking for her child, sent letters to Radley asking for her whereabouts, and penned even more letters to churches and charities up and down the state asking if they had seen her. Most never replied, and those that did knew nothing. Some even said it was for the best. When Joe was released, Toby bought an old ute with savings and borrowed money, and he, his wife, Joe, two married sons, their wives and five children all went looking for their daughter, sister and auntie.

At first, they didn't know where to start, as the years waiting for Joe's release and saving for the ute had made the trail grow faint, and everyone turned their query on Daisy. She was the one to whom the ancestors spoke most clearly. She told them that she must dream it, so they remained in the same place for several nights and watched as she twitched, sighed and blabbered with spirits in her sleep. Then one morning, before the sun had sailed over the horizon, she woke before the rest, rolled up her *swag* blanket, and sat in the cab of the ute waiting as if possessed. She told Toby that they would have to follow the girl's dreaming trail and ask at each place, and they had lost track of how long they had been doing that now, between stops for Toby and his sons to take on several months' work at a time so that they could replenish their supplies.

"We will have to stop for work again tomorrow, wife," Toby said as he steered the ute over a dry gravel road.

Daisy fanned the dust out of her face. "We're getting too close to stop; I can feel it." But she had felt close several times before, and they had seen or heard not a trace of the girl. Still, no one was

131

prepared to tell her that maybe her powers were waning, or the bitter cloud of grief had obscured her visions.

"We're running out of food, wife. The children must eat." He turned as if to garner support from their kinsfolk riding in the bed of the ute in weary silence. None had complained any of the way, and they avoided his mutinous glare.

"We can hunt, gather and eat bush tucker, husband. We mustn't lose time."

Toby stared at her, his annoyance drowned by rivers of empathy. Her hand was resting over her womb from where the child had come. It was as if her spirit had travelled more distance than the ute, trying to search the places that the girl might be before they arrived. "It's been dry here for some time. We may not find water, and there'll be little bush tucker. I've only seen one wallaby since yesterday."

"I'm not hungry, husband," Daisy said, as though her spirit was still miles ahead.

Toby glanced into the bed of the ute again, as if hoping Daisy would understand that they still had children back there and they had to survive too. "We're not on our land, wife. We'll have to ask the local mobs if we can hunt and gather on their land."

"They will not refuse us, husband. A *Koori* will never refuse another a feed, even if they are enemies." She thought of the amount of times the settlement managers had refused to give her rations if she broke the rules. Like the times she went fishing when they said it wasn't allowed, or if she spoke in her lingo instead of theirs, or if she was caught in a town after sundown, the blacks' curfew. "We've passed many white farms, husband. We can kill a sheep or cow at night."

Toby's eyes screamed his alarm. "Thou shall not steal, my wife."

Daisy cackled as if she was choking. It was so loud that the children in the back heard her above the groan of the engine and peered into the cab to see what had moved her spirit, because nothing had in the longest while. "Thou shall not steal," she repeated. "They stole our land, our culture and our children, husband. They don't believe their own words, so why should we?" She clapped her hands like tambourines and accompanied them with laughter again, clucking her tongue. "Have you forgotten what happened when you fought in their war against the Japanese, my husband?"

"It was our war too," Toby protested.

"Well, have it as you want, but when you came back they wouldn't even allow you into their precious RSL club to have a drink. You had to stand outside while they passed it to you through a window, remember?" Toby's eyes clouded over like a cataract had grown there. "You even saved some of those men's lives."

"They're just sick, my wife, and if we hold onto what we know to be true, maybe one day we can help them to get better."

"You better mind their sickness isn't catching, my husband; then we will all have it before we can help them."

The wind caused the dust to swirl into a migrating red forest, scorching all in its path and bringing on an artificial night. The ones in the back pulled a dust sheet over them to keep the grit out of their stone dry eyes, hair and mouths. They passed miles of fields where the grass was bare from drought and overgrazing. Earlier in the day they had seen stockmen driving a herd towards hills where they might find good grazing. One of the dust clouds opened like a stained window, and Toby saw two scrawny cows, stragglers, idling on the track. He swerved to miss them, but it was too late. He hit one a glancing blow on its hindquarters. The ute span one-eighty, and the occupants in the bed held tight to avoid being thrown out. The animal screamed in agony, but stayed upright. Toby jumped from the cab and inspected the front of the vehicle. The cattle bar was smeared with torn skin and blood, but the vehicle was undamaged. The two reddish brown santa gertrudis loitered on the track, gazing in forlorn misery at him. He went back to the cab and pulled his rifle from behind the seat.

# Chapter 11

Sean pulled up one of the drying heads of pineapples and handed it to Costos. "This is the second planting I've lost in this bloody field."

"I plant no more until we get rain, Sean. I lose money, sleep, everything."

They stared in wistful silence down the dying rows of pineapples. It had not rained anywhere near Malee for almost three seasons, and for sixteen months before that the rains had been dismal. The water table had dropped below a quarter, reducing pressure at the well heads, and the farmers were having to use increasing amounts of expensive fuel to pump water from deeper in the artesian bores, but it still wasn't enough to save their crops. The ground was like forged steel; it had broken several of Sean's ploughs, and he had borrowed money from Costos to replace them.

"We've got enough water in the tank and in the bore to keep the house and vegetable gardens going for maybe another six months," Sean said as he combed his fingers through his hair. Almost half the strands now ran to grey, deep lines gouged either side of his nose, and a gaunt blankness had robbed him of his youthful face. "I suppose we'll just have to wait it out."

"I speak to the Rossis. They thinking to sell," Costos said.

"Nobody around here is going to buy their land knowing the situation with water."

"That's what I tell them, but they say they don't know what else to do."

"Mr McDonald, boss." Nipper had been waiting at the edge of listening distance for some time, his hat in his hand. Sean's other workers were out in the fields pottering around, as there was nothing to do.

Sean sighed with heavy foreboding, "What is it now?" Each day without rain he had become more like a bull in musth.

Nipper bowed to avert Sean's venom, "I was wondering if we would be able to get some pay this week, boss."

"I told you last week, there is no money, Nipper. We haven't sold any bloody crop for months."

"The boys and I were thinking that maybe we shouldn't come in next week then, boss."

"What's this? Blackmail! You all formed a bloody union or something?" Sean's back was steaming, and a wet anger dripped off his face, as if to bleed him of his worries.

"No, boss, but we listening to the land." Nipper turned his hat by the band, as if considering a card player's hand. "We can feel the land, boss, like it's a part of us."

"So what the fuck's it saying, Nipper, hey? It wants to take a bloody vacation?"

"Yeah, boss, that's right about what it's saying."

Sean rolled his eyes in exaggerated frustration. They had practised this dance before. They needed him as much as he needed them. "There's some grog in my Coolgardie for any of you that wants it. When things pick up again you'll get paid. But if you leave you'll lose all that you've worked for." Sean turned back to his conversation with Costos. Nipper stayed glaring at his seeping back until he realised it would do no good, then he trudged out to where his kin were waiting.

"You know what I don't understand, Sean?" Costos said. "How come we are struggling to find water and I never hear one of them Abbos complaining?"

"They can find water anywhere Costos, they know where—" Sean stopped as if felled by an axe. He had never heard them complain about water shortages either. They had a camp maybe five miles outside town, and they never moved it. It had been there ever since he had come to Malee, and he had always heard that they liked to camp close to water and food. He watched Nipper console his kin with animated gestures, and he, one of his sons, and another man wandered off with sagging spirits in the direction of their camp. A fourth man slithered over to the Coolgardie hanging from the tree, took out the bottle of grog, and started to drink as he followed after them.

\*\*\*

From a bench on the veranda, Sean pulled on a cigarette and watched the wide orange gash in the sky recede. No matter how many times he had seen it, the light oozing from the cut always gripped him with its enigmatic awe and then calm. No sooner than that sight had disappeared, he held his smoky breath as a mirage of glinting stars materialised in the desert black sky, as far as the eye could see. Even with the lack of rain, the stunted growth in his fields, and little money in the bank, this filled his tank like fuel, so that he could go on another day. It made him understand why Nipper and his people had refused to leave this place, no matter how harsh.

He was about to throw his butt end onto the ground, but remembered how crispy dry the vegetation was and that Anne didn't like to see litter around the yard. He treaded over to the trash can, turned the lid upside down, and squashed the butt on it. A plume of smoke rose from it like fumes from a pyre, and he watched it with pensive eyes until he was sure it was dead. Fire was the last thing they wanted now. He turned the lid back the right way up and headed towards the water tank. Once he had climbed to the top of the ladder, he leaned his head over the side of the corrugated iron tank. The moonlight reflected off the water, which was well below quarter full. He sighed as if to acknowledge his impotence and came back down.

Ten minutes later Sean was in his ute, driving across the dusty land, on no particular track, towards the blacks' camp. He knew exactly where it was, but had never had any reason to visit the place. He stopped the ute in brush about a mile from the camp—if he drove any closer they would hear him coming—then he walked the rest of the way. He kept close to bushes and trees to mask his approach, and he heard pulsating chants and saw the flicker of flames before he made out the six rickety shacks standing in a clearing. The camp was always occupied, but Nipper had told Sean that sometimes a number of them went for *corroborrees* to other places with their kin. It seemed that their kin had come here now. There must have been more than sixty people—men decorated in animal finery sitting in a line by themselves, wailing women, and screaming children kneeling in five circles on the other side of the ceremonial site, chanting in submerged voices at something which was in-between them. An elaborate feast had been laid out in the middle of the ceremonial site, but no one was partaking of it. Sean leaned against a gum tree and went to light a cigarette, but he looked at the brittle vegetation around him and put it away.

The crying and chanting from the women and children leapt up like a barrier of flames as the men approached the five groups.

136

Several gangling adolescent boys, all in their birthing skins, stood up from between the groups of women and children, and the women held onto them and cried as the men tried to haul them from the women's circle. "All that born from woman is woman until the corrorborree makes them man." The men chanted this several more times in their tongue, still dragging the boys away. Sean stepped from behind the tree to see better, being careful to avoid the crisp vegetation which crunched underfoot. One of the boys was Nipper's son, but another ... It was ... it was Helen Cartwright's Aboriginal, Joshua. What was he doing out there? He certainly wasn't related to these people, at least not in any sense that Sean would have understood. Nipper appeared to be acting for both his son and Joshua. Joshua was now almost as tall as Sean. He had let his hair grow so that you could see the curls in it, and there was three-day-old stubble marking his squared-off chin which refused to grow any more, both of which had made Helen say that she was losing control of the boy. The men prised him free and Sean jerked forward into a stumble when he saw Margaret. She was part of the group of women from whom Joshua had been taken, and her protective arm was outstretched trying to claim him back. He started towards the circle but stopped when he thought of Anne; it would kill her. She was convinced that she had turned Margaret into a lady, and when he had seen the way she had grown, he had silently accepted it too.

Margaret glowed out there, like a dry field that had suddenly felt rain, or a nocturnal animal on the prowl at night, and it didn't escape Sean. Her slender, boyish limbs were gently rounded now, and they called attention to themselves as they jutted out in all directions to hold the initiates back. Sean turned away his guilty stare and with jangling nerves forced an unlit cigarette into his mouth. Then he followed the sound of the chanting back to the men and boys.

The men cut themselves on the wrist and let their blood run over the boys from head to toe, the blood of their second birthing. The boys had all been fasting for several days, because before they could be reborn, they had to be ritually dead to this world and its sensations. They were all drained of the slightest sustenance, but they knew the importance of the ritual and forced steadiness, like steel pins, into their legs. The men coated the boys' bodies in more blood, wallaby fat and red ochre. Then they decorated them with emu feathers. The women and other mourners were wailing with

137

uncontrolled anguish now. No longer would their relationships be bound as mother and son, adult and child. A man was able to swim with the voices of the spirits unaided, so he no longer needed the permission of his parents for anything. The boys were led feigning token resistance into the middle of the ceremonial ground. Finely painted men were dancing and chanting fiercely to ward off any evil spirits that might try to stop the boys from dying and being reborn into the world as men. On a chant which resounded like a bell's final toll, the men ran forward and knelt down next to each other, offering their backs as an altar for the boys to lie on. The fathers jumped up and straddled the chests of their prostrate sons, facing their penises. Joshua was lying next to Nipper's son, and Nipper sat astride both of them. *Nkuppa*, grandfather men, gave the boys boomerangs to clench between their teeth to kill the pain, and then they walked around the boys, like priests waving incense, to reassure them. Nipper pulled his son's foreskin up, twisted it carefully, making sure the head of the penis was out of the way beneath his thumb, and then he cut it with a quartz stone. He did the same for Joshua, who he called Nannup. The boys' eyes were flooded with water from the pain, and their wounds were dripping blood, but they would not cry in their manhood now. They stood up and went to kneel in front of a fire billowing gum leaf smoke, and it engulfed them, in the same way it had immediately after their first birth. Their elder brothers came to them, in Nannup's case his acting brother. "Here, brother," he said, "you have fasted long and you are now hungry; eat a piece of kangaroo meat, but swallow it and do not chew." Nannup opened his mouth and swallowed his own foreskin.

"You have swallowed your own boyhood spirit," Nannup's *Nkuppa* said. "It came before and so is the father of your manhood. It will impregnate you, grow inside you, and make you a strong warrior, a wise leader and a skilful hunter."

The ground then shuddered with the stomping feet of the dancers and singers as if tramped by charging herds. *Bullroarers* being swung overhead woke up the night for miles like millions of chattering insects. Sean watched all of the ceremony from the cover of the tree. Sometimes he imagined that he was one of the boys being dragged from the women to start his life as a man. For him there had been no ceremony, no mournful dancers and singers, no fathers and grandfathers who stood by to make sure he reached the other side.

He had simply walked away, when he was still younger than those being made into men now. If they had wanted it done some other way they would have found him. They had wanted it that way as much as he had, he assured himself. He wondered if his mother would have screamed and cried for him like they did, fought hard to touch the child once more like they did. He tried to remember how she looked, and his thoughts were like pieces of puzzles that he couldn't fit together. He wiped his eyes, which were stinging now, and turned away. He couldn't take anymore. What was it he had come for again? The water. That was it. A man had to do whatever it took to survive. He walked around the outskirts of the camp, taking care not to be seen. They had to source their water from close by. Any supply out there was unlikely to be very large, but it might lead to a bigger source. He couldn't sit back and watch his land turn to dust.

Sean spent several hours peering into bushes, investigating rock formations, following animal tracks by starlight, but the land out there was drier than his. He gave up before sunrise, and then stopped off at the place of his nocturnal excursions before going home.

***

Anne hurried down the stairs, still patting her hair into place, as she didn't want to be late. She went into the kitchen to fetch the cake that she had made for the occasion and put her nose to it. The fruity scent made her hunger bite, and she put the lid back on the box and went out the front, where Sean was waiting for her in the ute. He had promised to come in from the field early to take her, but she had considered walking, knowing that he wouldn't change out of his work clothes. As long as he let her out and drove straight back, she hoped no one would see him like that. She didn't know what he was doing out there anyway. Nothing would grow in the fields without water. She had cut back her baths to once a week early in the crisis, and now she had started to wash with half a basin of water like the girls. They were also wearing the same unwashed dresses to school for a week at a time. It wasn't proper for young ladies to have to do that. Even her vegetable garden had to be reduced to a quarter of its normal size to conserve water, and she doused each plant from a watering can now, as the hose was too wasteful. Why couldn't they live in cities like normal people?

"Is Andrew with you, Sean?" She peered past him into the cab to see if she could find the lively boy.

"Nope," Sean said, still chewing on a twig. Anne handed him the cake and went round the back.

"Andrew? Andrew? Where are you?" She heard a snigger suppressed by tightly sealed lips and turned to see the boy climbing up the bougainvillea on the side of the barn. He had a smile that softened her like churned butter, and deep groves tunnelled into his cheeks when he finally exploded with a laugh. The days she spent with him went far too quickly. Andrew had an on-tap energy that made her want to dance again, as she had done in London all those years ago.

"Get down from there."

"No."

"I said get down this minute."

"I'm a cat," Andrew said, and he continued to scramble with abandon up the shrubs. Anne grabbed him by the ankle and pulled him down. She caught him as he fell rolling and giggling with playful intent, but he was too heavy and she was too late, so she put him down.

"You'll get hurt if you keep climbing like that," Anne warned him as she hurried him into the ute.

"Where we going?" Andrew asked.

"We're going to Helen's house. Mrs Cartwright to you. She has invited all the ladies to have tea, and a discussion that she hasn't told anyone about."

"A secret?"

"Yes. And your mummy is going to be there."

"Yeah!"

When they arrived at Helen Cartwright's homestead, Aithra and Costos were waiting by their ute. Andrew scrambled to jump out of the cab and run to meet them, but Anne held onto him, licked her finger, and pushed his hair back into place first.

"G'day, Anne. He been good?" Aithra asked as she stroked Andrew's head. The gift God had sent to make up for all the others. He had his hand wrapped around her waist and his head pressed into her belly.

"Good day Aithra, Costos. Of course he has been good." Andrew shared her conspirator's smile.

Costos said g'day to Anne and went to speak to Sean.

"You give Mrs Cartwright this for me please, Anne." she handed her a spinach flan.

"Oh, Aithra, you are coming, aren't you?"

"We have much work to do, Anne. I can't leave Costos and the girl alone to do it." She avoided Anne's pleading eyes and threw a forlorn gaze towards her husband.

"It's just one afternoon, Aithra."

"I don't know what to say in front of those women, Anne. I'm simple country girl and I don't have education."

"They would love your company. You could tell them about where you came from and how you made this lovely pie." Anne smelt the pie as if she were drawing in the fresh scent of posies.

"No, no, Anne. You go. Thank you." Aithra hurried as if pursued into the ute with Andrew.

"Okay. Thank you for the pie, Aithra." She opened a palm, bearing acknowledgement to Anne, and then averted her gaze again.

Anne walked up the gravel path, which was lined with pink roses still in bloom despite the drought. Rumour had it that Helen Cartwright had trucked in several tankers to replenish her supplies. The O'Hares were probably the only other family in Malee who could afford to do that. The people of Malee were mainly poor subsistence farmers, although many would have argued with that description. She stopped outside to take a good look at the two-storey red brick house which was Billabong Lodge. Helen had described it to her and she had walked by on a few occasions so that she could describe it more accurately in her letters to Carol, but she had never been inside. It was three or four times the size of her homestead, and a wide polished mahogany porch ran around the entire property on both floors, encircled by intricate ironwork railings. The outhouses included a milking shed, and a beautiful sloping garden trimmed with massive rhododendrons, and gargantuan pines provided a natural border.

Maggie, one of Helen Cartwright's young Aboriginal servants, opened the door and Anne stepped in. She stopped inside the reception hall and sucked in a sweet breath. It was more than Helen had described to her. Chandeliers dripped from the ceilings, a curved stairway ran from two walls and met at the top, and oils of horses and riders littered the flock wallpaper.

"Can I take those from you, Madam?"

Anne looked twice, as she was not used to being addressed in such formal terms. "Yes, thank you," she said, and handed the servant the cake and flan. The luxuriant reception hall hypnotised her, and she loitered as if searching for light.

"Anne, don't stand out there, do come in," Helen called, having caught sight of her through the open drawing room doors. She stood up from the sofa where she had been sitting with Father Beir and beckoned Anne in with a wave of a feathery hand. She met her in the middle of the room with one of her toothy smiles and kissed her on both cheeks, as if they were best friends. Anne's face flushed the hot chilli shade of the wallpaper, but this was tempered by her pleasure at Helen's acknowledgement of her, especially because in addition to Father Beir, some of the women from church were there, and she was sure that Helen had not greeted them the same way.

"Would you like some tea, Anne?" Helen took hold of a cup.

Anne took a hanky from her bag and dabbed at her smouldering cheeks. "Yes, thank you. But could I use the bathroom first?"

"Sara— Sara," Helen called.

Another of the servants, a sprightly, more delicate girl, hurried into the room. "Yes, Mrs Cartwright?"

"Can you show Mrs McDonald to the main bathroom? And tell Maggie to bring some more tea, please."

"Yes, Mrs Cartwright." Sara curtsied then nodded at Anne, who followed her up the stairs. Anne crept up behind the girl as if she was afraid that her emotions might escape her and fly free, to nestle on each of the paintings and drink in their nectar, and this would somehow show that she was not worthy of these things. Sara opened the bathroom door for her, and she went in.

"Thank you." Anne closed the door and turned full circle twice, three times, taking it all in. Then she ran to the lavatory, lifted the teak seat, flushed, and watched as the water gushed away. She had held herself so that the first thing she would do when she came was to use the inside lavatory, but she forgot that and went to the bath standing on lions' paws in the middle of the room. She ran her hand over the cold, smooth enamel, and then she turned on the tap marked hot and held her hand under it until it scalded her pink. She picked up the bar of soap and drew in its perfume like soft drugs, and then she collapsed into a heap on the lavatory seat and started to cry. How had she ended up in a place like Malee, and if it had to be, then why not in a homestead like Helen Cartwright's? What had she done to deserve less?

Along with the other children of London, she had been evacuated to the countryside to avoid the German bombing during the war. Mrs Norma Sommers, a well-proportioned woman in a gabardine suit, had chosen her from a Somerset church hall full of anxious, homesick children, and she spent the rest of the war living on a thirty-acre farm with Mrs Sommers and her husband, Bernard.

The couple were childless, and they doted on Anne as if she were their own. The first thing Mrs Sommers did was to make new dresses for Anne, and she was enrolled into the local school. Whilst other children from the nearby village walked the mile or so to school, Norma Sommers drove Anne to school in her new Ford, and collected her at lunchtime and in the evenings. It was the first time that Anne had been driven in a car, as her parents had not been able to afford one.

Sometimes, for lunch, Mrs Sommers prepared a lavish hamper, and she drove to a nearby field where they partook of it. They talked about school, the farm, and the way a young lady ought to behave, whilst Mrs Sommers redid Anne's hair needlessly, in the hope that she could preserve the memories like her pickles in the pantry when the child returned to her parents in London. Anne did not have to do hard work on the farm, as she heard so many of the other evacuee children complain about, but the ruddy and cheerful Bernard Sommers, who had a wisp of his remaining hair combed over his bald patch, did show her how to milk the Aberdeen Anguses and feed the chickens, which supplemented his main business of growing root vegetables. Anne did this when she wasn't playing by the pond, sewing, cooking, reading with Mrs Sommers, or walking the collie, Goldie, through nearby woods.

Unlike other children who complained of being mistreated, overworked, underfed and unloved, Anne was sorry to see the war end, because she had to return to a life reconstructed out of rationed poverty—especially given that her father had died in the evacuation of the French beaches early in the war, information which her mother withheld from her until the war's end. But by then she was almost ready to go out to work, and she did this for several years in a department store in London, where she worked and went dancing with Carol, her lifetime friend, until she learned that there were farmers in Australia who were unable to find wives because the women were unaccustomed to farming life. So she determined to leave for Australia, and after only a few months of working to save enough money, that is precisely what she did, not telling her mother until the week of her departure. At that time it was easy to emigrate to Australia if you were British, the *ten pound poms* they were called because of the cheapness of their assisted passages. They could *assimilate and become good Australians* better than other races, or so the argument went, until it was realised that there were not enough British to fill the places for work, and so Germans, Dutch, Scandinavians and other Northern Europeans were invited, and when even these proved to be insufficient, they dug deeper into the barrel and invited those that some unkind people referred to as *dagos, ites, reffos* and the other darker tribes of Southern Europe, who, because they were less desirable, were first bussed to holding hostels to be registered as labourers or domestics—even if they were doctors, lawyers or teachers—and had to work in essential manual jobs for two years to pay for their assisted passage. But she had been amongst the first. The wanted.

It was shortly after she arrived in Sydney that Anne saw an advert for a wife by a farmer with three hundred acres in a place called Malee. She calculated that as it was ten times the size of Mr and Mrs Sommers's farm, the owner, Sean McDonald, must have been ten times as wealthy as the Sommerses. But she had never seen the outback, and it wouldn't take her long to realise that for one man to eke out a living in that sparse and barren land, it could take a hundred or even more times the land that was necessary in Somerset. But by the time she realised that, she was married to Sean McDonald, and it was uncommon for a woman to admit such a mistake at that time, and even less so for her to sever her nuptial commitments.

***

"Anne, where have you been?" Helen asked when she finally returned to the drawing room. "Aren't you well?"

Anne stopped dabbing at her eyes with the handkerchief. "I'm fine now, Helen. Thank you."

"You can sit next to me and Father Beir." Helen patted the seat next to them. "He has been telling us about his training in Italy and about Switzerland where he was born."

144

"Good day Father, good day ladies. Please excuse my manners," Anne said. A discordant chorus of cheerful g'days was returned. Then Helen poured Anne a cup of tea and put various slices of cakes and sandwiches onto a plate for her.

"Please continue, Father," Helen said.

He waltzed his way around the issue of where he was from as usual, not telling them that he had only spent a little time in Switzerland as a child, and that his father had tried to get them across the border before the war's end, so that they could not be blamed for what had taken place in their true homeland, because it was a part of himself he found too difficult to share. The ladies all listened with polite reserve. Being inside Billabong Lodge made them act more refined, as if they had shaken off the outback dust and their hardships for at least a few hours. Father Beir looked at his watch, as if anxious to change the subject and move on. "It is getting late, Mrs Cartwright. Do you think we should be starting?"

Helen called Maggie to pour some more tea, and when she was sure everyone was suitably settled, she tapped her spoon against the side of her cup, and all eyes nestled on her like a brood waiting to be fed. She had made the engagement a month before, saying she had something important for the community to discuss, but she hadn't made any mention of what that was. "Ladies and Gentleman, or shall it be Father Beir?" She looked to the priest.

"Oh—" He put his teacup back into the saucer. "Father will be fine, Mrs Cartwright."

She smiled encouragement at him and continued. "The reason I have asked you all here today, ladies and Father, is because as I am sure you will all already know, the Government has proposed a referendum for next year, to give Aboriginals equal rights." Mrs Wilson fidgeted in her chair then sat up as straight as the golden hair flowing across her wide shoulders. She took a calming sip from her cup. "The exact nature of the referendum is—" Helen picked up a document from the coffee table and opened it. "Yes, there will be two questions in the referendum. One is for the Commonwealth to make laws for Aborigines and have joint responsibility for them with the states. The second is for Aborigines to be included in the census. A yes vote to both these questions will mean that they have equal rights with whites." Section 51 of the constitution had said: '*The parliament shall ... have the power to make laws for the peace, order and good*

145

*Government of the Commonwealth [of Australia] with respect to … the people of any race, other than the aboriginal race in any state, for whom it is deemed necessary to make special laws…',* and then Section 127 had excluded them from being counted in the census. If you were trying to exterminate a people, then there was no need to count them. These were the provisions that Aboriginals found insulting and wanted removed, even though they never figured that other people had the right to vote yea or nay on their participation as though they were children.

Maggie shuffled in with more tea and started to pour for them. Mrs Wilson shoved her cup and saucer onto the coffee table with a rattle. "So why is that any of our concern?"

"Well, Mrs Wilson, if they are to thrive they must have full participation in the country. As good Christians, I was hoping we would all agree to get involved in a campaign to ensure that Malee, the outlying homesteads, and even Langley votes yes."

The 'good Christians' plea checked Mrs Wilson, and she sipped more tea as if considering her next move.

"So—how exactly would we have this campaign, Helen?" Anne asked.

Helen Cartwright turned to Father Beir, as if to signal her introduction was done. He put down his tea and with the gentleness of a breeze stretched his tree-trunk legs without bringing attention to them. "Well, Mrs McDonald—and … and ladies … We have planned to have banners to hang in Malee and Langley. We will hold meetings in the centre of both towns, and I will be speaking on it in church."

"We were hoping that some of you ladies would help to make banners," Helen said.

"Mrs Cartwright," Mrs Wilson said, "I know you mean well and all, but most of us don't have the luxury of trucking in tankers of water to help us through these times. What do you think is going to happen when we tell these Abb—" She caught hold of the word as Maggie was pouring her tea. "—When we tell these people that they're the same as us? They've already got the same wages as a white man, next they'll want a legal right to send their children to the same schools as us." She looked at Father Beir and her nose wrinkled as if at vomit-soiled garments. He had spoken in favour of the Aboriginal children going to the same school, saying the world had already seen too much divisiveness in the last fifty years.

146

"But they are the same as us, aren't they?" Mrs Jones said, and then hid behind her teacup from the glaring rebuff Mrs Wilson gave her.

"Well, my girl Margaret goes to the school. It took her a while, but she is getting on well now," Anne said.

"Getting on well? Sisters Agnes and Ruth don't even mark the bloody Abbos' work. My girl Laura tells me." The room fell into a tunnel of reproachful silence, because of the language whilst taking tea with Helen Cartwright and the Father more than the revelation.

"Well—I've seen Margaret's work and it is being marked. She gets good results too," Anne said, but a lump of doubt had lodged like bone in her throat, and she could tell from Helen's kind stare that she had heard it too.

"Who you going to believe, Mrs McDonald—your half-caste or my Laura?"

"Come now ladies, there is no need for this." Father Beir raised his pacifying palms to them.

"Well," Anne said, "I will have to speak to Margaret when I get home." She was aching to flee now. How could she have been fooled for so long? Now all these ladies knew, including Helen. How?

Mrs Wilson plonked down her cup and snatched up her bag. "Let me tell you something. My boy is fighting in some godforsaken place called Vietnam for this country. What have they ever done for this country? Where's that boy you keep, Mrs Cartwright? Is he fighting? You tell them they're the same as a white man and sooner or later they are going to be trying to kick us off our land. We ought to get rid of the whole bloody lot of them." She marched like thunder out the door, and Sara, who had been standing in the hall, ran to see her out.

"Right," Helen said, whilst most eyes were still fixed like locks on the door. "Would anyone like to be freshened up?" There was a cold silence. She took the teapot from Maggie and refilled everyone's cups. Still, it was as mournful as a child's wake.

Then, "I will make the banners," Mrs Rossi said.

"What words shall we put on them?" Mrs Jones asked.

"Vote now," someone offered.

"Vote for right," another said.

Anne was still drowning in the lake of deception.

"Vote yes for Aboriginals," Father Beir said, and all with the exception of Anne looked at each other and nodded in agreement.

147

Anne trudged all the way home in a pensive stupor, declining a lift from Helen. The girls were already in from school and had prepared supper. With the hard times they were having, it was Spam again. They called it camp pie in jelly, but Anne knew Spam when she saw it. She refused to go to the shop to buy it or even cook it, and she would only eat it if it was unrecognisable, which was difficult to achieve. Her mother had known a hundred different ways to prepare her ration of Spam during the war and afterwards when Anne returned from the countryside. Spam, you can do lots with Spam she used to say, Spam fritters, omelettes, roasts and just plain bloody Spam. She hadn't come all the way to Australia to experience a self-imposed ration of food and water.

Liz was sitting at the kitchen table, completing her homework. She was now the same height as her mother, and her hips and breasts were fully rounded, like ripened melons. Her auburn hair was left loose on her shoulders, and there were few signs of her youthful freckles. "Hello, Mum," Liz said. Anne returned the greeting, still in a sombre daze from her confrontation with Mrs Wilson. "How was Mrs Cartwright's tea party?"

"It was … was very nice," she said, and went to look at what was in the pots on the stove.

Liz turned to watch her mother. "So what did she want to talk about?"

"Oh, the referendum. Helen and Father Beir want to arrange a campaign for a yes vote."

"Oh, that's cool."

"Elizabeth, please don't speak like that. If you go to university in Sydney I'm sure the other students won't speak like that." Anne supported her wounded pride against the work counter. The bitter argument and exhausting walk had flushed all cheer from her, when the day had started out so bright.

"I saw Rose O'Hare. She's back from Sydney University for the holidays, and she speaks like that."

"Elizabeth, her parents sent her to Rutland Girls. She has the credentials of that."

"Kids that Sister Agnes and Ruth teach have gone on to universities."

"Yes, dear, but it's not as easy for them." Anne drank a cool glass of water, to dampen her smouldering rage. "Where is Margaret?"

"She's in her room taking a wash."

"I would like to take a look at both your homework papers for last week when I come down," Anne said, and she went upstairs to change.

***

Liz pushed open Margaret's door and Margaret cupped her hands over her pointed breasts. She had grown into some of her father's features and was only an inch shy of six foot, so her coming into womanhood had not been as pronounced as Liz's. Anne had learned how to use a hot iron to press out the natural curls in her hair, from a Sicilian woman in church, and it had now long been as straight as dried spaghetti, and hung an inch off her shoulders. "Mum says she wants to see last week's homework," Liz said. Margaret's narrowed eyes conveyed confusion. "You have got it, haven't you?"

"Yes, but she's already looked at it."

"Well, she wants to see it when she comes down." Liz spun to go then turned back. "If she finds out, I had nothing to do with it."

"She won't," Margaret said. "I tick it and write my B's just like Sisters Agnes and Ruth."

Liz left her and Margaret fished the brush they used to scour the floor white out of the basin. She shook off the excess water and circled one end in the bar of soap, then she put the brush to her face and gritted her teeth as she scrubbed with gentle circular strokes. She had been doing this behind her closed door and wearing her sun hat every day since she had first started to walk part of the way to school with Laura Wilson. When she was done she looked in the mirror to see if she could see the parts of her face that were getting lighter. Those were the parts of her that made her spirit fly. Her nose was a little too dark, but it wasn't as flat as others she had seen. She pressed it between her thumb and forefinger and dragged down and out, down and out ten times. Then she turned and looked at it from her right side. She had two good-sized blemishes, landmarks on a map, which were like Federico's hot butter colouring. Each time she scoured with the brush she was sure they grew a little larger and would eventually collide, like floating continents, and she admired them for the longest while. Then she cast a smile wide and silky with

149

perfection into the mirror, but still noting faults, the ones she thought the boys at school and the men in town saw when she caught them sneaking a look at her, as they often did, but she was oblivious to the real reason.

Margaret used the water she had washed in to rinse out the dress she had worn to school that day, because it was better than wearing it soiled. Then after she had emptied the contents onto the vegetable patch, she carried her homework in to Anne. Anne sat like a principal at the kitchen table comparing the ticks and grades in Margaret's and Liz's exercise books. Liz threw a glance filled with caution to Margaret, who was dishing up supper, as if to say something was wrong.

"You checked those already, Hmm." Margaret said. Anne ignored her and concentrated on the grades. Liz started to gnaw on her pencil like a hamster in its cage.

"The ticks and the B's certainly look the same," Anne said after a while. Liz put her head into her book as if she hadn't heard. Margaret's breath stuttered to a halt, and she spilled some peas onto the cooker. "I said the ticks and the B's look the same," Anne repeated, with fiery vehemence in her voice, as if she would scorch all those at whom she launched it.

"They ... they should do," Margaret said. "Sister Agnes and Sister Ruth marked them."

Anne shook her head in sharp spasms. "Don't take me for a fool, Margaret."

"No, Hmm." Margaret looked in forlorn hope to Liz for help, but she was pretending to swim in her work. Her eyes dropped like marbles to the floor.

"Do you forge A's as well as you do B's?" Anne asked. But she didn't wait for an answer. "Why didn't you tell me?"

Margaret shrugged her shoulders.

"Don't you shrug your shoulders at me, young lady." She waved a calloused finger at Margaret's face. "I was made to look like a fool in front of Helen Cartwright, Father Beir, and the others. Do you know what that feels like? Do you know how it feels to be the odd one out, the only fool in the room?"

Margaret reached out to touch that raw and tender sensation with ease. She had known it every day in her first year when the sisters wouldn't ask her questions if she put up her hand, so she gave her

150

answers to Federico, so that he could raise his. Anne may not have noticed, but each time they went into Langley and the woman pointed at her and said she can't try on the dresses, it knocked her back. She had cleaned Father Beir's church for so long now that she knew every crack in the floorboards, and on which pew the sun would cast its shadow in the late afternoon, but still he hadn't baptised her. She had even asked him about being baptised, and he had said that Sister Ruth had to recommend the older children for baptism, and then turned away from her with regret moistening his eyes. That had set her off to consider doing the thing that she knew would make Father Beir baptise her, but because she knew it was sinning, she was finding it hard to do it. Yes, she knew what it felt like to be the odd one out, and she was working as if in a hive to fit in. "No, Hmm, I don't," Margaret said.

"Where are your old exercise books?" Anne asked, straining to suppress her eruption.

"In my room," Margaret answered.

"Go and get them. Now!" Anne stabbed a begone finger towards the door. Margaret scurried to her room and returned with a box full of several years' exercise books. Liz continued to swim in her work, but she was floundering. Anne pulled open one of the exercise books and slapped it on the table. "I want you to sit here and erase every tick and grade until you're finished." She took an eraser and scrubbed out a few of the ticks to demonstrate.

\*\*\*

Just then the back door rattled as if a strong gust had buffeted it. "G'day, mates," a man's husky voice called out. Then there were three solid raps, which caused the door to shudder. All three women stared at each other, trepidation oozing from their skins like grease from a spit-roast pig. Anne got up and headed for the back door. The lazy dogs hadn't even barked to warn them. She stopped when she saw the dishevelled, one-eyed man pressing his grizzly face against the open wooden slats. "G'day, miss," he called out, and raised his tattered Akubra from his balding head.

"Bolt the front door and get your father's shotgun, Elizabeth. Stay out of sight with it," Anne whispered, and she continued towards the door. She pushed the bottom bolt with her foot and took out the key. "Good day, sir. How can we help you?" The man used his good eye

151

to stare past her towards Margaret, who was as rigid as a bronze cast statue. Then he looked over to the food by the stove.

"I'm a traveller, miss. I'm looking for some work and food to keep me the night."

"We have no work," Anne said. She followed his straining eye to the food. "We haven't much food, either."

"Just a little will keep me going, miss. And if I could fill my water bottle from your tank." He held up his empty water bottle.

Anne heard Liz come down with the shotgun and she signalled for her to stay out of sight with an urgent flick of her hand. Sean had offered to show her how to use it, but she hated the sight of guns. Where was Sean? He should be here at a time like this.

"You can fill your water bottle, and if you wait out on the porch, we'll fix you something to eat. But you won't be able to stay the night. My husband and his friends are due back soon."

"Thank you, miss," the man said, and he went to fill his bottle then sat out on the porch.

Margaret brought the man a plateful of food that they made up from their own plates. He was lounging as if at home on his rolled up swag blanket when she came. "My, you're a pretty one," he said, and grinned half a mouthful of rotten teeth at her. She stretched her arm as far as it could reach and handed him the plate. He ate the food with his grubby hands like a starving animal. When he noticed that Margaret was still there staring at him, he looked up and touched the raised scar on his face. It ran from beneath his egg-white left eye to the right tip of his nose. "What, this?" he asked. "Wild stallion kicked me a while back. Don't ever stand behind a wild stallion, girl." He looked her up and down as if another hunger had awakened, at the way the frock wrapped itself around her legs and found the hidden creases in her body; then he let out a guttural laugh laden with satisfaction. Margaret ran back into the house.

Anne locked the windows and they took refuge in the kitchen, watching and listening for movements and sounds. Liz clutched the shotgun to her chest with sweaty palms, and none of them could eat supper.

# Chapter 12

Sean waited on a log under a tree for Sammy, the way he had been doing for several weeks now. He opened the bottle of fortified wine he had bought him and poured half of it into another bottle which was already half filled with meths. Costos was the one who had come up with that idea. It would sweep the old Aboriginal onto the grog like flash flooding, he had said.

The moonlight illuminated Sammy stealing across the field, and so he stuck close to the cover of the surrounding trees. He kept stopping and peering behind him, as if he was being followed, then he hurried on a little towards Sean.

"G'day, boss," Sammy said, but his leering eyes weren't on Sean, they were caressing the bottle of grog like a lusted after woman.

"G'day, Sammy. How you doing?"

"Hungry, boss, hungry." Sammy pulled up his vest and rubbed his protruding belly. He glanced with bubbling anxiety over his shoulder again. "You got anything for me, boss?" He nodded towards the grog with reasonable certainty.

"Now you know that it's illegal for me to supply grog to Aboriginals, Sammy. You boys just can't hold your liquor."

"Not me, boss, I hold my grog real good." Sammy rubbed his hands together and his shoulders danced erratically as if the cold hand of reason had rested there, trying to pull him back.

"So, I give you some grog, what do I get, Sammy?" Sean took a sip of the half bottle of pure wine, making sure he kept the bottle mixed with meths to one side.

Sammy grinned a fake shyness and scratched his stubbly head. "What do you want, boss?"

Sean expelled his poisonous frustration with a sigh. They had been through this dance before. "I want your wife, Sammy! Come on, what the hell do you mean, what do I want?" Sean sipped some more wine. The bank in Langley had refused him a loan to tide him over. He could have asked Costos, he had saved well in the good years, but he

153

wanted to stand in his own shoes. Going up north and working someone else's land for a season or two would have helped, but he had never liked having bosses over him, that's why he had bought his own land. "You like grog, Sammy, we like water," he finally said.

"Been no water around here for a long time, hey, boss."

"Where the fuck you people get water then, Sammy, tell me that?"

"We eat lots of roots full of water, boss, and sometimes we get a little water from someone's tank. That's all, boss." Sammy spread his arms in a surrender to innocence then looked away.

"You had plenty of water to cook all that food you had at the ceremony for them boys you turned into men some time back."

"You see that?" Sammy's eyes flared with wild intention and he stepped back. "It's against our laws for you to see that."

"It's against our bloody laws for me to be giving you booze, Sammy." Sean held up the bottle and Sammy's head tracked it up and back down. Then he strung his hands behind his back and pursed his lips as if seeking out a tune on a horned instrument. Sean stood up and walked away. Sammy started after him, hopping up and down as if to prevent wetting himself.

"Mr Sean, Mr Sean, just one last time, Mr Sean."

Sean turned, opened the bottle, and started to pour the grog away. Sammy ran forward, inclined his head under the bottle and gulped down the spouting liquor, which ran down his mouth, neck and vest like an unfurling serpent. Sean pushed the rest of the bottle into his hand. "That's the last of it, Sammy," and then he walked away.

\*\*\*

When Sean arrived home he picked up the empty plate he found on the veranda. He pushed the door but it was bolted from the inside. Then he saw Liz inching down the hallway with the shotgun pointed at him, Anne and Margaret coming up her rear. He shouldered the door with a bull's snorting rage, ran forward, and grabbed the shotgun. "What the bloody hell is going on?"

"Daddy!" Liz fell against his chest and put her arms around him. Anne was clasping her hands together as if in prayer.

"A man—a beggar—came and asked for food and work. We gave him some food out on the porch and thought he was still there." Anne was still shaking with an uncommon fear.

154

"A *swagman*," Sean said as he uncocked the shotgun and took out the cartridges. "They like to travel and look for work where they can find it. Mostly they'll be no trouble to you." Still, Sean went out and checked around the homestead, and then he made sure that all the windows were locked and the doors bolted before turning in.

***

The time had come to confront them. Anne waited until the next time she had Andrew before going. Somehow she thought the sight of the boy with her would cause the sisters to relent, or at the very least, not to be too scathing of her. She sat under the overhanging roof of the schoolhouse, going over her words, whilst Andrew ran up and down the boardwalk. She would look at Sister Agnes when she said it; she seemed the more reasonable of the two, and the fact that she wore a dress instead of a habit made her aura less austere. "Andrew, get down from there," she called out. He was climbing one of the beams holding up the roof, and she went to pull him down and clutched his wriggling hand so that he stood next to her. The door swung open, and children streamed out into the yard to eat their lunch. Neither Liz nor Margaret saw her, and she slipped into the classroom and shut the door when the last child had left. "Good day, Sister Ruth," she said. Sister Ruth stopped wiping the board, pushed her spectacles up her thin nose and regarded her, as if trying to remember whose mother she was.

"G'day, Mrs McDonald," Sister Agnes called from the far side of the room, where she was collecting textbooks.

"Good day, Sister Agnes," Anne said, and she patted Andrew on the back. He said g'day and continued to study the room.

"Oh, Mrs McDonald," Sister Ruth finally said. "Elizabeth's mother."

"Yes, Elizabeth and Margaret," Anne reminded her.

"Yes," Sister Ruth said, as if she had swallowed a bitter taste. She put the duster on her desk and flicked through her diary. "I don't recall us having an appointment."

"No, Sister, we didn't. But I needed to see you, and it shouldn't take long."

Sister Ruth pointed her chalk-coated hand to the chair and Anne sat down. "Now if it's for this young man, we don't start them until

155

six." She wiped her hands and leaned across the table to ruffle his hair. "How old is he now?"

"Andrew is almost five, Sister, but it's not about him, it's about Margaret."

Sister Agnes put the books she had collected on a desk at the front, and instead of sitting in on the conversation as Anne had hoped, she took over the cleaning of the blackboard. Sister Ruth didn't ask what about Margaret, she sat and waited for Anne in stony silence. Anne swallowed her jitters, rising like aerated bubbles, before continuing. "I have been checking her homework, Sister Ruth, and it hasn't been marked."

Sister Ruth waited, as though signalling that she was only going to answer direct questions. Anne squeezed Andrew, so that she knew someone else was there, but he pushed her hand away and continued to discover the room from her lap.

"I was wondering," Anne said, "why hasn't her homework been marked?"

"We don't give her homework, Mrs McDonald, so there is no need to mark any."

"Oh. Can I ask you why she doesn't get any homework, Sister?"

Sister Ruth clasped her hands, placed them on the table, and sighed as if she were about to repeat an instruction. "Mrs McDonald, you do realise that they still have separate schools for them in some states?" Anne fought to hold her pinprick gaze. "When you first took in the girl I said there was no room in the school for any more Aboriginals, but you sent her anyway. As far as I can tell the girl has learned all she will ever need to know, so there is no need for her to be schooled any further."

Anne adjusted herself as if the chair had sunk beneath her. She was glad that she had practised how to keep her voice low and temperate. "Margaret is a very clever girl, Sister Ruth, and she could do with all the learning she can get. She already has enough disadvantages."

"What are you expecting, Mrs McDonald? That Margaret will become a lawyer or maybe even a surgeon? Even if she could, which I very much doubt, who would she treat? Our people are not going to allow her to touch them, and her own people are still practicing bogus medicine, Mrs McDonald."

156

"Then what is she to do?" Anne asked, gripping Andrew so tight that his face was contorted in pain.

Sister Ruth turned a motherly smile on Andrew and handed him a piece of chalk. "Go and draw something on the blackboard while I talk to Mrs McDonald, Andrew." The boy jumped off Anne's lap and ran with unchained excitement to the blackboard. Sister Ruth lowered her voice. "Mrs McDonald, your husband is a healthy man, isn't he?"

"Yes, but what has—?"

"And Margaret is a young black who is coming into womanhood." She paused in loud silence, as if hoping Anne would understand, but she didn't. "The Bible warns us of women like Jezebel, Mrs McDonald, and the Aboriginals' rampant promiscuity is well documented. I have witnessed it. Only by putting her to long hours of exhausting work can you hope to curb that sexual proclivity." Anne fell into a clear and pure silence, as if the beat of time had been preserved in thick amber. "An unrelated woman left around a man is a recipe for trouble. If you have no need for a servant, Mrs McDonald, then find the girl a mistress that will put her to work."

"Are you or I making supper for Father Beir tonight?" Sister Agnes asked out of nowhere.

"I believe it's you, Sister," Sister Ruth said with mild frustration at the interruption, but she appeared oblivious to the intent behind the question, as did Anne.

Anne turned to Sister Agnes, but she walked by, avoiding her gaze, which was lodged with appeal. She tried to speak, but her lips wouldn't part, and her mind was churning through a turbulent stream of thoughts. She cleared the numbness from her throat. "Thank you, Sister." Then she got up, took Andrew's hand, and walked to the door. She stopped and turned back to say something, but changed her mind and left. Elizabeth had to go to school there too, she had to live in that community. It wasn't all about Margaret.

*** 

That same evening, after a slow born dusk, Anne ran up to her room to change into her good clothes when she heard footsteps on the porch. It was too early for Sean, and she knew his sound. Liz called her down and said the person had gone, but they had left an old copy of the *Australian* on the veranda. "Did you see who it was?" Anne asked, as she took the paper from Liz.

157

"It looked like Sister Agnes, but I'm not sure."

Anne opened the paper to the page where the corner had been folded, and she saw the article clearly circled in red ink.

***

In the weeks leading up to the referendum, Father Beir and the ladies of Malee held meetings in their town, other outlying districts and Langley, and flew their banners and sang their songs: *Vote yes, for Aborigines, they want to be Australians too. Vote yes, and give them rights, and freedoms just like me and you. Vote yes, for Aborigines.* And on the last Sunday before the vote, Father Beir gave over mass to the cause. First, he read from the bible. And then he gave a sermon about all men being made equal, and how differences were one of God's ways of testing our true love. But inside we are all the same, he kept saying. "I don't know why we sometimes hate another people so, that we want to wipe them from the face of the earth." He sliced his hand through the air like a scythe, cutting down all before it. "Why, Father?" he asked himself as if in introspective confession. "Why did you belong to them?" And he held on to his dais to stop himself from swaying, and an unspoken shame filled his eyes.

Helen Cartwright glided up to the dais to say why she felt everyone should vote yes, without Father Beir having finished his sermon, and then she said she believed Anne McDonald wanted to say a few words. Anne stood in the pew, uncertain whether she should take her bag or not, her legs like a rickety table's. Helen caught her wavering eyes and nodded as if to throw her a lifeline. Anne took it, straightened herself, and carried the bag with her up onto the podium. She curtsied to Father Beir. "Good day, Father, ladies, gentlemen, and children." She started to unfold a piece of paper she had written her speech on, but she seemed to have folded it a thousand times now, and her uncertain hands tremored so that the words were swimming in front of her. "I am the mother of Elizabeth and also Margaret. Ah—she is sitting over there." Anne pointed to her, and Margaret slipped down in her seat as if she were sinking beneath still waters.

"Speak up, Missus, we can't hear you back here," a man called out.

"Yes ... Yes, can you hear me now?" Anne asked. The man nodded his silvery head.

158

"I said I am mother to Margaret. She is a half-caste girl, and I am trying to bring her up our way, the white man's way, proper. If we vote yes in the referendum, it will help me and any of you who look after these children, because they will know they are the same as us under the law." Her discomfort melted like lard left to the attentions of the sun, and she put the paper down on top of the dais and continued without it. "But to be the same as us under the law, they must have the same chances and opportunities." She fished the news clipping that someone had left on the porch from her bag. "I read a newspaper article recently about two Aborigines who are now at Sydney University. Yes, Aborigines at Sydney University. They are studying nursing, it says. Now I don't expect them to be able to look after our people, but they may be able to help some of their own kind. They might even be able to teach them the Lord's word." She directed this at Sister Ruth, who sat upright like carved marble. "Their teachers thought they were clever enough to do it, and those teachers must have been pretty smart too to get those kids through the exams. Now I know we don't have the same resources as a big city here in Malee, but we do have good teachers in Sisters Ruth and Agnes." An audible buzz of agreement rose from the aisles. "If there is a yes vote in the referendum, I don't want any other town saying that they can teach their kids better than Malee can. Please vote yes in the referendum." She grabbed her bag and hurried off the podium as the jitters caught up with her again. The congregation were silent, as if in contemplative prayer, and Anne dabbed at her watery eyes with her handkerchief. Margaret was still submerged in her seat, muttering something under her breath.

*** 

Helen Cartwright invited Anne around to watch the results of the referendum on her television, one of the few in Malee. She took the girls in their Sunday best, and they were served tea and scones in the drawing room as speaker after speaker came on the television saying why there should be a yes vote. The girls were animated and chatty about the television. They had seen them before in Langley, but each time Anne had talked about them, Sean had grunted with disdain and said too much work to be done to watch that thing. Now there wasn't enough money to buy one even if they wanted to, and Anne was not going to touch Elizabeth's university money. Helen had told Joshua to come home early from the orchards, where he had now decided to work alongside her hired hands, as he no longer saw any point in going to school. Even if he couldn't hear what was going on, at least he could see the historic moment, and so he sat there drinking tea and eating scones too. When the students from universities around the country came on in their dishevelled gear and cool-as-Coke talk, Liz drew closer, because she was hoping to go in little more than a year. She was burning, like a fire trapped in a room, for her freedom in someplace bigger than Malee. But when the blacks that spoke like whites came on, Joshua's face collapsed, but not so anyone would know he could hear what was being said, and Margaret twisted her strained gaze and once left the room.

When the *This Day, Tonight* signature tune came on, Helen sat forward on the edge of her seat. "This is it," she said, "keep your fingers crossed."

The young male reporter looked straight into camera. "The result of tonight's referendum was a resounding yes vote for the Aboriginal cause. Australians recorded a yes vote of ninety-one percent."

"Yes!" Helen leapt from her seat and hugged Anne. Anne hesitated before she could return the hug, but her arms were like butter and slid free easily. Liz beat her hands together like the wings of a dove, and accepted Helen's hug when she gave it next to her, then Joshua and Margaret. "Champagne for everyone," Helen said. "Maggie, Maggie, bring in a bottle of champagne and glasses, please." As they poured champagne, Joshua and Margaret searched out each other's vibrations across the room, as if to judge whether either could feel the texture of this new day.

\*\*\*

Sean sat on the veranda, smoking a rolled cigarette and watching clusters of stars, but not really seeing them. He hadn't bothered to vote—didn't see the point. It wasn't really going to change anything, was it? He had seen it all before. The blacks had got the vote a few years earlier in '62, but they hadn't been able to use it because Section 127 of the constitution had still stood: *'In reckoning [counting] the number[s] of ... people ... aboriginal people shall not be counted.'* If you can't be counted in a census you don't exist, so you can't be issued with voting papers. So what had changed? Yes they may get included in laws and counted after tonight's vote, but we'd still find a way. We're better fucking magicians than the bloody blacks, he thought. We can make it appear we're giving them something, long enough to quieten them, but if they ever managed to prize open the hand bearing the gift, they would find it was empty. Poor bastards. But it wasn't them he needed to be concerned for now. Most of his land had been sucked dry beyond hope, and so many of the serrated pine leaves had shrivelled and died, and nothing new had been planted. He had considered going into the church to pray for rain one Sunday, but he had only stopped outside long enough to watch Anne and the girls go in before dragging his festering carcass of despair to the pub. Some of the men had already gone north, to the cane fields, where they could earn enough money to send something back for their families. A few had abandoned their homesteads altogether and headed to larger towns or cities where they could find work. They would never survive. Once you have worked your own land you can never taste the fresh air of satisfaction with a boss-man over you. Maybe that's why the Abbos found it so hard to take. All this had once been theirs, and each man and woman roamed enough land to feed their family. Was that what it was like to lose control of the road map to your life? Would he descend into a state of drunken despair if he lost all this? No. It wasn't going to happen. He wouldn't lose it, whatever it took. Anne kept talking about moving to a city when the girls finished school. She would work as well, she said, life would be easier. We could have all the comforts. Cicadas hummed and a lizard scurried along the banister. The air was thick and had a ripe taste to it, like red wine. Sean smiled to himself; a crazy sort of smile, a dangerous kind, one filled with the knowledge that he would kill to keep his land. Sitting out there looking at them stars helped him to float free of his worldly worries. That was all the comfort a man needed, and a woman every now and then.

A whistle broke through the canopy of cicada songs. Sean looked up and the shrill squawk split the air again. He could just make out old man Sammy at the edge of the woods, signalling him to come. Sean stubbed out his cigarette and went inside to get a bottle of fortified wine. "How you doing, Sammy?" he said as he approached the woods.

"Not good, Mr Sean. I haven't had a drink for—" Sammy's feet were pacing as if to count the days, and he eyed the bottle in Sean's hand. Sean took a sip of the wine.

"So what do you want, Sammy?"

"I get in trouble if they know, Mr Sean. You can't tell how you find it."

"Find what, Sammy?" Sean wanted to wring it from him like a parched rag. He had already made him lose another planting.

"The water, Mr Sean," Sammy whispered, and then searched out the terror creeping up on him. The rocks were thought to have spirits that could hear, and if a possum or goanna happened to hear and the animal was then caught and eaten, it was said someone would know. Sammy stared at the bottle again, as though he needed fake courage to get him going. Sean handed him the wine, and he took two long swigs before trotting off, all the time looking about him, as though they could see him through the shrivelled eye of the grass that had been scorched by the sun, or point him out from high up in their birthing trees, and it was said that one of his brothers who had died had become a star, able to watch throughout the night.

They reached a place near the blacks' camp after an hour's walk, and Sammy bent down and crawled through the undergrowth. Sean slumped to his knees in disappointment, as there could be nothing worth his time in that space; but he lay on his belly and crawled in after Sammy anyway. This led them to a rock with a craggy opening, and they both crawled in.

When they were inside, Sean lit a match and waited for his eyes to meld with the diluted darkness. The roof of the cave was some way above him, and he stood up, but his head hit the ceiling before he was perfectly straight. "Shit!" Sean moaned, and he felt the sticky blood seeping from the wound.

"Be careful, Mr Sean," Sammy said, and he made no attempt to follow him further in. Sean bent lower than he needed and crept forward like a sinner paying penance. He took another step, but there was no ground. He tumbled a foot or two before there was a splash, and cool water broke his fall. He swallowed mouthfuls in his surprise, and flailed in the sunken blackness, forgetting to swim. He remembered so much then. How little he had to eat as a boy, competing with eleven others for the food on the table. His escape from the station, and having to walk for miles before he found somewhere to eat. Travelling with several swagmen from station to station for work. The one that tried to kill him and steal his few possessions one night. He had run off into the bush and come back

162

later with a stone, which he used to crush the sleeping man's skull, blood spattering his face. Had he lived? I want to live. My farm. Elizabeth. Sean gulped for air, but took in more water, and then he kicked. He kicked for the life that was being washed from him, and soon he heard wild splashing again, and he continued to flail until his fingers clutched a rock. Then he felt a hand against his, Sammy's, and he held onto it and hauled himself out.

Sean went directly to Costos' place, and they came back together with lanterns. This time he saw the immense size of the underground cave. It ran back for a quarter mile at a height that a man could walk, just. Then it fell abruptly so that the water lapped against the roof. They shone the lanterns on the cave walls, and white ochre X-ray figures of men, women, children, dingoes, wallabies, snakes, and all sorts of spirit figures performed centuries-old dances for them. They held the lanterns over the water and agreed it must be over thirty foot deep. Within a week, Sean and Costos had staked their joint claim on the land where the cave stood, and a few days after that the police had the blacks move their camp another two miles back from 'McDonald and Nicolaides' Underground Lake'. They could not resist. Sean and Costos visited homesteads that abutted the dry riverbed. The plan was to pump *their* water into the river, and those homesteads that paid for it could extract enough water to irrigate their fields. Nipper and his mob stayed away from work in the fields for a week or so, in silent protest. But their families had to eat, and there was no longer enough bush food to feed them all, as trees had been cut back for farming, causing game to die or leave, and they also needed a permit to hunt the little game that was left. Nor did they want to leave their country: the country that they had been born to protect as if it were a limb, the homeland whose dreaming they held in trust to pass on to their young ones. So inevitably, they drifted back to work, in order to earn the dollars that would buy them flour, tea, tobacco and tins of bully beef at the general store, as long as they didn't buy booze, and were out of town before sundown.

Sammy stayed away from the blacks' new encampment for weeks, but they knew it was him. He had been seen spending the reward that Sean had given him on bootleg grog. The elders sat together and tried him under customary law in his absence, and they determined what they would do to Sammy when they caught him.

# Chapter 13

A combination of Anne's speech in church, Helen Cartwright speaking to Father Beir, and he in turning speaking to Sister Ruth led to Margaret being given homework, and it was marked. Sister Ruth still didn't ask her questions when she raised her hand, but Sister Agnes did, and Margaret submerged herself in school more than she did before, even though Joshua and Isabel no longer attended.

She still sat at the back, but it was behind Federico, whom she would watch when she had finished her work. But then all the girls liked to watch Federico Rossi, even though he was too numbed with shyness to say anymore than g'day to them. He was now a shade over six feet tall, and although still slender, his bare arms were knotted like strong rope from work on his father's farm. He still thought schoolwork was like a boy chasing hundreds of sheep, but he tried hard, and Margaret loved the way the tight skin on his forehead wrinkled when he squeezed the last drop of learning from his mind. Only that morning she had checked his work in the woods before coming to school, and he had held her hand and said thank you Margaret, and then given her one of the pastries his mother had prepared for his lunch. She had already started to dream about Federico Rossi's well-cut smile and olive eyes when he said thank you Margaret, though she told no one about those dreams. But he still looked away if she stared at him, and so she preferred to pretend not to notice when he was caressing her with his gaze, until she felt well fed by his eyes.

After school, Margaret went into the woods and waited for Laura Wilson, as Laura had tied a yellow ribbon in her hair to signal her to wait, as she sometimes did. Laura loitered by the schoolhouse until the other children that went her way had gone, and only then did she go into the woods to meet Margaret. "Did you get that question right?" Laura asked as she walked up the hill, stealing more rapid breaths.

"Yes," Margaret said as she adjusted her sun hat.

"Me too," Laura said, and they continued into the woods. The trees shaded them from the scorching eye of the sun and the possibility that anyone else might see them together.

"What did Federico say when he walked past you at lunchtime?" Laura asked.

Margaret bit surprise into her tongue. She didn't know that anyone had seen them. It had only been fleeting words as they brushed by each other in the schoolyard. "Good day—he said good day, Laura."

Laura gritted a bitter slant into her face and jumped in front of Margaret, her peachy hands on her hips. "He said more words than g'day. I counted them, and he said about seven words."

"I really don't know, Laura. All I remember is that he said good day." Margaret kept going, and Laura walked backwards so that she could watch her empty face.

"Take off your hat. You can tell if you people are lying by looking into your eyes, my mother said." Margaret knew who she meant by 'you people', and it locked her jaws tight. She snatched off her hat and tasted blood seeping from her tongue. Laura looked into her translucent blue eyes. "Tell me again what he said."

"Good day, Margaret."

Laura snorted diluted scepticism and turned to walk in the right direction again, and Margaret put her hat back on. "You know I'm thinking of having a party?" Laura said.

"A party?" This time Margaret ran round to look into Laura's flaunting face.

"Yes. I was thinking of inviting you, but if you are lying to me I won't."

"I wouldn't lie to you, Laura, I promise."

They walked down the hill towards the Wilson homestead, Margaret hiding any words that might lose her an invite and Laura clutching onto its keys. They reached Laura's fence and stopped. "Do you think you can ask Federico to come to my party? And of course you can come if he does."

"Yes—yes, I will ask him," Margaret said. She was already wondering what she would wear. Maybe Mrs McDonald would get some cloth and she could make a new dress.

"Okay, then. I'll let you know when the party is going to be," Laura said, and then she went through the gate.

Margaret jumped as if to a jig and ran in the direction of home. Then she remembered and went the other way. "Where you going?" Laura called out.

"I just remembered I have to do something," Margaret said.

"I hope you're not going to see that Abbo girl, Isabel."

"No."

"Good," Laura said, and she stood there watching. Margaret changed direction, and when she was well out of sight she went back onto her route.

She climbed the fence of the Nicolaideses' farm and walked out of sight along a line of malee trees until she saw Isabel. She was eating a late lunch on the veranda whilst the Nicolaideses ate theirs inside. Margaret whistled, and Isabel looked up and saw her. She left her lunch and peeked through the window to make sure the Nicolaideses were still eating, and then she crept off the veranda and ran to the trees to meet Margaret. "G'day, Margaret." Isabel smiled as if she were being rescued and held her hand.

"Good day, Isabel," Margaret said, and then they walked a little further into the cover of the trees. "When you coming back to school, Isabel?"

Isabel kicked at the ground. "I'm not. They say I got to work on the farm now."

"Nannup—" Margaret stopped herself. No one else knew. "I mean Joshua—works on Mrs Cartwright's farm now, and he gets two dollars a week. But that's only because Mrs Cartwright is his foster mum and she likes Joshua a lot. How much they paying you?"

Isabel glanced with venom at the homestead and balled the hem of her skirt in her fist. "Nothing. I'm supposed to get fifty cents, but they don't pay me. Mr Nicolaides puts all his money under the floorboards. Some of that money is mine, Margaret."

"You complained?"

Isabel shook her shaggy head.

"We could write to the Welfare."

"All them bloody letters to me mother and we haven't had one back. I don't want to write any more stinking letters." She turned away to hide the tears that were gathering like marauding insects.

"We can still write one to your mother every Christmas," Margaret said.

166

"No! If she wanted to write she would have writ already. She won't want to know me now anyway."

"Yes she will, Isabel."

"No she won't, not after he done touched me." She stabbed a finger at the house and then the tears started to flow.

"Mr Nicolaides?"

"Yes, him, that bloody pig." Her face was in her hands, and she was bawling now. Margaret patted her on the back, and then some instinct told her to rub. "He said, 'You can't sleep in the house anymore girl, Andrew needs the room'. Then he sets up a room for me in the barn, and he keeps coming at night."

"You told his wife?"

Isabel nodded. "She says I'm a lying little black and she's going to cut my tongue out if I say it again."

"What if I tell somebody?" Margaret said.

"No! They will think it was me who caused it."

"But—"

"Isabel. Isabel." A shrill cry came from the veranda. It was Aithra. She scurried around looking for her and then went back inside.

"I have to go," Isabel said. She wiped the tears away with the hem of her skirt and ran back towards the veranda.

"I'll come back," Margaret said.

\*\*\*

After supper, Margaret went outside to where Anne was once again using the hose to water the vegetable patch. The plants had sprung into eager life, and there were runner beans climbing up poles, fat heads of cabbages eating up the sun, and unshapely green tomatoes dangling from their vines. "What is it, Margaret?" Anne said.

"Nothing." She continued to scratch at the dust with her foot like a hound that had made a find. Then, "If there was something really bad happening, who could you tell, Hmm?"

"Well, it depends what the thing was, Margaret." Anne squeezed one of the tomatoes, proud of her work.

"Suppose it was happening to someone you knew and they didn't like it?"

"Then I would tell them to stop doing it, Margaret. Whatever are you on about?" A silence more rapid than death engulfed them, and it lingered like a putrefying corpse sucked dry by the sun. Anne

167

switched off the hose and turned as if through thick slime to face Margaret. Sister Ruth had warned her when she visited the school, but she ignored her. "What is it, Margaret?" she said quite firmly.

Margaret turned her head, swirling with emotions, to the ground. "Supposing someone was touching this girl and she didn't like it?"

Anne dropped the hose and threw a hand to her mouth, as if to stop the vomit-scented scream that had already escaped her. Not in her house, it wasn't happening in her house. She marched over and slapped Margaret hard across the face, "You shouldn't speak such lies." Margaret grabbed her sizzling cheek. Work them to exhaustion, Sister Ruth had said, work it out of them. "I want you to scrub the floor in the kitchen and tidy your room before you go to bed. And you'll do that every night from now on."

"Yes, Hmm," Margaret said, and she turned and crept trembling into the house. Anne closed her eyes as if to expel the sinful vision when Margaret was gone. She would pray for them, that's what she would do.

***

It was after Mrs McDonald had slapped her that Margaret decided to have her vision. She had been dreaming it up for a long time now, and it would not only get her baptised, but also get Mrs McDonald to like her again and stop thinking that she was doing things with Mr McDonald. "I had a dream last night," she said as she, Mrs McDonald, and Liz walked the two miles to church. They both gave her raised-brow glances but said nothing. "I dreamed that Jesus was crying," she said.

Mrs McDonald stared a combustible rage at her. "Don't you dare repeat that anywhere, Margaret. It's blasphemy, and we don't want people to think we are fools."

"Yes, Hmm," Margaret said, and turned away, knowing now that it was done.

When they reached the church Mr Jones was running out like a fowl being pursued. "Good day, elder Jones," Anne said.

"G'day, Mrs McDonald. We've had a sign." He shook her shoulders and there was a believer's sheen to his face. Anne skipped back from his wild animated touch as though screams were raging in her ear. "We've had a sign, Mrs McDonald, go look and see. I'm going home to get my camera."

168

As soon as they reached the door they could hear the commotion inside. When they went in, most of the congregation were gathered like feeding vultures around the cross in front of the pulpit. Some were on their knees praying. Anne crept towards the front with the girls. A crying woman slipped away from the melee towards them. "Go and look, Mrs McDonald. It's a sign, go and look." Anne and the girls squeezed their way through the throng. When they reached the front, worshippers were trying to touch the cross, and some were pushing their children towards it so that they too could lay hands on it and be blessed. Father Beir and the sisters were trying to calm them. Anne gasped as if she had seen the Holy Ghost, then she turned to take in Margaret with the same hallowed stare. Congealed blood was running from the eyes of Jesus on the cross. The stain ran down His cheeks, onto His bare chest, and had dripped onto the floor.

Margaret knew they had a sweet tooth for miracles, even though they often denied it when they branded the local Kooris' ceremonies and beliefs as superstitious nonsense. She had remembered Mrs McDonald's teachings about the girl at Lourdes discovering the weeping virgin, and about how the people had sung up that girl. She had considered killing one of the Wilsons' chickens to do it, but when she slipped into their coop, they flapped into such a racket that she ran away. So eventually she had drawn her own blood by piercing the bottom of her foot where no one would see it. They were all burning hidden flames of desire for something exciting to happen in Malee, anything, so they wouldn't question it.

"Father, as we were coming to church this morning Margaret told me that she had a dream last night that Jesus was crying," Anne said, the way Margaret had expected her to. The commotion stopped and all turned to stare in rare awe mixed with fear at Margaret.

Father Beir stepped from the pulpit and the congregation parted so that he could approach her. He put his hand to her forehead. "My child, what did you see?"

"I—I saw Jesus crying, Father, and his tears were red." The lies were jangling on her nerves, but she said silent Hail Marys to abate them.

"Do you know what that means, Margaret?"

"No," she said, choking on the word.

"You have been chosen, Margaret; it means you have been chosen. You must be brought within the bosom of the church."

"Did you hear any words?" Sister Ruth asked, her eyes piercing like rays of sunlight peering through cracks.

"No, Sister Ruth," Margaret said, hanging her head.

"Father, if there were no words then we don't know what it means."

"Yes, but—"

"It could be a sign of wickedness and pain. We must wait to see before we mention it too widely and have people label Malee." Some of the congregation shuffled back now, as the pangs of fear in the mixture swelled. If it was that, then to mention it could make produce from anywhere near Malee unmarketable. Father Beir agreed to wait a few weeks to see if there were any more signs, and after that, if all was well, Margaret could start her training for baptism and Holy Communion.

***

Nannup was waiting for Margaret at the edge of the woods when she climbed out of her window in the night. She was glad he hadn't pursued the issue of running away, as she wasn't sure if she really wanted to go, not yet anyway. They had eaten most of the tinned food that they had buried in the woods, and over the years they had replenished them and the rotting blanket. He gave her one of the apples that had come from Mrs Cartwright's orchards, and she crunched on it as they walked.

"Mrs Cartwright's sister in Sydney is sick again. Mrs Cartwright's saying that if it gets worse we may have to go to Sydney," Nannup said.

"What's she sick with?" Margaret asked. Nannup shrugged as if to say all kinds of sicknesses were the same. The night was muggy, and a full moon drifted against a black canopy. Margaret fanned at a swarm of mosquitoes that had found the awakened riverbed.

They enjoyed the silence for a while, and then Margaret asked him what she had been meaning to. "Do you think the referendum will change anything, Nannup? Will we really be just like them?"

Nannup's eyes narrowed on her. "You still trying and hoping to be like them?" She didn't answer, but was sure he knew. "That night they decided we were all the same they took Nipper's people's water.

170

Them caves are where Nipper's people supposed to keep corroborrees so that the land remembers to bear fruit."

"Mr McDonald's pineapples have been growing since he found that water, and Federico's family are going to stay in Malee now that they can buy water for their fields."

"So you happy that they take the water?" Nannup snapped.

Margaret flicked her shoulders. "Mrs McDonald isn't happy. She said if it wasn't for that damned water they would probably have to move to a big town or city when Liz and me finished schooling."

"When you take something from the land, it will take something back from you," Nannup said, and hurried ahead, his mood bleeding dry.

They came to the spot that Nannup had cleared, gathered more dry sticks and threw them on the pile for the fire they would build later. Then they went out to find something to eat. Margaret still liked to eat bush meat caught and prepared in this way, but she also liked to sit at the table Mrs McDonald prepared on Sundays, with knives, forks, spoons, and napkins.

They spread out a little, so that they could cover more ground, and Margaret searched by moon and starlight for the animal tracks the way Nannup had taught her. She came across something and stopped. She hadn't seen these tracks before, and she stooped to touch their ebbing vibrations more closely. The oval tracks were about the size of a man's foot, and just outside the oval, on opposite sides, were two light brushstrokes, like paintings in the dirt. She picked up an eagle's feather from one of the scratches, then she whistled for Nannup.

"What you found?" he asked as he crept up on her.

"What are these?"

Nannup stared with unmasked concern at the oval tracks around him. He turned in a circle as though he couldn't tell which way they went. He knocked the feather out of Margaret's hand and yanked her up like a weed. "Come, we must go."

Margaret pulled away from him. "Why? I want to know what it is."

"We must go *now!*" Nannup said, and he grabbed at her arm again. She slipped his hold and started to follow the oval tracks, but she couldn't tell if she was heading to where they had gone to or where they had come from. "We must *go*," Nannup said, "it is the *Kaditja man.*" Margaret saw the spark in his feral-cat eyes, but she didn't want to say she didn't remember what a *Kaditja man* was. She turned back

171

to follow the trail and something brushed her face and entangled itself in her hair. She tried to get the twigs out, but when she felt, there were bits that were warm and soft like skin, and others, long, hard, calloused nails. She counted five toes before she looked up and screamed. Sammy, the giver of water in exchange for grog, was hanging from the tree with blood dripping from his spear wounds.

They didn't wait for the police from Langley to remove Sammy's body. The stench from the melting corpse had already started to travel on whatever little breeze there was in the morning heat. Sean and Costos cut him down, wrapped him in canvas to stop the seepage of liquefied remains, and buried him close by. Then they burnt their clothes and washed the stink off themselves. The police went out to the blacks' camp and questioned them, but no one knew anything, and in any case, they knew that the executioner, brought in from a distant clan, was long gone. Besides, it didn't pay to start asking questions as to why Sammy had been killed.

***

Sister Ruth said I told you so when they found Sammy's body. *Any vision by that girl can only mean disaster, and there'll be more, I tell you.* Margaret was finding it like stepping on thorny vines to get over her morbid discovery, especially now that Sister Ruth had blamed it on her vision. She kept seeing Sammy swinging from that tree, heard people screaming in feral alarm as flames licked around them, and saw someone gasping for air. Some of her visions also carried a pungent taste, and she wondered if God was punishing her for desecrating the Jesus man. She tried to push it aside by immersing herself in the preparation of her dress for Laura's party, in-between doing the additional work that Mrs McDonald was piling on her in order to extinguish any sinful desires. She made the dress with a cast-off piece of silk to tie around her slender waist, and a white lace collar. Now that Sean was getting in money from surrounding farms for access to the water supply, Anne had started to give the girls pocket money, as well as save up for one of those televisions. Margaret used some of her money to buy Laura a bottle of perfume, which they said at the store in Langley was from France, and she took all of one evening to make sure she had wrapped it nicely and tied it with a red bow.

On the afternoon of Laura's party, Anne saw Margaret and Liz off together. Liz had left her hair down and she kept wrapping and unwrapping her arms from around her body-hugging frock with an uncertain smile. Margaret's height and slight movements gave her a graceful poise, and Anne fussed over both the girls with motherly pride but worry at the same time. "You both look beautiful," she said as she stood on the veranda, holding onto Andrew.

"I want to go too," Andrew said, and he pulled away from Anne and ran down the path after the girls. Anne gave chase, but he evaded her and started to climb a tree.

"Get down," she said as she tugged him by the foot, and then she held him tight and watched from the path as the girls went.

They didn't take the short cut through the woods, because they didn't want to soil their shoes or have a branch hook onto and tear their dresses, but also because Margaret was still afraid of what she might find hanging from trees. So they stuck to the stony path that went most of the way there.

"Are you going to dance if one of the boys asks you?" Liz said.

Margaret covered the smile blooming on her face. "None of the boys are going to ask me."

"I think Federico will ask you. I see the way he looks at you."

Margaret dropped her eyes, and a hot wave spread out from her stomach to all parts of her. "What way does he look at me?"

"Like he is longing for something. Like Heathcliff looked at Catherine in *Wuthering Heights*."

Margaret laughed with abandon, her face flushed. "I dreamed I saw Andrew swimming last night," she babbled out, to change the subject. She hadn't dreamed for a long while before Mrs McDonald had accused her and discovering Sammy's body, and wasn't sure she knew how to read her dreams anymore. She had also dreamed about some travellers, but she didn't know who they were.

"Don't change the subject, you." Liz gave her a playful shove and they both giggled. "Andrew can't swim anyway."

"Who you going to dance with then, Liz?"

"I don't know. I like David, but I don't know if he'll ask me."

When they arrived at the Wilson homestead there were more than a dozen young people on the veranda drinking lemonade and chattering. Margaret and Liz gave their gifts to Laura and she took them with a curt thank you and walked away. The jerky tone of

Federico's reticent laugh was absent, and Margaret knew that was why Laura was stomping around. Liz went off to talk to her friends and Margaret stood in her own company, drinking lemonade. Laura walked by her to pour lemonade when no one else was near. "Where is Federico?" she asked, with her back to Margaret.

"I did ask him, and he said he would come."

One of the O'Hare girls came to pour herself a drink, and Laura and Margaret held their conversation and waited for her to go. "Nice party, Laura," Molly O'Hare said. Laura curved her lips in that thank-you-but-go-away fashion.

When they were alone again she said, "So why isn't he here, then?"

"I don't know. Maybe he is—There he is; he's coming now." Margaret pointed to Federico bounding up the path with a gift in his hand. Laura poured him a glass of lemonade and went to meet him at the steps of the veranda. He handed her an oval-shaped box and she handed him the drink. She stood in front of him, bouncing on her toes and smiling down at her gift, as if something had been forgotten. Then all of a sudden she said thank you, and tipped up and kissed him on the cheek before running into the house.

Margaret averted her eyes, which were clouded with jealousy when Federico saw her. She stood that way for the longest while, pretending to admire the Wilsons' rosebushes, which were coming back to life, but her legs were crumbling like porous rock. Then she heard, "Hello, Margaret," right next to her ear and turned to see his olive eyes a foot away from hers.

"Hello, Federico," she said.

He stared at the rosebushes as if they were words that he could read. "Are—Are you having a good time?"

"Yes," she said, and stung by his good looks stared down at her shoe, but she could still see his firm sapling legs in front of her.

"Me too." Federico leaned back against the banister, and neither knew what else to say. Then he asked, "Do you want some more lemonade, Margaret?"

She feigned surprise at the empty glass, which she had been putting to her lips for something to do, and said, "Yes, thank you." He brought back the lemonade and they stood the same way in a sheepish silence again. Margaret spied out of the corner of her eyes where on his cheek Laura had kissed him. If she kissed him there would he like it? Would he kiss her first?

Mr Wilson came out onto the veranda with his accordion and launched into a tune. By the second melody many of the young people were stomping dexterous feet to a square dance. They were spinning, skipping, changing partners, bending under outstretched arms, and hurling breathless laughs across the floor. Federico and Margaret watched it with wide grins. After a few more tunes Mr Wilson played a waltz. Federico glanced at Margaret's slender fingers wrapped around the banister rail and swallowed as if to calm his jittery gut. He put his hand on the rail and waited. Then he slid it along an inch and stopped. Another inch and stopped. Another inch and stopped. Until after three waltzes their fingers were touching. Margaret was tremoring like a windswept pool, and the vibrations crept up through her fingertips until she could feel him touching her all over. She slid her hand forward, until their fingers were entwined. They were still watching the dancing with cataract eyes, but only saw each other through the mirrors in their minds. "Would you like to dance, Margaret?" Federico asked, throwing away all caution.

"I—I don't know how," she said.

"I show you how, Margaret. We go slowly." He took her hand and moved towards her, and she stared up, hypnotised by his hot butter face as they first shuffled by numbers and then with more rhythm across the floor. By their third waltz they were sometimes gliding, and as Federico pulled her closer to him, she rested her head against his chest and could hear his heart booming like thunderous hooves. "Thank you, Margaret," Federico said when the dance ended, and she tipped up and had the briefest taste of his lips.

"We are going in to eat now," Laura said as she pulled Federico's hand from Margaret's and walked him towards the door. Margaret followed behind them, but Laura stopped at the door. "You can't come inside. Mum will pass you yours from the window." She pointed down the veranda to the window and disappeared inside with Federico. Margaret's feet clung to the boards as if sunken in mud as she waded down the veranda. She reminded herself to breathe the hot air, and blinked to hold back the flood that was rushing towards the corners of her eyes. Some of the others were watching her through the open door, and so, with her chest heaving, she joined them in singing Laura 'Happy Birthday' from out on the veranda, and gave three cheers after she blew out her candles. Then, after she had served all the other children, Mrs Wilson shoved a plate of cakes and sandwiches out of the window towards her, and pulled back her hand so that they wouldn't have to touch. Margaret took it and sat on the veranda. She played with the cake, not sure if she should eat bitterly given food. She was about to take a bite when Laura waltzed back out. She thrust Margaret's wrapped gift back towards her. "That's not what I wanted from you."

Margaret took the gift and a sharp ache soared through her, as if a part of her was being torn away. "What did you want then, Laura?"

"I'm not sure that you'll be able to give me what I want."

"I'll try my best, Laura, you know I always do."

Laura pursed her lips as if her thirst was near quenched. "You'll have to, or else I won't let you walk to school with me again. I want you to leave Federico alone." Margaret's hand dropped like loose tiles from the plate on her lap to her side. "Did you hear me?" Laura said.

"But he's my friend, Laura."

"You can have Federico or me as a friend, not both of us."

Margaret closed the door to hold back the fire burning inside her. Laura knew that Federico liked her; he had asked her to dance. All the other boys liked Laura. She could have had her pick of them. But she had wanted to walk with Laura ever since she saw her baptised. "I'll—" Before Margaret could get her answer out they heard a jeep trundling up the path. Laura ran inside to call her mother. A clean-shaven man in military uniform jumped out, glanced with knowing eyes around him, then strode up onto the veranda. "Is this the Wilson homestead?" he asked Margaret. She was about to say yes when Mrs Wilson came to the door.

"Yes, I am Mrs Wilson." The soldier stepped towards her, fingering the letter in his hand. Mrs Wilson gazed at the letter and her body became as hard as stone.

"Is your husband here, Mrs Wilson?" the soldier asked, and she fell into his arms without answering.

*** 

Margaret and Liz walked home without talking about the party. How could you talk about a party when the Wilsons' eldest son had been blown up in Vietnam trying to protect freedom? They didn't even understand whose freedom he had been trying to protect, although Sister Ruth had tried to explain it a couple of times at school.

176

As they walked into the yard they saw Costos Nicolaides. A nauseous scent swirled in Margaret's head and she wanted to wretch. She held onto her churning stomach to keep it down. His face was ruddy and he was sweating barrels-full. Then they saw Sean by the woods with a stick, pushing back the deep grass and shrubs. "You see Andrew, girls?" Costos asked, with worry lines ploughing into his forehead. Margaret shook her head and gave him a wide berth.

"He's not in here," Anne said as she came out of the homestead holding Aithra, who had already started to shake.

"What is it, Mum?" Liz said.

"It's Andrew, he's disappeared. I know he can't be too far. He was in the yard not five minutes ago."

Liz looked around her. "Didn't you say you saw him swimming or something, Margaret?" she recalled.

"No. I said I dreamed it. I dreamed I saw him swimming."

"We're not concerned with silly dreams now," Anne said. Margaret lowered her gaze, as she knew that it still took Mrs McDonald's full resolve to face the congregation at church after her previous vision, which, as Sister Ruth had predicted, had brought evil to Malee. "Can you girls look around the back? We'll help your father in the woods."

The girls went around to the vegetable patch and looked in the bushes, the dunny, and by the trashcan. Costos was shouting his son's name at the front of the house. Liz went under the water stand and asked the resting dogs if they had seen him, but they ignored her. At sundown they still hadn't found him. "Where haven't we looked?" Sean asked, scratching his head.

"He likes to climb," Margaret said. "We haven't looked in the trees, on the roof, in the—"

"In what, girl?" Costos said.

Sean followed Margaret's stalled eyes. She remembered. That's where she had dreamed him swimming. He ran and climbed to the top of the water tank before she could say anything. He had borrowed a tanker that the O'Hares kept on the back of a truck and refilled his tank from the cave's supplies. Andrew had seen him when he pulled the hose to the top of the water tank a few days earlier to pump the water into it. When Aithra saw him stretch over the tank and try to fish something out, she started to whimper as though she knew. Then, as Sean reeled in his catch, she saw her son's stiff arm swing out over the side, and she fell to her knees and let out a guttural

177

scream, which sent the birds resting under the eaves of the roof scattering.

They buried Andrew Nicolaides the following day, next to his twin and his other two siblings, none of whom had breathed a second's breath. Aithra wore a black dress and veil, shutting herself off from the outside world more completely than she had been before, and that was how she continued to live after the death of her first and only born out of four. She no longer bothered to take the short journey to church, and Costos would get anything they needed at the general store or in Langley.. Anne tried to visit her three or four times, so that she could continue to say and show how sorry she was, but Aithra would not see her, and Costos asked Anne to stop coming until his wife had gotten over it, which he knew she never would.

Margaret stopped cleaning the church and tried to get out of going on Sundays whenever she could. It was her fault for sinning and putting blood onto the Jesus man. Sister Ruth had said her vision could be a sign of wickedness and pain, and now the deaths of Sammy, Andrew, and Laura's brother proved it. Nannup told her it wasn't her fault, it was the land paying them back for taking Nipper's people's water, but she wouldn't believe him. She said Hail Marys twice a day to get over it, but the vision of that man hanging in the tree and Andrew's stiff arm kept visiting her.

Those parts of the Wilson boy that they brought back from Vietnam were buried in the cemetery behind the church, about a month after his sister Laura's birthday. The farmland, though, was coming back to life. There had still been no rain in close to two years, but the water from the caves was pumped into a newly dug channel that ran into a previously dry riverbed, and from there it flowed into the veins of the land, nourishing it, so that orchards started to blossom and bear fruit again, and the soil became soft enough to plough, plant, and hoe, and soon many of Sean's fields were packed with the serrated leaves of pineapples in various stages of growth, and he and many of the farmers signed deals to have their produce trucked to the Golden Circle cannery. With money in their pockets once again, the locals started to go to Langley more often, and a few more square dances and cultural functions were held—at the behest of Helen Cartwright—but these were undermined by the televisions that more people were able to afford, and Anne finally bought herself one and spent hours escaping from Andrew's death and her surroundings by watching episodes of *I Love Lucy, Perry Mason,* and more.

# Chapter 14

In the summer, Margaret and Liz began to revise for their exams. Liz was in her final year of schooling, and trying to achieve high enough grades to study medicine at Sydney University. Margaret still had a year to go, now that the sisters had more or less incorporated her into the class. Sometimes, she would say that she found it better to study out in the fields, and she wandered off into the woods where she and Federico would study together. She hadn't told Federico what Laura had said, but she had told him that she could only see and speak to him in secret now, because Mrs McDonald had forbade her to have anything to do with boys since that day she had slapped her and given her extra chores to do, which was true. She wasn't going to let go of Federico just because Laura said, and this way she could still walk with Laura to and from school some days.

Federico had come on some since she had first started to give him the answers to the sisters' questions all those years ago, but he still crept over the work like a feeding caterpillar and required her help now and then. Neither of them had mentioned the dance and kiss at Laura's party, but both would jump barbed fences to make arrangements to study together now, even when there was no need. They sat against trees, facing each other as they did their work, and now and again one of them would steal a look concealed by shyness at the other, and like teasing sparrows flit away again when their eyes met.

"What you going to do after the exams, Margaret?" Federico asked one day. It surprised her, because she had gotten used to his comfortable silences, which were like a travel companion's, except when it was to ask her something about the work.

"I—I want to go on and finish next year," she said. "And then—" She looked up, caught his saturating gaze, and turned away. "And then I don't know."

"I finish this year. Then I work with Papa on the farm." This forced Margaret's questioning eyes to him. How then would this

180

continue? "I still want to learn, Margaret. Will you be my teacher? We can meet here."

An imaginary ball of cotton lodged itself in her throat, and she crushed the hem of her skirt between her hands. "Yes," she said, and it brought on his perfect smile.

"I work with my papa for maybe a year, two, then he give me a piece of land for myself, Margaret. Then I marry."

Margaret looked away again, and her knuckles grew white as her fists tightened around the skirt. "I want to, Margaret, but I don't touch you until we are one." Margaret let out the slivering breath that had coiled itself around her chest. She could hear some of Father Beir's sermons preaching against it rumbling in her head, and if Mrs McDonald even thought she was thinking it, she would give her more floors to scrub. Her body was suffocating from this constant struggle which had invaded it.

"What are you going to do at the end of year ceremony?" she asked, to turn them to purer thoughts.

"I play my father's guitar, like last year. And you?"

"I don't know yet."

"You can sing, Margaret. I hear your voice above all the others in church. You can sing."

Federico walked back through the woods with Margaret to the edge of the McDonalds' place, and they held hands without talking. All the way there Margaret replayed the words Matron Blythe had said. *She will probably marry a half-caste or quadroon and at least her children would stand a better chance.* They were going to do better than that, and she wished she could shout it loud enough for Matron Blythe to hear all the way back at Radley. As they parted she dropped her head and turned it to the side again, and Federico's lips brushed it like butterfly wings.

*** 

The children sitting exams sat in their usual desks with their backs curled over their papers as Sisters Ruth and Agnes took turns to beat a path up and down the rows, when they weren't otherwise spying on them from their watchtower at the front desk. The air in the room simmered like soup, and someone had lent the school a couple of fans that whirred out a cool breeze to those lucky enough to be sitting near the front. Margaret sat at the back as usual, but it didn't bother

her now. She had done as much revision as she could, and she worked her way through the paper with some ease. A couple of times Sister Agnes had come and stood next to her desk to look down at her work, and this made her concentration fly out of the window, but still, she finished the paper with fifteen minutes to go. She scanned it two times to satisfy herself, and then she started to sift through ideas for the school ceremony, and how she would spend her summer holidays. Federico was fidgeting in front of her, and then she caught him glancing over his shoulder at her and swivelling back to chew on his pen. She looked to the front, and Sister Agnes was hunched over her desk, reading a book. Sister Ruth was hovering by Laura Wilson, glancing down at her work. Federico looked back again, and there was a reeling desperation in his eyes, as if he were being sucked below strong currents. "What?" Margaret whispered.

"I can't do number three," he said. Margaret turned to the front again, and Sister Agnes shook her head as if straining against strong winds. Margaret folded her arms and looked down at her paper. "I can't do it," Federico repeated. She raised her head, and Sister Agnes was spread between the pages of her book again. Sister Ruth was still by Laura's desk. She watched Federico's tightening back, not knowing what to do, but then he dropped a blank piece of paper on the floor and shoved it towards her with his foot. He knew she was good at copying other people's handwriting, and on several occasions had even written up his homework for him. Margaret wavered, like a child considering reaching out to touch flames, but still, she put her foot on the piece of paper and dragged it towards her. When it was under her desk she bent down to reach it. Sister Ruth stomped her foot on it first. She took Margaret's completed paper and with a curled finger summoned her to follow. Federico had already turned back and buried his muddled head in his own papers.

Outside in the schoolyard, Sister Ruth asked her, "What is this, Margaret? How is it that you have more papers than I gave you at the start of the test?"

Margaret shrugged her slumped shoulders. "I don't know, Sister."

"You have failed, Margaret." Sister Ruth ripped the paper in half, "And you have also failed all the tests you did earlier in the week."

"But Sister, I didn't cheat." Her flared eyes were stinging and a stream had woken in her nose.

"You are not allowed to have extra papers in the tests, Margaret. You will have to resit the year." Sister Ruth spun back inside without another word.

***

"I will tell them it was me, Margaret," Federico said when he caught up to her in the woods.

"That won't change her mind," Margaret said. "She will only fail you as well. Sister Ruth has never liked me."

Margaret asked him to go and wandered home alone, because she didn't want consoling company now. When she told Anne, she said she shouldn't have been so stupid, but Sister Ruth should not fail her in the other papers and make her resit the year because of that. She would speak to Helen Cartwright and ask her to have a word with Father Beir about it. Margaret felt there was more chance of rain flooding Malee, because she had stopped cleaning the church without telling Father Beir. After the Jesus man had wept tears of blood and then all those people had died, he had agreed with Sister Ruth that it had been a bad sign, and they had changed the cross to encourage worshippers to return and not even raised the issue of her baptism.

Margaret feasted on her worries until she was ill. She wanted to be an educated woman so that when Federico took her to his family they would know immediately that he had made his mother's choice. She had even planned to ask Anne to show her how to make Italian food, so that she would know when the time came. The school ceremony was to take place in the week before they broke up for the summer, and practising to sing for the sisters and the parents now was like planting seeds in a time of drought. If she had her way, Sister Ruth would rot in hell. She asked the Holy Mother to forgive her for thinking that and crossed herself two times, but she hated her so.

***

The desks were cleared from the schoolroom and the chairs arranged in rows along the back so that everyone could see. A small stage had been built up at the front, and a heavy black curtain was draped around it. In one corner of the room Sister Agnes was selling refreshments of lemonade, orange and pineapple juice, and tea and cakes, which had been provided by the mothers. A buzz like milling bees permeated the room as parents stood in-between the chairs

183

chattering, laughing, and exchanging greetings. Many of the men were there because they had to drive their wives and children home after the concert, and Sean sat next to Anne in a clean pair of pants and shirt, which must have pleased her. Aithra, Costos, and Isabel had not attended even though Anne had asked Margaret to drop off an invitation. Anne took up the program and fanned herself again, adding to the crinkling of paper reverberating around the room. Her finger ran down the list of events to seek out Elizabeth's name. It had been typed as Liz next to the poetry reading, which caused Anne's nose to wrinkle. At the bottom was Margaret's name. She had been given three minutes to sing a song.

"Margaret," Sister Ruth said as she walked along the line of performers backstage. "Your time has been reduced to one minute."

"But Sister Ruth, my song takes three minutes," Margaret said, whilst looking directly through her. If her eyes of rock fell on her, then she couldn't be sure that she would refrain from the wicked thoughts that she welcomed into her mind, and she was already saying too many Hail Marys to exorcise previous sins.

"Well, I am giving you one. I won't have you parading any longer than necessary before the men and weakening the moral fibre of this community," Sister Ruth said, and then walked off to peek from behind the curtain at the gathering audience.

Margaret ran outside, her chest heaving like a swollen river tide. She had practised with nerves and no encouraging lubrication for the song, but felt she knew it now. How could she change it like that? She sniffed back furious tears so that they wouldn't come, but that only swelled a bitter lake inside.

Sister Ruth went back to the remaining children, who were chattering with untethered animation and practising their performances. Then they gathered around her and listened to her words of encouragement before the performances started. She thanked them for lifting her spirits so that the deep breaths she took tasted like wine from the communion. She praised them for the aspects of her teaching that she could see in all of them: the way they carried their backs like staffs; many could have outstared a serpent, and all would eventually be capable of preaching a sermon. They were all her children, she declared, and this raised their chests and lifted their spirits so as to cast out any nerves that had accompanied them.

Liz's poetry reading was followed by Federico's solo on the guitar. Anne was still clapping for her daughter when he started, and Sean held her hand to remind her to stop. What Federico did not know in the classroom he made up for in his musicianship; and the tune, which he had composed himself, made the audience call for an encore, which on a nod from Sister Ruth he duly gave. Then a group of girls in Dutch traditional dress performed a folk dance, their clogs slapping against the wooden stage compelling the audience to clap in time to the beat. Their parents stood to give them uproarious applause.

The last performance was Margaret's. They closed the black curtains and called her twice, Sister Ruth rapping her foot against the wooden floor with burning impatience. Then the audience heard sniggers and giggles followed by howling laughter from the children concealed by the curtains. Sister Ruth shouted, "Do not open the curtains," and ran behind them, but the giggling boys at either end nodded their agreement and pulled them back anyway. Sister Ruth stopped struggling with Margaret when she realised she was in the full glare of the audience and ran back to the side of the stage. Margaret unfolded her arms from her white ochre painted torso to reveal her firm nipples, and she began to dance, like someone wading through water, but its consistency was getting thicker with each stroke that she took, until she could barely push it aside with her arms. Anne shot up and bolted for the door with a masked hand over her howling face. Helen Cartwright stood up and watched for a second before pursuing her. "What did I say?" Mrs Wilson said to the woman next to her. "Once a black, always a black. You can't train it out of them." Nannup was smiling in his seat, as if he had glimpsed a relative trekking home for a meet.

Father Beir and one of his deacons finally went up onto the stage and pulled the curtains, and Sister Ruth marched back centre stage and slapped Margaret hard across the face. But she didn't bend. She stood as straight as a desert oak and devoured, like precious water, the agony on Sister Ruth's face.

***

"At least she didn't take everything off," Sean said at the meeting that had been convened in Father Beir's office. "It wasn't that bad." Anne

185

gasped in horror and rushed her hand to her mouth too late to stop it from escaping into the room.

"It's the Devil's work. She must be expelled from the school this instant," Sister Ruth said, and she turned to Sister Agnes sitting next to her, expecting that she would concur, but Sister Agnes fixed her placid eyes on the four who were seated on the other side of the table; Sean and Anne McDonald, Margaret, and Helen Cartwright.

Father Beir kept unlacing his fingers and forming them into a steeple, then sewing them together again. "We have two days until the end of the school year," he said. "Shouldn't we spend the holidays considering what to do?"

"I think that would definitely be a good idea, Father," Helen said.

"I warned Mrs McDonald what they were like." Sister Ruth wagged her accusing finger, and Anne took her chastisement and stared into her lap with aching regret. "The other children saw what happened. Do you think they will know the difference between right and wrong if we don't punish her immediately?"

Margaret's gaze floated past the priest and the two nuns to the butterflies mounted behind glass in wooden frames on the wall. Father Beir's net for catching them was leaning up in a corner of the room. She felt trapped like one of the insects. She hadn't thought about the cannibalising distress for Anne when she did it, just how it would bite like fire ants at Sister Ruth, and in that regard she was unrepentant.

"I understand Margaret did it because you failed her in all of her papers," Father Beir said to Sister Ruth.

"She cheated. I will not have liars and cheats contaminating our school."

"It wasn't quite that, Sister," Sister Agnes said. She clasped her hands and let a gentle smile lift her stout face. "There was no evidence of cheating in the earlier papers—"

"Not that we know of," Sister Ruth interrupted.

"I didn't see any. Did you, Sister?" Sister Agnes turned with humble intentions towards her colleague, but Sister Ruth refused to respond. "And I think what happened in the final test was that the boy in front of Margaret—Federico, I believe—dropped his paper on the floor. Is that right, Margaret?"

Margaret looked at Sister Agnes as if she was caught short by her offer of help. She nodded twice and then dropped her welled-up eyes to her lap.

Anne slapped her on the shoulder as if to show that she would chastise her too. "Speak up, you have a tongue."

"Yes, Sister."

Sean's knee was bouncing and his fingers tapping his thigh with idle impatience. He had been persuaded to come even though he couldn't see the profit in it. There were more fields to be planted and he no longer trusted leaving it to Nipper and his boys. Ever since the water incident their exchanges with him had been like sharp axe blows, and when he walked close to them they would stop what they were saying and start up again when he was gone. He had even told Anne that everyone was giving the incident more weight than a three-year drought, as she had carried on as if Margaret had slept with half the boys in town; waving her arms, ranting about how her position in the community had been undermined, and refusing to speak directly to her. He gazed at Helen Cartwright, as if wondering when she would intervene.

"I would like to propose a solution, if I may?" Helen said, mainly to Father Beir. He sat forward, eager to listen, as though he didn't feel the iron-crossed confidence in his position that would allow him to overrule Sister Ruth.

"Yes, please do," he said.

"It's quite obvious that Margaret should be punished. Her behaviour was extremely rude and I am sure that Margaret will want to offer an apology." Helen turned to Margaret and waited.

"Yes, Mrs Cartwright." Margaret said. It wasn't enough. They were still waiting. "I am very sorry for what I did."

"Right, now," Helen continued. "To expel Margaret for one indiscretion—"

"Two," Sister Ruth reminded her.

"The cheating part is questionable, according to Sister Agnes," Helen said, "but all right, let's say it's two. To expel her for those and affect her for the rest of her life I think would be an injustice. What if we were to say that for the exam incident she has to resit the one paper and for the incident at the school ceremony she is punished in some other way?"

Father Beir sat up with fresh hope. "I think that sounds fair." He addressed it to Sister Ruth, but her face twisted taut, as if all balance had been leeched from it. "And of course, I will be putting your views about more involvement at Mass to the Archbishop in Sydney." She continued to drum her bony fingers against the elbows of her folded arms, as though her firm convictions would allow her to outlast any of them.

"Probably if Sister could decide the nature of the punishment, that would help matters," Sister Agnes offered.

A pious silence guided them for a while. Then, "She will be punished on Friday, the last day of the year," Sister Ruth decided.

"What—What will the punishment be?" Anne asked.

"I will decide the nature of that in my own time," Sister Ruth said.

***

On Friday morning Margaret slipped an exercise book into the back of her panties and put on her heaviest frock before leaving the homestead. She had seen Sister Ruth cane boys before, and as broad as some of them were in comparison to the sister, they still winced and often cried. She wasn't going to surrender her tears for the morbid pleasure of Sister Ruth, and if at all possible, she would try not to wince. Anne had offered her no advice, as she was still wearing the shame of the incident like some stubborn stain, and Liz decided to stay home that day.

Sister Agnes did not come to school either, so Sister Ruth called the register in the morning. Margaret had expected to take her punishment then, but before starting the quiz, which was the traditional way of ending a year, Sister Ruth started talking about sheep. She talked about how they were so foolish that they could not find their way. They had to have a dog show them the way, and even then many of them would backslide, and the dog had its work cut out to round them up and bring them back onto the right path. "But the black sheep," she said, "the black sheep are the most foolish sheep of all and easily led astray. That is why most farmers refuse to keep them; too much trouble." As she spoke she took a chair and turned it towards the class. "Jezebel was such a sheep, and as you all know, her example must not be followed. But as with all sheep, they must be sheared at least once a season." She took out the sharp shearing scissors from her desk and held it up. "Margaret, come and sit here."

Margaret stood up and crept to the front, as if to give her senses time to float free. Federico brushed his hand against her unsteady leg as she went by him. She sat on the chair, eyes cast down, her body shivering, having surrendered its true flame to where it could be shielded from winds of hate. Sister Ruth held out the shearing scissors. "Who will be first to shear the black sheep?" A number of hands shot up, but Federico looked away. "Federico, I think we will begin with you."

Federico stared at her, his olive eyes leaking juice. "I don't want a go, Sister."

"You will all have a go, Federico." She stretched the shears further towards him. Laura forced a crooked smile as he went by her, as though his aching voice had told her all. Federico stood in front of Margaret, hiding her lifeless tears from the class, and he stroked her head like precious stone before cutting an inch of hair. Then he slipped the lock of hair into his pocket before returning the shears to Sister Ruth.

"Who will be next?" she said. Laura's hand shot up, and three or four pupils scrambled over desks and chairs to try and reach the shears first. "Do not act like depraved animals, you will all get a go." The first boy took the shears and cut a lock of Margaret's hair, holding up his trophy; then the next, and the next. Margaret hid her face between her hands, and her shoulders shook to the rhythm of cold tears.

When Laura Wilson came up she grabbed a handful of hair and cast a poisonous stare into Margaret's face. "You're still seeing him, aren't you?" Margaret nodded. Laura yanked her head up, so that all could see her tear-stained face. Then she cut herself a large clump of hair and threw it on the floor. A loud cheer went up from some sections of the class. Sister Ruth finished the cutting, and she made sure that it was within a salt grain of the scalp. Then she asked Margaret to go to the lavatory, take off her panties, and put them on her head, and she sat like that, at the front of the class, for the rest of the day.

Some of the children waited outside to tease Margaret when the day was over, and she ran as if hunted into the woods. Federico tracked her, and when he was sure that they were far enough away so that the others wouldn't follow, he grabbed hold of her arm. She

189

swung around to hit him, screaming, "Nooahh!" But he caught her striking hand and pulled her towards him.

"It's me, Margaret—Federico." He held her in his arms and let her cry, draining it all away, and then he started to kiss her all over her face, on her shaved head, on her wet eyes, in her rust-coloured ears, and on her thin lips. He braced her against a tree, and they pushed against each other, like vines growing with no room. Margaret started to loosen his pants, but Federico grabbed her hand. "No, Margaret. I save it for when I am married, remember?" She didn't want to but did; still he made her spirit rise again so soon, and she rested her head against his heaving chest to tap its warmth and comfort, which were like the early onset of spring.

***

When Margaret arrived home she took off her hat to eat supper with Anne and Liz, and Anne served the food and said grace as if their world had stayed the same. Liz stared an open plea to her mother, imploring her to say something, but she appeared oblivious to Margaret's shame. When supper was done, the dishes washed and the floor scrubbed, Margaret put on her hat and went to sit on the veranda. "Sorry, Margaret," Liz said as she came out to join her. Margaret shrugged as if she didn't care and continued to watch a sprinkling of stars light up the evening skies, whilst remembering her afternoon with Federico. "I'm going to leave two of my hats when I go to Sydney," Liz said. "You can use those if you like."

Margaret forced a flickered smile. "What do you think it will be like in Sydney?"

"Exciting, I hope. Rose O'Hare says she'll show me around and take me to all the parties, but I'll have to watch out for the boys." Liz whispered the last bit and looked around to make sure her mother wasn't at the door.

"What about David?"

"I don't think he liked me that much," Liz admitted. "Anyway, he wants to live here in Malee. I think I would die if I had to live here forever. That's why Mum is the way she is sometimes, she doesn't really mean anything by it. I'm sure she was sorry about your hair too." Margaret turned away her shame, and Liz bit her lip as though she knew that she shouldn't have mentioned it again. She searched for something else to say. "How is it with you and Federico?"

190

Margaret shrugged from behind her reverie, but couldn't hold back the pleasure that seeped from her face like a candle burning from behind curtain lace.

"Have you—? You know, have you?"

Margaret shook her head in a shotgun burst. "No!"

"Oooh, I can't wait to." Liz brought her knees to her chest and squeezed her arms between her thighs. "Rose O'Hare says that's all they do in Sydney, and Laura Wilson says she has, lots of times."

They heard the clump of Sean's boots on the veranda steps before they saw him and hushed as they looked around. Liz said hello dad and Margaret said good evening whilst making her eyes wash over the floor. Ever since Mrs McDonald had accused her and given her more work, Mr McDonald had walked into her thoughts more often. She tried to shut her eyes and lock him out, but she still kept thinking he was watching her and wondering what to do; then she would say three Hail Marys and ask for forgiveness for thinking such lies. Sean nodded and looked at them. His sun-worn eyes held Margaret the longest. Then he went into the house, pushing the door behind him. "What the bloody hell did she do?" they heard him say to Anne.

"I don't like it either, Sean, but at least she gets to finish school."

"I should go down to that church and give her a piece of my mind."

"It won't do any good, Sean. Anyway, she only has a year left."

"That bitch calls herself bloody religious."

"Can you please not use those words, Sean."

They heard him snort with heavy derision, and then there was the clank of his dinner being shoved on the table and the stretched groan of Anne as she pulled off his boots. She came to put them on the veranda but stopped in the doorway. "Who is that?" The girls followed her worried gaze to the tree line. "Sean, does he want you?"

"Who?" Sean asked as he came to the door still chewing.

"That Aboriginal out there watching the house." Anne pointed the boots at him. The thin young man, barely visible in the dark, was hanging things from a tree.

"Oh, that's Nipper's son, Sonny Boy."

"What's he doing?" Anne asked. "He keeps hanging things from that tree and running away."

"It's *Djarada*."

191

"What?" Anne put her hands on her hips and frowned with stretched patience, as if to question his speaking to her in that lingo when he knew she didn't understand it.

"*Djarada*," Sean repeated. He's planting love magic. You said one of Margaret's panties had gone missing from the line. It was probably him who took it."

A scowl cut across Anne's face, and she stepped out into the centre of the veranda and puffed herself up like a cock, so that he could see her. "Elizabeth, Margaret, go inside now. And I want you to scrub that kitchen floor again, Margaret, it's not clean enough."

"Yes, Hmm," Margaret said, and both girls sauntered inside, still looking over their shoulders at the shadowy figure.

"Sean, you go tell him that I don't want him planting any of his mumbo jumbo love magic in our yard."

Sean shook his head as she brushed past him and went back inside.

# Chapter 15

Three days into the holidays Margaret walked down to the rusty tin post box sitting on its wooden stilt, and she found a letter from Mrs McDonald's friend in London. She felt it and was surprised that there was no Christmas card, as Carol usually sent one at that time of the year. As Mrs McDonald took the letter it seemed to bring all her skin alive. Carol hadn't written for several months, and although the letter felt thin, Margaret could sense that catching up on the news from England would be like oil to Mrs McDonald's creaking joints. She put the unopened letter in the centre of the kitchen table and left it as a treat for when she had finished her day of washing, cleaning the house, and tending to her vegetable garden, which she was able to float through that day.

As the girls prepared supper, Mrs McDonald wiped her hands, sat at the table, and filled her lungs with the serene pleasure of fresh air as she opened the letter. She took a sip of the tea that Margaret had made her and started to read. The teacup crashed to the floor and the chair tipped back as she flew up. Liz rushed to her shaking mother, but she palmed her off and ran up to her room. Liz ran after her. Margaret stood rooted to the spot, trying to trace the source of the madness that had just blown through the house like a sudden storm. Whatever caused it was contained in the tea-stained letter that lay on the table. She knew Carol from all of the letters she had secretly read, and now, was she sick like Mrs Cartwright's sister, or maybe even dying? She stood away from the letter bearing bad news until Liz returned to the kitchen.

"I've put her to bed," Liz said. "She's sleeping." Liz looked at the letter lying on the table. "Have you read it?"

Margaret shook her head. "No, but it's from Carol." Liz sat down and picked up the letter, and Margaret read it with her over her shoulder.

*Dear Anne*

*By the time you get this letter it will almost be Christmas, and I haven't even enclosed your card as I normally do, but guess why? I will be bringing your card and gift to Billabong Lodge myself. Let me just give you a few moments to get over the excitement—*

*I arrive in Brisbane on 12th December, where I will spend the week with Kenneth and Maureen Barkley, a lovely couple who I met in London last year. They will put me on a train which will get me as far as Langley by 20th December, and if you can arrange it so that your driver could pick me up and deliver me to your lovely home in Malee, where I will be able to stay with you until 2 January. From there I must go to see my brother who is now living in Sydney.*

*We have so much to talk about, Anne. I can't wait to see you, your handsome Sean and your two girls Elizabeth and Margaret.*

*Your friend always*

*Carol*

"What we going to do, Liz? Hmm will die if her friend finds out that it's all been a lie."

Liz covered her mouth with a hand and closed her eyes, as if to suffocate those embarrassing lies. "I want to go to Sydney before she gets here. Why did Mum have to tell her all those lies?"

"Because it made her feel better, Liz. Like more special inside."

\*\*\*

Margaret had arranged to meet Nannup that night, but Sean had been out pacing the yard and looking up at Anne's window after Liz told him what happened. He had climbed the stairs to Anne's door as though trying to work out what to do or say, but the only thing he kept mumbling was that she still didn't feel he had provided enough so that she could stand eye to eye with the likes of Helen Cartwright. He raised a hand to knock the door, but stopped and went outside to have a smoke. Margaret waited until she saw him go into the dunny, then she climbed out of her window and raced towards the woods. Before she reached the protection of the trees, Sean came out of the dunny, tightening his belt around his washboard waist. She leapt for cover behind a gum tree, not sure if he had seen her. Sean lit another cigarette and then walked towards her. Margaret backed deeper into the woods until she lost sight of him. The grasses and bushes were crinkly dry, and she walked on her toes to avoid awakening their cries. A clump of bushes opened enough to take her inside its womb, and she sat there to rest and hide. In wetter times there would have been a thick canopy in that part of the woods preventing the moon and starlight from penetrating, but many of the trees were near bald, and what leaves remained were yellowed and browned, and so reflected the light. A mixture of Sean's earthy smell with tobacco wafted by and made her feel hungry to the pit of her stomach, as if she had never been fed in her life. She waited a few minutes for her giddiness to subside, and then continued towards her meeting spot with Nannup. As she neared one of the large oaks that guided her, she heard rustling from a bush. She stopped. It could be a possum, but then again, maybe it was loud enough to be a man. Some years ago she would have been able to tell in an instant. There it was again, and again, but it was getting closer and moving faster. She broke into a run. Her heart galloped with blemished fear and her muscles tightened. He had looked at her too? She wasn't sure if it was the same way Isabel had said Costos looked at her, but he had looked. Maybe like a hunter he had bided his time. The bushes were whipping her arms and legs and tearing at her frock, but she ignored them and ran like a hunted mare. He grabbed at her arm from behind, but she pulled away. He slowed her. She stuttered in her gait and fought to get started again, but her knees buckled. She gritted her teeth and pushed herself upright, but he was up against her back. He pounced on her, a hand around her mouth, an arm around her waist and a leg around her feet. They stumbled into the undergrowth, him riding on her back. She closed her eyes. "Shh," he said, his lips pressed to her ear. They were panting near a mile's run out of their lungs. He waited to catch his breath. "It's me—Nannup." Margaret spun towards him, wild-eyed. He put a finger against his lips and then let her go.

Margaret's body was still tight, and she waited for it to unknot. "I—I thought you were Mr McDonald."

Nannup shook his head and beckoned her to stand up. "Mr McDonald doesn't want you." She felt a leaf of disappointment in that statement, hidden amongst the pages of fear that she had unearthed. "I catch you so that you don't run into him."

Nannup waited until she had reclaimed her breath, then she followed him to Billabong Lodge. They waited at the edge of the woods until they saw the light go down in Helen Cartwright's bedroom, then Nannup climbed up the iron post onto the balcony and pulled Margaret up after him. He waved at her to get down, and the two of them crept like caterpillars to Helen's bedroom window.

The window was slightly ajar, and they stayed hidden below the sill and listened to the groaning springs and moans drifting out to mingle with the muggy night. After waiting with the patience of a fisherman, Nannup raised his eyes above the sill, and when he felt it safe to, he signalled Margaret to come up. She shook her raging head. Mrs McDonald was lying at home all by herself, she was sure that was why she was angry. Nannup waved her up again with a jagged scowl distorting his face, and when she didn't move, he grabbed her by the arm and pulled her up. Mr McDonald and Helen Cartwright were locked together, like wrestling mud crabs, only they were enjoying each other.

Margaret slumped back below the sill while Nannup watched them for a while longer, then they climbed through another open window into his bedroom. He lay on his bed, watching her through the murky shadows, and she sat on the floor with her knees pulled to her chest, her lips pouting her distaste.

"What's wrong?" Nannup asked.

"Mrs McDonald is sick, and he is over here with Mrs Cartwright."

"What she sick with?"

Margaret didn't know how much to tell him. He would probably think it was a silly sickness. "Well—it's an unusual kind of sickness." Nannup waited. "Her friend is coming to visit her from England, and she thinks Mrs McDonald lives in Billabong Lodge and has lots of money. When she gets here in a week she's going to see that it's all a lie. So Mrs McDonald is in her bed sick, and he is over here." She jutted her chin towards Helen's bedroom and scorn briefly soaped her face. If she could get Mrs McDonald to cope with life again, then maybe she wouldn't be so mad about what she had done at the school ceremony.

"If you ask me, she have the same kind of sickness as all them people. They always want more, even if it's not theirs to take. Then when they take it they say no one else ever owned it." He shifted on the bed. "Nipper say they call that thing *Terra Nullius*. So they can go to Nipper's people's caves and say *Terra Nullius*, and from then the Government say it's their land and they sell it to Mr McDonald and Mr Nicolaides. That the lie, if you ask me." He turned on his back and looked out at a star, as if hoping its piercing light could draw his rising anger like poisonous pus. "Mrs Cartwright even get another letter from her sister's friend in Sydney to say how sick her sister is, but she say she's going to send them a letter tomorrow to say she can't come because there is no one to look after Billabong Lodge. But I think the real reason she don't want to go is because her sister always asking for some of her money. All this wanting things just cause so much trouble."

They listened to the hoots of an owl and clicking from night insects for a while. Then Nannup said, "I liked your dance at the school ceremony. It show you don't forget all your Koori ways." Margaret didn't look at him. "What they do to punish you?" She lifted her hat to show her sheared head. His fallow gaze remained unseeded. "It will grow back quick, you see."

Margaret left Billabong Lodge before Sean, with something Nannup said causing a dream to be born in her mind.

***

In the morning, Margaret finished her chores early and ran over to Billabong Lodge. Maggie, one of Mrs Cartwright's servants, told her that Mrs Cartwright had walked to the general store to post a letter. Margaret thanked her and cut across fields and then through the woods to try and catch Mrs Cartwright before she reached the general store. She raced down one side and up the other of a dried-out creek bed, and like treacle, she felt a thick vapour running over her, but she couldn't give it a name. She slowed to a brisk walk, thinking that it might be because she was tired, but the feeling grew stranger, like firm hands reaching out and clutching her. Then she remembered that if she had felt like that when she was younger, it usually meant someone was watching her. She saw him immediately she looked around, and Sonny Boy didn't attempt to hide his lanky, charcoal frame. "G'day, Margaret," he said, grinning ochre white teeth at her. "I work for your father, Mr Sean, now. I will build my own house one day, for me, my wife, and little ones." Any children he had would surely be blighted, Margaret thought. She screened off her mind and increased her strides. Then she broke into a run. She looked back, and he was right behind her, but he still appeared to be walking with gaping strides.

As she emerged from the woods panting she ran into Helen Cartwright. "Oh!" Helen exclaimed, jumping back and clutching her chest with sudden fright. "Margaret? What are you doing here?"

"I thought someone was following me, Mrs Cartwright." Margaret peered over her shoulder, but Sonny Boy had vanished.

"Who?" Mrs Cartwright said, following her wide-eyed gaze.

"It was probably a mistake," Margaret said.

"You're not still dreaming about that man you found hanging in the woods, are you?" Mrs Cartwright asked, concern clouding her face.

"No," Margaret lied.

"That's good." Mrs Cartwright gifted her a smile to bolster her confidence. "Anyway, I am just coming back from praying in church. Where are you off to?"

Margaret bowed her head as she thought about the sin Mrs Cartwright had to ask forgiveness for, and she hadn't even lost her hair. "I was just taking a walk. I'll walk back with you if you like."

"That will be very nice, Margaret," Mrs Cartwright said, and they started along the path, first checking over their shoulders one last time.

"What were you praying for, Mrs Cartwright?"

Mrs Cartwright regarded her through distant eyes. "My sister is very sick in Sydney, Margaret, and I can't leave Billabong Lodge to go and see her as there is no one else to run the estate whilst I am gone. I and my sister have never been close, Margaret, but she is the only family I have left."

Margaret had thought Mrs Cartwright would have regarded Nannup as family too, because he was family with Nipper's mob, even though they weren't his real mother and father, and he had asked her to be his sister when he was initiated, but she didn't bother to question it. "I'm sorry about your sister," she said.

Mrs Cartwright looked with softened eyes at her hat, as if she knew something good could be shaped from ill fortune. "And I'm sorry about what they did to you, Margaret." Margaret turned her gaze, stained with the previous night's memories, down to her skirt. He must have told her. She doubted if any of the others who knew had seen her, and as far as Mrs Cartwright was aware, Nannup still couldn't talk.

"You know Mrs McDonald keeps the books and does all the paperwork for Mr McDonald's farm, and I'm sure she would be happy to help. She would even stay at Billabong Lodge for you to make sure that the homestead was well kept."

"I'm sure your mother has far too much to do, Margaret."

"Some time back, her mother was very sick in England, and Mrs McDonald couldn't go to see her and she died. I think that's one of the reasons why Mrs McDonald is always so sad."

"Is that so?" Mrs Cartwright said.

"Yes. Family is really important, and if you part for good on an argument, then it eats at you forever."

Mrs Cartwright read her thoughtful face, and seemed to decide that it was full and brimming in experience. "Thank you for that, Margaret. You are very wise."

They came to the junction in the track where Mrs Cartwright turned off for Billabong Lodge. Margaret waited, but she said nothing except good day Margaret and kept going as though still wading through her thoughts.

***

When Liz had finished feeding her mother the broth, Margaret collected the lunch tray from her room. She left Liz reading her passages from the Bible. Sean had not bothered to go into the room and had kept snorting and shaking his head before going out to his fields. Margaret heard the car whisper into the yard whilst she was washing the dishes, and she ran to the front of the house. Only one car in Malee sounded like that. Helen Cartwright slid out of the driver's seat and climbed up onto the veranda. "Good day, Mrs Cartwright."

"Hello again, Margaret," Helen said. "Is your mother at home?"

"Yes, she's in bed. But you can go up to see her."

"I think I will, Margaret." Helen went up and Margaret stood at the bottom of the stairs, where she could hear them in muted conversation. Helen greeted Anne and commiserated with her illness. Then she told Anne about her own sister's deteriorating health and that she had decided to go to Sydney; for how long she didn't yet know. Anne said how sorry she was at this news and asked Helen to pass on her good wishes to her sister. Then Helen said she would like to know if Anne could keep an eye on things while she was gone. She could also spend as much time at Billabong Lodge as she would like. Anne said she would be happy to help out with the running of the place, but she couldn't stay there, it wouldn't be right. But Helen told her that she would be doing her a favour by keeping an eye on the homestead, and that Anne and her family had already done so much to lift her spirits that she didn't know how to thank her. Anne said no, you have done far more to support me, Helen, which in an unexpected sort of way was true, given Anne's revulsion for the intimate and Helen's energetic celebration of it, but then she conceded, well, once I feel better I will look in for you Helen.

***

Anne McDonald was out of bed and pacing the room in a well of internal dialogue before Helen Cartwright's car had completely left the yard. She could rely on the girls not to say anything, but what about Sean, and what if she met anyone from town? She really wasn't sure; it was a chance, but she decided to take it.

***

"What the bloody hell do you mean we're moving into Billabong Lodge for a few weeks?" Sean said.

"Please don't use that language, Sean—the girls might hear you." Anne put his dinner on the table and then went to scour the pot. "Helen has gone to Sydney—"

"Gone to Sydney? When?"

"Well, she left right after she came here this afternoon. Her sister is ill."

"She didn't—" Sean stopped himself.

"She didn't what, Sean?"

"Oh, nothing." He shook his head as if to throw off drops of rain and started to eat his dinner.

"We are only going to spend a few weeks there, Sean. Helen insisted, as I am going to be keeping an eye on the place. It will be like a holiday." Anne kept scouring the same clean spot in the pot, waiting for him to answer. But Sean was quiet, a tight frustration creasing his face.

"I thought it would also give us more room while Carol is here," she continued.

He banged down his fork. "That's what this is all about, isn't it? What? Isn't the home I've provided good enough for your friend?"

"It's not that, Sean." Anne squeezed the dishcloth with anonymous strength, as if to conceal what she was really thinking. "It's just that we can't have her sleeping with one of the girls, and—"

200

"If we slept in the same bed the way we were meant to then that wouldn't be a problem, would it?"

Anne swayed like a sapling caught by a sudden wind, and she breathed in deep rhythms as if to cleanse the vile thought from her. She didn't want to, but if it was going to get her through the two weeks, then— "I'm sure we can sleep in the same room at Billabong Lodge. And we can't really expect Carol to use the outside lavatory; she won't be used to that."

"It's a bloody dunny, not a lavatory. And if she's coming to experience the outback, then she'd better bloody well get used to going outside, and the heat, and the flies."

Anne swallowed any doubts, but she braced herself against the wind. "I and the girls are moving over tomorrow, Sean, to get the place ready." Sean threw his fork onto the plate and walked outside.

*\*\**

Anne, Margaret and Liz spent their first day at Billabong Lodge packing away any pictures, clothes or personal effects that indicated Helen Cartwright lived there. Anne tried a couple of Helen's evening dresses that fitted her and she kept those out to wear during the visit. Margaret spoke to the gardener and two maids, Sara and Maggie, and they agreed to cooperate for a dollar each at the end of the two weeks. Anne then familiarised herself with the homestead, making sure to examine the dairy where the four cows were milked each morning to provide the house with milk, butter and cheese. In the old coach house she found the Rover Coupe, which Helen's driver had returned after taking them to the station, but he had since left the area to visit family over the holidays. "Can you drive it?" she asked Bob, the homestead's Aboriginal gardener, who had a white salt and pepper beard and a stuttering gait.

"No, Mrs McDonald," he said. "I seen Mrs Cartwright drive, but them machinery and me, we don't get on."

"We have to pick up my friend from Langley in a few days, Bob. Can you practise here in the yard?" She pointed along the gravel track that wound around the homestead. "There'll be an extra dollar in it for you."

"Okay, Mrs McDonald, but if that there car gets hurt, then I won't take the blame."

"I'm sure it won't, Bob."

Anne reviewed the results of her work the night before going to Langley. They hadn't had to change much in the homestead, but by putting out some of her own things it made her feel more at home. Sean had refused to come, but she would say that he was camping out in the fields for several weeks with his men. Now all she had to do was hold her nerve, and fate and God's blessing would do the rest, as that's what they survived on out in these parts. She would go to confession after Carol had gone.

*** 

They started out for Langley a little after sunrise, but they could have done with starting earlier still. Anne had asked Bob to borrow a suit from a friend of his, and when he held the car door open for her and the girls the way she had shown him, he was still bending to turn up his pants' legs, which dragged in the dust. Bob stalled the car five times on the way to Langley, on each occasion saying how sorry he was. The car weaved drunkenly along the empty dirt roads, on one occasion almost running off into a ditch. Had the roads been used by more than the occasional car or truck, they would all have been killed. It was all Margaret and Liz could do to stop themselves from laughing as Anne told Bob how well he was doing, to encourage him, whilst her knuckles grew white around the door handle.

The car jerked to a halt a little too late outside the station and all the passengers were thrown forward as one of the front wheels mounted the pavement. Anne squeezed the cross hanging from her neck and stepped out of the car to ease her aching back. Liz and Margaret waited until Bob had gone under the bonnet to check the water, and then they released the laughs that they had been holding back, like overripe farts, all the way from Malee. They were more than two hours late, and Anne looked up and down the platform for her friend. Only then did she realise that they hadn't even exchanged photographs in the more than twenty years that had gone by, and she wasn't quite sure what Carol looked like now. She walked past the oddly dressed woman on the platform to the stationmaster's office and asked him if anyone had come in on the train from Brisbane. He scratched and shook his bearded head, then, as she was about to walk away, he remembered and pointed back down the platform. Before Anne had time to turn around, the woman in the batik sarong and

202

white cotton blouse was upon her. "Anne? Anne McDonald?" she asked.

Anne turned and stared in speechless awe at the towering, lean woman, whose plaited brunette hair with beads and trinkets dangling from it, and large round earrings, had made her look much younger from a distance. Now she could see that the woman's eyes sagged, though her thin face drew it in a little, and she had a few fine-as-hair lines around her mouth and across her forehead. "Carol Saunders? Is that you?"

Carol's sandals slapped against the platform and the bells on them jingled as she ran forward and threw her arms around Anne. "It's so good to see you," she squealed, and she started to cry.

Anne patted her on the back, "It's good to see you too, Carol." She looked around Carol at the girls who were standing outside the car, and when she didn't think Carol would release her, said, "The girls are here, come let me introduce you."

Bob loaded Carol's baggage into the boot whilst she gave Liz and Margaret the same lengthy hugs she had given to Anne. Then she gave Bob a hug, which was cut short when Anne said we should try to get back before dark, as Bob didn't like driving in the dark, whilst clutching her cross again, as if imploring it to act as her talisman in this her time of need. She knew she was doing wrong, but if God granted this one wish, made it succeed, then she would devote herself to Him. She had promised it in her prayer.

***

Margaret sat in the back of the car and Carol and Anne climbed in next to her. Carol held onto Anne's hand. "You know, I should have recognised it was you immediately, Anne. Apart from a few years added, you look very much the same."

"I didn't recognise you at first," Anne admitted, whilst reaching into her handbag for a rummage so as to break Carol's hold. "You still look so youthful."

"I haven't had a husband and two girls to bring up, Anne. I'm sure that's helped. Not that I would have anything against bringing up two such lovely girls." Margaret smiled from behind her perfect entrancement, drinking Carol's jasmine scent all in. She already liked the real Carol more than in her letters, although the frown she saw on Liz's face reflected through the driver's mirror said she wasn't so easily flattered. She wondered how Carol and Mrs McDonald, who were like differently cut patterns, had become friends. Had Mrs McDonald been more like Carol when she was younger?

They survived the fairground of a ride home, and Carol stepped out of the car in front of the homestead as the sun was retiring over the horizon. "So this is Billabong Lodge," she said. She stood with her hands on her hips and took in the red brick homestead and sloping gardens for a while. Then she breathed in the hot smells like the steam from freshly brewed coffee. "This will be good for my karma."

"What's that?" Margaret asked.

"My spirit, Margaret. It's that part of me that can do magical things."

Margaret's eyes glinted as if they had just been mined. She had never heard any of them talk about doing magical things, and Mrs McDonald had positively discouraged it.

"Come on inside, Carol," Anne said. "I'll show you to your room. You can freshen up and then we'll have supper."

In the morning Liz burst with bubbling animation into Margaret's bedroom. "Come and see what she's doing." She pulled Margaret out of bed to the window. Carol was sitting on the grass between the rose bushes. The soles of her feet were together, and her hands were trying to meet behind her back, one from the top and the other from the bottom.

"What's that?" Margaret asked.

"I don't know," Liz said. "I thought she was praying at first."

Carol adjusted herself so that she sat with her feet beneath her, and then she leaned her head back until her shoulders were touching the grass. An "Oh!" escaped from Margaret, and she covered her mouth and looked away, as if evading moulding memories. "She isn't wearing anything on top."

"I know," Liz said.

"But that's sinful."

Liz severed her weeping stare from Margaret's shaved head, which had barely begun to sprout back. Margaret took her hat off the dresser and put it on. She washed, changed, and went out into the garden and pretended to wander around before stumbling upon Carol. She was lying on the grass in shorts but no top, letting the morning sun gently roast her. The nipples of her pancake breasts

204

were erect and firm like rosebuds. "Good day, Carol. What are you doing?"

Carol shifted her shades to the top of her head. "Hey, g'day, Margaret. Have I said that right?"

"Yes."

"I'm tanning." She saw the mystery drifting over Margaret's face. "I'm trying to get my skin a little brown; it looks quite nice on me."

"Is that why you don't have a husband?"

"What?" Carol sat up with a wide-awake smile. "I don't have a husband because I don't want one. What makes you think my tanning will stop me from finding one?"

Margaret wanted to retract into her skin now, when her whole intention had been to explore her woman self in Carol's presence. "Just something I heard someone say."

"What happened to you hair?" Carol pointed to Margaret's wire-wool head. Margaret pulled the hat further down on her head. "I sinned." She saw that Carol was waiting to hear the extent of her sin. "I showed my breast at school." Her wandering eyes fell on Carol's nipples, and she pulled them away, as if to find the right path again.

"I guess I had better cover up then," Carol whispered, whilst folding a frolicking arm over her breasts as if they were being spied on from the bushes. "Come here." She beckoned Margaret next to her and took off her hat. She had a saffron scarf with her, and she folded it in half and tied it around Margaret's head so that the two ends fell onto her shoulders like plaits. Then she ran a few of the beads from her own hair up them. "That's better," she said as she held up Margaret's chin. "You're a very pretty young lady." Margaret looked away and pulled at the grass. "I asked Anne this morning what there was to do in Malee, and she said apart from farming nothing much happens here. Now I'm sure you must know of some interesting things to do?" Margaret pressed her lips together as if to say a travelled woman like Carol wouldn't find the things she did interesting. "Come now," Carol said as she took Margaret's chin and turned it back towards her.

Margaret and Liz spent the days wandering the forests with Carol, showing her the places where birds nested and possums curled in trees sleeping, and naming all the trees for her. They picked ripe fruit off the trees in the orchards for lunch, and then enjoyed the game of touring the homesteads whilst staying far enough away so that no one spoke to their visitor and gave their deception away. They didn't go to church either, which Margaret didn't mind, because she didn't have to subject her head to all of Malee's gaping scrutiny. One scorching afternoon Carol asked if there was anywhere that they could go for a swim. Liz said no right away, but Margaret hesitated, then said they could swim at the caves where the homesteads now had their water pumped from. Liz said that she needed to pack her books and clothes for Sydney, so Margaret took two lanterns and their lunch, and she and Carol walked the few miles to the caves. They lit the lanterns before going inside the widened entrance, and once in, they held them up to the ochre paintings on the walls. "These are fantastic," Carol said as she ran her hand over the walls. "How old are they?"

"Older than all things." Margaret repeated what Nannup had told her when he had brought her there.

"Do you know what they mean?"

"Some of them are spirits that the Koori people talk to when they have an important corroborree," Margaret said. "Those over there—" She shone the lantern on another wall. "—tell some of the dreamtime stories about how creation started."

"You mean like Adam and Eve in the Bible?"

"Hmm hmm," Margaret said.

Carol rested her head in the bosom of one of the X-ray women. "I can feel my karma in this place, Margaret."

Margaret could feel it too, but she hadn't said anything, because she had gotten used to burying that part of herself. "I can feel mine a little, too," she finally said.

Carol smiled as if she knew. "Don't ever deny it, Margaret. If something is right it never dies."

They stripped off and swam by lantern light in the underground lake, and after they had lunch they swam some more.

"You should bring Anne here, Margaret. I'm sure she would enjoy it."

"Mrs McDonald doesn't really like coming out into the bush."

"But it's so beautiful, Margaret. I suppose it can be lonely out here though, especially with Sean off working on the land for weeks at a time."

Margaret slipped her dress over her head without looking at Carol and pretended not to hear.

"Margaret?"

The two women froze in the booming echo of a man's voice, and Margaret's eyes widened in recognition. Sonny Boy walked into the lantern light, his manhood dangling before his naked body. "I know you will come to me, Margaret, I have sung djarada into your things." He held up her panties that had been stolen from the line some months earlier. "I am ready to take a wife, Margaret."

Margaret grabbed her shoes and one of the lanterns. "*Run, Carol, run!*" She ran towards the mouth of the cave without looking back, straight into Sean at the entrance.

"Margaret? What are you doing here?" he asked as he gazed around for an answer.

"I was swimming with Carol, and we saw Nipper's son, the one that planted them things in the trees and took my clothes, we saw him." She was panting like a well-run mare, and he held onto her to slow her. His firm, steady grip bit restraint into her skin, but still, she inched herself forward and inclined her head until it was resting on his shoulder. Sean seemed thrown by surprise and remained rooted to the spot. Then they heard someone coming towards them.

"Let me have that." Sean took the lantern from her and walked into the cave, holding it above his head. Carol strolled out to meet him.

"Hello, I'm Carol." She held out her hand, but Sean stared past her. "He's gone. He didn't mean any harm, I don't think."

"I'm Sean, Sean McDonald." He finally took her hand.

"I'm so pleased to meet you, Sean. I was beginning to think I was going to leave Malee without ever seeing you. You're even more handsome than Anne described you in her letters."

Sean grunted as if to conceal his cocktail of sloshing pleasure and confusion, as he hadn't known that Anne talked about him in her letters.

He drove them back to Billabong Lodge with Carol talking all the way. She told him how much she loved the country and was sorry that she wouldn't be able to spend more time. They seemed to like each other immediately, as Carol was as easy and natural as the land to be around. When they arrived at the homestead Anne was pacing a hole in a spot on the veranda. "Where have you been?"

"We went for a swim, and met Sean on the way back," Carol said. "I've persuaded him to stop working on Sunday and come over for dinner, so we can really meet." Carol waved to Sean as he pulled out of the yard, and Anne slipped on a muzzled smile and did the same.

*\*\**

Carol waited until she saw Anne alone in the garden, pruning the roses, before she went to her. Her time at Billabong Lodge was almost up, and they hadn't found time to have one of those unbridled chats they used to have in London all those years ago. Anne was always consumed by work. "What are you doing now, Anne?" she said as she crept up on her.

"Oh!" Anne jolted around as if her skin had been singed, and the pruning shears fell on the grass. "You surprised me, Carol. I thought you had gone for a walk with the girls again."

"No, Anne." Carol handed her back the pruning shears. "We really haven't talked since I've been here, so I thought this might be the right time."

"Oh, aren't you having a good time?" Anne kept on pruning. The lie was weighing like slabs of stone on her, and she couldn't ease them enough to face Carol.

"Yes, I am. The girls have been lovely, and the outback is so beautiful. You really should go out with the girls and enjoy it sometimes."

"It's all around us, Carol." She waved the shears. "You can't miss something this big. I can see lots of it from our kitchen window." She was thinking of the view from her own homestead and immediately corralled her thoughts. A raw chill ran through her, as if the Holy Spirit had rested judgement's hands on her.

It was Carol's hand on her shivering back. "But are you really happy, Anne?"

Anne chuckled as if on empty fumes. "As you've said, Carol, I have my handsome Sean, the girls, and our lovely homestead. Who wouldn't be happy with all this?" Her arm swept an arc around them.

"Sharon Jones wouldn't. You remember that toff that used to come into the department store and would only make her serve him?"

"Yes—" Anne scoured her memory. "Lord Fussy Boots."

"That's it, and he was a Lord too. He put her up in a Knightsbridge flat and she had three children for him, all hush-hush. He died last year and left her millions."

208

"Lucky old Sharon." Anne smiled. "I don't suppose she would want my life, then."

"I don't know, all this open countryside and fresh air—" Carol held her hand. "Why didn't you come home for your mother's funeral, Anne?"

Anne hovered over a wilted rose she was about to prune and closed her eyes. "I—I felt ashamed, Carol. Ashamed that I left without really telling her, and that I hardly wrote to her. She wouldn't have been proud of me."

"But she was." Carol rubbed her hand. "You had the guts to try something different. Everyone else just complained about the situation. She accepted you for who you are and I do too, Anne—I always will." Anne looked away, as her conscience was bearing down on her. "You'll have to come and visit when I get back."

"I don't know, Carol, it's been so long."

"Sometimes you need to see a bit of what you left behind to revitalise yourself and make you realise what you have, Anne. It's changed some, but there's a lot that you'll recognise, and you won't be out of place. You'll fit back in as if you had never left. It's your choice, but you can come anytime." Anne smiled like a drought-ridden flower and nodded. "Now come and show me this garden of yours," Carol said, and she pulled her off towards the rhododendrons.

\*\*\*

The only other times that Sean had worn the suit that Anne had bought for him some years earlier was when Andrew, Costos and Aithra's dead boy, had been baptised and buried, but Anne had sent Liz to tell him to wear it. He rolled his neck and eased his finger between the shirt collar in order to breathe, but it was tighter than a hen's fart. Maggie let him in with a "Hello, Mr Sean," made to sound as if she worked for him, and he grunted something back at her. She led him to the drawing room, where the ladies had been waiting for more than an hour.

"Sean." Carol got up, embraced him, and pecked him on both cheeks.

Anne followed her and touched her cheek against Sean's, then they both stepped back, not recognising this. "Carol, Margaret, Elizabeth, let's go through for dinner now, it's already overdone."

Sean didn't take the bait, not because he was too tired, but because he was never all there with Anne, and it passed over him. "I've got to go use the dunny," he said, and he hurried off up the stairs before Anne could correct him or quietly pass him a signal as to where to find it. As he opened the door to go in he saw her watching him as though a spark had flickered in her mind, but it was quickly snuffed out by her whirling anxiety over the dinner she had arranged, and she marched off as though her thoughts had hurtled back to making sure it was a success.

When Sean came to the table, Anne said, "As the head of the house, would you like to say grace, Sean?" She half expected him to say no, but he gave her a you-know-I don't-say-grace look and then bowed his head.

"Thank you for what we are about to receive. We also give thanks for Carol's visit and we all hope that she has enjoyed it, and will be able to tell her friends good things about Malee."

Carol gripped his hand. "I will, Sean, I will."

"You know I am not someone usually good for praying, but as I have started, Lord, I pray that you can help us all to be satisfied with what we have and not want that which others have. Amen."

He saw the vexed sting in Anne's eyes when he opened his, before she turned her attention to Sara. "You can start to serve now," she said.

"Yes, Mrs McDonald." Sara gave a modest curtsey and went to bring the food in.

"Did Nipper's people get any of their water back, Sean?" Anne asked, whilst still directing Sara with the serving. He shook his head and smiled as if she had trumped him. She coveted Helen Cartwright's home, and he had coveted Nipper's people's water, and taken it too. He didn't know she had this type of spirit in her. Maybe Carol's visit would bring out more about Anne McDonald that he didn't already know, which was probably most of her.

Sara served up fresh water trout with a vinaigrette dressing and Sean stared in ignorant dismay at the three-deep cutlery arrangement flanking his plate like some over-armed battalion which he was unable to command. The women picked up their outer pieces of cutlery and proceeded to surgically remove fish from the bone whilst Sean's mind wandered in confusion. Liz kicked him under the table and gripped her fish knife and fork firmly, so he picked his up and followed her in removing flesh from bone.

"So, how is your work in the fields going, Sean?" Carol asked.

"We've crated much of the harvest." He picked fish bone out of his mouth with his fingers. "And we're getting ready to plant another field."

"I wish I had time to come out and see you work, but I leave on Tuesday."

"Sean," Anne said, "will you be able to drive Carol and Liz to the station in Langley?" She showed him how to take fish bone out of his mouth on the back of the fork as she spoke. He ignored her and took another bone out with his fingers. Anne cleared her throat and removed an imaginary piece of bone from her mouth on the back of the fork.

Sean banged his cutlery onto the table. "Can't a man eat his food without putting on a performance?"

Anne forced an ironic smile. "Aren't you feeling very hungry, Sean?"

"No, I'm not," he said as his chair squealed back over the floor and he stood up, throwing his napkin onto the plate. "I'm going out for a smoke." He left the room.

"Desert should be good," Anne said, as if to divert minds whilst she hid spilt stains. "Maggie has made an apple and blackberry pie."

\*\*\*

A chilled night had drifted in and cicadas had begun to sing. Sean leaned back on the bench and watched the smoke he blew escape to freedom through the iron railings on the veranda. He had taken off his tie and pulled his shirt collar so that he could breathe. He heard the tiny bells jangling on Carol's sandals before he saw her. "Can I have a light please, Sean?" She rested a manicured hand on his thigh and leaned forward to light her joint from his cigarette. She took two quick draws as if she had been waiting for them all day, and they seemed to shake loose any small remnants of tightness. "Would you like to try one of these?"

Sean scrutinised the weed hanging from her slender fingers. "I'll give it a go," he said, and she lit another joint from her tin and passed it to him. He took a few drags and settled his head against the wall.

211

"You really have to bear with her, Sean, she needs a little bit of home to keep going."

"A little bit? If you ask me, she wants to bring all of home with her. What about trying to live by some of my ways sometimes?"

"I know, Sean, but the further you travel the more of home you seem to want to hold on to."

"She chose to leave, nobody forced her. If you keep harking back to things in the country you came from then you'll never set down deep enough roots to appreciate anything in your new home. You seem to like the place well enough."

"I do, especially those rock paintings I saw and the naturalness of the land. But I don't know if I could live here. I'd want to go native, and somehow I don't think that would be acceptable. I'm a bit of a nomad at heart." She seemed to read his cross-eyed retreat. "A wanderer."

"I used to do a lot of wandering when I was younger," Sean said. "Worked on a lot of stations and seen most things a man wants to see. But at some point you want to settle down and make something your own, to serve you when your wandering days are over."

"I suppose I'm a bit lucky in that respect. I sold my business in Kings Road and now I can afford to travel."

Sean examined the joint. It was freeing his tongue in a way that he liked. "Where did you get these?"

"I buy mine at a greengrocer's in Ladbroke Grove."

"You think any stores here will sell it?"

She laughed. "They're illegal, Sean." He looked at the shortening stick with renewed interest. "If you get the seeds you can grow it out here, no one will ever find it." Sean filled his lungs again, held it like a dam fighting flooded streams, and then let it out when he needed air.

\*\*\*

Margaret helped Liz to pack her books and clothes, and they sat up until late at night talking about what Sydney would be like. Anne didn't help with this or talk much about Sydney with her daughter, as if by not doing so would hold back the day, and, because she was bitten by envy, as Elizabeth was escaping this place without her. When Margaret went to her room, which was really Nannup's, sleep had not summoned her, and so she sat in the middle of the bed tying the headscarf that Carol had given her in several different ways. When

212

she thought everyone else had gone to sleep, she heard the bells on Carol's sandals stealing down the stairs. She looked out of the window and saw her running across the lawn towards the old coach house, where the cars were now kept. Carol had spent the whole evening on the veranda with Mr McDonald, time enough to arrange it. It ignited her flaming fury, especially after the way he had held her in the caves. She crept downstairs on the tongue of the flame and followed Carol to the coach house. She stood with her ear to the cracked door, but she couldn't hear them. The door squeaked its welcome when she eased it enough to get inside, but she managed to slip into the dark building unseen. The suspension on the car was rocking back and forth, back and forth, and Margaret could make out Carol's discarded nightie outside the back door. She stooped in a corner and took time to attune her ears, and after a minute she could hear Carol gasping for air. The back door flew open and Carol's arm fell out. A hand pulled it back, but she hadn't been able to see it through the velvet blackness, which was only intermittently cut by sprinklings of silvery moonlight slipping through cracks. Then his head rolled forward like a piston as he rode on Carol, and Margaret saw first his curly matt of hair and then Sonny Boy's glistening face. She covered her mouth in time to arrest her scream. Then she jumped up from where she was and bolted out the door. She dragged Carol's scarf from her head, threw it to the ground, and ran into the house, crying as if she had been bereaved.

Margaret went to her room and stayed there for the rest of Carol's visit, saying she was ill. On the morning Carol and Liz were to leave for Sydney, Liz came in to say goodbye, but when Carol came in Margaret sprawled in a fake sleep. She watched from her window as Mr McDonald pulled away in Helen Cartwright's car to take them to the station in Langley, and she prayed that Carol wasn't about to bring another of those blighted children into the world.

# Chapter 16

They were onto their third old ute—the old man, who now leaned forward at the waist like a withering maize stalk, his wife, whose hair had bleached grey and thinned, and the rest of the mob that rode in the bed of the ute. There were more heated silences between them too, as their arguments about when to stop the search for their girl—their stolen girl, she would remind him—only inflamed their molten rage. The old woman had encountered many visions, seeing the girl's trails in this place or that, hearing her call to them from some landmark not too far off, and always they had hurried there to find no trace of her. They had worked at stations along the way to earn enough to buy their food and fuel, and on four occasions they had stopped at stations for longer than the old woman would have wanted to: once to wait for their son Joe's three-year jail term to end, twice until they could afford another rundown ute, and once because Toby was seduced by the crinkle of money, now that he could earn the same pay as white men, after the trades unions had voted for equal pay for Aboriginals in '65—although that is not the reason he gave to his travel-eager wife. The constant moving had also kept their grandchildren safe from those who might want to take them away, too. But they were all corroded through laying themselves bare to the dust and heat, vibrations pounding their spines as the ute clattered over uneven roads, tracks and desert trails, and from not being able to wake in the same place each day. All except the old woman, that was. She was roused to a restless life by the need to find her girl.

The ute bounced over the open desert and spewed up choking dust. Daisy leaned forward in her seat, peering as if through billowing snow at a shadow in the distance. "What's that out there?" She pointed a wrinkled finger at the hazy figure. Toby scanned the flat horizon, but he couldn't see a thing. "Out there, man," Daisy insisted. Toby slowed the truck and squinted through the heat haze. He could barely make out the Koori walking towards them. The leather-skinned old man, supporting himself on a spear, stopped as they reached him. "G'day, Nkuppa," Daisy said.

The old man considered them as though examining a termite mound before responding, "G'day, *Yarmuk*. Welcome to our country."

The others all greeted him and he them.

"Thank you for your welcome, Nkuppa. Can we take you somewhere?" Daisy asked.

He shook his head. "No. I meet my mob. They only a little way over there." He pointed his spear towards the rolling hills some distance behind them.

"So this your mob's land then, Nkuppa?" Daisy said as she surveyed the barren scrub.

"Depends if you mean by white man's laws or our laws; we been here long before they come."

"Your mob's laws good enough for us," Daisy said, and she ignored Toby's sour reproach which had turned on her, as he had warned her about unbinding caution from her words before.

The Nkuppa blinked his gummy eyes at the bedraggled mob in the bed of the ute. "Them children look hungry, *Yarmuk*. You looking for a feed?"

"Yes," Daisy said, even though her stomach still cried out after she ate, and it would remain that way until she had her girl back, but the young ones had to eat.

"You find good tucker over there." He thrust his spear west. "Take what you need, and leave the land so that more can grow."

"Thank you, Nkuppa, we will." Daisy and the others waved to him as he continued towards the hills in the distance.

They reached the hunting grounds with enough daylight in store to gather food. They made camp by a small billabong, where tepid water bubbled up from between the rocks. There, they refilled their cans with the silky water that had flowed through the bodies of their ancestors for thousands of years and filtered its way back through the earth to wait for them. Then the children gathered firewood from fallen trees and branches, and followed Daisy to the bushes to search for tucker. She showed them how to dig for yams and leave enough of the root in the ground so that its life cycle would remain unbroken. They also gathered berries and seeds, which they would eat until the main meal was ready.

Joe carried the rock-wallaby that his father had shot back to camp, slung over his shoulder. He lit the fire and burnt the downy hair off the wallaby. Then he laid the carcass on a bed of gum leaves in the pit that his brothers had dug. His mother placed the yams around the meat, and then it was covered with more gum leaves, a layer of hot rocks and white smouldering charcoal.

Another fire was burning, and as the blue chill drifted in, one of the women took the children to sit around it and tell them a story about the dreaming while they waited for the tucker. They left Toby and Daisy by the pit oven, as they knew they had to talk. Toby sat on his spindly haunches and sifted sand through his fingers as if he were weighing time. "Our grandchildren are looking more hungry every day, wife."

"Our daughter is probably more hungry, husband."

Toby stopped, as there was not much he could say to that. Daisy was leaning back on her elbows and reading the stars for some sign.

"We should stop and earn some more money for food and gas. We haven't much left," Toby said.

Daisy snorted in open contempt. "Each time we stop you all don't want to leave, and she gets further away. I can feel her now, husband, she is very close."

"When will this end, my wife?"

"Do you love our daughter, my husband?" Daisy sat up and challenged him with a stare.

"Of course I love her!" Toby caught sight of the others by the fire and threw a noose around his voice. "What do you mean?"

"If you love her it must never end."

"What about them?" He flicked his head with heavy disguise towards the others. "They must live too. It is no life for them chasing after shadows."

"You think my visions are just shadows?"

"That's not what I meant."

"Did I not see your mother's death? Did I not see the birth of all of our grandchildren?" She raised her pitted chin towards the children playing by the fire. "Are you doubting me now? Did I not tell you that our youngest son, Joe, would not find a wife?"

"If we go back to our land he might find one."

"Joe is like me, his mother; he will never give up the search."

216

Toby bowed his head, as if to bury his betrayal. "I spoke to all of our children, wife. They are all tired."

"When? Why didn't they tell me?"

"They are afraid to disappoint you, my wife."

Daisy reached across and held his arm. "We are close, my husband, I can feel her like I am touching you now. Just a little while, give me a little while."

He didn't return her gaze, which was loaded with the visionary's appeal by which she always persuaded him.

The caramelised odour of roast meat rose from the pit oven, distracting the children from their story. Toby removed the charcoal and rocks. He divided the wallaby meat, placing the tail, the best piece, onto Daisy's tin plate. She placed the largest yam onto his plate and put the *billy* on to make tea as she called the others over for their tucker.

"G'day, mates." The voice sprung from unblemished darkness and snared all of their attention. The stranger stopped a few yards from their fire. Daisy signalled the kids to run and hide inside the ute. After all, she had heard that in some places they were still trying to take their kids.

"G,day, Mister. You eaten yet?" Daisy asked.

"No, miss. What you have there smells good."

"Come and sit down," Toby said. He made a space for the *swagman* between himself and Daisy, and the man slumped down and took out a tin plate and mug from his *swag*.

"Thank you for your hospitality," he said as Daisy put a piece of her wallaby tail onto his plate and Toby gave him half of his yam. He licked his greasy fingers after the first bite. "This is real good tucker." All were too hungry to talk and gorged on their food. Daisy poured the stranger's tea first and then the rest of them. That was the way when they had a guest.

The swagman caught Joe staring at his egg-white eye, and he tapped a finger under it. "Don't you stand behind no wild horse, mate, else you might lose your sight like me."

Daisy took a sip of her tea. "You come from far, mate?"

"I've been wandering all over. A bit of work here, a little there, seen most places. How about you folks?"

"We've been looking for our girl," Daisy said. "They took her a long time back."

"Yeah, I seen some of them kids that they taken on my travels. Some of them look real sad."

"Maybe you seen our girl—"

Toby grabbed her reluctant arm. "Don't be silly, woman."

She brushed him off like fine dust. "They called her Margaret."

"You know, I've seen so many of them poor children." He looked to the tarry sky as if to help his thinking. "I just don't know."

Toby, Daisy, and their mob took blankets and slept under the stars whilst the swagman rolled out his swag and slept close to their fire. When they woke, the swagman was still snoring. Daisy and her daughter-in-laws made damper bread and tea, and after their mob had eaten, they left some by the sleeping swagman and cleared the campsite ready to go. "We should tell him we're going," Daisy said.

"He's probably tired, let him sleep," Toby told her, but she shook him awake anyway.

"We're going now, mate. We left you some damper bread and tea if you want it."

The swagman wiped what Daisy recognised as vivid dreaming from his mattered eyes with the back of his hand. "Thank you."

Daisy went to climb into the ute. "Hey," he shouted to her departing back. "You say they call your girl Margaret?"

"Yes," Daisy said as she turned towards him with a flutter beating against her chest. "She'd be tall because of her father."

"There was this one girl I seen in a place called Malee, some time back. She just come into my dream for some reason. Pretty little thing, and I'm sure they called her Margaret. Had sea-blue eyes like yours. You never know, maybe you should check over that way."

"Yes, Mister. Thank you, we will." Daisy climbed into the cab, her heart racing like the engine. She squeezed Toby's arm and shook it. "Him coming here and dreaming our girl wasn't no accident, Toby."

***

After Carol's visit, Anne and Margaret moved back into the homestead with Sean. Anne was able to flow with more ease now. She had seen how Carol had changed over the years, and even though she never told her that Billabong Lodge had been borrowed, she sensed that Carol knew something was wrong, but whatever it was, their friendship was secure. At Easter she told Sean that she was going to visit Elizabeth in Sydney, and she packed her things and went for two weeks, also spending time with Helen Cartwright, who was still there. The city made her want to dance and sing in a way she had missed since her youth, and she promised herself that she would go back, and maybe even take up Carol's offer to visit England for a while.

Although Sean had a hefty mortgage from the additional land he had bought with Costos, he had more than enough money coming in from the other farmers buying water from the underground lake, and the orchards and pineapple fields around Malee were more crowded with fruit laden trees and serrated pine leaves than they had ever been. The surrounding land not used for farming was still bone dry, as there had now been no rain for almost three years, but the community were bolstered by scientific confirmation of the lake's supply, which, it was said, would last for years.

Carol left the headscarf for Margaret, but she threw it away and stopped reading the letters Carol sent to Anne, and when Anne told her that Carol had sent her good wishes, she raised her head like a cockerel and mumbled some inaudible response. Margaret's hair sprung back like rampant vines, and it had less of the curls, so it was easier for Anne or her to straighten it with the hot ironing comb, and she took this as a sign that she could outlast Sister Ruth's wicked whims. She had still been seeing Federico in the woods at the weekend, as he had finished school and now worked on his father's land, and she showed him what she had learned and brought him good books to read, because by now she had accepted that Federico would wait until their wedding night.

As her final exams approached, Margaret spent most of her time in her room revising. She had relished it like a favourite meal when Liz was there because they could do it together and ask each other questions, and also it stopped her from concocting wistful daydreams about Federico that could not be sated. She had kept asking him when would his father give him a piece of land so that he could take a wife, and he had said he didn't know, but she still asked each time they met. She told him that she needed to know what to do when she finished school. If they were to get married right away then there would probably be children soon after, and so it was best that she didn't try to find work. Then one day when she asked the same thing again, Federico threw down the sandwiches she had made for him and walked away. They hadn't met for almost two months now, and

219

even though she saw him in church, he hadn't spoken to her. He had talked about hiring himself out to other farms when work on his father's land was done, and in that way he could save more quickly to be married, and so she chose a pouting silence to convince herself that he was too tired to meet her.

The front door clattered when Sean came in, and he switched the television on. He had started to remove his own boots now, but Anne still placed his dinner on the table and took the boots outside. "Sean," she called as she placed the boots by the door.

"Hmm."

"There's that young lad again, Nipper's son."

"Yes, Sonny Boy. I told him to come by," Sean said.

Sonny Boy stopped by the edge of the woods. He was wearing his cleanest shirt and pants, and he had borrowed a half decent pair of shoes. A bunch of dried bush flowers stood solemnly in his hand.

"Well, what does he want?" Anne said.

"I told him he could come visiting Margaret." It was the only way he could think of to stop what he sensed was gathering like a merging fog inside himself and Margaret, and he was struggling to do it. But the two weeks that Anne had spent away in Sydney, when he had avoided being alone at the homestead with Margaret, had convinced him to do it. Anne marched leaden-footed down the hallway into the kitchen. "What did you do that for?"

Sean kept eating and didn't look at her. "Sonny Boy is now of marrying age and Margaret is about to finish school. We can't keep her forever."

"But one of *them*, Sean?"

"Sonny Boy's a bloody good worker."

"But suppose she wants to continue studying?"

"What the bloody hell for? She's going to be someone's wife, not the bloody Prime Minister."

"I've been looking at syllabuses for her to study nursing in Sydney," Anne said. She went to a drawer and pulled out some of the envelopes.

"Who do you think is going to pay for that?"

"I've saved a little and she can work while she's there."

"Who says that's what she wants? Maybe she wants to get married." The word sliced through his gut like a self-inflicted wound.

"Even if she did, she's been brought up to marry better than that, Sean," Anne cast a hand towards the lonesome figure loitering in the dark.

Sean banged his cup on the table. "What, like you were brought up to live in Billabong Lodge?"

"I didn't say that, Sean. When they let us have her it was on condition that she marries up. I have the papers upstairs, I can show you."

"You think that maybe she should have some say in this?" Sean sprung up and went to Margaret's door. He knocked hard three times, but there was no answer. When he pushed the door open she was asleep on the bed in her clothes. Sean went outside and spoke to Sonny Boy, and the lad trudged back the way he had come. He watched him go as he lit a cigarette and inhaled as if to cleanse his soul, wishing he had some of that pot that he had smoked with Carol nearly a year ago.

*** 

When Mr McDonald had come to her room, Margaret had only pretended to be asleep. She had heard him and Mrs McDonald arguing about her and Sonny Boy, but she was still thinking those things about Mr McDonald that she then had to say Hail Marys for, and the way he had held her at the caves when Carol was in Malee said he was thinking them too. So why was he trying to marry her off to Sonny Boy? But she had thought of Sonny Boy too. If Carol liked him then maybe she could, but always the thought of them blighted kids kept coming to mind, and could she be as good as Laura Wilson if she married someone like Sonny Boy, who hadn't been to a white school and learned their ways? If only Federico would ask her. She waited until everyone was asleep before climbing out of her window. She ran to the place where Nannup usually camped, but he wasn't there. He and Mrs Cartwright had only returned from Sydney in the last week, and she hadn't seen him since his return. She went to Billabong Lodge and hid in the brush. When she whistled, Nannup came to his window. She stood where he could see her, and he climbed down into the gardens. They hovered close to each other, like long lost siblings. Nearly a year had gone by since they had last met.

221

"Your hair looks good again," Nannup said. Margaret stroked it and smiled her thanks. "Come," he beckoned to her and they slipped off into the woods. On the way to his camping place he told her that Mrs Cartwright's sister had been very ill when they arrived in Sydney, but she had held on for more than ten months. Mrs Cartwright stayed to nurse her, and then when she passed, she sorted out her affairs before returning to Malee.

"Sonny Boy came to our homestead," Margaret said to Nannup after they had gathered wood and lit a fire.

Nannup pushed a piece of wood further into the fire. "Sonny Boy done tell me he wants to marry you before I went to Sydney."

"You knew?" There was a harsh ringing in her voice.

"Hmm. Sonny Boy is a good fella."

Margaret glared at Nannup through the flames. "Well, I don't want to marry him."

"You still wanting Federico?"

Margaret turned away from the dancing light so that he couldn't read her face. "I don't think he still wants me. We haven't met for two months, and when he comes to church he doesn't speak to me."

"He seeing somebody else?" Nannup asked. Margaret shrugged as if to hide her aching doubts. They sat in silence as Nannup mixed the dry earth with a stick, as if in contemplation. "I met some Koori people when I was in Sydney and they was real nice to me," he finally said.

"Did you talk to them?"

Nannup nodded. Margaret's face twitched and her stomach folded into a tight ball. He had only spoken to her in the past, and now that he was opening the door to others, it smothered her like a cramped room inside.

"Some of them Kooris get together and try to find people's mothers, fathers, and mob." Nannup waited, as if to hear how she felt about that, but she said nothing. "I'm going back to Sydney to help them."

"Mrs Cartwright won't let you," Margaret said. All those years of him burying supplies she had seen as a game. It would never come to this. Who would she have to talk to once Nannup had gone?

"I'm not going to tell her," Nannup said. "I'm going after the harvest picnic. Everyone will be too tired to follow me then." The community hadn't hosted a harvest picnic for several years, but they

222

were now into their second year of bountiful harvests, and the church and the ladies had organised one, to be held by a billabong hidden within rocks that were fed by the underground lake.

"How are you going to afford to get there? Have you got money?" Margaret asked.

"I got a little, and I was going to ask Isabel if she wants to come. She might take some of that money Mr Nicolaides has under his floor, for the work she's done on their place without any pay."

Margaret mulled it over like a fruit stone on her tongue. Now that Liz had gone to university, she was drifting alone in the McDonald homestead. Mrs McDonald seemed more at ease since Carol's visit, but she still busied herself each day as if work were a shield cast to protect her thoughts from chilling isolation, but it had proved too perfect a defence in that respect. Federico was acting as if he didn't want her anymore, although she wasn't sure, and Mr McDonald was trying to marry her off to Sonny Boy. She wasn't going to do that. "Can I come too?" she finally asked.

Nannup's grin flashed in the firelight. "Yes, I was hoping you would ask."

*\*\**

They agreed that Margaret should go to the Nicolaideses' place and tell Isabel of their plan. Margaret hadn't seen her in months, even though she sometimes walked by the Nicolaideses' farm. In fact, hardly anyone saw the Nicolaideses any more. When Father Beir had gone to minister to them they had locked themselves in the house and not answered his calls. They didn't come to church, Aithra didn't go to the grocery store, and only now and again was Costos seen picking up provisions and checking on his water supply with Sean.

Margaret arrived at the Nicolaideses' place the following day in a plummeting dusk, when she knew they would be inside eating supper. She was afraid she would come across Costos when she visited, and so she carried one of Anne's kitchen knives concealed in her dress.

Isabel wasn't eating on the veranda, her usual supper place, and Margaret crept along the wall of the barn where she slept and slipped inside. A sliver of fading light stole in through the one window, and she left the door ajar to let in another shaft. The mattress in the corner where Isabel slept was no longer there, and neither were any of her clothes. The barn smelt of dry hay and the maggoty, rotting

223

carcass of a pig hanging in a corner being worried by flies. A rat made a dash from behind an empty crate and Margaret fell back against some boxes, which crashed against the wooden slat walls. "Who's there?" Costos called from the doorway of the homestead. She gripped the knife inside her dress and peeped through a crack in the slats. Costos stood bare-chested with his man-breasts hanging over his sack of a belly like two empty udders. He stared at the barn for a while longer then spat frustration on the ground and went back inside. Margaret waited until she thought he had settled, and then she crept up to the homestead, hiding behind a tractor and the ute on the way. She climbed over the rail onto the veranda, tiptoed to the wall, and planted her back against it. Like a creeping vine, she worked her way along until she came to the first window. She pruned her rampant breath and pushed her hat off the back of her head so that she could peep inside. The oak sideboard and display cabinet that Costos had made were there, but there was nobody in the room. She remembered that Isabel had said they ate in the kitchen, and she slid along the wall in the other direction. When she reached the window she heard a *meow* from inside, and Aithra responded with baby talk. She peeped in the window and saw them sitting at the kitchen table. Costos was eating his dinner and Aithra was bent over a large reed basket, talking to the cat, which Margaret couldn't see. From the way Aithra was cooing, Margaret figured the cat in the basket had taken the place of Andrew. Costos looked up and Margaret pulled her head back from the window. The back door crashed open with a bang and she jumped back to the edge of the veranda. She hadn't heard his spongy footsteps.

"What do you want?" Costos demanded.

Margaret rested her hand over the front of her dress so that she could feel the knife, and the cold blade warmed to her heartbeat. "I came to look for Isabel."

"Who tell you to come here? No one invite you." His eyes were bulging, and he swivelled his fiery head to see if there was anyone with her.

Margaret shuffled to her side until she was in front of him. Then she took a taut step back off the veranda. "I—I just wanted to know if she's going to come back to church."

He caught her peering around him into the kitchen, and he signalled Aithra to go upstairs with a flick of his melon-sized head. She took the basket from where the *meows* were escaping with her.

"Isabel's not coming back to church," Costos said as he pulled the door behind him.

"Can I speak to her?"

"Why you don't go home?" He waved his shovel of a hand at her. "Isabel don't live here no more, she run away. You go home now." He waved her away again, went in, and slammed the door. Margaret could see him watching her through the window as she backed away. *Isabel don't live here no more.* It repeated itself on her like an insipid meal. If she was going then surely she would have told them; or was it that she could no longer put up with Costos' nightly visits? How long was it since she had last seen Isabel now? Almost nine months. There were all sorts of things she wanted to know. When did she go? Where would she run to? Why hadn't the Nicolaideses told anyone? Liz had gone to university in Sydney, Isabel had run away, and Federico was ignoring her. Soon there would be no familiar scent for her to fly to when in need of nourishment. She was decided. She would run with Nannup. Maybe when they reached Sydney she could make contact with Liz. She tried to remember the people she had left behind and forgotten, just to keep going: her mother, father, brothers, sister, aunties, cousins, her friend Lilly at Radley, now Isabel. She felt as if they were sailing with the stars, and for some she had held off the mourning for too long, until her emotions were withered and dry; but she found that when she gave them up, harboured no more hope of seeing them in this life, she could remodel her life, and eke out some kind of an existence.

*** 

For more than a week, trucks with empty crates pulled in at the Malee farms in the mornings, and by nightfall they would be on their long journeys to the cannery in North Brisbane, stacked with fruit. The district had received one day's showers about a month back, but it was far too little to have an impact on the farmers' own supplies of water, and so they still relied on that being pumped from the caves. Nevertheless, the showers had provided enough of a dousing to awaken the millions of hibernating grass seeds in the ground, and they sprung to a height of several feet within a week, and gum trees sprouted buds and leaves along their spindly spines. But as if out of spite, the sun had blazed more ferociously and had roasted the vegetation crinkly dry since that dousing. The trucks rolled along the narrow dirt roads, flattening the long yellow grasses that ran along the edges and sometimes right into the roads themselves. But the dry conditions baked the road surfaces as hard as concrete, and this made it easier for the long trailers to navigate them.

The harvesting of the fruits was sweaty, back-breaking work, but it was done with a tune on their lips and a bounce in their strides. They greeted each other with cut watermelon smiles and tales that made them laugh even when there was no need. The women made roasts, cakes, pies, and punch for the men gathering the crop in the fields, and they would do the same again for the church harvest festival and picnic that Sunday.

On the Saturday, a truck pulled up at the edge of Sean's fields to load his crop, but he directed them to Costos' fields first, and he followed them over with his Aboriginal workers to help Costos cut, crate, and load his pineapples. Aithra provided them with food and drink, but she set up a table out by the barn and let all the men eat it there, keeping them away from the homestead. Sean and Costos drank once again to their water find, and agreed it would last another three, maybe four years if they had no rain, but they were bound to get rain in that time. Sean arrived home aching like an arthritic after nightfall, and fell asleep on the kitchen table without eating his supper.

Margaret slipped out of the house sometime after Sean got home, and met Nannup in the woods. They hurried over to the Nicolaideses' homestead so that Nannup could check for himself, as he didn't believe Isabel had gone. They searched the barn first, where the reeking pig was still festering, and then they slipped into the darkened homestead by the unlocked back door. When they crept out of the kitchen into the hall, they could hear Costos snoring like a misfiring engine upstairs. They checked in the other two rooms downstairs, but they were empty. Nannup held onto the banister and placed his foot on the bottom stair like a wild cat out hunting. "Where you going?" Margaret whispered. He pointed up the stairs. Margaret grabbed onto his feline arm. "She's not here." Nannup shrugged her off snarling irritation and kept going. Margaret watched him disappear into the cloaked darkness. Her legs were shaking as if fatigued, and she wrestled her soaring breath to submission. Then she heard the *meow*. It was coming towards her, and Aithra blew through her teeth to quell it. Margaret hurried into the kitchen and hid behind the curtain beneath the sink as Aithra's footsteps descended the stairs.

The lights went on, and Aithra put the cat basket onto the kitchen table. "Hush, I get it ready soon," she said. She filled the kettle with water and a thimble full dripped into Margaret's hair from a leak. Aithra put the kettle on and went back to play with the bundle in the basket. Margaret peeped out from behind the curtain at Aithra's curved back. She was shaking the bundle and cooing. "Oh, I forget your thing," she said, and she put the bundle back in the basket. As Aithra went for the door, Margaret glimpsed Nannup scramble back on all fours into the living room. She pulled the curtains shut, sure Aithra must have seen him. She waited coiled with stone fists to her face, ready to scamper out. Then the curtains were tugged apart. She sprung to push Aithra back, but it was Nannup's startled grin that greeted her. He grabbed her fists and pulled her out.

"You found her?" Margaret asked. He shook his head and dragged her towards the cat basket on the table. Margaret lurched in a daze as Nannup pushed back the blanket from the *meowing* infant's face. The baby kicked with hungry impatience, and the covers slipped off his chubby legs. A crescent shaped fold of skin lacerated his calf, right where Isabel had worn hers. Nannup wrapped the baby in the blanket and picked him up to go. "No!" Margaret held him back, "We can't take him."

"He's not theirs," Nannup said.

"Look at his face." Margaret pointed at the boy. "He has Mr Nicolaides' face." Besides, where were they going to take him? At least here he stood a chance.

"Isabel didn't want to go with him, so he's not theirs."

"Nannup, I dreamed last night. Only two get away. If we take him, they will catch us."

The baby *meowed* its ravenous demands with urgent vigour now. Nannup and Margaret stared bitterly at each other, as if in a duel of wills. "All right, I'm coming. Don't wake Costos," they heard Aithra say as she hurried down the stairs. Nannup put the baby back in the basket and they scurried out the back door. They watched like doting siblings through the window as Aithra fed the baby that no one outside of that house, except the two of them, knew existed. Then

227

they started back home. Nannup was flooded with silence, as if dousing his blazing anger with Margaret for letting him leave the baby. But she was already wondering if, because the child had Mr Nicolaides' blood, he would not be blighted.

"Why were you up there so long?" she asked after a while. Nannup pulled a wad of notes from his pockets, which made her gasp with a covetous stare. "Mr Nicolaides' money?"

Nannup nodded. "I take some of it from under the floorboard where Isabel said it was."

"Won't he find out?"

"We'll be gone by then."

When Nannup left her they agreed to go to the Sunday picnic and to breathe normality's air. Then they would return home and go to bed, and he would meet her in the same place sometime after midnight.

***

Before Margaret reached her window, a sharp whistle pierced the muggy air. "Margaret, Margaret." Her knees buckled as Federico bounded out of the coarse darkness up onto the veranda and held her hands. "Where have you been, Margaret? I knocked at your window and you didn't come, so I have been waiting all night for you."

"I—I went to look for a friend and stayed too late." He hadn't visited her in almost three months, and he had avoided her at church.

"My father give me a piece of land, Margaret." His hopes and dreams were embedded across his wide-open face like a thick seam of gold. "My own land, Margaret." She looked up into his gleaming eyes and saw children even fairer than the one they had left in Costos' homestead. The women would call her Mrs Rossi and invite her to their tea parties, and their children would be baptised by Father Beir, even if she hadn't been. The previous three months felt as if they had been washed away by a flash storm. Sean's footsteps at the front of the veranda stopped them. Federico held her hands to his breast and they stood as if time were idle lovers. "You go to the picnic tomorrow, Margaret?"

"Yes."

"I have something important to say, Margaret." His awkwardness returned and he stepped back from her. She reached out as if to tear the message from him.

"Say it now, Federico."

The footsteps on the veranda drifted closer. "I tell you tomorrow," Federico promised, and he let her go and ran into the woods.

# Chapter 17

Sleep evaded Margaret as she tossed and turned all night, drifting between her pastel dreams of life as Mrs Federico Rossi and how to tell Nannup that she could no longer run away with him. She woke early, like a child on Christmas morning, and deliberated over what frock to wear. The two white ones that she wore to church were her best, but she would marry in white, so she picked out her blue frock with the yellow collar. She helped Anne to carry the Coolgardie packed with food to the ute, and Sean dropped them off at the church, where there was a convoy of vehicles waiting. Anne got into the car with Helen Cartwright and Nannup, but Margaret decided to travel in the open bed of the church truck, because she couldn't face him. When the last of the congregation arrived, they set off for the billabong.

*** 

The vehicles travelled in single file with Mr O'Hare leading in his jeep. Once they were out into the open brush, they cut across a plain of spinifex grass several feet high and jaundiced from thirst. In places, hardy mulga and malee scrub dotted the landscape, and they drove past desert oaks, some more than fifty feet high, their needle leaves hanging vertically to escape the full effects of the sun and reduce water evaporation in the hot winds. Red-sapped eucalypts, which had shed their leaves and branches so that their stems might at least survive the drought and rekindle life once it was over, had a few leaves growing along their trunks, encouraged by the showers a month back, but it wouldn't last without more rain. They hurtled by a flock of budgerigars that had died from drought, their little green bodies heaped under a slender desert poplar already being reclaimed by ants, mice, and a few crows that had survived.

Before midday they reached the hidden entrance to the gorge and the men shifted dozens of newly fallen rocks before the vehicles could get through. Huge boulders rested on the dry riverbed inside

230

the gorge, and the convoy manoeuvred around them like some gigantic snake. The red cliffs rose up steeply on both sides to more than one hundred feet, and ghost gums grew from tiny crevices in them, their huge network of roots clinging to and penetrating the cracks for support and moisture. Part of the gorge opened out more widely, but dozens of boulders made it impassable by car. The church party got out and humped their hampers around the boulders, and they lumbered out the other side into a hidden oasis.

The riverbed here was carpeted with a field of round-leafed parakeelya, their purple blossoms tickling at the ankles of the picnic goers as they waded through them. Behind this was a small sandy beach at the edge of a still, shimmering pool, about thirty feet across. All stopped to gorge their senses, Anne most of all. She flopped down onto a clump of parakeelya, and something welled up in her so that she wanted to cry. She said she had forgotten her Bible in the car, and she hurried back through the boulders and released her tears, a drop for each day she had held back. How could she have missed that she was surrounded by so much? The rugged cliff faces that had existed for millennia, plants that would eventually find a way to bloom, some of which may have even been foreign to the land—they all found some way to survive and on occasion thrive here, whilst she had spent her life dreaming of transitory things. I can find some way to live with this, I must find a way, she told herself, and when her sudden turbulence calmed again, she dabbed at her eyes and went back to join the others.

*** 

They were sitting in the same positions they occupied in church, with Helen Cartwright and Nannup at the front, and Anne sat on the sand next to Margaret. Father Beir had taken off his shoes, and he stood ankle deep in the water so that all could see him. From there he preached a sermon giving thanks for the bountiful harvest, and they sang hymns while Mr Wilson played the accordion. Then Father Beir asked for the four who were to be baptised to step or be brought forward, and he led them into the water one by one, carrying the two babies in his arms. Margaret still remembered the words, and she said them to herself as Father Beir poured water over the head of each child. She watched Federico looking on and knew he was musing with the same thought—their children would be baptised. He caught

231

a sight of her and turned away, still too shy to hold her smile in front of the others, but she kept sending it anyway.

After the service ended, the men set up a long table and the ladies laid out chickens, hams, potatoes, salads, pies, cakes, melons, pineapples, fruit juice, and more. Mr Wilson decided to continue playing his accordion while the people ate, chattered, and laughed as if unshackled from a ton of burdens. The plenty reaped from the land had given them much cause for celebration.

When she had finished eating, Margaret returned her plate to the table. That's when she noticed Federico by the rocks. He flicked his head, signalling her to follow, and he disappeared behind the boulders. Margaret waited a while, to make sure that no one was watching. As she was about to go, Nannup stole up to her side. He mouthed *tonight*, so that no one could see, and she nodded and said yes, then ran to the boulders. How should she tell him? She wandered through the boulders, her dislodged confusion slipping as if down a ravine, but when she saw Federico beckon her again she was sure. She looked behind her to check she wasn't being followed and then ran to catch him. They disturbed a black-flanked rock-wallaby peeping out from behind a boulder, and it turned in guarded haste and bounded away. Federico grabbed her hands and pulled her behind a boulder.

"Thank you for coming, Margaret," Federico said. She was breathing with nervous exhaustion, and he waited for her to slow. "My father he give me the east field." She knew the one; it was where they grew oranges and other citrus. It could bring in enough to keep two when water was in good supply, but they would have to buy more land when they had children. "I will start to build a small house on it soon with my father's help." She wanted to tell him how many rooms they would need, and she knew the best place to put the kitchen and the pantry, but she had come to listen today, that was a woman's role on a day like this. He held her hands to his cracked lips and closed his eyes. His hands were pale and she could feel his anxious tremor through them. She tightened her grip to help him. He took in a deep breath and let it out, as if he first needed to purify himself. "You are my best friend, Margaret. You help me a lot in school and make me do better." He opened his eyes and breathed again. "That's why I want to tell you myself. I have asked Laura Wilson for her hand in marriage."

She screamed and pushed him back.

"Margaret—" Federico lunged to take her hands again, but she hammered them against his chest, still screaming. Her eyes, her nose, her mouth were wide with a freakish rage and draining fluid. Her head spun like a felled tree's discarded leaf, so that she didn't know where she was. Was it really Federico in front of her? She ran to follow her reeling head. She stumbled against boulders, grazing her skin, crashed against the jeeps and utes as she raced by them, and somewhere she fell. It was eerie with a windless vacuum of thick blackness, and there was no bottom, she just kept falling.

Someone was calling to her in the murky darkness. *Daughter, daughter, can you hear us? We are near. Wait for us.* She could make out a grey-haired woman in a hurry. The man next to her was bowed at the waist, but you could tell that he had been strong as an oxen a few years earlier. And there were several of their mob supporting them.

"Margaret ... Margaret." This call was not floating in her head, and she felt Mrs O'Hare shaking her to prove it. "She must have fainted," she heard Mrs O'Hare say to someone, and then she felt water trickling into her mouth.

Mr O'Hare helped his wife to pull her up. "Are you all right there?" Two portly, ruddy faces were staring into hers. Margaret nodded with frail motions, so they supported her and carried her back past the cars and through the boulders.

"Let me rest here," Margaret said as they lumbered out of the boulders to where the children were playing.

"Are you sure now?" Mrs O'Hare said. Margaret nodded, and they left her, looking back a couple of times to make sure she was all right. She felt empty now, as if drained of all life. How could she have been so foolish? No one else in Malee had married a half-breed, so why did she expect Federico to summon up the courage to? She closed her bulging eyes, tensed her cheeks, and strained to squeeze out the pain, but when she opened them again, the laughter, smiles, and chatter on everyone's lips confirmed that they had always known. She glimpsed Federico sitting by his parents, but he was hanging his head as if shrouded in shame, and she looked away.

Laura Wilson's goat-sized brother Samuel slinked up to her. "Eenie, meenie, minie, mo. Catch a nigger by the toe. If she screams, let her go. Eenie, meenie, mine, mo." He coiled ready to bolt, but Margaret was too comatose to take notice of him. He started to flap his arms, which had fine blond hairs, and circled her, repeating his rhyme, over and over again. He fell by a boulder and screamed. Margaret jumped off her mourning rock and stomped her feet into the ground as if her life depended on it—that would extinguish her pain. The boy was screaming like prey at her feet.

Mr Wilson ran over and slapped her to the floor. "What the bloody hell you doing, you black bastard?" He scooped his boy up in his arms.

Father Beir was right behind him. "Mr Wilson—" He moved Mr Wilson aside and helped Margaret to her feet. Underneath her was the six-foot, thick-necked mulga snake whose skull she had crushed with her foot, her totem snake. Father Beir held up the kill by its tail for all to see. "Check if the boy has been bitten, Mr Wilson."

Mr Wilson ran his hands over the crying boy several times as the other picnickers gathered round. "He's all right. I didn't know," he said to Father Beir, his prostrate eyes seeking absolution. Mrs Wilson barged through the melee, prised her remaining son from her husband's arms, and hugged him. The gathered crowd wore their silence like stains on their consciences.

"Are you all right, Margaret?" Father Beir asked. She nodded with the slap still gnawing at her cheek. He looked out at the crowd as if imploring them to do something. Then, like a whirlwind, an impulsive thought seemed to overtake him. He took Margaret's wavering hand and led her through the centre of the crowd into the waveless pool. When Anne saw what he was about to do, she covered her mouth with a jittery hand to hold back her gushing gasps. Then she took off the white cotton scarf thrown over her shoulder, waded out into the water, and fixed it over Margaret's head like a veil.

"Thank you, Mum," Margaret said, and the word formed like well-patted butter for the first time. The orange sun was slipping behind the cliffs so that its light extended like arms and embraced that place. And there, Father Beir dipped Margaret's head into the water and joined her to Christ.

*** 

They were driving towards a rocky outcrop, which was being encircled by the dying sun's orange rays, when Daisy told Toby to stop the ute. She climbed out of the cab and wandered around the clumps of spinifex with her arms held out and her head up to the sky, as if her whole body were a serpent's tongue tasting the air for what news it carried. "What is it, my wife? Is it our daughter?" Toby asked. Daisy screamed. It travelled across the open plains like a thunderous wave. Toby jumped from the cab and the rest of the mob—sons, their wives, and children—climbed from the bed of the ute and joined her in the wailing, all of them.

"We can say her name no more, my husband. Ahhhhh. She is dead to us; they have killed our child. Ahhhhh."

When a few of them had emptied enough of their immediate grief, they surveyed the place where they had learned of her death, and fixed it in their memory. The rocky outcrops in the distance, the bent, bark-stripped gum trees—they would have to learn the myths and dreaming of this place, so that it could be held in the same esteem that their daughter, sister, and auntie had been.

When Toby was able to, he cut a fat branch to make the *morning star pole,* and his sons went with their children in search of feathers to put on it. He carved his daughter in the centre of it, because they had no body to bury, and in the centre of her abdomen he carved her clan totem design, which carried a vibrational affinity to the region in the sky where their ancestors resided. One of her arms was carved tied behind her back to discourage her spirit from going off to hunt or gather food. After painting on the other designs, Toby used a knife to scar himself about the arms, and his sons and the women did the same while they were singing death songs, which hinted at the dead girl's identity, but they never said her name. They let their mingled blood run down the pole, and they stuck feathers at the top of it to represent the star, above the painting of *Bural* the snake, which was coming out to see the light of the star.

The dead girl's spirit had split into three, and they had to ensure that all three departed in order to safeguard the wellbeing of the living. The *totemic soul* was the easiest to deal with, and they sang and danced in ceremonial ritual so that it could be returned to the earth, to animals, plants, mountains, sunlight, wind and rain, from whence it had come, and in that way what had been given to them by nature could be returned, and so the umbilical cord that tied them to the land would not be broken.

Then they continued the wailing, song, and dance so that her *ancestral spirit* could return to the Creative Ancestors of the Dreamtime, whose domain was the land of the dead in the sky. "*May from here your spirit reach the stomach of the sky.*" They chanted it like a winding stream, until that part of her spirit had departed to the unending, unchanging version of the gathering-hunting life, which she had lived on earth ... except that the game would be more plentiful.

Daisy dropped the hair that she had saved from the brush the day the girl was taken onto the fire, together with a dress of hers that she had retained. From here the mourning flooded the landscape as they wounded themselves and screamed out their anguish. Any sorrow withheld would form a link to which the girl's ego spirit would try to cling and delay its journey to the sky for months or even years. "*Don't look back at your mother or father now,*" they sang to the spirit. "*Don't think about your brothers, sisters, aunties or cousins. Keep away from our camp and don't follow us. You have to go the other way now to your own waterhole in the sky.*" The dancing, singing, and wailing grew to a frenzy as they tried to blow out a vibratory wave that would swell the sails of the ego spirit soaring to its place in the sky. But the dust cloud and noise that raced towards them threw up a gale.

***

Margaret rode back in the O'Hares' Land Rover, which led the convoy of vehicles. She had floated like Laura in the baptism ceremony, and even if Federico wouldn't marry her, she was now tied to Christ. Any children she had would be blessed by that union, and no one could take that away from her. She was one of them now, and she glowed warm at the bloated pleasure it had given Anne, who had told her she could keep her precious white scarf, which was now wrapped around her shoulder. "Look at that." Mr O'Hare pointed through the windscreen at the Aboriginals making ceremony around the campfire ahead of them. "*Blasphemy!*" he said, and bolstered by the intoxicating level of religious zeal which their day at the billabong had filled them with, he turned the vehicle towards the group. The rest of the convoy followed him, and Margaret joined them in the laughter and shouting as they stormed through the ceremony, sending the dancers scattering, and bringing it to an end.

# Chapter 18

Shortly after dawn, the screech of Costos' ute coming to a stop in the yard woke most of the McDonald household.

Costos and Aithra hurried up onto the veranda. He banged on the door, which had been kept locked ever since the swagman had passed through. Anne slid up with fraying nerves to open it. "Is that girl here? Margaret, is she here?" Costos demanded, with panic swilling in his eyes. Aithra had rock-hard fists to her mouth and was crying.

"She's in bed, Costos. She was baptised yesterday—"

"I don't care about baptism, Anne. Is she here?"

Sean came down the stairs, pulling on his shirt. "Costos, what's wrong?"

"Some of my money gone, Sean. And—" He stopped himself.

"So what makes you think it's Margaret?" Sean asked.

"She come by our house for—I know it's her." Costos pushed the door to come in but Sean blocked his way.

"Anne, go and wake Margaret," Sean said, and Anne scurried to rouse the girl who was still dreaming of her baptism. Margaret pulled on a dress and hurried to the door, and when she saw Costos and Aithra she remembered that she hadn't told Nannup she wasn't coming.

"You come to our house last night, girl?" Costos waved a stubby finger at her.

"No." She rubbed the sleep out of her eyes. The way Aithra was crying she knew Nannup must have gone back for the baby. Two got away, that's what she had dreamed.

"We lose everything. Andrew, now this," Costos shouted at her.

"Margaret, you know anything? Help us," Aithra said through cascading tears.

Margaret pondered with deep yearning how far Nannup had gone. Would he get away? But the baby hadn't even been baptised. He wasn't given a chance to float into a new life the way she had. "Joshua may have taken the baby," she said, then turned her still glowing eyes to the ground, not sure if she had done the right thing.

"What baby?" Anne and Sean asked with raised voices.

Costos turned to Aithra, to silently concur, and then returned to them. "Isabel must have been seeing someone and she have a baby," he said. He dropped his bulbous eyes from Margaret's searing gaze and continued, "She leave the baby and run away, so we take care of it. This morning when we wake, the baby and some of my money— gone."

"Isabel has had a baby and run away? Why didn't you say anything?" Anne said.

"We don't have time now, Anne, we need to find the baby," Costos said.

Sean dragged on his boots. "Let's go round to Helen Cartwright's place."

*** 

They roused Helen Cartwright from her sleep and she searched Joshua's room. "He's not there, Sean, and he's taken a couple of the blankets."

"We have to go look for him now, Sean," Costos said as he raced back towards his ute.

Sean grabbed hold of his arm. "Hold on. The two of us will never find him out there. Take Aithra home and stop by the Wilson and Rossi place. You can all head north towards the highway. I'll go for Mr O'Hare and whoever else I can find. We'll search out towards Langley."

***

Nannup had seen the glow of pure release on Margaret's face after her baptism, as if she had flown free of his world for paradise. Still, he waited in the woods for her as they had planned, and then he crept to her window and blew the whistle that she recognised, but she didn't come. He had been picturing that kicking baby all that time, and when he remembered Margaret dreamed that two got away, he decided that he wouldn't let them steal another child. He crawled into the Nicolaideses' bedroom under their snoring noses and took that baby right out of the cat basket. Mrs Nicolaides had been so happy to get some sleep that she didn't notice when the baby hadn't cried every three hours to get its feed, and it wasn't until she woke in the morning that she realised the child was gone.

Nannup went across country. He would try to board the train for Sydney somewhere past Langley, which would take him a day and night's trek. He wrapped the boy lightly to protect him from the biting night chill, and tied him to his chest. Then he started to trot across the bushland. In the morning the fierce sun bore down on him like a hunter toying with its prey, and the grasses whipped and stabbed through his clothing, but he had prepared himself by dreaming the run. Sometimes he picked up a fallen branch and dragged it in the dirt behind him as he ran, to erase his footprints, and at other times he jumped onto rocks and shrivelled clumps of grass, which held onto none.

By late afternoon they had caught up with him, and he heard the vehicles and shouting men in the distance. He ran towards where the malee trees were thickest, where they would find it most difficult to unleash their jeeps, but still they kept coming.

"There goes the black bastard!"

"Over there!" The cries kept coming, but he evaded them until dusk. They caught up with him as the forest thinned into a clearing. It was less than fifty yards to the thickest part, but he hadn't made it. Three vehicles encircled him like a raging river now. One of the men stood up in the back of a Land Rover and spun a tight lasso over his sandy head. He hurled the well-worn rope and it missed. The second time Nannup twisted his head to the side and the rope bounced off his shoulder. He grabbed the trailing lasso and threw it around a boulder, and as the man pulled back his rope, it dragged him out of the Land Rover. The driver braked sharp, and another vehicle in the circle crashed into the back of him. Nannup saw his chance and broke for the trees. The remaining vehicle stopped to check that the others were unharmed, and then it gave chase. Nannup dived into the forest before they reached him, and they had to slow and snake between trees to pursue him. Soon, the other two vehicles rejoined the hunt, and the chase trundled on for over an hour, until Nannup tired and they encircled him again.

"There he is," Sean shouted. Nannup melted into the shadows of a tree, wrapped himself and the child against the trunk, and branched out an arm. The vehicles encircled the tree with the bulging knot in its trunk, and the men scratched their throbbing heads as they tried to work out where he had gone.

A murky dusk was descending like wildfire, and Mr Jones pointed to the storm cloud that was billowing to blot out the receding sun. "Looks like we're going to have rain."

Sean stood up on the side of his vehicle and capped his hand over his eyes. "That's no rain cloud, that's smoke. It's coming from the direction of Malee." They didn't wait for more to be said. The men backed their vehicles out of the woods, and with urgent cries of dread, they raced towards Malee.

***

There were thousands of square miles of malee trees, gum trees, and bushes which had not yet been cut back for farming. Before the dry spells they had enjoyed two seasons of good rains that had fuelled the explosive growth of spinifex and other grasses. The three dry seasons had shrivelled these back somewhat, but the one-day shower they had a month back had fuelled the growth again, and the grasses were now yellowed, crisped and dried combustibles, several feet high. The fires raced through these fields, threatening the homesteads, and the men helped each other to cut and back burn wide firebreaks around each others' homesteads to prevent the flames from evicting them. When they felt their homes were safe, they went into the bush to join the fire services from Langley, neighbouring towns, and across the state, because all of them were volunteer firefighters. Let it burn, Nipper told Sean—the same thing he had told him when there had been smaller fires that might have burned off the combustibles and so prevented a larger disaster. His people had been practising firestick farming for thousands of years before the Europeans arrived. They had carefully burned small parcels of land, and not only had this prevented larger fires, but it had encouraged the growth of new, lush, sweeter grasses, and this had allowed bush game to flourish. But the European farmers had always been against this; if it wasn't knowledge that they had brought with them from their own lands, it was of no use. And so many of the early settlers had been forced off their land because the grass grew tough and bitter and was invaded by scrub, so their animals wouldn't eat it, or large bush fires would claim it. Sean was no different. No, he had always said to Nipper. How can you let good land burn? Many of those farmers would have at some stage wanted to cut down them trees and hack out those bushes to provide more farmland, but they wanted to control the destruction; no chance fire was going to cheat them out of exercising their power over the land.

The fires lasted six months. At their height there were more than nine thousand fire fighters in the bush wrestling them. The only water for miles around was at the 'McDonald and Nicolaides' Underground Lake', and millions of gallons of it were pumped out twenty-four hours a day, seven days a week, to douse the flames and dampen the land. When the men thought the fires were subsiding, a gush of hot wind or a cyclone would blow them onto another dry patch to start all over again. They jumped dry riverbeds and hedges, encircled towns and homesteads like marauding warriors, and sometimes they would hide unseen, and then erupt from the belly of the earth to ambush those who were fighting them. That was how fire razed the Nicolaideses' homestead. Sean had helped them to cut the firebreaks around their homestead, from which Aithra refused to emerge, weeping over the basket of the stolen child. But it was safe, they thought; they had done enough. Then one evening, whilst the weary Malee men were on their way home to take a few hours' rest, they saw the flames licking around the base of the homestead as if testing it for taste, but it hadn't caught yet. "Aithra, Aithra," Costos had called, but she refused to answer him or come out. The men tried to hold him back, but his buffalo strength and determination were too great, and he broke free and charged into the homestead. And that's when the tongue of the fire decided that it relished what it had tasted, and it devoured the Nicolaideses' homestead like a glutton.

The fire left the smell of molten charcoal hanging in the air and blocked out the sun with thick black clouds that at other times would have been a welcome sign of rain. Then finally, when no one expected any respite, the flames stopped their eating frenzy as suddenly as they had begun it, their hunger sated. Only then did all have a chance to take stock of what had been lost: the whole region's harvest for the year, except the little already transported, had been incinerated; thousands of square miles of farmland, scrub, and bush had given way to vast expanses of ash-covered red sand and blackened tree stumps; to the south where they were reared, the stiffened, charred carcasses of thousands of sheep and cattle littered the fields; the area's wildlife had been burnt or scattered; twenty-three

241

homesteads were no more; and thirty-seven men, women, and children were missing or dead, including Costos and Aithra Nicolaides, whose bodies were never recovered. It was only after the funeral service for the Nicolaideses that Sean noticed there was no water running into the streams, and when he checked the underground lake, it was as dry as a salt pan. Even with six months of pumping water onto the land, twenty-four hours a day, Sean sensed that the vast supplies could not have been depleted. It was as if the earth had opened up and drunk it all, and he wondered what trickery, which they called magic, the Aboriginals had played on them all.

The community for miles around were tired and numbed, but after six months of fighting to save much of what had been lost in the first few weeks, they did not have the strength to touch the tapestry of their shredded hopes, and it would take some time for them to stitch together their wounds. Sean spent days driving over the land, surveying it, and in a strange way it didn't seem like a land defeated. Blackened gum trees stood up boldly in the vast emptiness, and the land seemed at peace with itself, as if in some long overdue hibernation. And although he had some sense of this, Sean McDonald was from a people whose spiritual link to the land had been severed many thousands of years ago, and so he was already planning how he would tame and control this land, and eke out a living for himself once again.

\*\*\*

Sean sold the empty caves to Mr O'Hare and used his share of the money to pay off part of his mortgage. He couldn't figure out what O'Hare wanted with the property, as there was no good farmland out there. But O'Hare was a gambler, and he had figured that two seasons' good rains should fill the 'O'Hare Underground Reservoir' again, and when they had more bad years, which they surely would, he could sell underground water again. They also sold the Nicolaideses' farm and sent the money to their relatives in Greece.

Anne watched Sean in wistful expectation and waited. Waited for him to raise the matter, but weeks went by and he said nothing. Then one day Nipper trooped into the yard, and she sat on the veranda reading her Bible, but listening.

"G'day, Mr McDonald," Nipper said. He had his hands behind his back and was staring down at Sean's feet with caged anger.

"G'day, Nipper." Sean took out a cigarette, tapped it on the box, and lit up.

"I was thinking you could settle up with us fellas now, Mr McDonald."

"I was hoping that maybe I could settle with you after you planted that east field," Sean said.

Nipper gazed up at him as though he was crazy, then he turned away again as if not to rile him. "There's no water *now*, Mr McDonald." He struggled to control the roar in his voice, but it kept building. "I told you people to leave the fire alone, it would stop when it had a mind to."

"Don't you speak to me in that bloody tone, Nipper, or else you'll never work for me again."

Nipper wet his drying lips and swallowed like a drunkard. "We're moving on, and we want to get paid."

"Moving, now? Where to? How are you going to get work?" Sean threw the cigarette down and made sure he stamped it out good.

"We're not working here any more, Mr McDonald." Nipper bowed his head inches lower.

Sean gritted his teeth and nodded as if all was well. He wasn't going to go begging to them. "You realise no one else is going to treat you as good as I did, Nipper."

Nipper fought off an ironic smile. "Our water's gone, so we have nowhere to perform our corroborrees now."

"You thought about staying on for one more season?" Sean asked with mock nonchalance as he dug into his pocket for money.

Nipper glanced as if in mourning at the scarred land. Then it was as if he could hold it no longer. "Ever since you people come here you been trying to wrestle this land into submission and make it into something you recognise back in your own land. You brought your thirsty hard-hoofed sheep and cattle that turned the land to desert, and you kill the natural tucker to raise plants and animals that don't belong. It's as if you people think everywhere should be the same as the place you come from, and everyone should be the same as the people you sprung from. But if everything is the same, then when one catch a sickness, won't we all soon catch it and die? The land is telling us something, Mr McDonald. We been working it too hard, taking more from it than we been putting back; maybe it needs a rest now, and we should all move on to let it sleep."

243

Sean snorted with cold derision and shook his head. "Here, this is all I have. It'll have to do." Nipper took the money and looked at him one last time. They said nothing. Then Nipper walked away.

Sean stepped up onto the veranda and slumped down, drained by talk, drought, and money worries. "Lazy bastards desert you when the work gets tough. No wonder they don't have anything."

Anne put down the Bible. "He may have a point you know, Sean. We haven't had rain in three years, and with the water now gone, how are we going to survive?"

Sean looked at her as if she was wavering. "You too."

"Sean McDonald, I have put up with this way of life for longer than many would. I have grown accustomed to it and I'm willing to bear it if we can make ends meet, but we can't now. You still have that mortgage to pay, and we have to eat." Sean gazed off into the air, and Anne waited, but he said nothing. "I spoke to Mr O'Hare about buying the place. With what he would pay we could pay off the mortgage and buy somewhere by the coast, near Brisbane perhaps. Helen says a friend of hers went out there and they now run a successful guesthouse. We could try something else, Sean."

"I'm not selling my land, Anne."

"So what are we going to do?"

Sean reclined his head against the wall and closed his eyes. He could feel her stare crushing him. "I'm going to Brisbane to get a job at the canning factory. I'll work three weeks and come home every fourth week."

"What am I supposed to do in the meantime?"

"I want you to keep the place going, Anne." He rested his elbows on his thighs and leaned towards her. "I can't lose it."

"There has to be an end to this. When do we say enough is enough?" Her fists were bolted and her eyes moist.

"If we have no rain within the next year we'll leave, Anne. I promise."

Anne got up and drifted inside, where she hid in her room and cried. Then she got down on her knees and prayed for the drought to continue for at least another year.

\*\*\*

Margaret passed her exams and left Malee School. She wasn't sure what she wanted to do now, and spent her days at home helping

244

Anne to grow what little vegetables they could from the water Sean paid to be trucked in, and keeping her company while he was away working at the cannery. She watched from the charred woods as Federico Rossi married Laura Wilson, who wore the white wedding gown her mother had saved for her. Sometimes, she walked out past the piece of land Federico's father had given him and spied on them as they struggled to make ends meet on the drought-ridden farm, but even so, she noticed with smothered thirst how happy they were in their first months together. She wondered if Federico had waited like he said, or if he had been seeing Laura all along. It didn't matter now anyway, because she had been married to Christ when Father Beir baptised her, and even Mrs Wilson sometimes nodded to her now when she saw her in church or at the general store, especially if she was with her youngest son, who Margaret had saved from the snake.

Mr O'Hare bought up more land from the farmers who had bills to pay but no income with which to pay them. Some sold up everything and left Malee and the outback for good. Others sold little by little, and held on like addicted gamblers, hoping the next hand would deal them rain. There were others who did like Sean and travelled hundreds of miles to large towns or cities or to areas where they needed good farmhands to work. Then they sent their money back to Malee so that their women folks could buy in enough water to wet the vegetable patches and wash themselves. They weren't about to let go of what they owned. Mr Jones tried to hold on so tight that it drove him to throw a rope over the joist in his barn one night, and his wife found him swinging from it the following morning. All of Malee went to his funeral, and they shook their reeling heads as Mrs Jones wept, and asked themselves if it was worth it. But his funeral was soon forgotten, and they all shuffled back to their struggles, sure that they would win, that they could outlast any drought.

*** 

When Sean returned home from his tenth month of working at the cannery, his hair, which had only sported sprinklings of silver when he first left, was now awash with it, and had receded like poisoned weeds from the crown. He strolled through the charred woods in silent musings, which helped to air out his concerns as he rubbed the smooth spot on the top of his head, and sometimes he and Margaret

245

sat on the veranda, talking and laughing. Anne kept an owlish eye on them, going out to hang clothes if she saw them sitting out there, and asking Margaret to run an errand or tidy the house if she had been sitting with him too long. He didn't say much to her, and when the time came for him to return to the cannery, he was still loitering at home. "I'm not going back," he finally said to Anne over dinner. "You can start packing, and I'll speak to O'Hare tomorrow."

Anne stopped eating. "But you still have almost two months, Sean," she said with starved conviction.

"Nothing's going to happen in that time, so we may as well start now."

Anne took a deep breath, and it seemed to energise her. "Margaret won't be coming." She looked at Margaret, who said nothing. "She and I discussed it—she's going to Sydney to study nursing."

Sean nodded with a kind of rusted grating as if defeated. "Is that what you want, Margaret?"

Margaret gazed at the scrubbed kitchen floor, which seemed to pull her into its glaze. "Yes, that's what I want."

Sean kept staring. Her movements were so gentle, her skin so smooth, and he had wondered on more than a few occasions what it would be like to touch it, but he had fought those thoughts and incarcerated them somewhere. He looked away. Through the window he could see the evening sky on the horizon bleeding to merge with the red desert floor. He fought to hold onto that image. "It'll be tough to forge new roots—that's why folks don't move on so often, I suppose. But you know, after working my own land, being in that there cannery was like being imprisoned. Nobody talked about what they were doing or how much they liked it. All they cared about was whether they would be able to win something on the horses and get out of that place." His empty chuckle seemed starved of fuel. "If you ask me, the poor Abbo's a lot freer than many of them men I saw in that factory." His hand kept crushing and releasing thin air. Anne shifted as if to reach out to him, as though she finally understood that it wasn't only she who had been wallowing in a swamp of broken dreams, but something held her back. "You know I'm not a religious man, but if I was, I couldn't believe that some God had created us and sent us here to work so hard for—for nothing."

"It's ... It's not for nothing, Sean. At least we can sell the land and move on."

Sean gave a breathless laugh, which travelled nowhere. "I suppose all I'm trying to say is for Margaret to do what she feels good doing. We don't have all the right answers."

***

Sean saw Mr O'Hare the following day and they agreed terms. O'Hare said he should spend a day or two thinking about it and then come to see him to draw up the papers if he was still decided. He wanted land, he said, but he didn't want all the good people to leave Malee. Anne ran up a new dress and suggested they go to the square dance that night. Helen Cartwright had organised it, as she felt that even though there was nothing to harvest, the town's spirits needed lifting.

When Sean, Anne, and Margaret arrived, Helen's yard was already choked with cars, jeeps, and utes. Sean squeezed his vehicle in-between two cars and they headed towards the old coach house, from where they could hear music drifting. Dancing dust had been scattered on the floor, and several couples were already kicking it up as they twirled to country and western tunes that Mr Wilson was playing on his accordion, backed by two Aboriginals with flower box fiddles. The ladies were wearing mid-length dresses with gathered skirts, and the men wore wide-lapelled suits or clean shirts and khaki trousers. The musicians picked up the pace, and it seemed to make them all forget their troubles and whirl like blown leaves in the dust. Sean asked Anne to dance, but she said she would rather watch, and so he skipped around the dance floor with Helen Cartwright and several other ladies until they were all breathless.

Margaret stood by Anne, tapping her feet to the music until she saw Laura sitting in a chair because of her swollen belly. Federico was by her side. They were both nodding the same rhythm, and Federico had that buttery smile that had made her catch her breath so often, but now she could look at it and remain in control, she thought. When Mrs Jones sat at the piano to play a waltz, Mr Wilson danced with his pregnant daughter, who was now Mrs Laura Rossi. Margaret walked across the room to where Mr McDonald was standing. She knew it was scandalous, but something had driven her. "Could— Could I have this dance, please?" she said. Sean looked into her gum tree-rusted face and he couldn't pull away. He took her lithe body in his arms and they waltzed across the floor, trying to remain oblivious to the piercing stares which stuck to them like nettles. Margaret tremored as if a chill wind grazed her in his arms. She didn't know what moving on would mean. Would she have to fight to be accepted again? "I'll do anything if you let me stay," she said, whilst gazing at the floor. Sean stopped dancing and stepped back from her. They stared with unlatched cravings at each other whilst fighting for breath.

"I think your mum wants to try now," he said, and he hurried over to where Anne was sitting like a statue under the insinuating glares of the women, as though it was she who had violated their moral values. Sean took her reluctant hand and led her onto the dance floor. They moved like unoiled engines at first, but the longer they danced, the more at ease she became in his arms, until they were skimming over the dance floor together. Margaret stood ensnared where Sean had left her, with the Malee women ensuring their husbands gave her a wide berth, and then she left before the party had finished.

***

At ten o'clock the dancing stopped, and tea, cakes, and sandwiches were served for supper before everyone headed home.

Anne could hear Sean's whistling, which drowned out the songs of cicadas, as he prepared for bed. The night's dancing and his stumbling retreat from Margaret into her arms seemed to have made him forget that he would be selling his land to O'Hare on Monday morning. She knocked at his door and pushed it open, standing in her nightgown. "Sean, would you like to sleep in my room tonight?" she said. The invite struck him like lead in the gut, and he swayed back onto his heels. She hadn't invited him to her room in the longest while, and certainly not to sleep over after the act was done. She held out her shaking hand, and he took it and followed her to the room of flowers, and as they rocked in each other's arms, they heard thunder, saw lightning, and smelt the moistness rise from beneath them, before they both fell into a deep sleep.

They slept late that morning, and when Anne woke she sailed downstairs, singing with unbridled bliss. The fertile sounds and smells of the night before were still mingling in her head, and she realised it was the first time that she had surrendered control, and paradoxically, taken part. She dried some of the pots and decided not to use them again until they had moved, so she packed them in a corner. She started Sean's breakfast of eggs, bacon, and coffee, and as she buttered the bread the knife fell onto the floor. She glided to the sink to wash it, and it was only then that she noticed the film of cloud painted on the window. She wiped it with her hand and like an embedded axe froze, staring. Dark puddles glistened on the ground, and in one place she could see where a green shoot was already burrowing its way to freedom. She ran outside and trod the shoot back into the ground, but there was another, and another, and she ran from each trying to kill them before he woke. The skies wept again, and she didn't notice as she ran stomping into puddles and splashing muddy water onto her rain-soaked nightgown. Nor did she notice Margaret watching her from her window as Sean ran out into the rain. He was skipping and holding his hands up as if in grateful praise, and then he grabbed her and swung her around to join in his celebration.

\*\*\*

They had two weeks of non-stop rain before Margaret left, causing flash floods and vehicles to sink in the mud. Even so, Sean still went out and ploughed two of his fields to get them ready for planting.

They took her to the station in Langley, where she would take the train to Brisbane and then on to Sydney. Anne held her hand and then hugged her with a delicate strain, and Margaret went back to the car to say goodbye to Sean, who had decided to wait there. Anne watched her with sprouting envy as the train pulled out, knowing that she would probably never leave Malee, and she closed her eyes. Had Mrs Sommers, the woman who had kept her during the war, been so lonely? Is that why she had been unable to see her off at the station? She had to find some peace here; she couldn't live like this, always drowning inside.

# Chapter 19

The train from Langley to Brisbane took all day, and then Margaret changed for the overnight to Sydney, which took sixteen hours. The train pulled in at Central Station at midday, and Margaret's head swivelled like a weather vane, as she had never seen so many people. Businessmen in their khaki shorts and white shirts, uniformed schoolchildren, backpackers, and all sorts traversed the station. Their racket mingled with the clatter of trains from the marshalling yards and the hoppy reek of beer production from the brewery next door. She leaned to her side to balance the weight of her suitcase as she struggled through the crowd into the cavernous, echoing entrance hall. She put the case down and searched around her. The day-and-a-half journey had drained her, and she was like a lone fig tree in this strange place. Then she saw Liz approaching. Her jaw subsided like some foundation stone. Liz was wearing military fatigues and a Ché Guevara T-shirt, and her hair had been plaited with silk ribbons. "How you doing, country bumpkin?" Liz said as she hugged her.

"Good day, Liz," Margaret said, unable to mask her stark surprise.

"Comrade Liz, if you please. You're going to need a lot of re-educating." She grabbed hold of the suitcase. "What have you got in here?"

"Mum sent a cake and some things for you."

They walked out into the street, where a hot wind was howling. It lifted Margaret's hat and carried it down the street. She primed to give chase, but Liz grabbed her arm, "That's the first thing you're going to have to get rid of. Hardly anyone here wears those. If you want to look cool, I'll get you a beret." She pointed to a woman wearing one, and Margaret giggled two short bursts and shook her head.

They caught the bus out to Parramatta, and Liz pointed out Sydney University on the way. The bus conductor blew his whistle at every stop, and each time Margaret jerked around as if caught by surprise. They got off along the main road to Parramatta and walked down a side street to a three-storey brick house with a red corrugated iron roof. They dragged the suitcase up the steps and Liz put her key into the lock. A jazzily painted placard on the door said '*Only those against the war are welcome*'. The acrid haze hanging inside reminded Margaret of the cigarettes that she had smelled Carol smoking when she visited them in Malee. On the way up the stairs they bumped into a copper-bearded man who also wore military fatigues and a beret. "Bob, this is my sister, Margaret," Liz said.

Bob circled Margaret as if in a daze. "Cool, man. I'm Bob." He held up his hand, and Margaret gazed at Liz with quizzical eyes. Liz pursed her lips as if bored with Bob's antics, but she held up her hand, Margaret followed her, and Bob slapped her five. "Can I carry the case up for you?" Bob was already trying to take it from them.

"Fuck you," Liz said. It made Margaret jerk back as though she lacked recognition of the person before her. "We don't need testosterone to get a bloody suitcase up the stairs."

They dragged the case to the third floor and Liz opened the room she had secured for Margaret. Margaret went in and walked around while Liz lit a cigarette. The walls had been painted with various slogans, and there was a tattered wardrobe, table, and chair along one wall. A double bed lay in a corner of the room, but the mouldy sheets looked as if they hadn't been washed in six months. She peered out of the window into the overgrown backyard, where a wind chime was dancing in the gusts. "We all share the kitchen and bathroom," Liz said. "You'll like it after a while." Margaret gave a firm-lipped smile to swallow down her soaring disappointment. Liz sat on the corner of the bed and offered her a cigarette. She shook her head. "You know you'll have to get a job?"

"Yes," Margaret said. "I was thinking that maybe I could get a job teaching little kids. I'll have to do it before college starts."

Liz turned her back, but not before Margaret caught her wide-eyed glare, which suggested she was being too ambitious, but that's what their mum had taught her to be. "We're having a party tonight and you're invited. That cake would come in useful," Liz said.

Margaret took the cake out of the suitcase and gave it to Liz, who loitered as if she wanted to say something else but was constructing the line. Then: "Did you and Federico ever do it— you know?"

Margaret's head dropped like a sack of flour. "No."

"You know what these are?" Liz showed her a packet of her pills. Margaret shook her head in vigorous denial. "They stop you having

251

babies." Margaret's colouring flashed on and off like lightning clouds. "When you're ready, let me know and I'll take you to the doctor's."

Margaret shrugged from behind a kind of veil. "I'm going to wait until I get married."

"You'll be the only one in Sydney who is, so let me know if you need them." Liz got up to go. "Oh, and if any of the guys try to bother you tonight, especially that creep Bob, tell them to fuck off. Sometimes that's the only language they understand."

When Liz was gone Margaret opened the window and let the wind carry some of the weeks-old pee stench out. She found a broom and killed the cockroaches and bush crickets crawling over the floor before sweeping them away. Then she stripped the sheets from the bed, and washed and hung them to dry.

\*\*\*

The cicadas sang as soon as dusk fell, but Margaret didn't wake until music shook the floorboards more than an hour later. She searched out one of her nicer frocks and fixed her hair into a bun. She was going to dress and speak well even though Liz had made two years of Sydney brush oblique strokes onto her. A number of people lounged on the stairs chattering, drinking, and smoking the strange cigarettes as she went down. Many of them were dressed like Liz, and a couple of the women had on see-through kaftans, revealing their bra-less breasts, which made her recall Sister Ruth's punishment. Some of the revellers gazed at her frock with odd smirks as she squeezed through into the large kitchen where the party was being held. "You've arrived," Liz said, and put her arms around her shoulders. Her breath smelt like one of those Aboriginals that Sean used to buy alcohol for. "Everyone, this is my sister, Margaret," she shouted over the music. Several people said hello and then carried on with whatever they had been doing. "You want a drink?"

Margaret shrugged and scanned the room through the smoky haze. Everyone was drinking. Mrs McDonald didn't drink and had never allowed them to. "Just a little one," she said, pinching her fingers together. Liz gave her a double rum and coke and left her. The first sip bit her nose and throat and made her shoulders jump, but she liked the warm hug it gave, and the way it made her want to lounge in fortified comfort even when she was not. The lone black couple in the room smiled and raised their glasses when her searching eyes reached them, but she flitted away to study the poster of Lenin on the wall. She carried on around the room, past the couple snogging on the floor to the group who had congregated around the turntable grooving to the Rolling Stones and the Beatles blasting out of the speakers. She had heard the music a couple of times on the radio and TV, but she had never seen anyone do the dances in real life. The intoxicating rhythms were willing her body to move, but she poured down more rum and coke and pushed back the charge that was tempting her limbs.

"You want to fill in a *falsie*?" the voice next to her said again. This time the smooth-faced man held one hand by her ear as though speaking through a megaphone and then pointed to the documents he was carrying.

"I don't know what it is," Margaret admitted. He explained that he was getting the partygoers to sign bogus registration forms, to clog up the department of war's conscription efforts. Some had already signed as Mickey Mouse or Upyours Johnson, and some even received their call up papers. Margaret declined to sign one.

"Can I get you another one, then?"

Margaret stared at her empty cup. "Yes. Yes, please." She watched the tall, ivory-white man walk back to the table where all the drinks were laid out and fill her glass with rum, coke, and some ice. His black hair hung off his shoulders, but it wasn't as unruly as many of the others she had seen in the house.

"Here you go." Their fingers touched as he gave her the glass and she pulled her hand back, and then felt childish for having done so.

"I hear you're from the Deep South," he said. Margaret's shrinking face said she didn't know what he meant. "Queensland. That anti-socialist, fundamentalist Christian racist is still premier isn't he?"

Margaret shook her head. "I don't know." Then she looked away. She didn't like talking about that sort of thing.

"I hear he still doesn't allow you guys to have a drink up there."

Margaret fabricated an incomplete smile. She knew he meant the ban on Aboriginals drinking. "My mum is English and my dad is an Australian citizen."

"Well, my dad is an Australian citizen and my stepmother is a Martian," he said. Margaret saw the mischievous slant in his eyes and giggled behind her hand. He offered his palm. "I'm Matthew." He had a firm but friendly grip, and Margaret looked at his angular nose and sky blue eyes then averted her thick gaze again. Since Federico had left her she had taken to looking at men and weighing up which of their features would erase hers. If you put them together, what would you get? Matthew's would rub out a lot. "Do you dance?" He didn't wait for her to answer, but took her hands and swung from side to side like a rocking horse.

"No, I don't." Margaret pulled away and some of the drink spilled onto her dress.

"Sorry, that was my fault," Matthew said.

"No, it was me." Margaret wiped at the wet stain with her hand. "Excuse me." She hurried out to the bathroom.

When she sidled back into the room, he was gone. But then she saw him through the smoke, dancing with a narrow-hipped woman in the corner. Liz later told her that her name was Heng, and she came from Vietnam. She helped to organise marches against the war with her country, and Matthew went on all of them.

"How you doing, babes?" Bob stroked her arm, causing her to jump. He blew smoke from his joint into her face and she fanned it off, coughing. "Inhale, babes, inhale—we get two smokes for the price of one." His beard was tickling her shoulder and she could see the fillings and brown stains on his teeth. The room was crammed, like fruits into a crate, and Margaret couldn't move. She leaned her head away from him. "You and me could go to your room later, have a couple of joints and then—" He stuck out his tongue and curled it up to lick his rubbery nose. Margaret remembered the word that Liz had told her to use, but her foster mum had shown her how to act like a lady, and she had been baptised with a white scarf over her head. She retracted like a turtle into its shell and tried not to look at him. Bob blew more smoke her way. "Come on, babes, inhale." Margaret used her arm to push him off, but so that it appeared she was shifting her position. "What's wrong with this bloody sister of yours, Liz? She a virgin or something?" Unrestrained laughter came from all sides of the room.

"If you were the only fucking man on the planet then we'd all join nunneries, Bob," Liz shouted, to another cacophony of howls.

"If you ask me she's a bloody square," Bob said, weaving and searching for the laughs now.

"You think she's a square? Well, let me tell you what me and my sister did for our school concert." Liz was drunk and slurring. "We stripped naked, painted our bodies, and danced like two Abbos. No offence meant. You want to show them, Margaret?"

Margaret was stuck in her shell. Her arms slithered up to cross in front of her breasts. She felt naked. It wasn't the two of them, it was just her, and she wasn't one of them any more. Liz should have known that; she wrote and told her when she was baptised. Liz staggered over to Margaret, held onto her arm, and started to raise her own T-shirt. Margaret pulled away, and ran like a whirling storm to her room.

\*\*\*

In the misty morning, Margaret woke before the rest of the house, but it was still later than she had wanted. She had hoped to wake when the cockatoos nesting in a tree outside her window squawked the morning call, but when she looked out they had flown in search of food. She stepped over the bottles, cans, and plastic cups lining the stairs to the kitchen. Food and drink floated on the floor and work surfaces like a lake of garbage. The cake that Anne had sent looked as though people had torn off chunks with their hands, and there were several half-clothed bodies sprawled on the floor. Apart from Liz, Bob—who Liz explained was in hiding there because he was wanted by the police for dodging his Vietnam call up papers—one of the O'Hare girls, and herself, she didn't know who else lived there. She felt close to tears. With vexed care, she stepped over the prostrate bodies, cleared the rubbish, and piled it into boxes outside. Then she started to wash the dishes.

"Morning, Margaret," Liz said, whilst stretching her arms above her head.

"Morning," Margaret said, and her back stiffened.

Liz stepped over the bodies and put a soothing arm around Margaret's waist. "I was pissed last night, so if I said anything silly, I'm sorry." Margaret nodded but was coolly distant. "You want to go into the city today? I can show you where to start looking for jobs."

"Okay."

Liz went around the room and started kicking the squatters awake with burly haste. "Come on, time to go, let's have you."

\*\*\*

255

Liz asked Margaret if she wanted to work at a pub with her, but Margaret said she didn't want to work where people were drinking, so they took the train into the city. As the train screeched in on the raised section of track at Circular Quay Station, the sea breeze and smell of kelp smacked them in the face and seemed to sober Liz. Margaret was drawn to the Opera House, with its cream sails, which was still under construction after nearly two decades, and on the other side of the road, cement and granite giants rose up like steep mountains over the city, forming its commercial centre. They weaved through the crowds on the pavements and asked at various department stores. At first the managers smiled and nodded when Liz approached them, but when she pointed to Margaret, their faces set like concrete and they shook their solemn heads stiffly.

By early evening they still hadn't found anything and Liz took Margaret to work with her at a pub in Kings Cross. They hurried past a stretch of sleazy strip joints, tattoo shops, and nightclubs, shaking their heads when beggars stupefied from heroin approached them, and on a couple of occasions Liz had to string her arm through Margaret's and tell the soldiers on R&R from Vietnam that they weren't prostitutes, using the strong words she had mastered since coming to Sydney. Margaret sat in a corner behind the bar and watched the sailors and soldiers touch Liz as she took their orders, and the friendlier she was with them the bigger their tips would be. She was flooded with relief that she had decided not to work there. She would look for work herself the next day.

Two weeks later she found a job as a cook and waitress in a large burger bar on George Street. It was far enough away from the red-light areas to be frequented mainly by tourists and city workers, and she could work all day at the weekends and three hours two evenings a week, which would fit in with her studies. The money was barely enough to pay her rent and living expenses, but it was her first job, and she wrote to Anne immediately to tell her the good news.

She started her induction course into nursing at Sydney University in early February. The class was large enough for her to float in its pool unnoticed, and she rushed off to work or home to study at the end of each day, so she didn't have time to make friends. She was also wary of the campus life of constant demonstrations against the war and commercial development of the Rocks, the Loo, and other parts of Sydney. But most of all, she jittered with cold dread when anyone approached her to talk about signing petitions or marching for Aboriginal rights. She wanted nothing to do with it or them. She spent part of her first week's salary on paint to whitewash the graffiti from her bedroom wall, but the musty odour of hemp drifting through the house, the non-stop partying, the fact that none of the other residents cleaned the bathroom or kitchen—and when she did they thought she was square—and the itinerant hippies and draft dodgers she would find sleeping on the floors after a party or demonstration all served to unhinge her. So, without mentioning it to Liz, she started to search for another place to stay.

*****

The wind howled down George Street like a lonely dog and drove sheets of rain ahead of it. The extra wide drains were already flooded, and a large stream raged along the gutters so that people crossing the road had to jump it. Margaret served a customer and gazed out at the deluge. A man tried to leap the stream, but the hungry wind snapped at his umbrella and his feet landed in the racing torrent. He pushed open the door and entered the restaurant dripping. He placed his umbrella in a box by the corner and sat at a table. When he wiped the rain out of his sky blue eyes and back through his hair, Margaret recognised him. It was Matthew, who had spoken to her at the party on her first day in Sydney.

"Hey, you!" the stubby, bald man with a thick moustache, wearing shorts and knee length socks, called after her. The owner, Mr Gazis, was watching from behind the counter, and Margaret hurried to the irate customer.

"Can I help you?"

"What do you think this is?" He held open the half eaten sandwich. Margaret stared at the bun, not quite knowing what he meant. She could feel Mr Gazis' eyes searing her back. "Well, what did I ask for?" He started to play to an audience, and other customers swung prying eyes onto his table.

Margaret took her notepad out of her apron. "You ordered coffee and a hamburger, sir."

"I ordered a cheeseburger, I definitely ordered a *cheeseburger*. Did you hear that?"

"Seeing as your mouth's wider than a pig's ass, you could have stuffed three burgers in there and the whole of Sydney would have still heard you," Matthew said.

Baldhead turned towards him. "Well, you would think if they were going to employ them they would make sure they understood the language."

Margaret took his plate. "I'll get you another one, sir," she said in her best English.

"I don't know what this country is coming to," Baldhead continued.

"Sorry, can anyone interpret what he just said? I don't speak grunt." Matthew was performing now, and Baldhead turned away, pallid as a turnip.

Margaret brought him his cheeseburger, and he checked it with the rigour of an auditor to make sure the cheese was there, before biting into it without so much as a thank you. Then Margaret went to take Matthew's order. She didn't know if he would remember her, and so she played him for any other customer. "Can I take your order now, sir?"

"Have you learned to groove yet?" He clicked his fingers. Margaret's lips spread like butter and she shook her head. His stare refused to leave her and she dropped her blooming eyes to her pad. "I'll have a cheeseburger and a Coke, and I won't complain if you forget the cheese."

"You'll have to wait here until I've made sure it's okay," Matthew said with a wicked smile when she brought him the food. He bit into the burger and shook his head with satisfaction. "You seen much of Sydney since you arrived?"

"No, I've been working and I've also started studying." She played with her pencil and pad and pretended to look with assiduous regularity for other customers so as not to gape at him.

"What are you studying?" Matthew asked, his mouth full.

"Nursing at Sydney."

"I'm at Sydney doing my Masters in politics. Surprised I haven't bumped into you there."

"I don't hang around much after class," she said. Mr Gazis raised his football head to point her towards some new customers and she hurried over to them, trailing reluctance. She took their orders and waited while Gazis flipped the burgers and drained the chips. He put

258

all three plates on a tray and then wiped his hand across the apron that covered his ballooning belly. He was a quiet and easy-going man, and sometimes his wife and daughters, whom Margaret liked, would come in to help out. They hadn't been in the country long, and like many of the recent immigrants, he had seen a gap in the restaurant trade which meant he could be his own boss. He had been to the assimilation classes with his wife, and as soon as he had learned enough English to get by, he had set up the restaurant. Kebabs were what he sold first, but when he realised that it would take the Australians a while to get used to it, he had introduced things he already saw them eating, like burgers, chips, and fried English breakfasts. He had liked the fact that Margaret spoke well, and she wasn't someone who was going to feel she was better than him in his own shop.

Margaret flew around a few more tables in order to get back to Matthew, but when she turned around he had gone.

"You sure you don't want a lift?" Gazis said as he saw Margaret through the door. "I take half-hour to close up then I can drop you."

"No thanks," she said. "My bus will soon be here." She waved to him and hurried down the road. When she had started she hadn't worked until closing time, but after a few weeks in Sydney, she soon found that she could fill many needs with soothing jaunts to the department stores, where she could try on dresses like all the other customers before she bought them, and after, she sometimes stopped and ate the best foods at a restaurant, the type of tasty treat that she would have been refused when she was in the home at Radley, and she liked the money. The evening wore a naked chill, and a thick soup of dampness hung in the air.

"Hey, sister?" a dishevelled Aboriginal, reeking of mould, came out of a concealed doorway at her. She twisted to avoid his touch and increased her stride. "You got any change, sister?" She didn't look back, held her head down, and kept moving. Have nothing to do with them, her foster mother had said, nothing at all. His grubby hand reached out to clutch her and she stepped into the road. A car horn blared its irate warning and she swung around to stare into its blinding beam with a hand raised. Someone grabbed her by the arm and pulled her out of its path. She started to scream, but before it could escape her she saw it was Matthew.

"Sorry, I didn't mean to frighten you," he said. Her eyes were still caught in a glare and she was shaking. He put his arm around her heaving shoulders. "Are you going to be okay?" She nodded in a fitful swirl. The drunk was waiting a few feet away from them, and Matthew dug into his pocket and gave him a few coins. The stench of alcohol and mould receded like smoke on a breeze. "Where are you going?"

"Home," she said, relief coating her tongue like a stiff drink.

"Can I give you a lift?"

They were on the move again and he still had his arm around her shoulder. Margaret released a smile. "Yes."

They turned off the main road and he held open the door of his green MG sports car for her. Many of the other students didn't drive, and if they did, it was more likely to be an old Holden or one of those small Japanese cars. She took two attempts before she bent low enough to get in. "I live in Parramatta," she said as Matthew let the engine roar and then pushed the car into first.

"I know, I was at the party, remember?"

"You've helped me out twice today. Thanks."

"That's okay, I want to be of service to you." Their eyes locked and he grinned. Margaret skipped a breath and turned to stare at first her shaking knees and then the receding road. He had on a white T-shirt with something about Vietnam plastered across the front, and he wore forest-green kakis, which looked much smarter than the military fatigues many of the students were wearing. If anything, they looked like the troops and Matthew like one of their commanders. "So, when am I going to get to show you Sydney?"

"I'm too busy with studying and work."

"We don't live to work, Margaret." She spun around, surprised that he remembered her name. "Life is about more than that." She turned to hide her smile. That's what she used to think when she saw her foster mum running busy all the time, but how else could you afford a place like Mrs Cartwright's Billabong Lodge? Still, she didn't want to stir in the opposite direction to Matthew, so she asked him where he had learned that. "I've done some reading on Buddhism, and I spent some time in Goa. The people there have much less than we do in a material sense, but they have far more happiness." They travelled in comfortable silence the rest of the way, and when he reached her house he asked, "What time do you finish classes tomorrow?"

"About one."

"Are you working?"

"No, it's my day off, but I have studies."

"I'll meet you by the tennis courts at one," he said. She ran up the steps and through the door, but she left it cracked and watched him until he had pulled away.

***

They met a little after one, and Matthew drove into the city and parked somewhere off Circular Quay. Margaret had wanted to see the Opera House again, and he walked her past the unfinished building and told her that as soon as it was ready he would take her to a concert there. They strolled up through the botanic gardens, and Matthew said he was sure she could tell him about all the different kinds of trees and plants that were there. Margaret hesitated as if to question what he was really asking her. She had been brought up in a nice home with good food, and in recent years they even had a television. She wasn't brought up in the bush. No, she said. I don't know anything about them, and so she listened as he read off the names. When they reached the sea wall where they could look across Sydney Harbour at the bridge and the towers climbing skywards, Margaret stopped and put her palm against her chest. Not even Laura Wilson could have floated that high. There was a power to this place that was infusing her with new dreams. Matthew put his arm around her soaring shoulder and they wandered on.

They came to a bend in the path, and when they went around it, they saw the two warships anchored in the bay, with the stars and stripes fluttering from their masts. Four moping students were slumped on the sea wall with their banner of demonstration prostrate at their feet. Margaret felt Matthew's forearm tighten, and his arm slipped from her shoulder. He marched towards the sea wall and snatched up the banner. "Come on, lets give it to them," he said with a stabbed clench of his fist. "US navy— out now— Imperialist murders— out now— Nixon, Kissinger— out now—" The students stared at each other with re-torched eyes and reclaimed their banner and chants. Matthew scuttled off the path, plucked up loose stones, and started to hurl them at the ships whilst still conducting the

261

chants, but they were never going to reach, and his missiles, and those of the two students who followed him, splashed down harmlessly in the ebbing waters. Margaret rumbled with desire for his gaping passion and ability to draw people to his cause, and by the time they reached Hyde Park, she was sure Matthew had ensnared her, although she couldn't be certain that it was with the same force that Federico had held her.

"My father was in business, but he's going to run for labour at the next elections," Matthew said when she asked him. "I'm always telling him that he'll have to do something about Aboriginal land rights when he gets in."

"What does he think about the war?" Margaret said, changing the subject again. Matthew let it pass.

"Since we started to lose Australian lives I think he's changed his mind. He wants us to get out now, but he doesn't agree with the demonstrations. He says it can't be doing our lads' morale any good knowing that people back home are against them."

He held her hand as they sauntered up the steps into the Australian and New Zealand Army Corps War Memorial. They descended into the basement to look at the flags, medals, weapons, and attire of war, just so that Matthew could show her how foolish it all was.

"Hey you," one of the proud veterans on duty called out. Margaret turned towards the Japanese couple against whom his anger was vented, as they were about to take a picture of their country's midget submarine replica, the original of which was captured when it tried to sneak into Sydney Harbour during the war. "Can't you read? Show some respect for the dead, no pictures, no pictures." His crossing hands told them what he meant, and they bowed and put the camera away.

*\*\*\**

"He's so nice," Margaret said to Liz over their dinner of eggs, chips, and beans.

"Where did he take you?" Liz asked.

"We just walked around Sydney. I saw the Opera House again, and we went to a park. They have that statue of Cook there."

"Hyde Park," Liz said. "Did he take you to his place?"

Margaret's face prickled with warmth. "No, but he kissed me in the car." She giggled.

"You know he's about twenty-five and he's had a lot more experience than you?"

"You're beginning to sound like Mum, Liz. I thought you said I should enjoy myself?"

"I did, but it's not like being back at home where you meet someone and you're together for the rest of your lives."

"That doesn't happen at home anyway," Margaret said, with a ripened glaze to her face.

Liz pushed her shoulder in a playful tease. "We'll go to see that doctor tomorrow."

*** 

For the rest of the week Margaret saw Matthew on the evenings she wasn't working, and he drove her home on the evenings she did work. On Friday night they went to a bar on Oxford Street where they played live rock music, and he started to loosen her up with a few spirits and grooves on the dance floor. The basement was dark and smoky, the crowd young and noisy, and the band loud and hot. She laughed with wild yearnings when she made mistakes with her steps, and sometimes the drink made her lose balance and fall against him. As she supported herself, she felt his marble-smooth chest under his wet shirt. On one of these occasions, Matthew held her lithe body in his arms, stared into her eyes, which were unlatched with nervous expectancy, and then walked her to his car. They arrived at his one bedroom apartment five minutes later. It felt like a whirlwind, her losing her clothes and him kissing her in places she never knew could be cooled by rain. And when he entered her, she bit down and held him so that he would stop. When the pain dissipated, she made him rock again, and she did this several times until she felt she could take all he had to give. It felt better than when she had been baptised, all this white inside of her, and she remembered Matron Blythe's words that she would never have one of these men because they were reserved for better women, and she held onto her prize so that he could pump those words out of her, and near the end a scream echoed in her head, thank you Jesus, thank you for making me pure, and she sank back on the bed exhausted with tears running down her face. Matthew wiped back what she hoped he

263

thought was sweat from her face. "You are on something, aren't you, babes?" She nodded with cushion-closed eyes, because she knew that anything which came from her now would be pure, and so would be registered in the annals of the church as belonging.

***

They continued to see each other over the following weeks, and Matthew began asking her to stay over for a night or two, until soon Margaret was spending most of her time at his apartment. When he realised that she was still searching for a place, he asked her to move in.

"Are you sure you know what you're doing?" Liz asked her as she packed the last of her things. Margaret stopped, so that Liz could feel the gentle breeze that she was swaying in. She had never been so sure.

# Chapter 20

By the end of the week, Margaret had moved into the neat but sparse apartment without fuss. Less than four years previously it would have been illegal for the races to cohabit, not that Margaret saw herself as any different to Matthew now. With tacit conspicuousness, she set about turning what had been a bachelor apartment with bare walls and few ornaments into a home. She put flowers in vases around his Ché Guevara poster, and when he didn't say anything, she bought pictures of children playing and hung them on the walls. Each morning she rose and swept cockroaches and the black Sydney dust, which had flown in on the wind, from the apartment before she left for college or work. Then she waited for Matthew's pat on the bum or smile, anything to say that he liked what she had done, but they never came, and she remembered that was how her foster father, Sean, had been, and put it down to men's ways.

Matthew's energy threw her into a swirl. He did his studies at the university with copious amounts of work at his desk in the living room, and then he spent as many hours with his friends from the Sydney Push—a loose confederation of intellectuals, artists, renegades, radicals, and commies of all ages that led the city's counterculture. They sat in smoke-filled bars and rooms listening to poetry, jazz, and rock, planning strategies for demonstrations and what the new society would look like, before they stoned themselves on pot and booze. Margaret tagged along like loose fittings to some of the meetings, and when his friends saw how *down* Matthew was being with his new girlfriend, they forgot that his father was a rich businessman who had now turned to politics, even if it was for the Labor Party. So Matthew started to insist that she come with him when she had a spare moment, and even at times when she didn't. Margaret never refused, but mostly she would sit and drink with chilled interest while they planned protests.

Margaret told Mr Gazis that she had to go to the doctors so that she could get the afternoon off to go to the demonstration. Gazis didn't yet feel comfortable enough with his Australian citizenship to consider protest, and with all that he had gained from coming to the continent, he was sure that he and everyone else should be eternally grateful. With sudden convenience, Margaret had forgotten the *Moratorium on Vietnam* T-shirt that Matthew had given her to wear, and she eventually found him at the university near the front of several thousand other demonstrators preparing to march through Sydney. Marches had also been planned in other cities across the country to call for a stop to the conscription of young Australian men to fight in Vietnam. The American president, Lyndon Baines Johnson, had visited Australia in '66 to bolster support for the war. At the time, most Australians supported their superpower ally or paymaster, depending on which side of the fence one stood. But, instead of continuing Johnson's policy of withdrawal as he had promised, Nixon had deepened the war, and dozens of Australians were now returning home in body bags.

Tens of thousands of marchers, twenty chests wide, wound their way from the university up Broadway towards the city centre. Many carried placards with the inscription *Withdraw All Troops Now!* and banners stretched the full width of the crowd, swinging uneasily in the breeze. The roads had been blocked off and traffic backed up for miles. Black-capped police marched single file alongside the demonstrators. At first it had been rumoured that bus loads of them were waiting behind buildings to attack the marchers, but when they saw that the marchers were from all walks of life, the plans quickly changed, and some of them even lifted their lapels to reveal their hidden moratorium badges. Grandparents marched with their student grandchildren, and mothers and fathers who had lost sons or were trying to save sons from the draft, children who had lost fathers, teachers, university professors, farmers, bus drivers, dustmen, trade unionists and politicians, rich and poor, all sections of society were there. The crowd were jovial in their comradeship, some singing and laughing, and black caped, white masked actors staged guerrilla theatre for them, some playing American soldiers chasing and shooting or stabbing others dressed as Vietnamese. When they reached Hyde Park, thousands more melted into the throng for the march to the Town Hall. This would be the ground on which they would vent their anger in Sydney, whilst others did the same in Canberra, Brisbane, Melbourne, and other cities. Margaret stuck close to Matthew as the crowd squeezed in around them and forced them up the street like herds into a pen. They joined in the chant of the crowd as they went, Margaret with doused emotions. "*One, two, three, four, we don't want any bloody war. One, two, three, four, we don't want any bloody war. All troops*

*Out Now*
*Vietnam*
*Out Now*
*Australian troops*
*Out Now.*"

By the time the pushing and shoving had stopped, they were in the middle of the crowd on George Street from where they could see the stage on the steps of the Town Hall. Office workers were leaning out of their windows, waving banners and cheering them on, and some of the protestors had climbed onto roofs and canopies to get a better view. Speakers from the peace movement and the mothers of 'Save our Sons' gave anti-war speeches, and the crowd cheered and clapped each one, regardless of how good they were. A loud cheer went up when three draft dodgers, who were on the run, were smuggled onto the stage, and they gave impassioned speeches about the plight of the Vietnamese and the numbers in which they were being killed. Margaret recognised Bob, Liz's flatmate, amongst them, and he gave a lucid speech which brought the house down before he and the other draft dodgers had to be rushed off stage to escape the advancing police. A schoolgirl went onto the stage to let the demonstrators know that schoolchildren were against the war, and then various folk singers and hippie bands gave performances.

As dusk fell, the demonstrators lit candles and marched towards the football stadium for a concert, singing the protestors' anthem, 'We Shall Overcome'. Matthew asked Margaret to wait, and he went over to speak to two Aboriginals. He pointed back to her, and the Aboriginal man and woman, both of whom had big Afros, nodded their hellos. She didn't respond, but she could sense the man's eyes still scouring her. He started towards her, and she felt herself tightening into a ball, like the day the Aboriginal drunk had approached her a few weeks earlier. She searched out the rest of the crowd. Most of them were like her; if he tried anything, they would help her. Why did Matthew have to go and speak to them?

267

"G'day, don't I know you?" the man masked by the Afro and beard said. Margaret stared into the distance as if she hadn't heard him over the tramping of the marching crowd. "Margaret?" She looked at him with a narrowed gaze. She recognised his rasping voice, but not his hairy face. "Margaret, it's me, Nannup."

She flung open her mouth in astonishment, and then she tried to slam it shut until it produced only a frightened smirk. He was about two years older than when she had last seen him, but he seemed to have filled out into his man's body, which he now carried like someone who had lived his learning. "Hello," she finally said, and looked past him, hoping that Matthew would hurry back.

"What are you doing in Sydney?" he said, his arms opening to embrace her, but being warned off by her cringing shoulders.

"I'm studying to become a nurse."

"That's great, we need people like you. I thought about you a lot and wondered if I left you by mistake or—"

"I live with someone now. I just want to be left alone."

Nannup followed her bolted glare to Matthew as he came back towards them. Matthew slapped him on the back. "This is my girlfriend Margaret, Nannup. Do you two know each other?"

"No," Margaret said before Nannup could contradict her.

Matthew shook Nannup's hand. "I'll see you at the party, then?"

"Yeah, sure thing, mate," Nannup said, and he left, looking over his shoulder as if tethered to an irrefutable past.

*\*\*\**

Margaret waited until they arrived home before asking him, "What party?"

"Oh, didn't I tell you? My father's having a barbecue tomorrow evening."

She dropped the potato she was peeling. "I—I can't go. I haven't got anything to wear."

"It's just a barbie; any of them dresses you have will do." Matthew opened the fridge, grabbed a beer, and took a swig.

"But it's the first time I'll be meeting your parents."

"Don't worry about it, it'll be cool." He wandered into the bedroom as if untroubled. Margaret stole to the linen cupboard in the hall and took out the bottle of wine she kept hidden between the sheets. She drank one mouthful then another, and when she heard his

268

creaking footsteps she shoved the bottle back and wiped her mouth with the back of her hand.

***

In the morning, Margaret went out and bought a bottle of wine for Matthew's father and some flowers for his stepmother. Her lips were dry, and she creamed her hands several times before they left, as well as swallowing two gulps of confidence from her hidden bottle. The autumn day was unusually hot, with the temperatures reaching into the mid-eighties. They headed down Macquarie Street and onto the expressway leading to the harbour bridge. Before reaching the bridge they caught the first glimpse of the sails of the Opera House, but it wasn't so interesting to Margaret now, as her stomach had not held anything all morning. They sped out past the many bays and inlets along the northern shoreline, out past the three-hundred-foot rocky cliffs of North Head, which formed the northern side of the entrance to Sydney Harbour. The spaces were more open now, with bark stripped gum trees and green and yellow vegetation dominating. They welcomed the cool breeze which blew in from the pacific as they cruised along the highway towards the more prosperous northern suburbs. Matthew turned into a road leading down to the water level, and Margaret could see that there was only one large mansion down there, behind which lay a curved sandy beach and a turquoise lagoon. She needed a stiff drink now more than ever.

A number of cars were parked along the road, but Matthew drove up to the gate. The gateman recognised him and the gates eased back with the whirr of a motor. "Matthew!" a lady shouted as she stepped out of a car and hurried towards the gate. It was the same woman who had been with Nannup at the demonstration, and he was behind her. The woman seemed much older than Nannup, although with his beard and Afro he had managed to disguise the gap. She bent down and Matthew leaned his head out of the car and they touched cheeks.

"Hello, Joyce."

He parked the car just inside the gates, got out, and shook Nannup's hand. "Margaret, you remember Nannup from yesterday, don't you? And this is Joyce." She nodded and accepted Nannup's and then Joyce's hand. "They are both with the Aboriginal Advancement League," he continued, but Margaret was blocking them and their Advancement League out.

Matthew led all of them around the back of the house to the well-manicured lawns where the garden party was already in full swing. The house was newly built, he said; his stepmother had persuaded his father that a new wife needed a new home, and he had built her a white Spanish villa without sparing any expense. Dozens of people were gathered in clusters around the swimming pool, eating finger food, drinking wine, and chattering like birds. Jazz melodies rose from a quartet of piano, bass, drum, and saxophone players at one end of the pool. As Matthew wound his way through the party, he nodded and pumped several hands. "Matthew!" a man called out. It was obviously his father. He was a shade smaller than Matthew and his hair had receded from the centre, but they had the same sky blue eyes and sharp nose. He also moved with the same formal gait as his son as he strode across the lawn, shook his hand, and embraced him.

"Dad, these are friends of mine, Margaret, Joyce, and Nannup."

"Pleased to meet you," Bob Stevens said as he took each hand with both of his and gave them a firm politician's handshake.

"Am I going to be introduced to your friends, too?" said a smiling woman with a heavy accent. She embraced Matthew briefly and touched both cheeks against his. He did not hug back.

"Helga, these are friends of mine."

She shook their hands with the same pasted on smile, and they introduced themselves again. Helga's brunette hair had been moulded into a beehive, which made her stand inches over Bob Stevens, and she was also bigger in body. Like most of the ladies there she was wearing an evening gown, which melted Margaret's spirit from burning shame in her best frock.

"Would you young people like a drink?" Bob Stevens asked. They all said yes, and he called the waiter over to serve them. "Were you at the demonstrations yesterday?" he asked his son.

"Yes, thousands turned up."

"How long do you think it will be before we get out, Mr Stevens?" Joyce asked. She was a sharply studious woman who took her time to weigh up people or situations before she stepped forward. She was more than ten years older than Nannup, but their relationship had been good for him. The movement in Sydney had been her life for some years, and she had been able to guide him in that as well as other things.

"It will be up to you young people," Bob Stevens said. "If you vote for the Labour party at the next elections, we will begin to pull our troops out immediately."

"That's what you're going to do for your people, but what you going to do for ours?" Nannup said. Margaret took a glass of wine from the tray the waiter offered and stepped a few feet away from them to listen to the music now. This was none of her business.

Bob Stevens waved a manicured finger in the air, as if he was on a dais. "We will certainly look into the land rights issue. I think we can do something there."

"Don't you think the first thing any new government should do is give an apology?" Joyce held Nannup's sturdy arm, which Margaret glimpsed from the corner of an eye was growing tense with unpruned irritation, and his voice was travelling so that other guests were turning to look.

"I will admit that many wrongs were done in the past, by governments and individuals," Bob Stevens said. Helga strung her arms through his, as if to support him whilst he was campaigning. "But I am not in the habit of apologising for things for which I had no responsibility."

"A company wouldn't get away with saying 'The chairman's left so we're no longer responsible.' So shouldn't there be some continuity of responsibility for a government's actions, whoever was at the head when it happened?" Joyce squeezed Nannup's arm to rein him in, although his muscles were still knotting, and he was shaking like a well-run colt.

"You know, the most effective apology for a past wrong is to correct it in the present," Joyce said. "But if those in the present don't feel there is any need for an apology, then the wrong can never be corrected." She studied Mr Stevens as if to see if she was having any impression on him. "Maybe the reason you think as you do, Mr Stevens, is because our peoples are very different spiritually."

"How is that?"

"Well, we Koori people believe that we have a link with all that comes before and after us. We still talk to our ancestors in ceremonies, for example. So whatever they did in the past is a part of us."

Bob Stevens nodded. "Yes, that maybe it. What do you think, Margaret?"

271

She turned back to them, flush faced. "I'm sorry, I wasn't listening. I'm not feeling very well." She touched her churning stomach. But she had heard everything, and she didn't believe what Mr Stevens had said. She had been to that ANZAC war memorial and the museum with Matthew, and there they acknowledged through solemn exhibits the things their ancestors had done for them. They said they had fought in two world wars to protect them, to give them a future. But hadn't they also stolen land, killed its inhabitants, taken their children so that they could give theirs what they thought were shallower steps to climb? Maybe like weak mortar they could only carry so much weight; so they lay claim to the good that their ancestors had done for them, but they couldn't bring themselves to face the bad, and so they would deny it was for them, or cloud it in some false glory.

"Hearing you speak, Joyce, I think you would do well in the women's movement. We need people like you," Helga said.

Joyce's lips curled a touch. "At the moment the women's movement would break up our community even more by splitting us off from our men. We spent years being encouraged not to do men's things, not to marry our men, and to walk on the other side of the road when we saw them, so our community needs to reconnect with them. It took me years to let an Aboriginal man touch me, Mrs Stevens." She stroked Nannup's arm and Helga recoiled.

Margaret walked away, clutching at her stomach. "Excuse me," Joyce said to the others, and followed after her. "Do you want to sit down over there?" She pointed to the quiet patch of grass by the bed of petunias. They walked over and sat in the grass. "Smell them," Joyce said, and she put her nose towards the petals. "Sometimes it can make you feel better." Margaret followed Joyce and drew in the scent of the flowers. "Do you remember doing that as a little girl?" Margaret pulled away from the flowers and sat straight-backed. "I'm sorry," Joyce said, and stroked her back. "Nannup told me about you. He said how smart you are, but also that you might need help." Margaret swung further away from her, with blind fight stiffening her back. Joyce stopped stroking it. "Our organisation helps to trace mothers, fathers, and their children. We've been quite successful."

"My mother lives in Malee," Margaret said, without facing her. Why was this woman doing this? She spoke nice and was even fairer than her. If she tried, she could pass as well.

272

Joyce pressed her lips together and her mouth spread wide, as if caught between a smile and a frown. She took a card out of her purse. "Our office is in Redfern. Here—" Margaret wouldn't take it, so Joyce rested the card on her lap. "If you change your mind, come in anytime." Joyce got up and went back to where Nannup was waiting.

Margaret looked around for Matthew; she wanted to go. This was worse than being caught in a downpour without an umbrella. He was standing alone at the buffet table, and Helga slid up alongside him. He said something and Helga looked dismissively in her direction and then back at Matthew. She seemed pricked with irritation, and she said something to him as if she were giving firm orders. Matthew stared with tickled nonchalance at her, bit on a piece of food, and walked away while she was still lecturing. Helga folded her arms under her ample bosom and gazed pure venom across the pool at her. Margaret turned her delirious head to the ground and plucked at the grass like the strings on a solemn guitar.

***

"I don't think your parents liked me," Margaret said the next morning as she got ready for college.

Matthew rolled over onto his back. "Don't be silly, my father is very open-minded."

She sat on the bed to put on her shoes. "What about Helga?"

"Helga just likes Helga." He pulled her back down onto the bed, but she pushed him away.

"I've got to go."

Matthew threw a pillow at her. "Are you going to bloody mope all day?" Margaret picked up the pillow and put it back on the bed as if there was no one there. Matthew raised his head and sighed in insipid frustration.

As Margaret was going through the door, the phone rang. "It's for you," Matthew shouted. She came back and waited for him to tell her who it was, but he pushed the receiver in her direction and climbed out of bed.

"It's Bob. Liz isn't well; I think you need to come over."

"I'm on my way to class, and then I have to work today," Margaret said.

"Look, I think this is serious, someone needs to be here."

"I'll come after work," Margaret said, and put down the receiver. She was getting tired of nourishment flowing one way along the umbilical cord that tenuously held her and Liz together. Usually it was money. She knew Liz drank, but many of the customers at the pub bought her drinks. Margaret stole to the airing cupboard, slipped her bottle from between the sheets, and downed a mouthful before she left.

***

After classes she took the short bus ride to work. When she hustled through the back door to change, Mrs Gazis, who looked as if she and her stumpy husband were twins—including the hair on her chin—told her that someone had called to say her sister wasn't well. Mrs Gazis said that she would cover for her if she wanted to go early, but Margaret said that it could wait, as she had to make up for missing work when she visited the doctor, although she sensed that they suspected she had gone to the demonstration. She did half of her shift behind the counter frying eggs, burgers and chips, and was glad when she could move to the relative cool of the dining area to serve instead. The unhurried calm out there gave her more than a moment's breath to think, and she cooked up all kinds of worries. Liz had always called herself when she wanted her, and that had never been at work. Was it their mother back home, or had Liz fallen out with her latest boyfriend?

When she finished work she hurried out the door and caught a taxi to Parramatta. Bob met her at the house and told her that Liz had been rushed to hospital. Rose O'Hare had gone with her. When Margaret reached the hospital Liz was lying in a bed with drips running into her arm. Dark circles gnawed at her eyes as if trying to extract them, and she was asleep. Margaret told the nurse that she was her sister and wanted to know what was wrong, but the nurse folded her arms and slapped her foot against the floor as if to say she was no fool. Rose O'Hare was still there and told the nurse that it was true, and so the nurse read the chart to Margaret. "Heroin," she said. "Seems she overdosed." Margaret staggered back onto the chair at the side of the bed. They had talked about the crazy people they saw weaving aimlessly along Kings Cross and had both said they couldn't. She knew that Liz took vitamin B shots when she had poisoned herself with too much alcohol, but this? She called Helen Cartwright

274

on her recently installed telephone, and she said she would drive over straight away to tell Sean and Anne, as they didn't have one.

***

It was two days before Anne reached Sydney. "Your father couldn't afford to come too," she said when Margaret met her at the station. Margaret was caught by surprise that she would admit they couldn't afford to do something, but then they hadn't seen each other for some time. She gave her mother a thick jumper to protect her from the bone-gnawing winter breeze, which she was not used to, and they rushed straight to the hospital. Liz was awake when they arrived. The swelling around her eyes had reduced, but she was still as drawn as a wilted leaf. They had been giving her small doses of methadone to wean her off the heroin without the severe symptoms of withdrawal, and the nurse said she was doing well. Anne kissed her cheek and held her wasted hand. They stared into each other's tear-breached eyes for a while, and then Liz turned away as though she had glimpsed the shadow of her mother's disappointment. "I'm sorry," she said as she started to cry.

"Why?"

"I don't know. It's not easy being away from everything you know. I just couldn't cope."

Anne closed her eyes and brought her daughter's hands to her quivering lips. She had known it too. To tear yourself from all you knew and sew your soul into the fabric of a different world. It wasn't easy, and she had been dropping stitches for three decades. "Do you want to come home?"

Liz shook her head as Anne stroked her sallow cheek as if touching it for the first time. "No."

"I can stay for a week or two. Will that be all right?"

Liz nodded and wiped back a tear.

"Is there anything else you need?"

"Well, I'm behind on the rent," Liz said.

"Your father and I won't be able to help out much; things are still fairly difficult on the farm." Anne turned to Margaret with the question written in her eyes.

"I can do some extra hours at work and help out," Margaret said.

***

After they left the hospital, Margaret took Anne out for a meal before taking her back to Liz's room in Parramatta, where she would stay for the duration of her visit. The rank odour of dirty clothes and half-eaten food smeared them like tipped garbage as they stepped into the room. Anne was stunned silent. She put down her bags, opened the window, and started to clean the room with Margaret's help. When they were done, Anne patted a place next to her on the bed, "Sit down for a while before you go, Margaret." Margaret sat on the bed with apprehension unfurling its crumpled leaves in her stomach. Anne brushed her arm with short halting strokes. "I want you to know how much you helped me, Margaret. Not around the house or in the garden or things like that, but the way you helped me to accept this place. I watched the way you changed from what you were when you came to us into who you are now, and that made me realise that I could find a way to be alive here." Margaret looked away, as if trapped in her own world. Wasn't it Anne McDonald who should have helped her? Isn't that what a mother was for? Did she think it was just she and Liz who had been away from those they knew?

"I have something for you," Anne finally said. She dug around in her overnight case and pulled out a stack of letters. "About four years ago I received all of these from the welfare." She placed the letters between them and Margaret slid back as if they were hot coals. "They are from your mother, but they held on to them until they thought it was appropriate to send them. There is no forwarding address; they cut those out. They said it was up to me whether I showed them to you, and I probably should have done so a long time ago." Anne covered Margaret's jittery hand with her own. "I want you to have them now, and if you need any help to find her, please let me know. I'm sorry." Margaret's arms felt as stiff as poured concrete, and Anne had to place the letters in her hand.

It took an excuse that she had to be in class early in the morning for Margaret to get away from Anne's apologetic ramblings. She trudged down the road carrying the secret letters, which weighed like a heavy burden. Why now? She was settled in her new life, why try to tell her she was someone else's child now? Did they think it was a role she was playing, where she could just learn her new lines and then begin her performance? She had forgotten her jumper at Liz's place, but she didn't feel the cold. The unleashed rage inside of her was burning like a furnace. Do you think I was a good mother? Anne had

276

asked her before she left. What else could she have said but yes? Anything else would have seemed ungrateful, and she wasn't, she was sure she wasn't, but her thoughts were awash with questions. She stopped at a liquor store, bought a bottle of wine, and took a furtive swig before she caught her bus. The letters sat burning a hole in her lap all the way home, and when she reached her stop she placed them on the seat next to her and got off.

***

Anne stayed in Sydney for the week Liz was in hospital and another week after. Two months after that, Liz dropped out of Sydney University and flew to Europe with friends to work and travel.

***

Even though Margaret no longer needed to work the extra hours to help with Liz's rent, she kept working them. She bought new dresses, ornaments for the apartment, which Matthew didn't notice, and booze. Then when she fell asleep during lectures and one of the students offered her uppers, she started to spend her money on those also.

***

Late one evening, Margaret arrived home. The burning light signalled that Matthew was there and not at another pointless meeting with his revolutionary friends. When she opened the door she saw Heng, the Vietnamese woman from the party, coming out of the bathroom. "Hello," Heng said, and she gave a curt smile and drifted into the living room. Margaret followed her, and Matthew was sitting at the table with Nannup and Joyce talking in urgent tones. She said hello, and they greeted her with fleeting breaths and went on with their discussions.

"Can you fix us all a drink please, babes," Matthew said. She bought them beers and wine, and sat back in the lounge with her own glass. They were talking about going to Canberra, to join the protestors at the Aboriginal tent embassy there. Matthew said that they would have to carry food, sleeping bags, and clothes to keep them warm and protect them from the damp conditions. Nannup and Joyce were saying that they could stay for a week, but Heng said she would stay for as long as Matthew was staying.

277

"I'll come too," Margaret said, although uncertain of what was going on.

"Are you sure?" Matthew asked.

"Yes, I can help out with some of the cooking and so on." She hadn't yet thought of what excuse she was going to give to Mr Gazis for missing work.

"Okay, babes." Matthew winked admiration at her.

"Would anyone like some tea?" Margaret asked. They all said yes and she slipped out to the kitchen.

When the kettle boiled, Nannup crept through the open door. "Can I help?"

Margaret jumped around with sudden fright. "No, I've got it." Blanking him out, she turned back to pour the water into the teapot, but she didn't hear him leave. He made her giddy standing there.

"I waited for you," he said.

"What?" She kept working with her back to him, as though she didn't know what he meant.

"I waited outside your window the night I ran away. I whistled and knocked, but you never came."

"I was happy where I was," she said. She was hurrying to mix the tea now so that they could go back outside and join the others. She knocked over one of the cups and spilt tea on her dress.

"Are you okay?" Nannup put a hand on her back, but she hurried from his touch to the sink and wiped herself. He started to mop the floor.

"I went back to the Nicolaideses' place and took that baby and ran for Langley. I got on the train past there. They nearly caught me an' all. I saw Mr McDonald and that Mr O'Hare looking, but I was well hidden in the bush."

Margaret cut through him with a glare. "There was a fire afterwards. It lasted for months and killed Mr and Mrs Nicolaides in their homestead."

Nannup's lips fell apart as if tasting the sour information. "I didn't start no fire, but they probably deserved to die for what they did."

"They would probably have given that baby a better life," Margaret said.

"That baby is in real good hands now, and very happy."

The furious clink of spoon against china broke the silence between them as Margaret mixed the tea. "Somebody found some letters on a bus and brought them into the Aboriginal Advancement League's office. They were from a mother to the welfare about her daughter." Margaret's mouth hardened like a craggy rock, and her fault lines were sliding into a violent seism. "The woman says them people changed her daughter's name to Margaret." Nannup went over to where Margaret had put the cups on a tray and he prised the shaking tray from her hands. "We can find her for you, N——"

"My name is Margaret, and my mother lives in Malee. Margaret, that's who I am." She tore herself from the spot, pushing him and two chairs out of her destructive path, and bolted to the bedroom.

***

They drove the one hundred and seventy miles from Sydney to Canberra in three hours. Heng pulled out at the last moment, giving Margaret no time to frame an excuse not to go, so she and Matthew travelled in one car whilst Nannup and Joyce went in their own. Hundreds of blacks had begun arriving in Canberra on Saturday, on foot, by car, and by the bus load. The police had forcibly removed the 'Aboriginal Embassy', which had stood in a tent on the lawns opposite Parliament House, and they were there to re-erect it. It had been established there on Australia day, the 26th January 1972, to embarrass the Government for bringing out a mineral exploitation policy that did not recognise Aboriginal land rights, and to symbolise that the Aboriginals were foreigners in their own land. It had stood for nearly six months, in spite of repeated attempts to remove it, but the Government had grown frustrated and told the police to stop drinking wine and coffee in the tents with the protestors and dismantle it. The young Afro-wearing Aboriginals who had manned the tent with the help of their white student colleagues were educated and proud of their heritage. As the tent was re-erected, blacks and whites linked arms three deep around the embassy and sang, "*Black and White together, we shall not be moved*," to the tune of 'We Shall Overcome'. The adopted flag was raised and fluttered over the tent, its black symbolising the Aboriginal peoples, its yellow circle the sun, and the red the earth and their blood spilt in the battle for it. Hundreds of police looked on, not sure what to do.

The demonstrators were waving dozens of placards protesting about the stolen land and mineral exploitation of Aboriginal reserves, and a number of speakers spoke to the crowd, including Joyce.

When Joyce had finished speaking, they squeezed through the crowd into the tent. A few of the older activists jumped up and ran screaming to hug Joyce. She introduced them to the others, and told them that she had been on the '65 'bus rides' across New South Wales with some of these people, which had been inspired by the black 'freedom ride' in America. They gave the newcomers tea and food, and laughed as they reminisced about driving through those towns to protest that Aborigines on reserves and the fringes of towns were not allowed in public areas such as clubs, hotels, swimming pools, and public toilets, and had to sit in the front stalls at picture theatres. Some whites had spat, thrown food, and sworn at them, and on more than one occasion the police had intervened to pull them apart, but they agreed it had been worth it, it had probably shamed the country into having the '67 referendum. Joyce asked the others if they remembered coming to that town where the white men had been out in force, adamant that the protestors would not speak there. But when the Aboriginal women who lived in a camp on the edge of the town learned that they were there, they had hurried into town, some with their hands on their heavily pregnant hips, and they had called the names of the white men who visited the blacks camps at night, and those men had run back like chastened sheep to their homes. All except Margaret laughed with solid breaths at this.

As night fell the crowd guarding the embassy did not disperse, and their chattering, singing, and laughter kept all awake. Margaret stumbled out into the bitter night, and her stomach lurched as she pulled back the tarpaulin and squelched through the soggy mud inside the makeshift latrine, which gave off a rank, foul odour that stuck to her senses even after she had retreated. She played with the insipid food that was served up inside the tent, and watched with a caustic squirm twisting her face as Matthew joined the others in singing protest songs and comparing war stories of demonstrations up and down the country. It wouldn't last, she told herself. She had seen the older whites, how tired they looked. They eventually moved on to fight over good paying city jobs and forgot about protest and revolution. She would get Matthew to herself some day.

In the morning the police moved in to the chant of "Zieg Heil, Zeig Heil," from the crowd. Three hundred and sixty-two of them marched four abreast to encircle the embassy, and others pushed back the crowd. Those who had been there longest realised that the police were more bolstered with steel and organised than they had been on previous occasions. They ploughed in, en masse, and this time those who resisted were punched, kicked, and beaten. The protestors fought back with inflamed spirits. Men and women writhed on the ground screaming, and those who fell broken and unconscious were put into cars and rushed to hospital, and the blood of protestors and police mingled to soak the ground. Margaret allowed herself to be carried off the lawn with grateful ease, but some of the others held on to each other, the poles of the tents, trees, anything to stop themselves being taken. The operation lasted a little more than an hour, and by the end of it the police had arrested eight people, including Matthew.

Robert and Helga Stevens squeezed through a cordon of photographers to get into the police station. The reception area looked like the northern cattle markets, with the friends and relatives of those arrested frantic to negotiate their release. Everyone was shouting to be heard at the same time, and they were pushing against each other to get closer to the sergeant's desk. Mr Stevens saw Margaret on a bench with her jaded cheeks in her hands. He pointed her out to Helga and they went over to the bench. "Margaret?"

She jumped up. "Oh, Mr Stevens." He didn't move to take her extended hand, and she dropped it back to her side.

"Where is Matthew?" he asked, his jaws set and his manner terse.

"He—He's in the cells downstairs. They won't allow me to see him." Mr Stevens had already spun and gone. Helga looked Margaret up and down as if she were searching for exactly what Matthew saw in her. Margaret stepped aside and gestured towards the bench, but Helga forced her sealed lips to curl upwards for a second and didn't move. Margaret looked away and sat down again, but she couldn't escape the pungent smell of perfumed powder that rose off Helga like steam.

"You do realise that you are not the first," Helga said.

"What?"

"Matthew likes to choose those less fortunate than himself." Margaret stole an envious look up at the huge monument towering over her and turned away again. "Before you it was a little Indian girl," Helga continued. "Then he was into Hinduism, or maybe it was Buddhism—you can never tell with Matthew. I thought his next

281

charitable project would be that Vietnamese girl we've seen him with—after all, we are bombing their country."

Margaret wanted to ignore her, but she couldn't; Helga was too large a presence.

Bob Stevens strode back through the melee, mopping his brow. "He'll be released on bail in one hour, they are processing his papers," he said to Helga. "I think it's best if you return to Sydney by train, Margaret." He pulled some notes from his wallet and held it towards her. "There are cameras outside and we don't want to cause any confusion. I'm sure you understand. We'll wait for Matthew and meet you back at the apartment." Margaret got up and walked away without taking his money.

***

When she reached Sydney Margaret still had time to rush to the market. She would show them her true worth. She set pots to boil and put in a roast, and whilst they were going she cleaned the already spotless apartment again, then set the dining table with candles in the centre. The pots clanged against each other and the stove, and the broom rattled against furniture and the skirting board as she laboured to expel the choking vines of doubt climbing in her. Every now and then she went to the linen cupboard for stiff relief, and when she was finished she washed off the grime from the dusty tent she had spent the night in and slipped on the flowing red gown she had bought after the Stevenses' garden party.

Matthew arrived with his father and Helga shortly after eight. When he saw Margaret he jolted back with a carnal desire in his eyes, and then he saw what she had prepared and made a show of kissing her. "Great going, babes. See, I told you she's a gem," he said to his father and Helga as he went to wash and change.

"I hope you don't mind," Margaret said to Mr Stevens and Helga, who were standing by the door. "I thought you would stay to dinner."

Mr Stevens looked at Helga as if to seek her advice, and she gave him the same curl of her lips that she had given Margaret earlier that day. "Thank you," Mr Stevens said, and he strode towards the chair Margaret held out for him.

They waited for Matthew to return and carve the meat before they started. Helga spent most of her time cutting her food into small portions, and ate like a mouse. Mr Stevens ate with unbridled hunger.

"This is very good, Margaret, very good." She gave a wavering smile and Matthew stroked her cheek. When Helga smirked, he did it again. Helga glared at Mr Stevens. He set his cutlery down, wiped his mouth, and cleared his throat. "As you both know, the elections are to be held in December, five months from now."

"Labor are going to sweep those bigots aside, Dad."

"Nothing is certain in this world, Matthew. That's what thirty years in business has taught me."

"Dad, the country wants out of Vietnam, people are demonstrating for Aboriginal rights, we want change."

Mr Stevens cleared his throat again. "Excuse me. Yes, yes. But to get change one must also be responsible. There's no point in pursuing desires of the minute if that delays grander opportunities of the future. Do you get my meaning?"

Margaret shook her head.

Matthew threw his napkin onto the table. "I think I do. Dad's talking about *us!*" Margaret's spinning head swung from Matthew to his father and back again.

"Calm down, Matthew. One must look at the bigger picture here."

"Don't tell me to bloody calm down. What happened to 'We're all the same, we must fight for everyone to be equal'?" He drained his glass, slapped it onto the table, and spilled more wine into it.

"And we must, Matthew, but all in due time. We must act in a way to ensure it succeeds."

"And how is that?" Matthew asked, with sarcasm hanging from his tone.

"Well, for one thing, we could see to it that Margaret has enough money to finish her course."

"I don't bloody believe it." Matthew pushed back his chair and stood up. He tramped over to the window, shoved it open, and drew air into his lungs as if to cleanse his words before delivering them. Then he turned back to face them. "Is that the way you conduct business, to bribe your way to a solution?"

"Matthew, don't be so bloody rude and ignorant," Helga said. "Your father has been asked to be in the cabinet if Labor wins. Just think of what he could do."

"Oh yeah, he could reintroduce the law against interracial relationships, that would appeal to some of the electorate! You're a bloody politician, Dad. You should lead the way through people's ignorance."

Mr Stevens wiped his mouth and stood up with a flawless calm. "I can see we are not going to get anywhere."

"No, not on this one, Dad. You're not choosing who I can date."

"I've instructed the lawyers to make Helga a trustee of your trust fund," Mr Stevens said.

Matthew snorted and nodded with a knowing smirk oiling his face. "I can get a job, I'll survive."

"I think that will be good for you, Matthew," Helga said. "Far too many of you young people don't know what it's really like to do a hard day's work—that's why you protest so much." She spoke with seasoned authority. She had come to Australia with nothing and had struggled to set up boutiques and salons, sometimes failing. Now she headed a consortium that had expanded back into her home country, and she had denied herself all until she had succeeded. Mr Stevens pulled back her chair and they left.

Margaret's head spun, bruised like one of the tennis balls she had seen smashed across the courts at the university campus. "It might be best," she said.

"What? To listen to that?" Matthew stabbed a shaking finger towards the door.

"I can't pay the rent on what I earn, and I don't want to be responsible for taking you from your parents."

"I haven't got parents, remember. I only have a father."

"Your real mum got taken by God, Matthew, so it's not Helga's fault."

"You going to fucking start turning religious on me now?" As the engine of his father's Rolls hissed into life, he looked out of the window, only turning back when the sound of the car had receded. Margaret sniffled. Her tears were splashing dark stains onto her beautiful gown. Matthew came and knelt by her side, wrapped his arms around her heaving waist, and sunk his head into her lap. "I'm sorry," he said. He raised his head, wiped the tears from her sodden cheeks, and kissed both her eyes. "Margaret, will you marry me?" She was trembling, her pulse racing like water through a cavern. What did he mean? Was he serious? "I love you, Margaret. Will you marry me?" She nodded with a strangled breath, and then wiped cascading tears into his hair.

284

# Chapter 21

After Matthew's proposal, Margaret wrote to Anne to tell her of their plans. She and Matthew would marry in January after she had finished her exams. It would be a simple wedding with few guests, but she would bring her new husband out to meet her and Sean as soon as possible. She didn't tell her about Matthew's father and stepmother not liking their union, as she prayed they might resolve that before they travelled to see Anne. Anne wrote back to say how pleased she was and told Margaret to give thanks for her blessings, as she had prayed for her and those pleas had been answered.

Margaret was working longer hours now to help with paying the rent. She also took more of the uppers to keep her awake during classes. Matthew had a little money saved, but it wouldn't last them long, and each time she asked him he said he hadn't been able to find work as yet.

She was serving a customer at the restaurant in the afternoon when she glimpsed Nannup outside, waving with wild excitement at her. She turned away, hoping he would think that she hadn't seen him. When she went back to the counter to pick up more orders from Mr Gazis, he pointed the dripping spatula over her shoulder. "You know him?" She shook her head without looking. "He's been there ten minutes now, Margaret. When you finish this order you speak to him and tell him to go away."

Margaret served the food and then stomped out into lunchtime George Street. Office workers were hustling to get as much into their one hour breaks as they could. She bustled through gaps in the rush. "My boss says to go away. I could get the sack."

"We've found her, Margaret, we've found her." Nannup was beaming and bouncing like a child.

"Found who?"

"Your mother, Margaret." Her mind froze as if he had stung her with venomous poison. So she didn't hear as he explained how they had used the letters brought to their offices by someone who had

285

found them on a bus to trace the welfare office that had sent them to Mrs McDonald. When they phoned and explained, the people there said they didn't know, there were lots of papers in storage. But there was a Koori Advancement League office close by, and they contacted someone there who had been willing to go to the welfare office and search through the papers. Five days it took them. Five days to trace the files on the girl whose mother kept phoning and sending letters, and then one day it all stopped as still as death. She sent them her numerous addresses over the years and addresses of relatives to contact if they couldn't find her. They had traced the woman, Nannup said. Margaret came back to him now, but she was swaying in the sudden humidity. The thick, rainless clouds bore down on her like the lid on a coffin. "We told her that we couldn't give her your details unless you agree, but she insisted on coming to Sydney," Nannup said. "I'm meeting her at Central Station at seven o'clock."

"My mum is in Malee," Margaret said, bubbling like hot grease.

"Look, Margaret, we can't insist that you see her, but I think that you should."

"I don't want anything to do with this, can't you leave me alone?" Her words gushed out and passers-by slowed down to stare.

"I think it will help, Margaret." He stretched out to hold her hand, but she pulled away from his stuttering reach and turned back to the restaurant. "I'm going to meet her at Central Station, Margaret. I'll wait an hour, and if you don't come I'll put her on the train home."

***

Margaret stomped around the dining area like a bad heartburn. Customers who saw her ruffled face tried not to attract her attention and waited for the other waitress. What did they expect her to do now—run crying into some woman's arms, someone she didn't know? She didn't even know that this was real. That's it; it could all have been arranged by Matthew's father and his stepmother. They didn't want them together; they had arranged to bring this woman here to destroy her new life. Nevertheless, when work was finished she found herself trudging in a helpless daze down George Street towards Central Station. She stopped outside and stared up at the clock tower sitting atop the Victorian building which ate up a block. It was seven-thirty. Nannup would probably have put the woman on a train home already. She climbed up the incline, through the car park, and into the entrance of the domed ticket hall. She stopped just inside and looked about her, the blood in her ear gushing over the echoes of the crowds milling about, announcements being made, and trains pulling into and leaving the platforms. With measured steps, she started down the tiled hall, searching about her. It took nearly five minutes to comb from one end of the hall to the other, but she couldn't see them on the platforms. She turned to go and gazed straight through the plate glass window of the tea room opposite platform nine. Nannup and Joyce were sipping tea and talking to a silver-haired woman. Margaret stared as if ensnared, and when Joyce looked out of the window, she stepped back a little and stood with her shoulder against the cast iron post leading to the platform.

*** 

"If she doesn't want to make contact, we can't go ahead," Joyce said. "You do understand?"

"I don't know that she is my girl anyway," the silver-haired woman said. "I felt her die a long time ago and we give her a ceremony our way, you know." Nannup and Joyce smiled in sympathy and watched the woman's wrinkled hands as they rolled her paper napkin into a log. The woman appeared to think of something and stopped.

"What is it?" Nannup said.

"You know something, I never feel that girl got a good ceremony. Okay, we never have her body, but we still try to do it right. Just when we was to send her ego spirit—" She stopped and touched Nannup and Joyce's hands. "You a Koori boy and girl, you still keep your culture and know what that is, hey?" They nodded. "Good, good." She patted their hands. "Because not everyone wants to keep it now you have all these modern things. My grandchildren want to be watching the television and playing the football, and I say 'What about you learn to fish or I tell you a story about the dreamtime?' Sometimes they agree, but most of the time I can't get to them. It's like television and these modern things is their parents, but things can't bring up our kids." She sipped some of the tea to moisten her drying mouth and made an ugly face. "This not tea. You should tell me to bring some of that stuff I have back home. Modern stuff— bah!" She patted her lip dry and looked around her. "What was I saying again?"

"About sending her ego spirit—"

287

She patted Joyce's hand. "Yes, yes. We tried to send our girl's ego spirit to its place in the sky, and just when we were doing it these white fellas drive their cars and trucks right through our corroborree. So I feel part of our girl's spirit is still stuck here." She dabbed at the corner of her eye with the napkin, and Joyce rubbed her shoulder.

"What about the rest of your family? Do you see them much?" Joyce said.

"We stay out in the bush until we hear they stop taking the children and then we move back to near where my husband was born. He took to the grog after we stop looking for the girl, and it kill him. My youngest son, he never marry, but they found his body floating in a river." She wiped nothing out of the corner of her eye. "Say he drown himself because of depression. But my boy wouldn't do that."

They sat uneasily for a while. Nannup looked at his watch, "Your train will be leaving in fifteen minutes." She nodded, and they all got ready to leave.

***

The old woman walked with a shuffling limp, and Joyce and Nannup guided her across to the platform side of the hall and all the way back down to platform one. Margaret hid until they were far enough down the hall, and she crossed to the opposite side and followed them from there. Nannup and Joyce waited with the woman on platform one for a while, and then they hugged her and said goodbye. Margaret stood in the alcove by the toilets and turned to her side as they walked back down the platform and left the station. The woman was still on the platform. She contemplated getting on the train and then changed her mind. One of the guards walked by and she spoke to him. He looked at his watch and nodded, and then he pointed her down the platform towards the toilets. She took her time in getting there, but Margaret didn't move. She stood by the door waiting, divided with doubt as to whether she wanted it to be her. The woman opened the door and limped into the toilet without looking at her. *She didn't know me. I can't be hers then, I can't be hers.* Margaret wiped her stinging eyes and running nose with the back of her hand. The woman came back out and their eyes met, as if in brief recognition, but then she shuffled on. She took two steps, stopped, put her hand over her heart and looked up into the curved corrugated iron roof. "Ningali?" she said,

288

even though she knew she shouldn't say a dead person's name. Margaret wanted to answer to her mother's curving back. Her mouth opened and she implored her voice, but it was being stifled by her hard won desires. "My daughter, tell your ego spirit to stop following me. You must be tired now, my daughter; go to sleep, go to sleep." With that the woman shuffled off and boarded her train. Margaret watched the train from outside the toilets until it was gone, and then she sat on one of the benches in the middle of the hall and cried.

***

It was gone ten when Margaret got home. As soon as she opened the door, Matthew pounced on her. "Where the bloody hell were you, then?"

Even in her thick reverie he stunned her. "At work, why?"

"We were supposed to go to the theatre, remember?"

Margaret's hand shot to her mouth. "I'm sorry, I forgot."

"Forgot." Matthew pushed past her. She hadn't seen him this way. He went to the linen cupboard and pulled out a half-empty bottle of wine. "This what makes you forget?"

"It's just a little drink, I—"

"And this." He pulled her bottle of uppers from his pocket and emptied them onto the floor. She stared at the little red pills, shamefaced.

"I'm sorry, I've been tired and under pressure, Matthew."

"You under pressure." He stabbed an accusing finger at her and threw the empty bottle at her feet. "My father's trying to get elected here—what do you think the media will do if they get hold of this stuff?"

"I don't know, Matthew." She slumped into the chair. She had cried all she had on the bench at Central Station and had no tears left for this.

"Crucify him, that's fucking what—crucify him."

"Matthew, I'm sorry. I didn't think it was that serious. I was tired and needed something to keep me going. If you could get a job then I could give up some of my hours and—"

"So it's me, is it? It's my fault that you're taking this shit." He scraped some of the pills from the floor and threw them at her.

"I didn't say that." She rested her throbbing forehead in her palm. Sleep, that's what the old woman had said she should do, sleep.

Matthew threw on his jacket and stormed out the door, slamming it. Margaret got onto her hands and knees and collected the scattered pills. She counted forty-three of them. When she had finished, she took off her clothes and climbed into bed with the half bottle of wine and pills for company. She threw back her head and swallowed one of the pills, helping it down with a mouthful of wine. The others glistened like tasty treats, and she considered them for an hour or so between mouthfuls of the drink. It would be easy to make the raw emptiness melt even in the shade of the bedroom. She fumbled to put the cover back on, stuffed them into her pillowcase, wrapped her arms around it as if securing them in a safe, and fell asleep.

*** 

Days went by, and both Matthew and Margaret drifted in and out of the apartment with little acknowledgement of each other. Margaret threw away the pills and put the wine she had hidden in the cupboard out where Matthew could see it. The December '72 elections were weeks away, and a buzz of activism and anticipation pervaded the city as students campaigned for Whitlam's Labor Party, which many hoped would bring their conscripts home from Vietnam. Margaret put Matthew's strict quietness and inattention down to this, and one evening on her way home from work she stopped and bought him some flowers to which she attached an apology. As she turned into their road, she saw his father's Rolls parked outside and the light burning in their apartment. He had probably returned to polish over their differences, but when she looked through the window she saw them arguing. She turned around and walked back up to Oxford Street to give them time together, but also because shooting nerves perforated her when she was around his father and Helga. For a while she sauntered along, staring into shop windows. She hadn't chosen a wedding dress yet and wondered if it was still acceptable for her to get married in white. It didn't matter what colour it was anyway; she would have a name she had chosen— Mrs Stevens. She sat down at a table outside a restaurant and ordered a tomato juice, as she was trying to restrict her alcohol to the times when Matthew was around, with varying degrees of success. But after one she ordered a bottle of wine and almost finished it. When she felt enough time had elapsed, she strolled back into their road and the Rolls had gone, but the light was still on. She was glad that he was still up and she would be able to surprise him with the bouquet. Maybe they would make love tonight for the first time since they had argued. The stairs moaned softly as she climbed them and opened the door. The apartment revealed eerie silence. "Matthew!" She rushed from room to room searching, but he wasn't there. Then she stopped at the kitchen door and stared across the empty chasm to the table. His scribbled note was leaning against a bottle of wine in the centre of the table. Her enthusiasm for reading letters and notes had evaporated. She shuffled across the hardwood floor as if she was sinking in mud, pulled out the chair, and sat in front of the note. She read Matthew's large, bold script, and it said he had gone to a meeting and wouldn't be back until late. She sat there staring without relief at the note, and it spurred her on. One day it would say he was going for good, she knew it. Either he would wake up and realise with sudden horror that she wasn't the same as him, or he would get tired of arguing with her and blame her for him not talking to his father. She closed her eyes and squeezed to summon up the courage. If she was going to do it she had to do it now. She had been thinking about it for weeks. She opened the bottle of wine to help her and packed as much as she could get into her small case. Then she wrote her message on the other side of Matthew's note. It said she didn't want to steal him from his parents. She wasn't sure she felt anything after she had done it. If you're empty, how are you supposed to feel? She put the bottle to her mouth and drained it; then she looked in the linen cupboard, not remembering that she had taken out the bottles she used to hide there. She picked up her case and headed towards Kings Cross, where Liz worked. The car headlights seemed to caress her as they approached and then slipped by. She walked closer to the edge of the pavement to encourage their hugs. The street was stirring with people and most of them were chattering and laughing about her, she knew they were, and she started to shout and laugh back. The neon lights blinked on and off at the place where Liz worked, and the woman inside was shaking her head and saying no, Liz left for Europe some time ago, don't you remember? But she couldn't hear her above the humming vacuum in her head, and so she ordered a drink, sat in a corner, and downed it. Two American soldiers on R&R spotted her from their table and joined her. They asked her if she would like a drink, and she said yes and laughed at everything they said, as it was all so clear now, nothing had meaning anymore. They laughed, drank, and touched, and the soldiers were sure they could make out tonight—thrust the fear, loneliness, hatred, mutilations and death of that gruesome war out of their systems, for one night at least.

They half carried her between them down a lonely street. "Where do you live, honey?" one of them asked.

"Nowhere," she said with a bitter laugh, and then took another swig from the bottle of wine she carried. The soldiers looked at each other, and a well-practised understanding that had saved their lives on more than one occasion in the jungles of South East Asia flowed between them. They turned her into a dark alleyway, put down her case, and pinned her to a wall. Their sharply liquored lips tried to stick to her face like plaster, sealing her wounds, but she pushed them off with a growling, "No!" The shorter of the men came back for more, his stocky hands probing at her taut body like a healing surgeon. The fear lit a spark in her, and she lashed out before she could control the flame. Her first strike broke the bottle across his head, sending him reeling. Then she slashed at his neck with the jagged edges. His blood spurted over her like a human fountain.

"What the fuck you doing?" his jarred-awake friend screamed. He slapped the broken bottle from her hand, fell to his knees, and grabbed hold of his buddy's oozing neck to stem the flow of warm, honey-thick blood.

The sharp, metallic taste of the soldier's blood on her lips jerked Margaret's head around, and her dizziness cleared a little. She wiped her bloodstained hand on her dress, grabbed her case, and ran out of the alley, leaving one soldier clinging to life and the other screaming for help.

Margaret hurried through the streets, not knowing where she was going. She managed to slip into St Mary's Cathedral on the corner of Hyde Park, and she slept in fits and starts in a pew at the back of the church. In the morning she prayed and said several Hail Marys, knowing it was a sure thing that the police would find her soon. Her body shook like a chill blown tree, and her mind slowed to a frosted crawl. She searched through her bag to see how much money she had, and the card that Joyce had given her fell out. Police sirens were wailing like mourners in grief, but she ventured out in her bloodstained dress and called the number on the card. Nannup answered, and she told him that she was in trouble. Half an hour later he picked her up from the cathedral and drove her to Joyce's place.

# Chapter 22

For a few days, Nannup and Joyce kept Margaret hidden at their place, waiting for the high police presence on the streets and the talk about the Aboriginal woman to die down, but they wouldn't. So, in the middle of the night, Nannup drove her out of the city. They headed north for more than a day and a half, sometimes coming off the highway and driving overland if they suspected a police roadblock to be up ahead. All the way, Nannup could get no more out of her than what she had told him when he picked her up at the cathedral: she had killed a man, an American soldier. They weren't to call Matthew because she had left him. For three days the papers carried reports that the American soldier had not died, but was in intensive care, fighting for his life. The police had even come to the offices of the Aboriginal Advancement League to question them. That's when they had decided to take her out of the city.

Margaret rolled over and opened her eyes. It took her a while to adjust to the untamed dark, but there was an old woman in the bed next to hers and she nodded and gave a toothless grin. She had been watching the newcomer all night. Margaret jumped up and looked about her, wondering how she had gotten there. Three metal beds with thin mattresses were arranged against one whitewashed wall of the small room, and a screen was stored in a corner on the other side, next to a desk, a filing cabinet, and a refrigerator. She heard singing coming from a distance, and she hurried outside and stood on the veranda. A bush church sat on the other side of the outstation, with a few one-room shacks that had wide verandas surrounding them. Metal beds with thin mattresses were on some of the verandas, to keep the people connected to the outdoor life. A fire had been lit between the buildings, and the Kooris had gathered around it for a corroborree. "Hello, cousin. I'm Lonnie." Margaret swivelled to her right with a start. The woman who appeared slightly older than her had been sitting in the shadows on the veranda all along. She had a flat face and an apprehensive smile, and her hair still had the look of having had hot irons pulled through it for years, although she had stopped styling it now.

"Good day," Margaret said. "Where is Nannup?"

Lonnie pointed out towards the singers and then continued to weave her fingers unconsciously. "He said if you wake and want him, you should tell me."

"Where are we?" Margaret asked.

"It's them Kooris' there outstation. I been with them nearly two years and I work in this here clinic." She pointed back to the room where Margaret had been sleeping. Margaret ignored her and looked out at the dancing figures around the fire. She wanted Nannup to come so that they could leave. She wasn't used to this kind of place. "Nannup say you was brought up by white folks too," Lonnie said after a while.

"What did he tell you?"

"Nothing. He just said we're sort of the same, me and you. I can maybe help you to get used to this here place and you could help me in the clinic. He said you been studying some nursing, you know."

He had already told them too much. The police would already have known that she studied nursing in Sydney. "I need to speak to Nannup," she said.

"Okay, I'll go and call him for you." Lonnie got up and sauntered barefooted through the red dust out to the fire. She returned with Nannup and an elder.

"You had a good sleep?" Nannup asked.

"When are we going?" Margaret asked, her flickering glare urgent.

Nannup drew back and stared at her. "We're not going. This is the best place for you to stay. They won't find you here."

She saw the man waiting patiently next to Nannup. His white whiskers were unkempt, like a shaggy cat's, and his drooping, wise old eyes had taken her all in after just one stare. She turned away from him, but she could still feel his knowing gaze. How was she to stay here, when she had spent the last few years crossing to the other side of the road when she saw these people?

"My name is Barry Anderson. We're not used to your ways either, cousin, but we'll try to understand while you're here." He spoke with crawling precision and dropped his gaze to the ground to ease her discomfort.

"You have to stay for a few weeks at least," Nannup said. "Maybe we can think of somewhere else in that time." The objections appeared to slide like thick gruel off her face. Barry nodded sagely and gestured for her to follow. He showed her around the outstation, which he said was funded with mineral royalties from mining on their land, which they hadn't agreed to. Some of their sacred sites were close by, and he pointed them out and said she would not be permitted to go there. Then he told her that they allowed no drinking at their camp, as it had destroyed too many of their people. And finally, if she wanted to help at the clinic, she had to observe their decision as to how a patient was to be treated, with white fellas' medicine or their own. Under promptings from Nannup she agreed to all of this.

The first thing Margaret did at sun up was to take a broom to the insects crawling into the clinic. A number of the children gathered outside and rolled about laughing, because as she swept the ants turned around and marched back up onto the veranda and headed for cracks in the building. Lonnie came out and gazed at her with gentle understanding. "They're just searching for some place cool to stay, cousin. When I first come, Barry's wife told me to 'kick your shoes off, girl, and go walk on the land, that ways you'll remember how it feels to be on your own land.'" Margaret ignored her and swept more vigorously. Lonnie played with her fingers and then went back inside. Margaret wasn't sure why she was doing this. Was she still trying to keep house the way Anne had taught her? Was she trying to show them that she was better than them? Or was she trying to forget the spilt blood of that soldier? She remembered what they had tried to do to her, and she felt herself strangling the broom. She stopped when a woman climbed onto the veranda and said she wasn't feeling well.

Throughout the day more patients than usual turned up at the clinic. They mostly complained of sore stomachs, or that they were feeling a little dizzy, and most wanted to be treated by the new nurse. Margaret told them several times that she wasn't a nurse, not yet at any rate, but they ignored her protestations and called her 'cousin' or 'auntie nurse' all the same. They watched her face as she felt their stomachs and listened to their chests—first tentatively, and then with fast learned assurance—and each time she came up with a perplexed frown masking her face, because she couldn't find anything wrong, they flitted away their gaze and grimaced as if in pain. By late

295

afternoon she realised what was happening and started sending everyone away with a lump of sugar. "You're going to do me out of a job," Lonnie said, and she waited for Margaret to smile before she was at ease enough to give one back.

"Can I ask you something, Margaret?" Lonnie said, as though she had been waiting to ask ever since Margaret arrived.

"Yes, what is it?"

"Do—Do you still see the people that took you in?"

Margaret sat on the edge of one of the beds and stroked the worn fibres of the blanket with her thumb. What would they think of her now? Mrs McDonald had seemed so much more relaxed when she last saw her, as if she had somehow started to accept her life and look for the pretty things within it instead of holding out for something more, something that she couldn't quite define. Even Helen Cartwright's homestead couldn't have satisfied such an imprecise desire. "Yes—" She considered again. "No, I haven't seen them for a while. They lived far from Sydney."

"I haven't seen the ones who took me in since I left." Lonnie's fingers were knotting and un-knotting themselves faster now. "They were good enough, but—it wasn't like having a family where you know you're one of them, and you're not in your room wondering how you can look more like them so that people can't tell you're different. Do you know what I mean?"

Margaret nodded and closed her eyes so that she could examine her festering wound. All those years of scrubbing her face with the floor brush, of saying she had work to do when Anne called her to watch the black singers on the television, and more recently, of running to the other side of the road when she saw an Aboriginal coming. She could feel the desire to be like them racing through her veins even now, and its greed cannibalised her energies so that the hunger in the pit of her stomach was sharper than it had ever been, but she was slowly beginning to realise that it wasn't possible to shed her skin, even though she hadn't quite accepted it yet. None of that desire had changed the outside part of her, but it had made her stirred up on the inside, stirred up in a way that they hadn't seen, and she had only recently started to recognise it herself. She put her face in her hands as if she was about to cry. But then she started laughing; without any prompting she laughed like a cockatoo squawking from

296

its high point, where it could see all. Lonnie waited as if to make certain it was real, and then she joined her.

***

In order to check if it was safe for Margaret to return, Nannup drove to Sydney and then back to the settlement. The soldier was expected to survive, but the police had extended their search all over New South Wales for her, he said, and so she was better off where she was for the time being. She made herself busy at the clinic, and sometimes she helped to teach the children how to read and write. She treated one boy of about three or four years for runny ears, and every day little Eddie came back for another lump of sugar. Sometimes, she would get him to practise a few words from a book before she gave in and let him have the sugar cube.

One afternoon, when Lonnie dressed up in her hat and gloves so that her husband could drive her into the small town nearby to pick up provisions, Margaret asked to come. They looked at each other concerned, but she promised to stay in the car. Margaret slipped into the pub whilst they were in the grocery store and bought several bottles of port, which she hid in the car. She drank them mainly at night whilst the others were at the corroboree. Lonnie or Nannup would come and ask her if she wanted to come round the camp fire with the others, but she always gave some excuse that she was tired, or had to keep an eye on a patient, but secretly she was still afraid of the older members of the mob, although she could relate to the children and some of the women with flowing ease.

***

During the night Margaret sat at the desk in the clinic, drinking from the bottle. There was only one patient in the clinic, a stringy middle-aged man with a wheezing chest, whom she was treating for incipient glaucoma. She thought he was asleep until she heard his *"Psst."* She jumped with a start, hid the bottle in the desk drawer, and went to the man's bedside. "Can I have a drink, nurse?" he whispered.

"I'll get you some water," Margaret said as she turned to go.

He grabbed hold of her arm. "No. I want some of what you're having." He flicked his head towards the desk. Margaret remembered what the wise-eyed elder Barry Anderson had said, but the man had seen her. She gave him a drink, and when he left the clinic the

297

following day, she gave him a bottle also, which he hid in his pants. Her supply could be replenished if she went to town with Lonnie and her husband each week.

***

In the afternoon a police car pulled into the outstation. Nannup ran into the clinic and told Margaret to stay inside. They watched from the window as the shrunken-kneed policeman extended himself from his tiny car and asked one of the children to call Barry. Barry Anderson took his time to shuffle across the red dust to where the policeman waited for him. They exchanged greetings, and the policeman turned towards the clinic as he asked if they could talk out of the soaring heat. Barry directed him to sit under a tree instead, and asked one of the children to bring them cool lemonade. They talked about local matters first, such as some of the Koori youths coming into town to siphon petrol from cars so that they could sniff it, and Barry promised that they would find the ones who were doing it and punish them. Then the policeman asked if anyone new had come to the outstation in recent days. Barry had heard that Margaret had been into town, so he told the officer that a cousin of one of the women had come from up north, near Arnemland, so that she could attend ceremonies and the likes, but they were out visiting other kin nearby. The policeman looked with a detached air about him, wiped the sweat streaming from his crinkled face, then thanked Barry for the lemonade and left. They all knew he was thinking about the incident in Sydney, although he didn't say. It would have been the highlight of his dour outback career to bag a city criminal.

When the policeman had gone, Nannup asked Margaret why she wouldn't come to the corroborrees, once again. "I have work to do, and—I'm not ready."

"You see how hard Mr McDonald used to work. Do you think it made him happy?"

"I don't know, Nannup." Her tone was like pine needles. "I just don't think I can deal with this right now."

"Them people back in Malee used to work so hard they couldn't live."

"Maybe *they* need to do some more of that," she said under her breath, and nodded her head at the people outside, but he heard her.

298

"To the point where you don't have no time left for the living? Isn't that why we're really here, Margaret?" She sighed and turned her head from him. "You can lose all them material things, Margaret, but when you got your culture inside here—" He banged his fist against his chest. "—You can keep it with you wherever you go. They're saying that you don't join in anything with them, you even eat by yourself." She swayed like a desert-wary traveller. What did they expect of her? She sat at the desk and pressed her head between her hands to ease the bald madness. She needed space, somewhere to think. If only they would give it to her. "You still wish you were one of them, don't you?" She looked at him. Her eyes were like plump fruit, days past picking. "Milk on its own is just that, Margaret, but once you mix in some cocoa you can't change it back."

"But if you mix in more milk at least your children will stand a better chance," she said. He shook his head and walked out into the yard.

***

A few days later, Margaret was standing on the veranda when the young man approached with a rifle. She had treated him the previous day for an ear infection, and he looked like a teenager whose muscles had just started to ripen. He had said something to her when he left the previous day, but she hadn't really taken notice. "You want to go hunting now?" He held out his rifle towards her. She shook her head. Then she saw the man she had treated for glaucoma and given the grog weaving his way up towards the clinic for the third time. He was coming for more.

"I've never fired a gun," Margaret said. Her breath was short as she looked from the youth to the weaving man.

"I can show you if you want to learn." She hurried from the veranda and followed him, looking over her shoulder to make sure that the drinker had not seen them. "We go this way so that we don't go too near the town." He pointed through the trees with the rifle and she raised her head to question why. "White fella says we can only hunt at certain times now, when they give us a permit. So when we can't feed ourselves we have to go begging in town." He walked with long bounding strides ahead of her, so sometimes she trotted to keep up. She could hear Anne's words that it was men's work and not ladylike, and for a while they wanted to hold her back, but she took

299

off her shoes like Lonnie had said, and when the hot earth licked at the soles of her feet, it made her simmer with warmth inside, as if it had woken to welcome her back. She giggled with sharp surprise, as she hadn't believed it. The youth looked back at her and smiled a hunter's understanding. "My father says that when his grandfather was a boy the bush was full of tucker, and our people hunted all the time." They kicked their way through the tall, sharp grass, and Margaret glimpsed flashes of a little girl doing the same, and always running to be at the head with a dripping honeydew laugh on her face. She caught herself running and laughing with the girl, but she stepped with novice care onto plants jutting out, while the little girl bounded wallaby-style over them. Flies that the girl ignored bothered her, and she caused bushes to rustle so that a flock of galahs resting in a nearby desert oak exploded into the sky on a hundred wingbeats. She had lost any sense of being in this place. Tears bit at her eyes like grit, and she wiped them away with the back of her hand.

They were almost two miles from the outstation when the youth's loping strides narrowed and suddenly stopped. Margaret pulled up behind him and crouched in the long grass in the same way he had. He pointed through a gap in the grass in silence. Margaret's eyes followed the line of his lean, black arm, but all she could see were a few crooked gum trees. "I don't see anything," she said. The youth tapped a finger to his mouth twice, still staring ahead. He held up the rifle and aimed it towards one of the trees. For ten heartbeats he froze in perfect stillness, with not even his sweat rolling down his face or his chest rising from his breath. Keeping one hand on the rifle, he waved Margaret to his side. When she was settled, he transferred the rifle to her without changing aim. She took the offered rifle, in spite of the thunderous rumble coming from her chest and her surety that she couldn't do this. The youth made sure that the butt sat in her shoulder, and he supported the shaft of the gun with one hand and her back with the other. Still, all Margaret could see were crooked trees. She sat that way for the period it took a tree's shadow to visibly fall, with streaming sweat threatening to blind her, and when she felt a firm, slow squeeze on her shoulder, she closed her eyes and pulled the trigger. A shaft of lightning flew out of the barrel and a loud crack ricocheted through the air. The boy leapt up, shouting, "Yee!" He grabbed the rifle from Margaret and ran to one of the trees, where he clubbed the dying kangaroo with the butt to finish it off in the traditional way.

They brought the carcass back into the outstation, slung over the youth's shoulders a short race before dusk, once again avoiding the town. He threw it to the ground near shallow bushes, from where he produced a cutlass and started to divide the animal. Margaret went back to the clinic, and later the youth came and offered her one of the leg joints. She said no, she had enough to eat, but he told her that everyone else had been given a share, and insisted, so she took it and went inside.

Within minutes of the youth leaving, a young woman marched to the door, shouting, "He is promised to me." A small group of women gathered behind her, laughing and encouraging her. "I have sung djarada into his gun, he belongs to me." Margaret staggered onto the veranda with sleep in her strides and confusion in her eyes.

"She wants him for her husband," one of the women shouted, and this seemed to rile Margaret's accuser into a storm. She scooped up a handful of dirt and threw it onto the veranda. Margaret could see that the woman was carrying a piece of the kangaroo meat. She moved behind the banister as if it were some barrier between her and the woman's scalding temper.

"I'm sorry, I don't understand."

"You cannot come here and take him because you think your ways are better." She was about to throw more dirt when the youth grabbed her arm. Somehow, when they stood there together in the sultry shadows, Margaret could see he was not a youth after all, but a young man.

"Come," he said to his woman, "she has done nothing wrong."

"This is women's business, Kati," one of the onlookers said. "You should go away." Kati's woman palmed him off, and the other women moved between them so that he couldn't get to her. She turned her fire back to Margaret.

"His best cut of meat should be for me, his woman." She slapped her chest. "I sang djarada into his gun to make him strong." Margaret went to get the leg of meat and held it out for the young woman. She snatched it, threw the less prized cut she had been given onto the veranda, and walked away with her group of supporters laughing and singing up her courage.

301

Margaret shuffled inside and curled up on the bed. There was a full outstation of people around, but she was still imprisoned within her own thoughts, the same as she had been living in the apartment with Matthew. She remembered the woman that Nannup had brought to Central Station and she had spied on from the alcove. Was she really her mother? Would she want to know her now? She pulled the blanket over her, but continued to tremble from a feverish cold, as if she were warding off some illness. Then she remembered the bottle she had hidden behind the filing cabinet and she drank herself to sleep.

***

Many of the women began to ignore Margaret now. When they walked past her they raised their arrogant heads into the air, and if they, their men or children needed to go to the clinic, they insisted that Lonnie treated them, as long as they were not in a forbidden kin relationship where Lonnie could neither look at nor touch them. Under those circumstances they asked to be treated by the *Nagankari*, and if that was not possible they dragged themselves to Margaret and then complained that she prodded them too hard, tied their bandages too tight, or worked too slow.

Lonnie ran up onto the veranda, as she was late for combing Margaret's hair. Margaret was already sitting on the floor in front of the chair. Lonnie sat down so that Margaret was held between her knees and she put her bag by her side. "You forgot the paper?" Margaret said. Lonnie shook her head, but her wide-eyed stiffness gave off a dead prey's scent. Margaret opened Lonnie's bag and the paper was lying folded on top. She took it out and started to read as Lonnie pulled the comb briskly through her hair. The article was on page three. It gave the name of the American soldier's assailant as Margaret, a half-caste Aboriginal woman, and it said that police thought she had now fled the Sydney area. The police had interviewed Sean and Anne McDonald, her guardians, who lived in Malee, and they had said they couldn't explain it; nothing in the girl's upbringing indicated that she could be capable of something like that. She hadn't contacted them they said, but if she did they would tell her to turn herself in. The article said nothing about Matthew Stevens being her boyfriend. Now that Labor had won the elections and his father was in the Government, they had probably been able to arrange that, in the same way that his draft papers had not been selected. Margaret put the paper back into the bag and wrapped her arms around her knees.

Lonnie parted her hair and rubbed grease into her scalp with a finger. "You don't need to worry, cousin. They won't find you here."

"Some of those women look as if they're ready to give me up."

"No. They are just jealous because their husbands look at you, but they would never give you up to the cunnichman."

Margaret looked up at her. "Are you so sure?"

Lonnie's eyes were roaming and contrite. She pushed Margaret's head around. "Let me do the other side."

"How many times have you had to change, Lonnie?" Lonnie's hands stopped moving. She snorted and pulled a masked smile. "Sorry," Margaret said, and she touched her hand. The skin was smooth, gentle and fragile, like a child's. Lonnie started to part her hair and grease the scalp again.

"When I was with the foster family I forgot all our ways and practised everything they taught me. I went to church, worked money to buy clothes and all sorts of things, but even though I did all of that they still didn't let me feel like one of them. It's as if they did all that changing so that they could tell me what to do, how I should do it and when."

"Control you," Margaret said, from some place far off in her mind but still close enough to hear.

"Yes, that's it," Lonnie agreed. "And if they make all of us the same it's easier to do that controlling. Like that piece of machinery I worked on one time in a factory. They had rows and rows of them, all doing the same thing." She continued to work on Margaret's hair in silence, taking a handful and pulling the comb through it to untangle it and trap the dead ends.

"How's it been since you've been here?" Margaret asked.

"It was hard at first. I really got used to roast dinners, going to church, working long hours, and being so tired that I was sleeping all the time. I still can't sit still to look at the trees and the sky sometimes. I have to find something to do." She giggled, as though glad she was able to share it with someone. "If you try to do the things that they do and forget all that other stuff the white fellas taught you, then you'll be okay."

303

Margaret remembered the way she had gone hunting with the youth, with the white fellas' rifle, even though they had finished off the kill in the traditional way. "But supposing you like some of those things?" Margaret said. "Maybe some people change so much that they can't go back. They feel they're part of both and they can't be one thing anymore."

"Then you hide it, and only do it when you go into town or you're by yourself."

"I'm tired of doing that, Lonnie. There are so many things that I'm holding in here because I'm scared to let them out in case that's not the way someone else wants me to be, and I feel like I'm going to burst. Will they accept me if I just let them out and be me? Whatever that is, because I'm not sure I even know anymore."

"I don't know, Margaret, I'm scared for you. Look." Lonnie slipped her hands under her dress and pulled out her rosary beads.

"You had Holy Communion?" Margaret fingered the beads with her eyes and mouth agape. Lonnie nodded, brought the cross to her lips, and kissed it. "With a white dress?"

"Yes." Lonnie smiled. This time it was real. "If they hadn't tried to force all their ways on us Koori people and take away all that we had, because some of it was good stuff that they could have learned as well, then our people would be more willing to listen." Lonnie finished greasing the scalp and started to massage the whole head. "You can't hear what someone is telling you when they're holding you down. You too busy wriggling and kicking to get out."

Lonnie finished Margaret's hair and went inside the clinic to wash her hands. When she came back, Margaret was standing at the edge of the veranda watching the commotion out by the ceremony site. Lonnie walked through the yard towards it and Margaret followed her. As they got closer, Margaret could make out the drinker in the middle. His battered wife was on her knees, with blood seeping from where he had struck her on the head in his drunken rage. Margaret stopped when she saw Barry hold up the bottle.

"Our laws say no drinking," Barry said. "This man was caught with a bottle of grog. Look what he's done to his wife." Barry pointed to the cowering woman and then circled the bottle over his head so that everyone could see. Murmurs of disapproval stabbed at the air. "Where did you get it?" The man looked up with an acid stare. He caught a glimpse of Margaret's blood-drained face and turned away.

Barry gripped the bottle and shook it at the drinker. "Where did you get it, I said?"

"I went to town. I can drink if I want." He spat on the ground. His punishment was certain, so it didn't matter now.

"You know what the punishment is. Why?"

"When they take our land they cut off our limbs," the drinker said. "I need a drink for my crutch."

He started walking before Barry told him to. He had been banished from the community for two years. Margaret held on to Lonnie and asked if there was nothing they could do, but Lonnie told her it was customary law and they would have to let it be.

***

To block out her vision of the banished man's departing back, Margaret took the half bottle of wine she had left and drank herself to sleep. During the night she was woken by a commotion. A woman came in carrying Eddie, the little boy she had read to until the women had started to ostracise her. Margaret climbed out of bed and went to the door where Lonnie was standing. "What is it?" Margaret said.

"He was bitten by something during the night."

"Are you going to look after him?"

"No, I can't," Lonnie said. "He is kin now, he and my daughter are promised to each other, so I can't look at him or touch him." Lonnie had already explained the forbidden degrees of relationships to Margaret and pointed out the people who couldn't look at or touch each other. It hadn't occurred to her that it would be followed so strictly in an emergency.

Margaret looked back at Eddie. The woman had placed him on one of the beds and she was stroking his stiffening face. His eyes kept rolling back into his head so that only the whites were visible. Margaret slinked over to feel his forehead, but the woman brushed her hand away. "The *Nagankari* is coming. He will treat the boy."

"But it may be too late by the time he gets here," Margaret said. She knew he had gone hunting two days earlier with two other men. The woman turned her back on Margaret and covered the boy with her arms so that she couldn't get to him. He was hot, sweaty, and wheezing. Margaret walked around the bed and examined him by sight. As her eyes travelled down his legs, she saw two small fang marks on his calf, but right below this was a half-moon fold of skin,

305

the same birthmark as Isabel, his mother, whom she had last seen in Malee. The breath hissed out of her and she jolted back, slapping her palm over her heart. She knew she had to help him now. The women had gathered outside and they were singing curing songs, whilst shuffling their cupped hands out from their bodies to send healing powers to the boy. Margaret looked at them and shook her head; how was this supposed to help him? She went to the fridge to check what vaccines they had. There was a box of anti-venom, but she didn't know if it was the right type. How was she to get it to Eddie with the woman still there? She sat on the edge of a bed, watched, and waited.

Before dawn the Nagankari arrived. He was an older man with curly hair and oily black skin. He hurried to the boy's bedside and waved away the woman who had been protecting him. She got up and backed out of the room to join the others, who were still singing outside. The Nagankari felt the boy's head, chest, and legs, and within seconds he found the bite wounds. He asked Margaret to fill a small bowl with water and bring it to him. Then he clamped his mouth around the wound and sucked. The first mouthful he spat into the bowl was blood, and the second was a small piece of stick. Margaret couldn't see where it had come from, and rolled her sceptical eyes. The Nagankari held up the bowl. "Let me throw away the evil spirit that got into the boy and give him some bush tea before you try the white fellas' medicine," he said. He took the evil spirit out to dispose of it in the bush. All the while the women had still been singing, first to invoke the presence of the Nagankari so that he could enter the boy and remove the source of the pain, and then they moved to rain dreaming to sing the wound shut.

Margaret went to the fridge and drew the anti-venom into a syringe. She held it down by her side and walked past the open door to the boy's bed. He was in a light sleep, but moaning and rolling his head from side to side. She wanted to take control, sure that these people didn't know what they were doing. With her hand shaking, she found some flesh on the boy's bony thigh and stuck the needle in. As she pulled the needle out, the Nagankari hurried back into the room with the bush tea. She hid the syringe under the boy's pillow and stepped back. The Nagankari stared at her guilty stance and rushed to the boy. Within a minute he had taken a turn for the worse, and his head thrashed from side to side and his body convulsed so that his chest jumped from the bed. "What did you do?" the Nagankari said.

306

Margaret shook her head but was too frightened to say anything. The boy's thrashing was causing the bed frame to squeak, and the women stopped singing and gathered around the open door. The syringe rolled from under the pillow onto the floor. The Nagankari picked it up and held it aloft as evidence of whose fault it was. He called in one of the women, who helped him to hold the boy down while he fed him sips of the bush tea. After a while the boy's thrashing slowed to intermittent jolts and coughing throughout the night.

The women wailed in the dark and threw handfuls of dust into the air all night. They sang that Margaret wanted the boy to die, she had not wanted him to live in their world, and so she had inflicted her sorcery for Nannup having brought the boy to them. And then they started to sing her to death.

In the early hours, the Nagankari came out of the clinic to tell the people gathered outside that he thought the boy would live, but it seemed the leg where Margaret had injected him might be infected. After, most of them went back to their huts to catch up on sleep.

In the late morning, Nannup headed for the small hut that Margaret had been sent to so as to keep her away from the clinic. As he walked across the compound, he saw oval shapes in the dust, about the size of a man's foot. The last time he had seen these they had led him and Margaret to the man that Nipper's people had speared and hung from a tree. He broke into a run and kicked open the door of the hut. Margaret was by the table pouring tea, and he startled her. She watched with tired eyes as he looked around the room. "What is it?" she said. He shook his head. She continued pouring tea. "Would you like some tea?" Nannup lunged across the room and slapped the cup from her hand as she was about to drink. He grabbed her by the arm and pulled her through the door. "What's wrong?" she said. Nannup pointed to the oval tracks, which stopped right at the edge of the veranda. She remembered them too, and her knees buckled. Nannup kept hold of her and hurried to his car. The engine spluttered lazily, and then it backfired. It woke everyone.

Nannup turned the car towards the desert. If he went out that way, he could lose them in the gorges and then join the road later. "Let me explain it to the elders," Margaret said. "It wasn't my fault, I'm sure they will understand."

"They sent the kaditja man, Margaret. They've already made their decision."

They drove out over the hard dusty ground for less than twenty minutes. Then the car coughed, spluttered, and rolled to a halt. They climbed out of the car and looked back from where they had come. Red dust was racing towards them.

Two utes caught up with them, and a large group of the outstation's residents—men, women, and children—climbed down from the bed and encircled them. They opened their circle so that Barry could walk through. He supported himself on a long spear. "The Nagankari said the boy will live," Nannup said.

"But he will not be able to walk properly, so he cannot live the hunting gathering life that has been passed down to the rest of our mob," Barry said.

"She was trying to kill the boy because she didn't want us to have him," a woman shouted. "She still thinks he would be better off with the farmers."

"Is it true? Do you think he would be better off elsewhere?" Barry asked.

Margaret didn't answer, which signalled to the mob that she was guilty.

"You know she has to be punished," Barry said to Nannup.

"She is not one of us," Nannup retorted.

"I didn't do anything wrong," Margaret finally claimed in her defence.

Barry pointed his spear at her. "Did you inject the boy?"

"I did what I was taught to do at nursing school." She pointed at the Nagankari. "He couldn't help the boy."

Murmurs of outrage came from the gathering, and Barry's face grew ashen. "When you're Koori, there are things that come before what they taught you, cousin—things that we could teach you if you'd slow down enough to listen." He slapped the flat of the spear against her ear, and she clutched it. Fresh blood soaked her hand. "You don't come to our corroborrees or join in the singing, dancing or talking that would help you to remember our ways. But you can't survive without them out here." He pointed the spear into the desert. "You think you're better than us, but if you listened to our stories of the dreaming, you'd know how the Nagankari can heal the boy's spirit— even if he can't heal his body. I've seen a white preacher done it once, too." Barry walked around her and shook his head with pity. "They pulled up all your roots and left you without a way to get nourishment, didn't they?" Tears streamed down her face, as though she knew how true that was. "The elders have decided that you must be punished for breaking our law—"

"She is not subject to our customary law," Nannup argued. "She is a white woman and so she is subject to the white man's laws."

"So why did you bring her here?" someone from the mob shouted.

"Because they don't want her," someone else said, and there was general laughter.

Barry stopped in front of her. "What are you?"

Margaret shook her head and sniffed back the tears. "I don't know."

Nannup held her arm. "Tell them you're white; they can't judge you then, Margaret."

Her head was spinning in the heat. How many more times would she have to change? How many? She had changed a little to satisfy Matron Blythe when she was at Radley, but that wasn't enough. Then she had transformed herself to be accepted by the McDonalds and the people in the town of Malee, and even now she still didn't really feel like one of them. Then she had shifted some more, to fine-tune her white self for Matt—

She swallowed and closed her eyes; even now she couldn't bear to think his name—if she ignored it for long enough then it too, like those past selves, might fade away. Now these Koori people—her people they told her—wanted her to transform herself again. Was there a self that they could all accept? She remembered Nannup's story about the gum tree having its lifeline so deeply sewn within it that it could only be scarred on the surface, and it would spring back to life at some point. Her changes had been far too profound, her scars too deep. How many changes could one person go through and still feel like someone? Even a butterfly only had to go through four or five changes, Father Beir had said, before realising its full self. And for its final change, didn't it become more beautiful? But when its time has come, if it belongs to no one, then who will remember to mourn its passing? They had asked her if she wanted to be a part of them, even under these circumstances. She couldn't remember anyone having done that before. Others had shown her how to be like them, and then held her at bay. But even now, these Kooris had

309

asked. "Judge me as Koori," she said, accepting all that would come with that.

Barry huddled in a group with the other elders, and the punishment was decided again. "Because of what you've been through, we've decided you should only be banished for a week. After that you can decide if you want to be replanted into our community," Barry said. As the rest of the mob turned their backs on her and walked away, Nannup gave her a bottle of water and whispered to her to stay by his broken down car; he would be back.

Margaret woke in the afternoon, leaning against the hot body of the car. The sun bore down on her like an unwanted lover. She put her hand over her forehead to block its glare and scanned the vast empty plains. She saw a quandong tree nearby, and went to sit in the shade of its sparse cover. By nightfall Nannup had not returned, and she had finished the bottle of water. She decided to try and find her way to the road. The night was still and cold, and she clutched at her body as she wandered over sandy dunes and rocky outcrops. In the morning when the sun rose she was grateful for its warmth again, but within minutes it had sapped her energy and made her tongue swell to fill her dry mouth. She wasn't certain which direction she was moving in, and her vision was blurred and her head spinning. She stumbled, exhausted, onto a cluster of yellow top. Its stems and buttercup flowers had begun to wither, precipitating its demise, but at the same time, the dry, furry seeds of the next generation appeared. They already held within them the vision for new life, because it is said that all that there is has existed from the beginning in the dreaming of the Creative Ancestors as an enduring potential. And so all living is reliving, there is nothing new to the universe. Those seeds harbouring the next generation would be scattered by the wind and feeding birds to places where they would lie dormant in the red soil, waiting. And when in the following months, or years or decades the next rains came to nourish them, they would rise up to reveal their secrets from the dust.

# Other books by George Hamilton:

**Carnival of Hope**

"Compelling and intelligently written." - Marilou George (Confessions Of A Reader)

" The contrast in lifestyle between the poor and the rich is absolutely shocking..." - ElaineG (KUF Reviewer)

A poor idealist forced to teach in secret, and reluctant to abandon his mother. A determined young woman, desperate to escape the struggles and tragedies of a dangerous Brazilian shantytown. A carnival competition offering hope of a better future in the South...

But what lies behind the sinister practices of carnival?
What's become of former winners who have disappeared?

The route out to a new life is not as easy as it appears, and as the competition spirals into a corrupt and perilous deception, it plunges the young loves into a fight for their lives.

## Reviews:

5/5*
I found this book extremely compelling and intelligently written. I highly recommend this book to all readers who want to be immersed in a story that will take you on a journey that you would otherwise never have taken. (Marilou George @ Goodreads)

4/5*
In the end, CARNIVAL OF HOPE is a love story that examines a society, warts and all, with an ending that allows room for the reader's imagination and sense of wonder. I would recommend it to anyone who wants to be immersed, not only in a love story, but in the culture of the Brazilian favela during carnival season, the superstitions and longing of its people. (Susan Russo Anderson @ Goodreads)

5/5*
Tomas in his heart is a good person, but who knows how far we would be pushed before we do bad things like he reluctantly has to... . I was thinking of Tomas and Thereza long after finishing the book. (Joo @ Goodreads)

5/5*
Carnival of Hope is a story that should be on reading lists everywhere as a wake-up call to conditions that really exist in our modern world. (Alice D @ Readers Favorite)

5/5*
I thoroughly enjoyed this book, extremely well written with wonderful characters and very clever plotline. (ElaineG's @ Amazon)

## The Disease

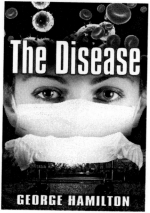

Doctor Ludmilla Toropov is a Gold Cross bearing Daughter of her Nation, a champion advocate for President for life, Emile Sakovich. Her estranged daughter, Olga, has joined the student dissidents. When a deadly virus sweeps the world, wiping out millions in weeks, her repressive East European nation, under sanctions from the international community, becomes the first to develop a vaccine. But with their antiquated production facilities, they are only able to satisfy the demand of a small section of their population. Doctor Toropov can either watch hundreds of her patients die, or defy the state that nurtured her by attempting to smuggle the drug out to the West to be synthesized. One choice will pit her against her daughter, the other could unearth unpalatable secrets, and land her in a gulag jail.

## Reviews:

5/5*

I thoroughly enjoyed this book which is set in an unnamed Eastern European country … Set in a world where it seems that even the very walls have ears and nobody can be trusted and nothing is really as it seems, the story is a gripping, thrilling read … (ElaineG's full review at Amazon)

5/5*
It is an interesting plot, well written, good character development and entertaining. (J Adamak's @ Amazon)

4/5*
George Hamilton writes a very good story … He makes the characters believable even though they are a long way from what you know. (Joo @ Amazon)

5/5*
Dr. Toropov is forced into making life or death decisions on every step of her journey, but will she make the right choice ultimately …? The Disease is wonderfully written, and impossible to put down. (Kathryn Romeo @ LivingInAFictionalReality.com)

## Connect with George Hamilton:
Website: http://browsingrhino.com
Facebook: http://www.facebook.com/browsingrhino1
Twitter: https://twitter.com/browsingrhino

Lightning Source UK Ltd.
Milton Keynes UK
UKOW040602250413

209723UK00001B/57/P